THE MYSTICAL VILLAGE THAT REWIRED REALITY
- *Journey to Gylodon* -

Justin Nathan

Mystical Literature for the Age of Transition

Join our village @
JustinNathan.com

Copyright © 2017 Justin Bruce Nathan
All rights reserved.

Cover design, logo and illustrative images* by Justin Nathan

Editing by Bruce A. Nathan

All characters and events in this story are fictitious.
Any resemblance to living persons is coincidental.

ISBN: 978-0-9985001-0-2

Duplication of this work in any form, without the author's consent, is illegal and punishable by law. Please support independent artists and purchase only authorized editions. Thank you for your support.

*Attributions: The female figure on the cover and on the imprint logo is derived from Botticelli's painting, *The Birth of Venus (1480s)*, which is in the public domain. The male figure on the cover is derived from Lucas Cranach the Elder's painting, *Adam and Eve (1520s)*, which is in the public domain. The internal illustration, labeled *Separation of the Astral Body* is derived from the work of Luigi Schiavonetti, titled *The Soul Leaving the Body* (1808), and is in the public domain.

First printing: April 2017

1. Metaphysical and Visionary – Fiction
2. New Age & Spirituality – Fiction
3. Magical Realism

Author's Website:
www.JustinNathan.com

To the memory and spirit of Dennis J. Valdez, a man who lived one hundred lifetimes in forty years, and died too young doing what he loved most—flying off mountains.

Dennis was a real-life hero, an explorer, an artist, an innovator and a warrior of the highest caliber—and he left deep footprints where few humans dare to tread.

He served this world in many capacities—as a naval officer and combat veteran who led covert missions in the special warfare community, surface warfare officer working jointly with the German and Japanese navies, leader of rescue missions to retrieve people stranded on impassable mountaintops, advisor to numerous families on kidnapping and ransom cases that successfully recovered many loved ones, triathlete, mountain climber, racecar driver, videographer, photographer extraordinaire, elite scuba diver, skydiver, BASE jumper and wingsuit flyer. He traversed vast expanses of this planet, not the least of which included driving a motorcycle from Georgia to the southern tip of South America, crisscrossing every country along the way. His insatiable quest for learning drove him to speak multiple languages and enabled him to share his gifts across many cultures.

Above all things, though, Dennis was a kind and generous person—a stalwart spirit who inspired all who knew him to embrace their dreams and savor life.

Even though he has departed this world, his fire still burns hot and his legend lives on in the hearts of all those who were blessed with his friendship.

Thank you, Dennis. You are loved and missed.

Contents

Prologue……………………………………..…….1
Chapter 1: Age of Transition…..………....…5
Chapter 2: The Seed Bearer……………..…12
Chapter 3: Womb…………………….…..…15
Chapter 4: Gylodon………………………22
Chapter 5: Inipia……………………....……30
Chapter 6: Altered States……………….…..37
Chapter 7: Wandering Mind…………....……43
Chapter 8: Astral Realities……………..….…52
Chapter 9: Endings……………...…………...62
Chapter 10: Lost………………....…….…73
Chapter 11: Surrender……………..…...…79
Chapter 12: Beginnings……………...……82
Chapter 13: Healing……………………94
Chapter 14: Master Unschooler…………112
Chapter 15: Bandwidths………………..121
Chapter 16: Animal Energy……..………131
Chapter 17: Falling……………………135
Chapter 18: Illusions ………………….140
Chapter 19: The Demonstration………...150
Chapter 20: Consciousness Cloud……….156
Chapter 21: Elements……………...……163
Chapter 22: Changes…………………...170

Chapter 23: Initiation……………………..181

Chapter 24: Readiness………………...……187

Chapter 25: I Am………………………..195

Chapter 26: Astral Museum……………....199

Chapter 27: Love + Lucidity……………..203

Chapter 28: Hunters……………………...207

Chapter 29: Answers……………………..212

Chapter 30: Nightmare…………………...219

Chapter 31: Elders……………………….225

Chapter 32: Woodlands Encounter………..231

Chapter 33: Tristis and Twins……………..243

Chapter 34: Plant Medicine………………..245

Chapter 35: Mountain Preparation………...261

Chapter 36: Ode to Tristis………………...265

Chapter 37: Departing…………………....270

Chapter 38: Valley of Below……………...278

Chapter 39: Animal Companion…………286

Chapter 40: Middle Ground……………...292

Chapter 41: Highland……………………298

Commentary………………………….318

Acknowledgments

★★★

Thank you to the innovators, activists, healers and spiritual warriors of the world. Keep challenging the status quo. Your spirit is the backbone of this work.

As to the task of writing it, and molding it into a fluid story that is rooted in important ideas, I have some folks to thank; first, Bruce Nathan, my father, who tirelessly edited this work through multiple drafts, calling upon his years of experience as an editor for The Associated Press to transform this story into a worthwhile experience. Thank you, Dad—I am forever grateful for your efforts.

To Mom, for always wanting the best for me, even when the way was unclear—thank you for your energy, love and support.

To Cris Parque, a true friend and seeker of truth, thank you for reading my earliest drafts. Without your kind words and encouragement, we may not have arrived here.

Thank you to the talented Ryan Dodge, my speechwriting brother-in-law, for reading my earliest draft and providing structured, critical feedback that altered the course of this book in profound ways.

To my dear sister, Lauren Nathan Dodge, for her constant support in all capacities, not the least of which included feedback on the earliest draft and manuscript support—thank you.

To my former navy shipmate and close friend, Commander Jonathan Paz y Miño, for his photographic support, and for keeping my priorities aligned—thank you, Brother.

To the healers and teachers in my life, past and present—Jackie Rolandelli, Itzhak Beery, Ipupiara Makunaiman, Natalie Berthold, Peter Goldbeck, Rob Murphy, Louise Jenner, Richard Unger and so many others—thank you for your light. You have forever changed me.

To friends and acquaintances along the way—like the New York Shamanic Circle—thank you for your magic, support and friendship. Likewise, I have boundless gratitude for the friends who have indirectly inspired aspects of this work—your spirits are woven into the pages like roots in earth.

Finally, thank you to all the invisible helpers and guides—those that dwell in the other realms—for your wisdom and inspiration; you are the ethereal foundation of this work.

"Just when the world seemed dark and gray, and the prospect of happiness a dying ember, he wandered to the edge of the pain and looked beyond. The shadowy landscape was fraught with fear and doubt, but already the pain of not changing was too great to endure, so he closed his eyes and leapt. To his surprise, in his surrender, he landed softly on the bottom, still alive, and on the far side of the darkness shone a single ray of light. It was bright like a diamond, crafted of color and love, and it vibrated with the song of eternity. He crawled toward it, feeling his way, more hopeful with each moment, and the ray of light grew into a rising sun. Just beyond that sun, on the far side of the horizon, was the village of *Gylodon*."

*–**Master Unschooler***

Prologue

***

From a watery womb, we plunge into the mud of mortality. Grasping for a handhold—or any kind of anchor—we seek balance, as our feet slip to and fro, sinking into the depths of adversity, challenge and pain. It is here, in the classroom of earthly life, that we rise and fall, adapt and grow, die and live again. Our existence is an ever-evolving storyline—and the only constant is *change*.

Somewhere, amid the chaos of our daily lives, there is a place of peace, a locale of unrivaled beauty and fulfillment. It lives just beyond our view, obscured by a veil of physical pain, fear, ego and our own wandering minds. Sometimes its beauty graces us with its presence, and we are touched; but, alas, our memories are short, and the experience is fleeting.

As we ride through this adventure, we are active participants, quiet observers, and far too often—unconscious autopilots, asleep at the wheel.

But every now and then we awaken from our unconscious daydreams. We look up from our work stations, turn away from our computers and gaze out the window; it is then, with uncommon clarity, that we find ourselves in the throes of war—held captive in an invisible prison—and the battle is for nothing less than our *personal sovereignty*. Like indentured servants, we follow the designated routine—working to earn money while striving for sustenance. At the same time, our consciousness is under attack from all directions by forces that seek to control our minds and amputate our hearts. Never in the history of humankind has *consciousness pollution* been so rampant—shaping our reality through an endless slew of media portals, while inhibiting our basic self-awareness. Our lives have become blinding tornados of constant distraction, obscuring our most fundamental gifts.

But we are not blind, nor have we ever been, and even as we stand in the eye of the storm, our power grows like a climbing vine. It adapts and regenerates, always moving upward. For each of us, the time to rise is now, as we stand at the gateway to humanity's grand transition—one that is destined to free minds and open hearts. Profound change is upon us, and even as you read this, reality is being rewired.

Before moving forward, please understand something. There is a universal truth that is both well known and scarcely understood. It is the secret hidden in plain view. It is about who—*or what*—we are. We are perfect arrangements of *organized energy*—consciousness in motion—molecular works of art, crafted of magic and measured by science. But science, at present, cannot measure the scope of our consciousness, nor the infinite, subtle layers of energy of which we are built. Even our personalities are composed of organized, intelligent energy, as is love, which has shape and form. Indeed, our world is a mysterious soup of science and spirit.

If you can take a leap of faith and accept the premise that we are *spirits*—or perhaps, self-aware energies inhabiting physical bodies—then you may presume that we are here having an earthly experience. Let's call it an adventure. These adventures are both dark and light, devastating and exhilarating. They are the stories of human mortality.

But sometimes our spirits are seeking more. Much more. And therein lies a lesser-known truth of our human experience. It is that each night when we sleep, our spirits leave our bodies to wander into alternative planes of existence, in pursuit of their own adventures. These planes of existence are both infinite and reachable—and they are as real as the air you are breathing right now. They are the divine playgrounds of limitless truth, spaces of unimaginable beauty and horrific darkness—manifestations of thought, emotion, light and sound, mixing and melding, forming the fabric of consciousness. And now—*more than ever before*—these planes of existence are within reach.

PROLOGUE

Just beyond the edge of human experience, on the cusp of conscious awareness, is a sacred community—the mystical village of *Gylodon*. Its inhabitants live by a different code—an alternative framework for reality—built to nurture humanity's finest gifts. But the path to Gylodon bends and twists in peculiar ways, and many will be led astray. For those who stay the course, however, Gylodon is the way of power, a magical school of arcane lessons on mental mastery, energy, consciousness, healing and reality sculpting—timeless tools of transformation. For those who walk the path, it is a place to find *purpose, freedom* and *love*—the birthrights of humanity.

Throughout history, only a few were destined to find Gylodon. But the currents of life are shifting, as reality becomes more fluid and humanity enters the *age of transition*. In the days to come, many more will journey to Gylodon's gardens, where they may plant the seeds of heaven on Earth. *Perhaps you'll be among them.*

Age of Transition

✶✶✶

"Are you *lucid*?" Honaw asked, scanning the crystalline skyline with astral eyes.

"Not yet. Give me a moment," Donja replied. She'd just separated her conscious awareness from her physical body—as had Honaw—and required intense focus to ground herself in the new environment. It was not an easy task, but she'd done it many times before. Briefly, Honaw examined her ghostly form; it was the visual projection of her self-image, both conscious and unconscious, and it radiated power like a storm. Back home, in her physical body, Donja was a stout woman with salt-and-pepper hair and sun-beaten skin, but here—in the astral realms—she was semi-transparent, and even semi-formless, teeming with colorful aberrations that reflected aspects of her emotions, personality and even old memories. She was divine.

"I'm ready," Donja reported, flexing her energy-body.

"Good. Come now, let's fly."

As they took flight into the shadow world—traversing the in-between spaces that are invisible to human eyes—Honaw could not help but revel in the beauty. The stars glistened, revealing their full spectrum of colors, each dancing with the next, as if their pulsing patterns created some infinite and unknown melody that shaped the cosmos. Grandmother Moon was as vibrant as ever, buoyed by the sun's warm light on her globular cheeks. Honaw could feel her power, pushing and pulling on his energy-body, just like her effect on the tides, and it was an odd sensation. He tempered his emotions, refraining from excitement, lest he accidently reconnect with his physical body back home. Emotions could do that, and he would not let that happen tonight during an important astral investigation—not with Gylodon in danger. Both and he and Donja carried special knowledge—a burden, really—about the fate of their village. Gylodon was being hunted, and for the first time in recent history, the darkness was close. It was their job to understand the threat. So, they carried that knowledge, quarantining the fear, so the others could thrive.

Their investigations of the outside world, and more specifically, those who hunted them, leveraged an uncommon skill set—one that transcended the boundaries of physical matter. As *astral travelers*, they could separate their conscious awareness from their physical bodies, defying three-dimensional paradigms, and visit any location at the speed of thought. While their bodies slept at home, their lucid awareness—in the form of an energy-body (also called an *astral body*), traveled to distant places.[1] So profound was their mastery that they could merge their experiences and travel as a group, as a cluster of specters in the night.

Tonight's investigation took them inside a sterile and white-washed research facility, deep in the mountains of Colorado. The entire locale was peculiar, as if ruled by some unseen overlord who sucked the marrow out of its human inhabitants. People scurried around like rodents, and nowhere was laughter present. It was a dead place, devoid of trees or vegetation, and only its white walls brought any sense of light. As usual, Donja and Honaw observed from another layer of reality—a different wavelength—cloaked in invisibility. Sharpening their focus, they calibrated themselves to the local environment while observing two men engaged in conversation. They'd watched them before.

"We'll have to see what we find," reported a balding man, donning a coffee-soiled lab coat, disheveled pants and a nervous disposition. "I suggest we put it to the test."

An emotionless figure with dark, manicured hair, perfect nails and a custom-fit, ash-blue suit looked down at the ground before responding. "The funding for this project is not unlimited, Doctor Dalton. I don't know if *putting it to the test* will be quantifiable enough—but I will await the demonstration, nonetheless."

Dr. Dalton nodded respectfully, masking his unease, desiring only to escape his benefactor, or rather, his benefactor's liaison. He'd never actually met his benefactor. The entire project had been mired in secrecy from the start, leading him to doubt his own safety. Sometimes he wondered if his scientific expertise was the only thing that kept him alive. It was a disturbing thought. Still, he did love the work—it was an unrivaled opportunity to pioneer new technologies—but the personalities, and agendas, of those who funded him left him unbalanced and uncertain if he'd made the right choice.

Honaw repositioned himself, now hovering four feet above the men. As he turned, he glimpsed Donja's energy-body—it had transformed from an amorphous ball of light into a humanlike silhouette. It was a common occurrence—a self-projected image.

"Let's have a look down there," he suggested. Honaw swooped down between the two men, like a ghost, partially passing through the shoulder of the scientist, who looked straight through him while conversing with the other. For a moment, it seemed, the scientist had shivered—an involuntary response to the interaction with Honaw's energy-body.

Gracefully, Donja glided in behind him and they moved toward the edge of the room where a large silver box, housing electronics, was situated. The room was as unremarkable as the entire facility, too clean and without character. But there, in the center, as if on a pedestal, was the box. It was hard-wired to a series of servers. As they approached the device, they could feel its electromagnetic fields playing harmlessly with their own. They examined it. According to their prior investigations, this device was designed to find energetic anomalies around the planet, allegedly with uncanny precision. Their concern was that it might be used to discover the location of their village. They didn't know its full capabilities, but both Honaw and Donja understood the risks. Too much was at stake. Their village was an uncommon treasure, a breeding ground for a better tomorrow. It served as the nucleus of humanity's unrealized gifts, a pivot point of planetary destiny, and they were its guardians.

The Mystical Village That Rewired Reality

Gylodon could not be discovered. Not now—not after all this time.

For too long the shadows of illusion had descended upon humanity, leaving it to stagnate in an unnatural state of normal, balancing people on the cusp of suffering and basic sustenance. But now the discomfort of "normal" was becoming too much to endure. Slowly, people were waking to their predicaments, rising from long, unconscious slumbers, and the time of change was near.

Invisible heroes, like Honaw and Donja, born on Earth, yet blessed with uncommon power, observed events, ready to assist with the transition. Their requirements for change were two-fold—a *free mind* and an *open heart*. To most, these were nebulous concepts at best; nonetheless, they were the building blocks for a revolution of consciousness, destined to alter humanity's course. While these requirements were simple, they were extraordinarily difficult to attain.

The heroes could access these superhuman abilities, despite a fog that blinded much of humanity. In Gylodon, heart-consciousness and mental mastery were the foundations of daily life, empowering its inhabitants to sculpt realities with extraordinary precision and speed. It facilitated transcendental experiences, like astral travel, or profound healings through energy manipulation. But it was their collective power—all the villagers working together—that shaped the path of humanity. Their effect on the planetary *consciousness cloud* was profound, forever blazing a path toward love and unity—for all humans. Their extraordinary talents, and the light they shined on the planet, had not come easily, and to some people on Earth, posed a threat.

For centuries, powerful corporate, governmental and religious sects had hunted them. Through sheer will, and an unrivaled mastery of energy, they'd learned to live in an alternative layer of existence, concealed from sight. Their location was earthbound, in the woodlands, but existed at a different energetic wavelength than the rest of humanity, offering invisibility from those who sought to destroy them. A long while back, they'd discovered how to do this.

Their ability to alter energy and matter had been a natural offshoot of their consciousness development, and it offered them access to multi-dimensional realities. They used their gifts to support humanity's progression, always striving to transform the planetary *consciousness cloud* into love and light. As masters of energy, they could transmute molecules into the very essence of love—by altering their frequencies—like alchemists sculpting reality, and propagate their creations throughout the world. The geometries of reality, expressed through thought, emotion and vibration were a language with which they were well acquainted, and they used it to create balance across the planet. Their astral explorations, a critical activity, kept them up to date on the changing world. Tonight's investigation had revealed new information—but not without a price.

Donja scanned the room, processing the scene, watching the strange men discuss their peculiar agendas. She didn't feel right. Her emotions bubbled like molten lava, admonishing her for the invasion of privacy. Suddenly beset by a wave of guilt, her energy-body flashed blackish-green, reflecting her mood; spying was not aligned with Gylodonian values—it violated the spiritual laws. Still, it was necessary, and it was a sacrifice that she was willing to make. But the surge of guilt had already disrupted her focus, reconnecting her with her physical body, and the environment began to blur, as if viewed through a vacillating lens.

"Let us return," Donja suggested. "My lucidity is wavering."

Honaw nodded, as best he could without a physical body, and they both shifted their attention from the silver box back to their sleeping physical bodies, nearly two thousand miles away. Within a blink, each reconnected, waking in their beds, recalling every detail of the investigation so they might precisely relay the experience to the Council of Elders. Honaw was grateful to be back in his body in Gylodon. The research facility had been like a vacuum, devoid of humor or love; it was an alien thing, and a bit unsettling. He let the emotions pass before curling back up under his blankets.

The Mystical Village That Rewired Reality

Historically, it had been critical that all villagers in Gylodon hide far from the outside world, lingering in the shadows, standing as external observers and record keepers of humanity's illusions, while protecting the wisdom of the ages. They had climbed to the peak of human potential, and were prepared to step forward when the time was right. That time was approaching.

On mainstream earth, a free mind and open heart were nearly impossible to attain amid a world of prolific *consciousness pollution*, where independent thought and empathy were battered by mood-altering drugs, environmental poisons, suggestive advertising imagery, negative news, violent video games and messaging of all types.

The planetary wealth gap had only widened over time, leading to unprecedented levels of oligarchic, global control, with leaders viewing humanity as little more than "useless eaters," pointing blame at them for an imperiled planet, when in fact it was their corporate greed that drove global deprivation. The businesses they controlled had rights like humans, but were devoid of any moral compass. Nature was trampled as power consolidated into the hands of a nameless few.

Preferring a world of workers to a world of thinkers, these enemies of freedom sought ownership of humankind's mental faculties, shaping beliefs and implanting fears whenever possible. Their greatest failings as human beings were excessively quantitative minds, at the expense of empathy. To them, compassion was a lost emotion, buried beneath layers of logical, power-seeking agendas, while using Earth as their personal chessboard.

Fortunately for humanity, there were those who would stop them. They understood the transition that was under way. Theirs was a deep knowing, from a place outside of three dimensions, where fractals of truth emerged from the guidance of their hearts, coupled with the complete ownership of their minds. They watched as the elite rulers consolidated power, taking dominion over the consciousness of humanity through their monopolistic platforms and messaging.

Biding Earth's progression, the heroes awaited the moment when they would have the proper leverage to shift humanity's fate. As keen observers of the illusions that kept minds enslaved, they watched as people were spoon-fed belief systems that promoted conflict and separation. Humanity had unconsciously accepted black-and-white paradigms like *right vs. left, privilege vs. poverty, choice vs. life, masculine vs. feminine* and *right vs. wrong*. Despite innumerable shades of gray between differing perspectives, humans routinely aligned with polarizing belief systems that had been implanted into their consciousness. This polarity created infighting, bleeding their power while suppressing independent thought; it trapped them within a matrix of someone else's making, forever prodding them toward addiction and escapism for relief, while suppressing their own innate wisdom.

The invisible guardians trusted that underneath humanity's cloud of confusion loomed powerful, capable beings that had forgotten who they were. It was their role to help them remember. Through the restoration of free thought, self-love, unity and purpose, they would tip the planetary *consciousness cloud* back toward light. These were the birthrights of humanity.

The Internet had been the last bastion of free thought, but the so-called elites had finally seized that too, regulating it to their liking. Humanity, however, had fought back, finding a plethora of workarounds for the predicament. Still, free minds were a minority, and the heroes bided their time, watching for the signs, waiting for the chosen ones to find them. They'd always known that select outsiders, those born in mainstream earth, would find them. These individuals were not those who hunted them, but rather those who would join them. They would act as bridges, or *mediators*, between Gylodon's wisdom and the rest of humanity, paving the road to transformation.

The Seed Bearer

***

Forty-five years prior to the boy's birth, in the far recesses of nature where the wildest creatures know peace, a man whispered to a seed. "Little One, send forth those who would join our cause. May those who are ready find you at just the right moment, in just the right place, and may you share with them our message, if their hearts are open and willing to receive it."

He blessed the seed, holding it to his lips and further infusing it with the necessities of its mission. He spoke not only with words, but also with heart. The vibrations and patterns of his emotions penetrated deeply into the seed and became a part of this tree-to-be's destiny. The man completed his prayer with an exhalation, casting off the seed while watching its wings lift it over the surrounding brush. Then he chose another seed from the pod and began the process anew.

The seed remained on the ground for two days when a voracious, gangly turkey came upon it. For reasons that only fate can fathom, the bird gazed at the seed, cocking its head, and then left without taking its meal.

With Mother Earth's sustenance, this seedling became a delicate sprout and then, in time, a proud and powerful birch tree. Although growth is in the code of all seeds, this seed's plan was uncommon, for it carried a message that it would pass along to its own seeds one day.

The old man, or Seed Bearer, as he was aptly named, walked delicately through the forest touching the trees and blessing the plants, all the while allowing their leaves to brush along his exposed body. Aging lines, carved from experience, creased his broad brow, marking him as an elder and wisdom keeper. Old, but entirely unwithered, he stepped with a ballerina's grace and a warrior's precision, dodging any sprouts or fragile plants. This man had a lifelong relationship with the forest, and in turn its plants provided him endless bounty and medicine; its leaves would caress and cleanse all that ailed him and above all else, its trees would guard his message until it was ready to be received.

When the old man completed his tasks for the day, he lifted his head to the sky and softly uttered words of gratitude to entities that only he could see.

Shifting his attention to the earth, he squatted and buried his paw-like hands into the rich, wet soil below. The soil examined his fingers and Mother Earth knew him; upon his fingers sat ten perfect whorls, the fingerprint markings of an earth steward.[2]

He spoke a silent prayer: *Mother, I am your servant. Thank you for letting me walk upon you, for providing me all that I need. I am made of you, and it is to you that my body shall one day return. But for now, I renew my lifelong pledge to honor you, to act as your steward and to help maintain the balance to the best of my abilities. Thank you, Mama, for all your blessings. I love you.*

His prayer completed, he returned to a standing position, flexing tree-like legs chiseled through a lifetime of nature hikes. He touched base with his primal intuition—a gift shared by all creatures—before pausing deliberately, reading the wind and sun, and stepping in the direction of his home.

Waves of light, outside the visible spectrum, radiated from the man's body toward the trees, enveloping them in an ethereal hug. The trees, in turn, touched him with subtle waves of energy with each step he took. Of course, one would need access to the fourth dimension, simply known as *four*, to see this.

En route to a place known by few people, where all inhabitants carried the power of *four* to varying degrees, the Seed Bearer strode with an open heart, rippling with the fifth-dimensional resonance, a power that many could feel, but few could see. He could not help but smile.

He calculated that his journey back to Gylodon would take one day, but first he would look for some nettle and brew some tea.

The Mystical Village That Rewired Reality

Keen at the prospect, he thanked the forest, and again asked her to lead the chosen ones home. They had been waiting a very long time for the *mediators* to arrive.

WOMB

✷✷✷

Back in New York City, the conception was a good one, exercising just the right balance of love and animalistic release. Or so, the parents felt. And just as the sperm and egg found each other, like soul mates colliding in some far-off land, a ripple of change sounded its call, putting the world on notice. A new destiny would soon be hatched—and with it, a new timeline of possibility would unfold. As the embryo grew into a fetus, its plan became clearer, and it revealed a unique blueprint for an uncommon existence—one of heroism.

This hero-fetus was a sponge, pure and unsoiled, ready to suffer and learn in the classroom of life. Unblemished by humanity's grime, he remained in a state of grace, floating freely in his mother's womb, immersed in the soup of life. But even within this sacred space, the outside world pressed upon his awareness, offering the full spectrum of mortal drama. He heard sounds, sensed sadness, swallowed frustration and anger, and was touched by joy, hunger, love, sex and silence. His reality was a shared experience—at his mother's mercy—a conjoined truth, in the web of life. The womb was a place of profound learning, an opportunity to sit still and absorb the vibrational patterns that found a home in the cells of his body. And while his mind could not rationalize it all, his emotional body was highly attuned to absorb information, and did so with insatiable thirst.

This information came endlessly, and already, at the tender age of seven months in the womb, had taken its toll. His mother worried incessantly about something she felt she needed more of, but always struggled to attain. His father was gone much of the time fulfilling "his duty"—whatever that meant. To the little unborn hero, the words were only sounds, but the sounds carried vibrations deep into his solar plexus, lower stomach and his root, and the information changed him. Still unborn, his purity was already being diluted by the drivel of life, even by the ones who loved him most. Without knowing what it was, he carried his mother's fear and felt the absence of his father. He was, after all, human.

Deep in the womb, the hero-to-be could still remember his plan. As he grew older he was destined to forget, only to remember again. Such is the cycle. When his spirit took residence in its developing body, it brought with it an architecture; some would call it genetics, others a life purpose, and still others might call it a destiny.

His blueprint included a collection of propensities, aptitudes and yearnings that would drive him throughout his life. They did not change. While he might forget them, be distracted or even reprioritize them from time to time, these elements were omnipresent. They were his pathways to fulfillment and gateways to joy, acting as a compass, pointing him home.

The boy's life purpose was already encoded in his unborn body. It lived in the lines of his hands and the ridges of his fingertips, like secret maps awaiting revelation. Even his name and birthday would shape his destiny. Such codes are not causative, but reflective; they are flexible, bending to free will, but never breaking. Serving as markers for civilizations that are willing to look beyond a three-dimensional understanding of reality, they are signposts for a life well lived, for a culture destined to thrive.

Still unborn, the baby could already use his senses extensively. Unconsciously, he was aware that all of earthly life was a dream, an elaborate illusion crafted of consciousness, forged with energy. Soon he would be birthed into this world, carrying his destiny with the innocence of youth.

It was, however, a destiny that society would continually challenge because it threatened the dreams that society had woven, the kind that governments and big business channeled right into the educational systems, molding the minds of young children. Instead of fostering and empowering their unique gifts, the system churned out loyal, rule-following workers, laden with debt, who would find their motivation through the unconscious worshipping of money. Their daily work was dedicated to its attainment, at the expense of their natural-born destinies. Short-term escapism supplanted long-term fulfillment, while fear of poverty and escalating bills reinforced destructive illusions. In time, many would lose their connection to nature, leaving them blind and vulnerable. Not everyone chose to dream this dream, but nearly all were under its influence.

Despite these societal constraints, new dreams are always being born, and powerful dreams can transform. Such is the cycle. Coded into the boy's fingerprints were the markings of an innovator, destined to view the world through an irregular prism. In his hands, heroism was plainly written, and in his heart burned fire. Predestined to challenge conventional thinking, he would share his unique worldviews with those who would listen. Most would laugh, still others would sigh with exasperation, but some—*some*—would understand. It was a blessing, it was a curse, but it was all learning.

✱✱✱

He'd been swimming in womb water for nine months and three days, and it was nearing time to get dry. Still, the hospital seemed an odd place to make an entrance into the world. It was too empty, as if all color had been systematically erased, leaving behind metallic beds and white plastic tables adorned with vapid, processed foods. And while the workers had big hearts, the building itself lacked warmth, as if the echoes of death had subdued the joys of birth. But at least there was safety and security.

The mother-to-be was mildly distressed as a hospital staff member pushed her through a sterile, harshly lit hallway in a creaky wheelchair, her husband at her side. Clearly tired, the skin underneath her eyes puffed just a bit, creating dark lines, and her swollen body was ready for release.

"Is everything OK?" she asked, voice quavering, as she looked

The Mystical Village That Rewired Reality

to her husband for support.

"I'm just waiting for confirmation," he responded, forcing confidence. "But the C-section is all scheduled. Soon you'll be fast asleep and won't remember a thing. After that, well, we'll have a son." He cracked a reassuring smile and squeezed her shoulder.

The thought of sleeping through the birthing process gave her some comfort and she relaxed. "Make sure they give me the good pain killers," she said, forcing a smile.

"Let me go see what I can find out," he said as he left her side.

Preparing to enter the world, the hero-to-be baby felt the energy of this strange place they called a hospital, and he throbbed with wonder. When his mother took painkillers, he felt peculiar. When she tensed with anxiety, he felt distressed and when she experienced physical pain, his tissues absorbed the emotional imprint like the sponge that he was.

Nonetheless, at 3:33 p.m., in relative peace, he entered the world of humankind, weighing eight pounds and eight ounces.

When his mother's anesthesia wore off, the child was removed from his isolation cot and prepared to meet her.

"Where is he?" she asked, eyes heavy with fatigue, yet vigilant and eager.

The nurse brought the infant to his parents, and they swooned with gratitude. Holding him high, they bequeathed upon him a name they long had coveted. *Anax.*

Only time, another one of humankind's twisted, albeit useful inventions, would determine how this unusual name would shape the boy's life and sculpt his dreams.

While a life of free will awaited Anax, his blueprint was already drafted, and in time he would learn to embrace it. There are few things in the universe more powerful—and challenging—than finding and embracing one's destiny. Too often they fly in the face of those who love us, confronting the fabric of society and expectation, evoking our deepest fears while provoking calls for obedience and order. But for those who find the courage, destiny opens the doorway to heaven, where fear and resistance dissolve in its blazing bright light, illuminating the path to fulfillment. To embrace destiny is to love self, and this is the foundation of true power.

Nothing can match the power of a mother's bond to her newborn child—life creating life. A simple touch bridges their consciousness like an electric arc, uploading all information needed for growth. All of eternity can be transmitted in a single touch, and so it was that Anax knew his mother loved him; and through her touch his immune system strengthened, his mind gained understanding, his heart learned trust, and his spirit basked in love.

Dreaming colorful, worthwhile dreams for her son—dreams of joy, contribution and success—his mother cradled him in her arms. These dreams were honest and pure and carried forth a powerful message to the cosmos. In that moment, she wanted nothing but the best for her child and she cast no judgment on what that path might be; in that instance, on her son's behalf, she dreamed from her heart. She dreamed for her son.

My son. Anax. I love you so much. You're a part of me, and I'm a part of you. I promise to care for you and provide a stable and loving home, to keep you healthy and happy. I promise to be a good mother to you and help you grow up to be a good man.

And yet, amid his mother's love, the battle for *personal sovereignty* had only just begun. For Anax had entered a world with an architecture and agenda of its own.

As life progressed, many of the motherly dreams from that time forward would emanate not from the heart, but from the mind—a place of good intention and even greater potential, but a place that was far too vulnerable to the crooked dreams of society. They were the kind of dreams that cast aside individual expression in favor of conformity; the kind that teach one to swim with the crowd without making too many waves. And while cooperation is a powerful ideal, cooperation within a culture that promotes false ideals is not.

Little Anax was born into a world without mother's milk. She tried for a couple of weeks, but it had proven too painful. And besides, society had dreamed a new realization. Formula would work just as well as mother's milk. Or so they said.

While a lack of breast milk is certainly not to be blamed, the next stretch of Anax's life was a series of bland events, devoid of power, illusive and common. Nowhere was heroism present. The fire in his heart remained, but the flame was low.

***

At age sixteen, Anax's life was routine, without much room for change or inspiration. *Time for swim practice,* he thought, for the five-thousandth time. Up at dawn to head to the pool, along with his younger sister, then shuttled to school for six hours, followed again by swim practice, then dinner, homework, TV and sleep. It had been that way since he was eight years old. Always he was moving along the required path; it had been chosen for him, without any real consent, as best as he could recall. If that wasn't enough, the path moved in a soul-crushing circle, as well, with no ending in sight. He felt like Sisyphus dragging a boulder up the mountain, over and over again—and he burned enough calories to justify it. No matter how much he ate, he could not gain a pound; at least he'd finally broken the one-hundred-pound mark. That put him just above the pipsqueak weight class, but did little to repudiate his swim-team nickname of *Squid*.

Life was an endless cycle that left neither room nor inclination to contemplate other things. It was a blur of chlorine, exams, and the occasional drunkenness with friends. The drunkenness, of course, assumed he didn't have swim practice the next day. During the school year, he lived for the weekends when he might catch a moment's rest.

Daily worries were limited to fear of physical pain in the pool, cold water, poor grades, exclusion by friends, and on occasion, rejection by some girl. That was about it. The only time of year that brought any real fulfillment was summer. Summers were times of freedom. Sure, swim practices continued and the outdoor pools brought icy discomfort in the early part of the season, but the days were largely open for more enjoyable pursuits. Lifeguarding and coaching young swimmers were gratifying activities, particularly when shared with friends.

Anax lived outdoors in the summer and this only heightened feelings of health, freedom and joy. *If only life were always like this*, he thought, as he sat astride the lifeguard chair, keeping watch on the pool. Summer's rays brought his freckles into full bloom, and he wore a baseball cap to shield his skin. His baby-face and scrawny body did little to lure women, but that didn't stop him from looking. Scanning the beach, he located a flock of young mothers clad in bikinis, and he could not help but imagine what wonders awaited him when his body filled out a bit. His time would come.

Redirecting his attention, he fantasized about the grilled cheese and french fries awaiting him at the snack bar when he got off watch. He needed some grease on his stomach to soothe the remnants of his hangover.

GYLODON

✶✶✶

Deep in the old-growth woodlands, and energetically shielded from the prying eyes of satellites, planes and other invaders, a village hummed with a potent vibration, thriving at a wavelength that nurtured beauty, while safeguarding it from the outsiders who sought its destruction. A new day had arrived, and sunlight trickled through broad green leaves before greeting the soil and exposing the underbrush. A peaceful, gentle wind stirred the leaves in perfect rhythm, and the birdcalls had morphed into a single song—the song of morning. The villagers rose from their beds in a state of wonder as small cook fires eased the chill, and the scents of hot cereal and herbal tea wafted across the village. Smiles abounded as people departed their cottages, headed to the communal dining area for a laughter-filled breakfast.

Gylodon was a place of magic, manifested and maintained by the collective consciousness of its inhabitants. Although these inhabitants were human, they were pure and powerful in uncommon ways. Having never been exposed to constrictive thought patterns or language, they knew only how to create. They lived largely without fear, because they were never given anything to fear, nor told of the concept of fear. No such word existed in their language. And when things happened that an outsider might deem fear inducing, the villagers perceived them as part of a natural order of perfection. Some lived to be hundreds of years old simply because they carried no expectation of when death should arrive. And when others departed their bodies sooner, they communicated with them in the astral realms and held joyous celebrations to honor their lives. Death was never a separation, just a metamorphosis.

Their language was constructed to be positive and enhancing, encouraging optimism, while training their minds to view the world through filters of endless potential. In many ways, they were shamans, with one foot on Earth and the other in the spirit realms, but they had little need to dabble with darkness because they had created a community where only light could shine. Protected by an energetic web of unbreakable love, the villagers thrived, as did the animals and plants. Still, their extreme bias toward positivity and love was also their greatest vulnerability, leaving many of them blind to the physical threat posed to their home.

Recent scientific advancements in the outside world left the village more vulnerable than at any time in its history. Those who hunted them did so at the behest of a small group of people with endless resources. It's unclear how they knew about the mystical village, but they did. For seventy years, they'd known, ever since the knowledge resurfaced through folklore, but only recently did they have the technology to pose a threat. And so, the hunters intensified their search, fueled by a rapacious hunger for global dominance. They were determined to identify—and eradicate—any resistance to the illusions that they forced upon humanity.

The people of Gylodon, excepting the Council of Elders, were unaware of the threat. Most were not equipped to handle its implications. Their mental mastery left little room for fear-based thought, and their commitment to heart-consciousness blinded them with love. They were innocent, and to some extent, naïve. It was only the council members, along with select others, who carried the burden of Gylodon's vulnerability—only they were equipped to step into the darkness, to face lower-vibration realities.

Despite the secret concerns of the elders, life flourished in Gylodon, laden with radiant realities and elegant creations.

✱✱✱

The moon was whole, excessively bright, and all were ready. Three hundred villagers surrounded the ceremonial altar, blessed with fertility, as they prepared to bring new life into the world. In the shades of their faces one could find evidence of every lineage and ethnicity on Earth; indeed, their ancestors had touched every phase of human evolution. The union of these three hundred souls bridged the history of humanity.

Tonight, for the birthing ceremony, they wore their finest ceremonial gowns. Flowing red capes dyed with local berries and herbs complemented an array of beaded necklaces, many of which were sacred power objects displaying the Gylodonian rainbow pattern. These rainbows were uncommon, revealing three new colors not visible in the outside world. Gylodon's unusual wavelength played with light in peculiar ways, expanding upon the traditional color spectrum. One of the new colors appeared to be both red and green at the same time, while another was simultaneously yellow and blue.[3] The third took on a luminous star-like quality that sparkled with movement, reflecting frequencies of light that were invisible beyond the village boundaries. Each color had appeared over time, as more energy had been invested into the village. They represented the community's progression over the centuries. To touch them was divine. To wear them was a celebration. Tonight was a celebration—twins were arriving.

"Everybody spread out and surround Eva," the father-to-be announced. His tan barrel chest reflected the moonlight, revealing geometric patterns scribbled across his skin. He was the holder of the masculine energy—as was his right—for what was a profoundly feminine ceremony. There always needed to be a balance.

The villagers moved toward the altar, forming a large, near-perfect circle around the expectant mother.

"The hole has been dug, and all is ready; it has been blessed," another man declared.

One of the healers, Inipia, held the woman's hand, offering motherly comfort and smiles. Eva, the expectant mother, who had conceived her babies in the nearby woods, was now preparing to birth them into the shallow hole. She rested comfortably on a reed mat, surrounded by flower offerings, a bowl of water, candles, honey and sweet fruits. Her white gown fluttered in the breeze, flaunting the moonlight like ripples in water. She was profoundly grateful to be birthing *the twins*—honored, really—as she believed herself to be carrying the prophesied twins, destined to alter humanity's course. She knew it in her soul.

For the benefit of the younger children, who were witnessing their first birthing, the father-to-be explained, "These infants were conceived on the earth's floor, their bodies are made of the earth and it is to the earth that they shall one day return, as will all of us. When these little ones enter this world, they will be greeted by the soil first, so they know who their first mother is. After that, they will be handed to their second mother for…"

"Izzzzz time! Hooooahhhhh…" Unleashing an ecstatic howl as she brandished an ear-to-ear smile, the expectant mother proclaimed her readiness. She'd never been more beautiful.

The group shuffled closer, falling silent as they raised their hands in the air, their palms toward the woman, completing their circle. It was a medley of color and power. Holding space in this way, and sending supportive energy and love, was a long-held tradition in the village; it was both spiritual and practical, playing a central role in the birthing process. Births in the village were relatively rare, and having twins was an exceptional omen.

"Hooooooaaaahooooo!" All that could be heard was Eva's heavy, controlled exhalations blending with the flittering leaves.

"Hoooaaahooooooooooooooo!" The smile never left her face except when she widened her mouth for air; even then, her eyes still smiled.

With a peaceful heart, and one final gulp, she pushed her babies into the earth, one after the other. They were scooped up, almost immediately, just as the soil graced their skin and baptized their spirits. Eva held them close and they knew who their second mother was. Soon they would learn of their third mothers and many fathers—all the village elders would play a parental role in their lives. Once things settled down, Inipia would read their little hands and fingerprints, check their astrological leanings and ascertain the direction of their destinies.[4]

For children born in Gylodon, growing up was akin to living in a fluid, multi-dimensional amusement park. The youths were revered for their natural gifts and visions. Just as children in the outside world had "imaginary friends," Gylodonian children routinely interacted with spirits. The distinction was that their perceived realities were supported while children on the outside were told they were illusions. In this manner, Gylodonians lived free of *consciousness pollution*, seeing reality as relative to personal experience and not subject to external judgment.

In fact, all Gylodonians could see spirits. Within the village boundaries, these occurrences were a natural offshoot of the wavelength and energetic frequency at which the village existed. Its frequency was much higher than mainstream earth, opening spirit portals that otherwise went unseen. The phenomenon had become increasingly prevalent over the centuries, as Gylodon had raised its frequency, year after year.

The effects were nothing less than otherworldly, and the result was a magical landscape where ghosts, nature spirits and even concentrated thought forms became visible to the naked eye.

***

Wind whipped the leaves like a thousand rattles, twisting light that bounced off crystal fragments strewn across the ground. It was the kind of day that inspired the spirits to come out and play.

Five years had passed since the twins' birth, and not one moment of that time had been taken for granted, as curious infants grew into capable boys. The twins—named *Huta* and *Zevi*—had grown rapidly, as had their skill sets.

Blessed with uncommon power at the age of five, the boys were anomalies, even in Gylodon. It was believed that their birth portended humanity's grand transition, a shift in conscious awareness, and that their gifts promised fuel to the cause. So, the elders gave special attention to their lessons, which the boys hungrily embraced.

An elderly man with weathered skin, who still carried himself with the stature of youth, motioned to his great-great-grandson, Huta, directing his attention to the perimeter trees.

"Do you see the swirl forming over there? Watch closely now, and use your fourth power," the man encouraged.

The shirtless boy, wearing a youthful smile while displaying absolute focus, looked just beyond the pines. In the distance, a cloudy mist floated, taking form as if growing limbs, and then it twisted, revealing silver, fluffy wings. Within moments, the shape faded into the skyline. "I see it, Papa," he said. "I see all of it. It's a Sylph."

The Elder gave a nod of satisfaction and a smile. "Very good, Huta. And the element?"

The boy paused for only a second. "It's of the air, Papa."

His grandfather's eyes crinkled with satisfaction. "Excellent," he said. "Stay here and observe; when you are ready come find me and tell me everything that you learn." Huta nodded enthusiastically, as if overflowing with excitement, and his brown eyes widened, revealing the underpinnings of his Native American and African heritage.

After a pause, the man turned toward the community center and departed, leaving the boy to his lesson.

For a villager with access to the fourth power, which included all manner of mental psychic abilities, it was a life far apart from the outside world. Upon the wind, multi-dimensional melodies floated freely to the ears, providing ecstatic experience from a passing gust. Dazzling arrays of colors flickered among the gardens, only to take form into one of the legendary garden spirits. These energetic life forms interacted through feelings, as well, often inspiring spontaneous explosions of love and compassion in the villagers.

In addition to a culture of constant learning—through personal experience—the villagers would come together to channel their power for the betterment of Gylodon, as well as the larger planet.

They were *warriors of light* and their actions helped restore balance in the outside world.

While they knew little of the change their intentions created, their very existence guided the planet's evolution, waking minds and opening hearts. The transition for humanity—an awakening to self-love, purpose and free thought—was nearing its tipping point, and they were at its fulcrum.

Only the elders knew that pain and suffering would precede the transition. It was inevitable. Humanity would endure a calamitous era of earth-rattling change and environmental devastation, catalyzed by a failure of integrity among its leaders. Darkness would rise upon the wings of greed and discrimination, and demagogues would seize power, hastening the collapse of old systems. Humanity would hit bottom, forcing absolute surrender, freeing minds and opening hearts to the things that mattered. Only when they had lost everything would the people release the illusions that held them hostage. It was at that moment that certain Gylodonians would depart the village to wander out into the world of pain, serving as guides toward freedom and love. They did not know how events would transpire, or exactly what their role would entail; they knew only that they were awaiting the omens. They had been waiting for hundreds of years.

Children of Gylodon; hemp canvas.

Inipia

***

She'd just returned from an arduous journey to the outside world that lasted months, and Gylodon's vibration had never felt so good. Inipia's smile transcended physicality, as if affecting more than her lips, and coupled with her nurturing green eyes, was enough to warm a room. She shuddered as warm, tingling energy rose in her spine, acclimating her body to the village's higher frequency. It had been a long time since she'd been gone this long. Departures from the village were exceedingly rare, reserved for a select few—and returning home always felt like a rebirth.

She'd seen true darkness on this trip and it had taken its toll; in one instance, she'd inadvertently stumbled into an animal kill shelter and was empathically overwhelmed by the fear and hopelessness. Her legs had collapsed before she'd reestablished her energy protections. She'd spent the better part of a day there after that, doing a healing on the entire facility, and each creature in turn, both those still living and those that had passed. The employees had thought her a bit odd, to say the least, walking around to each cage with her hands in the air, but they were inexplicably soothed by her presence and allowed her to stay as long as she liked. Each of the animals had fallen asleep afterward, as well, creating an eerie silence in a normally bark-ridden room. The employees were utterly baffled. She advised them that the animals would need extra water when they awakened. They had agreed without an ounce of resistance. In the end, they too received healings, after she acquired their permission, of course.

Inipia's return to Gylodon was a celebratory event, and many came to greet her, bringing gifts and warm embraces. She was a true village mother and healer, loved by all. The reunions brought her a sense of completeness and community that had been absent on the outside. But it was with particular joy that she opened her door to find Zevi and Huta, the twins, now eight years old, standing outside. How quickly they had grown.

Before she could speak, they erupted into their usual giggles. Bending a knee, she extended her arms, wrapping the two youths in a motherly embrace. They were not her biological children, but ones she'd helped birth years before; nonetheless, they *were* her children. The boys had grown a great deal, and their once supple baby skin had transformed into tiny muscles wrought with scratches and all the markings of active boys. They'd acquired deep tans and full heads of curly, dark hair.

"Look at the two of you, sprouting like jade vines!"

The boys caressed her face, silent, as if she were a newborn, reveling in her return and her softness, while connecting with her energy. Zevi laughed again.

"My favorite young gigglers, what adventures have I missed?"

What the twins only peripherally knew, but Inipia, along with the elders, had long realized, was that the codes in their fingerprints and hands, analyzed at birth, had revealed extraordinary talents for energy mastery. Their birth astrology had corroborated the findings.

They were destined, it seemed, to play a role in the world's tipping point, perhaps even altering the planet's *consciousness cloud* on a significant level. Among the council members, there had even been talk about them being the prophesied twins who would reincarnate when the world was ready, able to alter realities with uncommon ease. But to Inipia, they were children, young and growing, and rascals at that.

"We have been making friends in the forest," Huta replied, very adultlike.

"Yes, and we have learned to play the chute flute," Zevi offered. "And we can sing a lot more songs! Fourteen new ones."

"Fifteen!" Huta corrected.

"Yes, fifteen!"

Their enthusiasm was electric. As twins, their personalities overlapped synergistically, but Huta had always been a bit more reserved. Both were avid adventurers, tree climbers and inquisitive learners. Their curiosity was one of experience and interaction, always seeking to touch and imagine the object of their lessons. Imagination played a key role in their energy manipulations, and came naturally, while their parallel personalities amplified their creative powers in strange ways.

Inipia had wanted to bring them gifts, but there was little in the way of "stuff" the outside world could offer. Most things would be detrimental to their innocence and growth, but she'd been clever. Pulling a tiny satchel from her bag, she gave the boys her grandest smile, before pouring the contents into her hand.

"For my two young energy masters, I have these very special apple seeds. New kinds that do not yet grow in Gylodon. Take them, share them with your family, and transform them into magnificent trees, full of juicy fruit, to share with all!"

The twins held the seeds with reverence, knowing their power, and then hugged Inipia in gratitude. She put them back into the satchel for them, which they eyed with intrigue; it was constructed of a foreign material, like an alien technology. Occasionally, such items made their way into the village and were sources of curiosity. Most important to the twins, though, were the seeds. Apples were their favorite fruit, and new varieties provided an exciting prospect to young, growing boys who loved to eat.

When the twins had finished envisioning the "trees full of juicy fruit" and how they might accelerate their growth, they departed to the forest for the day's adventures.

***

Sunlight flickered on flapping leaves and an enchanting, perfectly temperate day shone forth. Only in a place so untouched could natural beauty thrive. The young twins frolicked in the wilderness, lost in a world of wonder.

Gylodon was a bubble of beauty—a sanctuary in the midst of a profoundly imbalanced world. The boys had no knowledge of the pain and suffering of the outside world; little did they know that just one hundred miles from where they stood, communing with animals and plants, were factory farms—and institutionalized animal torture—where something called money was the impetus behind extraordinary suffering. Little did they know that there were people out there who wanted them dead because of the love in their hearts, and the power that they held. They were not equipped to understand these dark realities, and so Gylodon's *consciousness cloud* shielded them from humanity's harder truths.

Their village was nearby, but the boys were equally at home in the forest. Jumping and rolling in the leaves, they screaked birdcalls and laughed until their bellies hurt. When they caught their breath, one of them would squawk again and reignite the entire process. By the time they were done, they were so tired of laughing—and so in need of oxygen—that they could only lie in the leaves, savoring each breath while staring upward through the canopy at the wispy clouds.

"This one is a hummingbird," Zevi said, as he pointed skyward.

"And this one is a flower," his brother responded, pointing upward before scratching his back.

After a pause, Zevi released another low-pitched screech, and the two of them burst into another laughing fit.

"I would like to see a hummingbird *and* a flower," Huta added.

"Yes!" his brother responded, flashing white teeth through a buoyant smile.

They looked at each other as if the matter was settled, then shifted their bodies to lie shoulder-to-shoulder and hip-to-hip. Instinctually, they closed their eyes and quietly accessed their imaginations, emotions and focused intentions. As children born in the village, dreaming things into reality was a daily activity and had become as natural as eating. They practiced this form of manifestation with absolute faith in the outcome, as they knew nothing else. Their language did not have a word for doubt, and so they operated from a place of true power. In fact, the outcome was never something to be achieved, but rather something that already existed. They were just making it visible in their current density and reality. Operating with youthful purity, they could create realities faster than many of the adults in the village. As twins working together, however, they could harmonize and amplify their intentions and were quickly growing into the most powerful *reality sculptors* in the entire village.

And so, they shared a dream of a hummingbird on a flower. When they finished the process of visualizing the scene, feeling it fully and knowing it to be reality, they rose slowly and walked deeper into the forest. They walked without expectations or a care in the world, simply absorbing the beauty around them and interacting with it in countless ways. A dream of this magnitude, they knew, would usually take less than one day to manifest itself.

The boys had strong relationships with certain trees, knowing them by name, and would frequently visit certain knotty pines and towering oaks. The boulders by the spring had names as well, as did the spring itself. Speaking with the nature spirits through the power of *four* and loving them through the power of *five*, the children rambled along, smiling and free, engaging life fully.

When they reached their favorite cluster of wild raspberry bushes, they stepped around them and then found the access point; stepping inside, they were swallowed by brambles that towered overhead, like a secret garden offering bright red capillaries of delight.

"May we have some of your fruit?" they asked. The plant waved back and they giggled. Plucking the berries lovingly, they searched for the ripest, those that were ready; and when they ate them, they consciously absorbed the color, flavors and life-force with which they were imbued. Eating was a multi-dimensional experience, and the flavors exploded in their mouths, evoking laughter but never taking their attention away from the experience. They lived in the present moment with every bite. A single, wild raspberry was a full sensory experience, and the twins expressed gratitude for these simple pleasures.

As much as they were prone to laughing fits, the boys were mature, growing rapidly in all ways, and their time of acknowledgment was near.

Zevi (lying down) and Huta; hemp canvas.

Altered States

***

Flute music filled the night and Gylodon was reborn, as was the tradition. The community members, wearing their finest ceremonial clothing, gathered in the field around the fire, beneath clear skies, to call forth magic and commence the initiation. Blades of tall grass swayed with the breeze, as the scent of wild lilacs drifted across the field. Melodic frequencies enlivened the natural elements, giving them form, and patterns of light swirled before flashing, just as the stars moved closer to observe. Even the spirits partook. Festivity overflowed, dripping alongside dancing feet, open hearts and unbridled celebration.

It was their first rite, a true initiation, and the twins were being honored for their mastery of *four* and *five*, as well as their destinies as village manifesters, or *reality sculptors*. Frenzied ecstasy, tapered only by haunting flute music and spontaneous explosions of light, catapulted the villagers into altered states of consciousness. Dancing and spinning, they became one with the melodious trance, carried by wind, and the geometries of the earth drum, vibrating beneath their feet.

Two elders, donning red cloaks and a multitude of rainbow beads around their necks, hoisted the boys upon their shoulders while circling the fire as the village mothers looked upon them with love. They were the youngest in the village's recorded history to attain such mastery. Eight years old. "Might as well be eighty," one jested. They carried a purity and power comparable to any elder. It was only experience that they lacked, and that would come in time. For now, though, they'd celebrate.

A beautiful, dark-haired woman called Tristis looked on, and her heart swelled. The children reminded her of her own family who lived in the outside world. She wished her little ones could be exposed to such opportunities. Alas, it was her path, and hers alone, to be here acquiring power. It would still be many moons before she could attain comparable mastery to that of these two small boys. She was one of three people in more than one hundred years to arrive at the village from the outside world. Though she was grateful for the opportunity, her mind drifted to her children on the outside. She regretted her inability to share the magic with them. Instead she sent them love and knew they felt it.

A villager bumped her playfully, wakening her focus, and she returned to the festivities. Moving back toward the spinning circle of bodies, she allowed the magical resonance to consume her consciousness.

The flute players journeyed to other realms, playing entirely under trance and channeling whatever came through; sometimes their vocal chords took on unusual physiology, capable of new sounds. During these brief episodes, they could merge mind and heart, capture the multi-dimensional melodies that lived in the astral layers, then re-release them into the village as newly constructed geometric structures, frequencies and colors. It was raw creativity and the villagers relished it, merging with spirit through ecstatic dance.

The twins, climbing down from tall shoulders, moved toward the fire. At once, the melody slowed, the movements unified, and the circle closed around them. Now was the time for the initiates to offer a silent intention for planetary healing.

As they stepped toward the flames, ready for their moment, the peace was disrupted, as a loud and violent sound ripped through the village, like a warning from the gods. It echoed across the field, like a drumbeat of death. It was a gunshot, several miles away, outside of Gylodon's boundaries. The elders turned to look at one another, and the firelight cast feathery shadows through ornate headdresses, but it did little to disguise the foreboding sadness in their eyes. They were the only ones who knew the truth of what a gunshot was; most villagers had accepted it as a rare, natural phenomenon. It was better that way—they were not equipped to understand the existence, or the implications, of weapons. Regardless, there was no immediate threat—Gylodon was protected—but still, it seemed that the animal hunters came closer every year. The elders sent their protective prayers to the forest creatures.

Seamlessly, the villagers returned their attention to the ceremony, as the twins prepared to offer their prayers for the planet. Gazing into the flames, the boys remembered their teacher's adage, *sculpting high-vibration realities is the path of a warrior of light.* That is what they intended to do. No words would be spoken during the process, but all the villagers would channel energy toward them as a show of support and to multiply their powers of creation.

Mostly the villagers wore red, white and brown ceremonial clothing, ornamented with colorful beads; but some decorated themselves with woven twig headdresses and still others sported elaborate flower wreaths around their necks. Collectively, the group looked like a shape-shifting serpent, and its energy pulsed like ocean waves, driven by wind, amid the perfect storm. Within the storm's eye stood the two young initiates, embracing their destiny.

Always in sync, the twins smiled at each other, and their eyes shone with power, tainted only by a glimmer of mischief. First, they'd offer their planetary intentions, and then they would have their fun.

Their prayers came easily, penetrating the earth and nearby astral spaces. In time, they would become realities that healed nature. The process felt good; it was as much about feeling—channeling nurturing energy—as thinking, and it came back to them like a reflection, flooding their hearts. The energy the twins felt from the villagers surprised them; they'd never had concentrated power directed at them before, free for use. It was nearly overwhelming, but they handled it well.

They'd told nobody about the second part of their plan. With their prayer complete, they looked at each other one final time, eyes bright, then shifted shoulder-to-shoulder while standing, summoning all the power at their disposal.

It didn't take long. A fluttering sound disrupted the silence and eyes began to open. The villagers, previously immersed in their energetic projections while holding space for the boys, cast glances left and right, unsure if what they were seeing was a magical manifestation from another realm, or something straight from the forest.

Just within the circle, surrounding the boys, in a near-perfect halo, eight hummingbirds hovered; the firelight flickered upon their ghostly figures, but they were not ghosts. They had flown directly from the woodlands to partake in the ceremony. If that wasn't enough, they had aligned themselves with each of the cardinal directions, and each point in between. On occasion, the villagers had experienced such displays from the spirit world, but never from their own world. It was unheard of. Nobody had ever had the power to manifest such realities with the woodland animals.

Tristis, born in the outside world, observed the spectacle with reverence and awe; it stirred something deep within her, something intangible, and for a moment she was lost. She'd always had a powerful bond with animals, touched by their innocence and presence, and moved by their unconditional love, but she'd never witnessed anything like this. Such a feat was worthy of veneration—a parade of possibility made into reality.

The focus quickly dissipated and the birds scattered, returning to their nests. Time paused as sporadic whispers morphed into collective joy. The flute music ceased and everyone began speaking at once about the omen and how powerful it had been. The twins just giggled, looking at each other in the bouncing firelight, as others rubbed their heads and squeezed their shoulders, offering congratulations.

Before long the music began anew, and it carried the joyful flight of hummingbirds dancing on air, as the villagers synchronized their movements and chanted like warriors. The ecstasies were reignited, the bonfire fed, and the people danced until dawn.

Life was raw and free, and to the villagers it was normal, but it was always revered and appreciated. Gratitude was as natural as water consumption, and love lived not just in their hearts, but also in the leaves, the rivers, the rocks and the air.

***

Bedraggled and delirious with fatigue from the night's celebration, the twins called upon the residual adrenaline coursing through their bodies. Despite a visceral need for sleep, they sought a brief escape into the woodlands, where they could be alone with each other.

Creeping around a moss-laden rock face, they searched for a new cavern to explore. They were approximately a half-mile from the village, near a favorite spot, when the hairs along their spines stood erect, awakening their animal instincts. From the shadow of the rock, they crouched, peering into the surrounding woodlands; the bird songs had changed, portending danger, and the land's hum had been disrupted. Their eyes fell upon an emerging silhouette, which they assumed was a forest spirit, fully embodied. But it lacked the hallmark signs of wispy energy; instead, it moved like an uncoordinated man. As the truth became clear, it exceeded their wildest imaginings. A white man, sickly and uneven, bumbled through brambles, nearly tripping. With vacant, bloodshot eyes he seemed to have no awareness of where he was.

The boys were not afraid, but they became like the animals of the forest, dissolving into invisibility within the uneven shadows.

Zevi whispered to Huta. "It's a man! And his colors are all crooked!"

Huta just stared, nodding in shocked assent. They had never seen anyone whose energy fields were so disjointed and irregular.

"Let's tell Ini!"

They slithered, dodging sporadic patches of light that illuminated the forest floor. When they cleared a hillcrest that shielded

The Mystical Village That Rewired Reality

them from sight, they ran full speed to the village to report the strange man who had breached the village's *consciousness cloud.*

Wandering Mind

***

Anax had grown up. Or perhaps he hadn't. Kicking back in his office chair, he rode the momentum as it slid off the cheap, sticky plastic sheet below. It was a little trick he adopted to divert his attention from the perils of deadlines and project work. It made him feel like a kid again. He took a deep breath, quieted his mind and immersed himself in silence. Something irked him. He'd recently read a study published by NASA that indicated that all the water on Earth might have originated from outer space by way of ice comets.[5] The implications spun his imagination into overdrive.

As a rule, his mind ran out of control, connecting one thing to another, seeing possibilities everywhere. He was a man of ideas. Too many of them. Finding focus was akin to great achievement, and any semblance of thought discipline remained just beyond reach. To him, the universe was a mystical place, full of intrigue, mystery and interconnectivity. He believed that quantum physics, among other things, supported his feelings about the magical nature of the world, but he never had the patience to look deeply into the subject. Prone to outlandish perspectives, rarely backed by proof, his philosophies were often met with quizzical stares and overt resistance.

Nonetheless, he did have an unusual way of seeing patterns and codes in the world, where others did not. His odd angles on life fostered a contrarian mindset that sought to unbalance mainstream, routine thinking. It rarely made for relaxed conversation. His sensitivities easily flared, and he often felt frustrated—or even lonely—when others failed to embrace what he deemed to be immutable truths.

Today, Anax's mind was plagued by the origin of water. *If water comes from outer space, what does that mean to us? Our bodies are primarily composed of water—something like sixty percent. Hmmm. So, sixty percent of our bodies are not really from Earth, but from out in the universe somewhere. So, NASA is indirectly saying that we're from outer space. Right. That explains it.*

Through the western-facing office windows, the sun streamed in, and the already-too-small room was sweltering, disquieting its inhabitants and igniting short tempers. Anax swept back a lock of dirty-blond hair and squinted blue eyes into an annoying sunlight reflection from the neighboring building. He adjusted his position. Still dousing himself with the implications of water, he yearned for a shower, a cold one at that, and not because of the attractive new team member with whom he'd started playing bumper chairs as of late.

So, Mother Nature recycles her water. That means that the water in my body could be the same water that was in a caveman's body, or a dinosaur's body millions of years ago. He recalled his roommate telling him that over the course of our lifetimes, we will likely ingest the same molecules of water more than once. *Don't other people wonder about this stuff? Not enough.*

It was 2:30 p.m., and despite the oppressive heat, he was alert. In the past, he'd be stricken by a post-lunch coma by now, fighting the urge to crawl into the fetal position and hibernate under his desk. But now, since he'd shifted to a vegetarian diet, he didn't get drowsy after lunch. The change afforded him new vitality and mildly improved focus.

Ann, the project manager, pulled him out of his daydream. "How is that presentation coming along?"

"Oh, pretty well, I should have it cleaned up in about ten more minutes," he responded. He liked Ann, but felt that she stressed too much about things that were out of her control.

Silently, frustration crested in Anax, tipping him toward despair. It was a daily occurrence and it wasn't healthy. *What a waste,* he thought. *So tired of it. How did I end up here? I wasn't born to be shackled to this stupid desk. I'm 31, and this is where I am? God help me.*

And still, he did not have the courage to leave.

Life felt like a stage play that he was forced to endure, but could not enjoy. Living in a state of constant inner conflict, he suffered. A restless spirit who longed for an unconventional existence, he fantasized about mystical subjects like magic, energy and adventure. He dreamed of exploring wilderness, uncovering obscure mysteries and becoming a warrior. How he could earn a living doing that, he had no idea. Money-related fears kept him from deviating too far outside of his corporate existence.

In the past, his entrepreneurial spirit had led him down some exciting paths, none of which had resulted in financial success, and at least one of which had taken its toll on his natural, risk-taking propensities. So, he hid himself in a corporate culture that fostered company allegiance, all the while confronting his own internal resistance to authority figures. Living in a constant state of imbalance caused his health to suffer at times, and he daydreamed about a better life. Still, he could not move forward.

Nonetheless, through his challenges, he was beginning to access deeper self-awareness. This only added to his restlessness, as he did not know how to act on it. He'd long been attuned to his personality type, having studied various systems while seeking answers about his purpose in life, but new things were beginning to present themselves—things that defied normalcy. His intuition was stronger than ever, and he sensed interconnectivities among things, although he could never quantify them. He embraced his newfound awareness openly, but recognized that the office environment seemed to stifle it.

On his way home after work, he picked up some cleaning supplies to tackle the apartment dust balls that appeared spontaneously and grew like overfed puppies. *They are an absolute puzzlement*, he thought. *I don't get it.* Of all the life mysteries that he was prone to examining, city dust balls held a special place.

Cleaning supplies in hand, he climbed the stairs to his walk-up apartment and crossed paths with another tenant exiting the building.

"Hello," Anax said, smiling.

"Hullo," came his muffled response, from a face fixated on the building exit. Anax shook his head. *Another oddity. How can we live so close to one another and not know each other's names?* City life was indeed a peculiar experiment; people living on top of one other without any sense of community or fraternity. *Strange.*

***

Date night was a bizarre ritual—one of equal parts expectation and pleasure; it served as both a display of financial security—depending upon how expensive the restaurant was—and mandated face-to-face intimacy. Dialogue danced between shallow topics like weather and emotionally charged ones like love, or life purpose. Anax hoped that tonight's dinner discourse would hit the spot, and if for some reason, it did not, he hoped to at least find fulfillment in the first and second course. Followed by the intercourse, of course. That always hit the spot.

"What would you say that you're most driven by, underneath it all?" Anax asked.

His girlfriend Elizabeth laughed. "You always ask the oddest questions. Not one for light conversation, are you, Hon?" She leaned across the restaurant table.

"Nope," he responded, modestly drunk, as he leaned forward to meet her halfway. The candlelight captured her Irish-Italian features just right, granting poetic justice to jet-black eyebrows and distinct, high cheekbones that complemented pristine teeth. She was exquisite.

"My career is very important to me, as you know," she continued. "Proving myself, being successful, having a family and being happy, I guess." She paused, thinking. "What about you?"

He was disappointed by her answer; it was trite and lacked heart, like a greeting card. Anax liked to peel away the layers of people, right down to their core; when he asked a deep question, he wanted a deep answer. Maybe he was being too serious, or too hard on her, though. Her eyes twinkled in the candlelight, and he forgave her.

"What about you? What drives you?" she asked.

He looked down at the table, taking a sobering breath. *The endless possibilities in life,* he thought. *Opportunities. Infinite permutations of sex, vegetarianism, puppies, love, energy, music, freedom and nature. Yes, nature. Reverence for nature. Oh, and of course, understanding the nature of consciousness and pushing its boundaries. Magic. Real magic. Hmmm. Fighting the status quo when it's broken? Then again, that just gets me riled up. Animal rights. That's a good one. Alternative healing modalities—that turns me on too. My God, there are so many. Oh—can't forget about innovation and creativity, those are always sexy. How about finding innovative solutions to end unnecessary suffering in the world—for humans, animals and all of nature? Perfect. Done.* Then again, he realized, he wasn't doing too many of these things, and he blinked, sequestering his onslaught of thoughts in favor of a commonplace, greeting-card response.

"Those dimples."

Her lips tightened, holding back a mischievous smile. "Thank you for the compliment, Hon. Now, seriously, what is it for you?"

He sighed. "Happiness, certainly. Finding that natural state of happiness that I believe is inherent to all human beings." He contemplated expanding upon the concept, but thought better of it. Besides, he hadn't quite uncovered that natural state of happiness himself, so preaching about it was fruitless. And he wasn't about to strip away any of his own layers, exposing his true self; their relationship wasn't that deep. And if it did go that deep, he knew, it would rip apart at the seams.

Like many young men who were unsatisfied with their livelihoods, Anax turned to his relationship to fill a void in his life. And she filled it well, with dimples cut like gemstones and a knowing smirk that invited laughter.

"Lemme get a bite of that dimp," he said, as he leaned in for a quick peck on the cheek.

Elizabeth obliged, but her cheeks flushed at the gesture. Sometimes he wondered if they'd be together without those dimples. Their belief systems clashed, and no matter how hard he tried, he could not envision marriage. Instead, he saw empty space. Far too often he felt like an alien around her, so he avoided esoteric subjects and let their relationship slog along on autopilot. It was better than sitting at home alone.

"Hello, folks," the waiter intervened. "Are you ready to order?"

Anax had staked out one or two vegetarian possibilities on the menu; he wondered if they would satisfy him. He settled on mushroom risotto, which he hoped would do the trick. If not, some wine would curb the hunger pangs.

"I will have the veal," Elizabeth said, looking content with her choice. Anax bit his lip and steadied himself in his chair. He waited until the server departed.

"Did you seriously just order *veal?*" He mustered his finest expression of utter disbelief.

"Yes, I did. And the problem *is?*" She squinted her eyes and snarled her lip, just a bit, as if daring him to answer. Her dimples were nowhere to be found, he noted with concern.

"Well, I don't want ruin your meal, but that is not really a morally responsible food choice."

"Anax, I don't want a lecture. Please stop." Her voice was firm like a stone wall—and not the crumbly kind with loose rocks.

"OK, no problem," he said, choking back his frustration before slamming into her wall; he raised his hands feigning submission. It wasn't worth ruining the evening over. Never had she seemed more like an alien to him, though. *A sexy alien, no doubt, but one whose food choices reinforce the commercial torture of baby cows. Lovely. Well, I guess we aren't marriage material.* He smirked indelicately.

The thought of marriage was peculiar. He'd found it odd as he watched all his childhood friends marry and create families. In his youth, he never imagined living a lifestyle so divergent from them. Now, nearly all of them had at least one child and a white-picket existence to which Anax felt a deep-seated resistance. Adamantly opposed to following other people's expectations, or any sort of societal norm, for that matter, he just watched as everyone around him built lives, while he wallowed in loneliness. Refusing to settle for what others deemed normal, he accepted the loneliness and tolerated nonfulfillment.

When he was not in a relationship, his married friends ceased inviting him to social gatherings, and he did not seek them out. As he aged, he only felt more distant, isolating himself in his world of oddball beliefs and otherworldly perspectives. Though he was a loner in many ways, he unconsciously longed for a community to which he might belong. Such a place seemed far away.

Fortunately, his romantic relationship provided a much-needed reprieve from his self-imposed isolationism, and the hardest times of his life—or at least the most boring—were when he was single. Still, he did covet his time alone; unfortunately for him, far too much of it was wasted exploring unusual topics on the computer instead of living life. His existence was introspective and quiet, and so far, quite a disappointment.

"Shall we?" Anax asked. The check had been paid. She nodded. They rose and made their way outside. Oppressive and moist, with the sweet redolence of restaurant garbage, it was a typical summer evening in New York City.

They strolled across the street until the crosswalk light flashed and then rushed to cross the avenue. Elizabeth was walking faster than Anax, skillfully stepping out in her silver spikes. Anax trailed about five feet behind, lost in his thoughts, as usual. In a flash, his conscious awareness returned. *No. Wha...*

A car barreled through the intersection, its horn resonating like a muted echo in Anax's wandering mind. Then blackness came, followed by light. No pain. None. Only freedom. Magnificent freedom. The episode reverberated in Anax's consciousness like a soulful melody.

In those few moments, Anax shed his body, but kept his

consciousness.[6] He could never quite express what happened. Or, perhaps, people couldn't understand his explanations—it was all too personal. Time was not linear. It was not even real. It was one of those things that a person had to experience to comprehend. Whether one called it a near-death experience, or an out-of-body experience, Anax had never encountered anything so vivid.

There was no fear or pain. Just seamless floating. Clarity of thought. Acute awareness. *This feels so natural,* he thought. *How can this be?* Excitement surged.

He floated above the accident scene, able to identify every detail, hearing every voice. He could decipher every license plate. Razor-sharp awareness, and yet, his body lay strewn across the intersection like an external appendage that he did not recognize. Lifeless.

But I'm alive, he thought, attempting to reconcile the two realities.

He observed the bystanders chatting on their cell phones, squinting to see what had unfolded. They stood around watching, but few reacted. Briefly, he thought about how many people disassociate from the hungry and homeless, stepping over them on the sidewalk, without so much as a glance.

Fortunately for Anax, a few reactive pedestrians called 911. *Thank goodness.*

And then, as if the spigot of life had ruptured, he was flooded by lost memories and misplaced emotions; they intruded upon his awareness like long-forgotten acquaintances, and he wasn't ready for them. Remorse. Sadness. Joy. Choices—right and wrong ones. Visions. His consciousness was inundated with life insights, playing like a movie. He could remember how it was intended to be. *So many opportunities, so many paths left to walk.* All the pieces fit together like a four-dimensional jigsaw puzzle.

There were fleeting glances into a time before his birth, when he chose a blueprint for this lifetime. *An elegant blueprint.* He'd been excited about the prospect for growth this time around. He'd chosen parents from whom he could learn a great deal. And, likewise, to whom he could teach a great deal. *That was the contract*, he remembered.

He'd adopted a personality that was entrepreneurial, inventive and even mystical. *So much potential. So much left to do,* he thought again, as he reviewed his life as an external observer. His story floated, danced, and played in frames like a film. *I see things clearly now,* he thought, as his visions muted the screaming ambulances.

Sudden awareness rattled him.

"I'm not finished!" he yelled. But nobody heard.

And then—darkness—momentary and transient. Eyelids lifting. Sharp light and pain returning like an unwelcome guest. He'd reclaimed his broken body.

Numb, dulled and cloudy, he scanned the room. *Where am I?* Dazed, but fully aware of his body, his heart swelled; a new reality was upon him, tearing apart the fabric of his lifelong perceptions. Emotions filled the holes. He knew, beyond any doubt, that consciousness could exist outside of the body. *I will not forget,* he told himself. Still, his head throbbed, his mind was unreliable and he worried that he'd forget.

A spontaneous memory displaced his fear. His roommate, pontificating about memories, once said, "They come and go, like blurry glimpses of another life. The ones that are most difficult to comprehend are easily forgotten, relegated to a gray abyss of forgotten truths." He chuckled at her zealotry; she loved poems and was prone to histrionics.

This memory will be different, he promised himself. But his mind was already lost, and he slept.

Astral Realities

✱✱✱

In and out of awareness. Strange scenes, merging, and then awakening to a whitewashed hospital room. More unfamiliar landscapes, people, no sense of body. Barely lucid. Then a fluorescent bulb biting into his vision.

With one foothold on the hospital bed and the other in alternative realities, he wrestled with death. He'd suffered a traumatic head wound, one that few would have survived, and his legs were shattered, presenting kneecaps like twin purple eggplants.

When he awoke, they told him that his brain was stable. *They seemed surprised,* he thought, feeling a twinge of humor. Then he slept for days.

Along with immobility, pain and evolving depression, the next two months in the hospital continued to shake his foundation.

One evening, lying extra still, he directed his attention to the repetitive, electronic hum of the hospital machines. The sounds lulled him into a deep trance, while keeping his attention focused. Before long, he drifted into the dream realms, and something happened. Again. It was different, yet the same. He never really fell asleep, but instead teetered on the cusp of consciousness. It was a strange place wedged between wakefulness and sleep where his body slept, but his mind maintained awareness. It felt not so different from his near-death experience following the accident.

What's going on? His heart rate seemed to escalate. *Is it?* Next came vibrations, then noise roaring through his solar plexus and into his head. *This is odd,* he thought, and felt no fear from the sensations. The vibrations grew stronger, consuming his awareness. *It's ripping.* The next thing he knew, he pushed out of his body. He willed it. His thoughts were his own, but he felt a strange sense of freedom that was almost all consuming. *Just like the accident,* he thought. *Am I dying? Hell, I feel great.* He didn't know if he was smiling, but it sure felt like it, as if his whole body were smiling. But he didn't even have a body. This time he'd experienced no trauma. Rather, he was in a peculiar, sleepless mind state that allowed him to shift into this odd place.

Anax floated around the room. *It looks different,* he noted. Puffy, dark clouds floated in the corners and near the closet. Other than that, though, he could discern most of the details in the room. It was as if he'd passed through a mirror into the hidden side of life, accessing a reflection of reality. It was an odd feeling, to wonder if he'd just died, and yet, to feel so alive. He glanced at himself lying in the bed. *Hi there. You alive?*

As he tried to distinguish his face, the environment blurred—like fog on a windshield—and he felt his energy-body drop, expecting to wake up on the floor. Instead, he opened his eyes and found himself in bed.

Whoa. That was wild. It was 11:30 p.m. He'd only attempted to go to sleep twenty minutes before. *That was no dream.* He'd consciously felt himself separate from his body; he'd been in control, and grasped details. He savored the experience for a few more minutes, willing himself to remember, and then drifted off to sleep.

The next few days were daunting. At times, Anax's head felt like a collection of loose bone fragments, held together only by flesh, and when he failed to take the painkillers, the headaches assailed him like merciless war hammers, thumping his skull. But he was alive. And though his legs were shattered, he was determined to regain mobility. He pictured himself running, and directed his thoughts toward his legs. It was a technique he'd read about somewhere—and damn it—he had nothing else to do anyway.

***

Anax spent more than two months in the hospital, and the only things that kept him sane were his *astral projections*—a new term that he'd learned to describe his out-of-body experiences. He embraced the phenomena, like an avid student of occult magic, and they occurred with increasing frequency.

How ironic, he thought, smiling before cringing again at the head pain. The prospect of exploring the astral realms, and their endless possibilities, had reawakened his long-suppressed spirit of exploration. It was the ultimate journey, devoid of limitations. No legs needed. Life was more than flesh and dirt. He could heal himself; he just needed the right path.

Without these experiences, he would have quit. But instead of dying, he took vacations outside his body. Realities widened. Bone and blood were replaced by energy and spirit, and despite his immobility, he traveled to the edge of the universe and to the spaces in between.

Hospital visits from family softened the doldrums of waking boredom. They challenged him, though; a widening chasm now existed where communication once flowed. Unable to express how he'd transformed in a manner that they could understand, he floundered.

When his mother, a loving and protective entity, visited she was overwhelmed by his injuries.

"How could you not be paying attention when crossing the road? Oh Anax, your legs. Your legs. My poor boy." Her heart was centered, but her mind ran rampant with devastation.

"Mom, please, I am aware of my legs," he responded. "Let's not fixate on what's wrong. Be grateful that I'm alive."

She nodded, but positivity amid the suffering of her child was difficult.

"Another thing, Mom, remember how I told you about being out-of-body after the accident, floating above the scene?"

"Yes, I remember," she said, looking down.

"Well, this is going to sound strange to you, but those kinds of experiences have continued while I've been in the hospital. And, well, they've been transformational. Let's just say that I've been able to travel to alternative realities several nights a week." Anax instantly regretted his choice of words, but he was too tired to recant them and too vested in truth to deny them.

She gave him the courtesy of looking him in the eye. "Sweetie, you are on a lot of pain killers and have a serious head injury. Don't you think they might be causing these dreams?"

Crimson flared in his cheeks, and he accidently bumped the food tray, sending a fork clattering to the floor. "Mom, they are *not* dreams. They are real. As real as you and me, sitting here right now. I'm fully conscious and aware of everything."

She inhaled a deep gulp of air and her eyes reflected anguish. She was tired.

"Look," he continued, "I just want you to know that in some ways this has been good for me, and changed me for the better."

"Sweetie, you're scaring me a little bit," she said. "Are you OK?"

He lost it. "Look Mom, it's not my fault that you don't believe in the eternal nature of consciousness. Up until a few weeks ago, I didn't either. But I'm telling you that it's real, and that I have repeatedly experienced it over the past few weeks. I'm OK. In many ways, I'm better than OK. My body is busted, but my spirit is experiencing new worlds."

She half acknowledged his comment, but her filters were like walls. "I don't know what to say, Anax. I can't relate."

Despite his throbbing cranium, his frustration exploded and he lost control. "You don't need to relate, Mom. Just accept and acknowledge. I understand that it's my experience and not yours. Still, it wouldn't kill you to share in my joy a bit."

"Honey," she responded, "I just don't believe in that religious stuff. I believe that when we die, well, we just die. That's it."

"Huh? What does *religion* have to do with any of this? I'm talking about *spirituality*, and maybe even *science*—but not *religion*. Very different things. Your generalizations make my head spin. My God. You know what? That's fine. You're entitled to your beliefs." Still he was frustrated. "I just want you to know that in some ways I feel quite blessed right now. That's all."

"Blessed?" It was too much for her to accept.

"Yes, blessed!" He raised himself on his elbows.

"Well, good, I guess," she said, her voice barely audible. A moment of awkward silence followed, the result of shared guilt for flaring tempers.

Anax loathed losing control of his emotions. It was weakness and he regretted it. *Jeez,* he thought, *what is it about parents that can instantly reduce us to rubble?* He suspected that it was rooted in their long-held beliefs about their children, unable to bend, even in the wake of obvious change. Somehow, parents could project their perceptions back onto their full-grown offspring, who unwittingly absorbed them, igniting old dynamics that reduced them to squabbling, insecure children.

"Mom, I will heal. I believe it and so should you." His expression softened, offering peace, and she returned the gesture.

He knew a thing or two about healing, or so he thought. The mind-body relationship and the power of positive thinking were subjects in more than a few of the books he'd read. His shelves were cluttered with personal-development books. At one point, he was so brazen as to buy out the entire self-improvement section during a library liquidation sale. And while he had not read all those books yet, or even a fraction, he knew a bit about healing. Or so he thought.

He recognized the mind-body relationship was something that had been proven in every major clinical study ever done. It was called the placebo effect. It was real. How powerful it was, nobody knew. *And now I've experienced the power of intention through my astral projections,* he thought. *I've seen firsthand how we can alter reality. Anything is possible. Even healing.* He decided that he would use everything in his arsenal to recover from the trauma that had broken his body.

He could fix it.

His mother spoke. "Well, visiting hours are over. I guess I

should get going, Hon. Love you."

"Love you too, Mom." After a hospital-bed hug, she turned to go, looking back upon her exit; her eyes reflected the same sadness that he'd seen ever since the accident. His father would have been there too, but he had a tennis match that evening. Likewise, his sister, who had visited several times that week, had a charity event that evening.

Once alone, Anax relaxed, recalling a conversation from yesterday. His roommate Alina, a German woman with esoteric leanings, had stopped by to visit and had offered some advice about seeking a holistic approach to healing. She went so far as to suggest that he seek the counsel of a *shaman*, or healer of relationships between self, community and planet. He wasn't quite sure what that meant, but he liked the idea of it.

***

Hospitals are repositories of both despair and hope; they are strange amalgams of our most tragic moments and our most profound rebirths. In their hallways one may encounter kind-hearted people, like nurses, working in service to others, but one will also find an abundance of death, stagnation and ghosts.

Anax was on fewer and fewer medications, by his own request—and his mind was a bit sharper. He noted with quiet resignation that his wardrobe was lacking—limited to white gowns of limited style—and his hair did not get the attention that it deserved. At least he managed to brush his teeth each day. That was something. Sleeping was a challenge and he awakened regularly throughout the night. He refused the sleeping pills because they prevented him from dreaming, but he continued with the painkillers, which helped his body to relax.

That night, after a modest helping of painkillers, he dozed off, and the vibrations came on again, and this time he was propelled out of his body with ease. Reveling in the freedom, he eagerly scanned the hospital room. As he'd experienced before, it was largely the same as his waking life, except for some dark clouds floating in the corners and a few things that seemed oddly out of place. The subtle distortions were peculiar. Regardless, it was extraordinary, and as far as he was concerned he'd traveled straight down the rabbit hole and through the looking glass. He waved his arms in front of his astral eyes, and was fascinated by their translucent nature and bluish-green color. *They're pure energy*, he realized. *Just like me.* Before he got too excited, he decided to roam the hallways, and have a look around. At the speed of thought he was there, floating just off the ground, when a large gurney rounded the corner, passing straight through his left hip. *Sweeeeet!* He waved at one of the nurses; she was oblivious to his presence. He'd not traveled far, but his clarity was extraordinary; he was the invisible man—empowered beyond belief.

Gliding into the next room, he explored the premises. At the foot of the bed, he spotted a strange man gazing downward, cradling his head, as if he could scarcely believe his bad fortune. Anax was surprised to see the man slowly turn his head and look at him from the corner of his eye. *You can see me?* Anax asked. From what he could discern from the man's profile, he looked to be about seventy years of age, with thinning hair—and, in a strange twist—he had a seatbelt wrapped around him. Suddenly, the man's focus shifted to Anax.

"You, there! Come here and talk to me. I want answers!" he screamed. The man turned his head, revealing a mangled cheekbone, concave and bloody. Where his right eye should have been was a dark, hollow cavern. Anax recoiled as the man charged him. "Tell me where my daughter is! She was in the passenger seat! Damn it! Why won't you answer me? I need answers! You're gonna give me some…" The man ran straight at him, and through him, and Anax was instantly jolted back into his body; he opened his eyes and found his pulse racing. *Jesus. That wasn't much fun.* He felt violated. His room had an eerie silence, as well, and he could not help but wonder if the spirit he'd encountered was still in that room, or if he'd followed him into his own.

After this one disturbing encounter, the out-of-body experiences continued, as frequently as four or five times each week. Fortunately, most of them were intriguing, not frightening. And many were much broader in scope—taking him far beyond hospitals, and even planet Earth. The more he contemplated the experiences, the more they seemed to happen. They were all that he could think about, so long as his medicine kept the pain in check.

The process was always the same. As his body slept, his mind suddenly came awake, leaving his awareness disassociated from this physical body. Next, he'd hear a roaring noise surging through his body and into his head; physiologically, it felt like his pulse was throbbing and his body was vibrating. Then he simply rolled out of his body. Sometimes he was pulled right back in, and other times, he could resist the pull and break away. The sensation of tearing away from his physical form was common. Perhaps most incredible of all, though, was that he could travel anywhere, so long as he kept his focus.

During one astral projection, he found himself visiting a house located across the street from his childhood home. After exploring the trees in the yard—which reflected light like glitzy rhinestones, he wandered inside. He could not say what lured him into the house, except that normal boundaries seemed meaningless in the astral world.

The interior was common, like any old house, but then he encountered a woman, or spirit, who welcomed him into the kitchen. She appeared to be in her thirties, with chestnut brown hair and attractive features. Her disposition was friendly and casual when she asked, "You're not from around here, are you?"

Anax didn't quite know how to respond; he attempted to explain that he was in fact from another dimension, but had grown up across the street—in the earth plane. He chuckled at his explanation. But the woman gazed at him more closely after that, as if examining him, and asked, "Are you a *traveler?*" In that moment, he was overwhelmed with excitement, a result of her realization, and the environment began to fade, like a dimming light, and he awoke in his bed.

After considering the incident, he concluded that the woman was probably a ghost or spirit residing in that astral plane, and that somehow, she'd been able to identify him as a temporary visitor, or astral traveler. Maybe his energy-body had appeared different, less dense or something; he could not be certain.

On several other occasions, he found himself in completely alternative realities—colorful landscapes, rural and urban, with other people, or spirits, that both confused and enthralled him. He was on the super-highway of transcendental travel, exploring microcosms of infinite possibility—and it felt good. Colors had new meaning and aspects, like personalities or multiple forms of expression, and matter was not solid, but empty space—a collection of molecules loosely held together by conscious consent. The very architecture of the universe had infinite layers that comingled in both a random fashion, and one of perfect order. The excitement of his new awareness was always enough to distract him from the frustration of immobility.

Remarkable, he thought as he pondered his experiences. Outside of his physical body he was indescribably free, and no longer carried the burdens of physical injury. He could even fly—if he willed it.

There were a handful of experiences that plagued his curiosity more than others. On three separate out-of-body occasions, he'd found himself in the same stretch of wilderness observing strange, cottage-like structures in the distance. They called to him, tugging on his awareness, but he could never reach them. For days, they haunted him. *What is this place? And why do I keep returning to it?* Whenever he attempted to fly in for a closer look, he would lose focus and reconnect to his body in the hospital room. It was frustrating.

Separation of the astral body; hemp canvas.

Endings

***

Distant hospital sounds crept into the room like an invisible guest. Within a half-hour, a dull, distant beeping lulled Anax into unconsciousness. When he awakened a short time later to his girlfriend's voice, he knew that he was not dreaming.

Things had been on a slippery slope with Elizabeth since the accident, and it was becoming apparent that a fairy-tale ending was not in store for the two of them. They had different belief structures, and the passion that had characterized the relationship early on had dissipated. And now, with his body in a state of disrepair, there was little to salvage.

That's the funny thing about relationships, he thought, *in the beginning two people choose only to see the good in each other. As things progress they tend to focus on negatives and become more judgmental. When the focus on the negatives becomes too dominant, the bond crumbles.* Today was no exception. Elizabeth was standing beside the bed, looking far too beautiful for a hospital, and Anax could feel the tension like a corkscrew lodged in his abdomen. Clearly, she'd attempted to dress more formally, perhaps to cage her feminine power, or at least not to flaunt it, but still it flowed outward like a laser beam, cutting straight through his paper hospital gown. It felt foreign and far removed. It was not for him—not anymore.

"How are you?" she asked, halfheartedly.

"Just dandy," he responded, half smiling, half lying.

The strain between them was visceral, and he could feel it sucking the energy from his limbs, reducing them to achy mounds of flesh. Nausea pitted in his gut.

"My roommate Alina came by yesterday and thought that perhaps I should take a more holistic approach to my healing. Mind, body, spirit kind of thing. What do you think?" Elizabeth rolled her eyes, not even attempting to conceal her disdain. He knew her filters were on. She had a strong allegiance to the medical industry, having worked in it for several years, and already she'd been frustrated by his refusal to take some of the drugs that the doctors recommended. The ugly cycle was continuing.

"Why don't you take your meds?" she asked.

"I don't want steroids in my body. It's that simple. I know some drugs may be necessary but a lot of them simply treat symptoms at a price that I'm not willing to accept. You know that. We've been over this. I just think the body is resilient so long as we don't flood it with synthetic toxins that suppress the immune system." On the verge of one of his over-the-top medical tirades, Anax pulled back, but too late. Elizabeth became visibly irritated, and emotion carved hard lines in her face. Her dainty dimples had never seemed so far away. If he could only kiss them and start over, then all would be well. Instead, he sensed a tidal wave and tensed in anticipation. A brief and awkward silence filled the room—it was a silence of separation, an invocation of loneliness. It was the feeling in one's gut just before the rope gives way.

"Look, Anax. I don't think that this is going to work. I just… I'm sorry. I can't do this."

"What? What are you talking about, Elizabeth?" Anax asked, breathless, but knowing.

"Wait," he persisted. "Let's just relax for a minute." He was not prepared. "Can we talk about this? What's bothering you?" But he knew that her words had been eerily decisive.

"I'm sorry, Anax."

"How can you be so cold about this?" Desperation tainted his words as he searched for any reason why they should remain together. Nothing came.

"I don't know," she said. "I don't feel the same way about you as I did before. I'm sorry." She looked down at him with executive-like firmness and severed any remaining emotional cords with butcher-like precision.

"I have to go." Without pause, she turned and walked out of his life.

"Elizabeth, wait—*Elizabeth?*"

He might have followed her, but a twist of fate had rendered his legs useless. *Perhaps I am useless,* he thought. *My life is useless.* His solar plexus knotted and he felt ill. It was the worst kind of pain. If he did not take control of it, it would destroy him. Lying there in his hospital room with his broken body, he attempted to rationalize the situation. It was his coping mechanism. *It's for the best,* he thought, only half believing the words. His body was not functional. Their personalities were too different. Elizabeth had a sharp edge, after all. She was a true corporate woman with a fixation on climbing the ladder somewhere; she was the sort of person who could separate her emotions from physical intimacy. She was a natural in New York City, but not in Anax's world. He knew it.

But that did not quell the feelings of loss, particularly at a time when the entirety of his existence had fallen into an abyss. He tried not to beat himself up, recognizing that self-immolation could be destructive for years to come, while proper thinking could be the catalyst for change, or even a galvanizer for greatness. In truth, he just wanted to heal.

Over the next few weeks, Anax did what he could to channel his erratic emotions into constructive thoughts. He was rarely successful. *One door closing will lead to the opening of others,* he told himself, only half believing at times. *Such is the interconnectivity of life. Cause and effect—always seeking to balance our lives, offering lessons along the way. Even this car accident gave me the opportunity to explore the eternal nature of consciousness. Not a bad tradeoff, I think.* Despite his efforts, depression still seeped through the cracks in his emotional armor.

The next few days bled together, and his head hurt more than usual. He was told there was still significant risk from the head injury. He didn't care. Contemplating death was strangely liberating, raising topics of deeper meaning to the surface. *Is that what it takes?* He wondered incessantly about his purpose in life. Despite his past explorations on the subject, he still lacked clarity. Since the accident, this question plagued his consciousness, rattling his old value systems. He couldn't shake it. He'd been given insight into the fragility and beauty of life, and his breakup now pushed his mind's wanderings to the edge. *What is my role here?* The question ate at him. *There has to be a reason for all of this.* He had, after all, gained deep insight during his mystical experiences. He'd seen endless possibilities; he just needed to remember them—to keep the flame burning. In the face of daily living, the passion slipped away too easily. Old fears and limitations concerning money, as well as health, crept into his thoughts, diluting the power of his otherworldly journeys.

What can I do with my life? Do I search for the perfect path, or do I simply create it? How can I make any of this work when I don't know what to do, how to make a living doing it and don't even have a body to carry it out? These were questions to which he had no answers. And they invaded his mind, in a near-debilitating fashion. He needed direction. Shaking his head, he returned to the present moment, and his pains came with it. *I'll figure it out.*

He looked over at his cell phone. It had been on silent mode. Two messages. The first message was from his father. The second message was from his roommate Alina. She'd found a shaman.

***

Another long month passed. Anax's sedentary lifestyle gave way to painful mobility, and ultimately, tolerable discomfort. His crutches gave him the extra push he needed. His headaches never ceased, however, and the threat of his injuries had not waned either. For too long, his optimism had been stymied and his body carried the burden. On this day, however, he pressed on—embracing whatever came his way.

As he climbed the stairs from the depths of the West 4th Street subway stop, he was reminded of the day's grandeur. Cool air soothed his skin, like a long-forgotten friend. Emotions once buried were rekindled, and his relationship with nature began anew. He inhaled the fresh air as if it were medicine.

His love radiated outward, and a lightness of being filled his limbs, despite his limp. *Hello, trees. It's good to see you. It's been too long.* It was like being in a museum; everything held renewed intrigue and color. Autumn had long since arrived, and already half the leaves had fallen. *Man, I have missed sunlight.* To most, the trees were invisible. To Anax, they were living creatures, slow moving sentinels of this great city, and surely, they were aware of all the pedestrians. They had a story that was worth knowing.

He hobbled across the street and commenced his three-block walk to the shaman's office. Passing Washington Square Park, he noticed a disproportionately high number of dogs and smiled. It had been a long time since he'd seen so many people, let alone dogs. Rounding the corner onto the block, and feeling a bit nervous, he found himself at his destination. He had no idea what to expect. The buzzer indicated that this was the office of an advertising agency and he hesitated before pushing it. A subtle fear of the unknown pierced his gut, but it was fleeting. He buzzed and the door buzzed back; entering, he walked toward the elevator.

Reaching the third floor, he walked down the hall to the shaman's office. Outside the door, he noticed a few tied-off small plastic bags that appeared to contain the remnants of eggs. The bags reminded Anax of those used to pick up after a dog, and he exposed a perplexed smile. *What am I doing here, again?*

Having arrived ten minutes early, he knocked tentatively at the door. Muted voices and strange rattling sounds echoed from within. A head popped out, and in a hurried foreign accent said, "Please give me a few minutes."

"Sure," Anax responded, uncertainly. He laughed again to himself about the entire scene—it was peculiar, indeed. Comical even. The man appeared to be in his fifties, of strong stature, light-skinned and was dressed in all white. *I wonder where he is from—he is definitely not from South America. European? Middle Eastern, perhaps?*

ENDINGS

A few minutes passed and the door opened. A woman came out, gave Anax a knowing smile and made her way to the elevator. He entered the shaman's office—or lair, as he perceived it—and it was dark and musky. A sage-like scent, coupled with other alien smells, wafted throughout the space. His olfactories struggled with the smoky aroma, and he nearly sneezed. *So strangely out of place here in the West Village*, he thought, rubbing his nose. The shades were drawn but still light crept in through the blinds, along with noises from the street below. The sounds were foreign, as if emanating from another layer of reality. Indigenous artifacts lined the walls, juxtaposed against computer monitors. His imagination expanded with each passing moment. He couldn't help wondering how this office could double as a mystical shrine and a professional advertising agency, yet there was an odd, symbiotic relationship between these two worlds.

His internal dialogue was in full swing and the hodgepodge of scents only added to his intrigue. The place seemed so far from corporate America—a mystical oasis amid a city of suits and deadlines.

"Hello, it's nice to meet you. Please, make yourself comfortable," the shaman said.

The healer's demeanor was soothing. There was no air of judgment—simply a calm and open energy that transcended boundaries. Inviting and unhurried, he moved with a grace that defied New York City. There were no clocks in the room. This was not a sterile physician's office with patients to herd through. In this realm, time did not exist, and schedules were only manifestations of our own morbid creation. Anax felt at ease.

The shaman, who was observing him, awakened him from his daydream.

"Please, have a seat," he offered. His knowing smile connoted a deep understanding, and Anax felt as if he was somehow deciphering the machinations of his wandering mind. He reined in Anax's attention with a simple glance. In front of them on the table sat a collection of miscellaneous goods—a smooth, black lava rock, rum, tobacco and a few items that he did not recognize.

The two men sat in silence. It seemed like a test of wills, a waiting game. The shaman observed him on a deeper level, and Anax, ensnared by his contemplative gaze, did his best to remain relaxed. A shyer person would have squirmed under such a knowing stare, but his laid-back nature, coupled with an openness to all things mystical, left him unfazed.

Smiling, the shaman broke the silence. "Your mind is very busy."

Jolted into awareness by his prescient comment, Anax could only stare, and nod. His mind *was* busy—never resting.

Delicately, a vibration struck a chord in Anax, and it awakened something long dormant. A spontaneous flow of knowledge penetrated his conscious awareness. There was something to be said about living in the present moment and being in control of one's thoughts. He realized that far too often his mind ran rampant, like a runaway train, living in a gray no-man's land, concerned only about the future, or remorseful about the past. Like invasive weeds, the worries multiplied; they needed to be plucked, lest they overwhelm the garden. In this realm, Anax realized, fear ruled, often reigning as king until the host decided to reclaim his rightful place.

He had always prided himself on his busy mind, connecting one thing to another. It made him feel a little bit like Edison, Tesla or Da Vinci—or so he liked to imagine. And now, for an instant, he questioned that belief. Perhaps, after all, he'd only ever had an overinflated sense of self. Humbled and shaken, a small piece of his ego dissolved that day, rooted in the realization that perhaps his mind's wanderings were not an attribute, but rather a symptom of undisciplined thinking.

A single, well-placed comment had reinvented his mindset. Perhaps he gave more credence to the words because of the messenger, or perhaps it was because he'd sought his counsel. Either way, one thing was evident—living in the present moment would become a hallmark of Anax's future endeavors.

The shaman stared into his eyes, and with a smirk said, "Don't worry, my mind is busy too. You are of the air and intellect—a dreamer. Your head is buried in the clouds. It is important that you learn to be more grounded and focused. This can be learned. Also, don't be so serious. Life is just a silly and mysterious journey, after all."

The healer pulled back his gaze and looked down at the black volcanic rock while dropping a small quantity of fluid on it. The silence returned, clutching Anax in its grip—one that only his unceasing curiosity could endure. But instead of speaking, the shaman handed him a white wax candle. "Take this and rub it on your body," he instructed.

"Rub it?" Anax said, with uncertainty, slowly simulating the action of brushing the candle over parts of his body, all the while watching the healer for any sign of approval. None came. But neither did disapproval, so he continued. When he'd covered all major body parts, he nodded, and the shaman raised a flame, making a motion to light his candle, and Anax obliged. Gingerly, the shaman took the burning candle from his hand, and shifted fierce, hawk-like eyes onto its flame, seeing straight through it, and then began to speak.

"You are a person of ideas, seeing the world through an unusual lens; this makes you innovative but also challenges you to follow through on any single idea. You likely get bored and move on to the next idea before you finish anything. But finish you must. Until you finish, you are incomplete. While it is important to be materialistic in this world, you must let go of your fears about money and status; you must lose your self-created sense of grandeur. You must let it all go before you can find what you seek. And stop analyzing everything—it blocks you from finishing. You don't need to break everything down into a million pieces. You need only to pick a piece and start on it. Your path is not something to be discovered through analysis and rationalization. It is to be actively created and navigated by your heart."

He paused and Anax stared.

"And while you are mostly *air* right now, you will become *fire, water* and *earth* before it is done. And if you choose, you will find rebirth when the time comes; you are destined to shed your skin more than once. Now, lie down on the ground; there is one more thing we need to do. You will journey for guidance."

Anax had no words to question, nor will to resist. He stretched out on the reed mat, suddenly tired, and rested his head on the cushion. A peculiar sense of déjà vu grabbed him. *How did I wind up here?* He was beset by a feeling of interconnectedness, a knowing that somehow his accident had led him to this exact spot. He was supposed to be here.

The shaman gave instructions and began to rhythmically beat a large animal-skin drum above Anax's flat body. Closing his eyes, Anax felt the vibrations deep in his core. They were tribal, and oddly comfortable. This continued for some time until he was lulled into trance, relaxing each muscle of his body.

The healer guided him, slowly at first, pausing for several minutes between each suggestion. Anax's imagination expanded, going deeper into the visions, feeling every element. He was in a forest and could smell the moist bark and touch the trees. *Where am I? Am I creating this?* A path of natural wood chips lay strewn out in front of him, leading out of the forest. The path fed into a stream, approximately six-feet wide and one-foot deep. The water was cold and alive. Smooth round pebbles, with reddish hues, rested patiently below the surface. He crossed the water and it chilled his bones. Climbing the opposite bank, he stumbled upon a dizzying field of red and white flowers, ephemeral and sweetly scented. Above him the skies were ominous, presaging a storm.

Before him loomed a cliff with rugged stairs carved from stone. *Three long flights.* Climbing the stairs on all fours, he struggled to maintain balance. *Why am I having such difficulty standing up on two feet?*

Upon arriving at the top, he paused to observe his surroundings. Atop the small cliff was a grassy knoll, replete with cherry blossom trees and a large boulder. Beneath the boulder was a large, dark hole, to which the shaman guided him. Having never used his mind in this way before, he hesitated before climbing into the earthen, musty space, mildly fearful of the darkness below. *This is silly—I am imagining this. Or am I? What is there to fear?* Squirming through the narrow hole like a worm, he was squeezed by a sense of claustrophobia as his shoulder dug into dirt, crumbling walls, and he was relieved to see that the tunnel opened into a small cavern up ahead, offering some freedom of movement. He made his way toward a light at the back of the cave. Trepidation flooded his body as he inched forward into the rocky recesses. Something lurked just beyond. He felt it, like a visceral announcement of impending shock. Out of the darkness, a gut-rattling roar echoed, sending his heart racing. Loud and shattering it came, but with no intention to harm. It was a display of power. He'd met his totem. His helper. A large brown bear emerged from the darkness and lumbered before Anax. The shaman instructed him to ask it for guidance.

Do you have a message for me? No response came. Somehow, he knew the bear was female, and was comforted by that awareness. For a time, she walked back and forth, piercing him with her large, dark eyes—sizing him up. He waited patiently, and asked again. *Hello, do you have a message for me?* Unsure of the proper etiquette for discourse with an imaginary bear, he let it flow. Again, no response came. For a moment, he felt small. She walked and he followed, guiding him out of the cave and down the backside of the cliff. It sloped perilously, but he simply glided over it, impervious to its pitfalls.

At the bottom, they entered a forest and he followed her through tall, straight birch trees bearing distinct, striped bark; light crept in through the canopies partially illuminating the bedrock. *Where are we going?* She stopped and seemed to be telling him to move onward without her, but he was unwilling to continue alone.

So, he waited. *Do you have a message for me?* Again, she pointed to the forest. Then she lowered herself, placing her chest against the ground, repeating the gesture several times. *What are you saying?* Again, she repeated the gesture as if imploring him to join her on all fours. So, he did. In his consciousness, he heard the words. *Connect to the earth. CONNECT with it.* He emulated the bear's gesture, bringing his chest to the earth, allowing his face to lie in the dirt. The soil comforted him and he relaxed, listening. *Go to the forest.* The words made little sense to him, but he let them come. *Connect to the earth. Go to the forest.* Over and over again, they repeated. And then an image of woodlands flashed into his mind's eye; he recognized the location. It was up north, a place he'd camped as a child. It was as if the memory had been extracted from the depths of his consciousness and fully restored. It was a welcome gift, from a kinder time.

The drumbeat shifted and sped up, the sign to depart his journey, and he retraced his steps through the forest, back up the cliff, down the stairs, through the flower fields, across the river and back to the trail in the woods. The drumming ceased and he lay silent, reconnecting with his body. It took him several minutes to move. None of it made sense, but he was grateful for the experience.

He sat up, suddenly overwhelmed by fatigue and dehydration. The day's adventure had come to an end. In a daze, he paid the shaman and departed.

LOST

***

"Anax, do you have that analysis done yet?" It was like a flashback, except it wasn't. He was here again, tethered to a desk, inside a cubicle; the only difference was that he was working part-time, and lived with chronic pain. *Lovely. I am actually here again. Bloody Groundhog Day.* He pushed the emotions back. His manager, John Billsby—aka *Bullsby*—in honor of the invisible horns atop his head, was nice enough but far too passionate about project deadlines. He also aligned his identity too closely with his job for Anax's taste. Then again, Anax was at the other end of the spectrum, deeply disconnected from the work.

"Anax? Hello? The analysis—have you made any progress?"

Anax cringed before turning. "Ummm, no. Not yet. I have ten other things to do first that seemed like higher priorities."

"Well," replied his manager, "I need it *a-s-a-p* for a meeting this afternoon." He liked to sharply enunciate the letters.

"This afternoon? That's kind of short notice, don't you think? If you had a hard deadline on it, you should've told me."

"Well, Anax, I didn't have a hard deadline until thirty minutes ago. I don't need complaints; I just need the analysis. Can you do it?"

"Not sure if I'll get it done, but I'll try."

Bullsby walked away, shaking his oversized head. Anax was certain that his horns would scatter the ink cartridges stacked atop the file cabinets.

Three months had passed since his visit to the shaman, and life had become only more difficult. At first, he'd been hopeful, believing in his ability to heal. But soon life crept in, sidetracking him into old patterns as the power of his experiences bled away. The memories he'd pledged to keep became shadows as he fell into old frustrations and fears. He'd returned to work part-time, still on crutches, but his position was tenuous, at best. Casually dismissive of his bosses, he missed most project deadlines and couldn't concentrate on his tasks, let alone take any of them seriously. Twice Human Resources had warned him. It wasn't the injury that bothered his employers; it was his attitude. Even the smallest things could send him into a spiral of anger; mostly, though, he'd bottle them up inside, unwilling to argue or fight. Instead, he was aloof, storing the poison within, unable to process it. Everybody around him felt it, and their understanding stretched only so far.

With his semi-functional legs and daylong headaches, life turned bleak. *How did I wind up here? It's not supposed to be like this,* he thought, sitting at his desk, once again feeling restless and caged. He was confused by how rapidly things had deteriorated. Somehow his exposure to out-of-body experiences, shamanic mysticism and extra-dimensional realities had only made life that much more difficult. His awareness of a larger picture of reality ungrounded him, leaving him unable to take his job seriously or cope with the systems, rules and judgments conceived by society.

He could not relate to his old friends any longer. Instead of bringing strength and vision, his awareness made him feel trapped more than ever. With a dead relationship, a faltering job, ruptured legs, constant headaches and no way to escape a world he now viewed as superficial, death started to seem like a tempting option. He'd catch himself thinking about it sometimes, then dismiss it. But it would rise up again like something that needed to be acknowledged. Now that he'd experienced it, he didn't fear it, and some days he even looked forward to it.

On his way home from a painful walk, he was feeling particularly sorry for himself. He hobbled, eyes down, mind lost and heart vacant; like a corpse, he was too far gone to even notice his agony. A homeless man approached, asking for change, and he walked past him without making eye contact. His aloofness fueled more guilt and anger. *Have I become so hardened that I no longer feel compassion?*

LOST

Locked in a mental cycle of internal resistance, he was unable to resolve the conflict. He fantasized about running away, but knew that such an act was unlikely to resolve the pain. Besides, he needed functional legs for that.

The loneliness of a weak body, cloudy thinking, impending unemployment, and an inability to relate to others had taken its toll. His fears about money would become more real if he lost his job and could no longer afford to pay rent. *How do I function in a world that I don't believe in, but still need to pay rent?* Questions like this plagued his already unstable disposition. The cycles of self-pity were like a revolving door that sped up, slowed down and never stopped turning.

When he attempted to speak to friends or loved ones about his out-of-body experiences, he was delicately dismissed and the conversation shifted to a topic that was more comfortable. He felt alone. The veil into alternative realities had been lifted, but without a healthy body and the ability to enjoy these new experiences, it felt empty.

Three more weeks passed and Anax trained himself to walk without crutches. It was painful, and he limped, but he also improved a bit each day—until he had a bad day, that is, and the pain in his legs and head surged in unison, launching him into a state of despair that bordered on hell.

He'd carried that hell into the office, in the lines of his brow, as he sipped his coffee. *At least I didn't spill it all over myself today.* Last week he'd burned his inner thigh with a cup of boiling coffee, then walked around all day with the crotch stain to prove it—as if his self-esteem wasn't already low enough.

"Anax, would you come with me?" His heart dropped into his stomach and his diaphragm clenched. It was Jennifer, the head of Human Resources, sporting a colorless pantsuit.

"Um, OK. I guess. Everything OK?" He knew it wasn't.

"Just come with me, please. I'll explain."

He was led into his manager's office and Jennifer closed the door behind him. He took a seat. It's difficult to describe the sinking one feels in the face of rejection. The anticipation is the worst part—knowing you are about to be dumped. Employees with whom you'd been friendly minutes before suddenly switch sides, drawing a line of emotional demarcation. The experience sliced self-confidence with surgical precision, leaving one to pick up the pieces, alone, and with no way to pay the rent.

After shifting in his seat, Anax noted that Bullsby's forehead looked particularly broad and unusually shiny. Then he saw his face. It was ghostly. He'd always given Anax a bit of leeway considering his physical challenges, but the line was suddenly pulled taut. Bullsby looked up from a piece of paper, emotionless.

"Anax, I need to let you go. I want you to know that this decision had already been made prior to the accident, and is entirely performance-based. You'll receive eight weeks of severance. You may gather your items and Jennifer will escort you to the door."

Stupefied, but not surprised, Anax just nodded, mumbling, "OK." It's not like the topic was up for debate. The walk back to his desk was a strange affair, passing co-workers who nodded at him as if all were well; his legs suddenly wobbled. It was an emotional mixed bag, with some feelings of release and freedom, but mostly it was a blow to the gut, leaving him winded, unable to reconcile the sudden void. Not only had his performance been rejected, but he was being exiled from a community of friends, as well.

In a daze, he gathered his items. A co-worker sitting in the adjacent desk mumbled something casual, but he barely heard him. Jennifer was hurrying him along, deflecting dialogue with others, and that only heightened his sense of alienation.

On his way to the exit his manager came out and shook his hand, expressionless, wishing him well, and Anax actually found himself thanking him for the opportunity. The words were hollow, an automated response.

The following days were ugly. The rejection felt worse than anything he'd experienced physically; it was like a reflection of his emotional and spiritual catalepsy, and it came on all at once, inflaming his entire being.

Several days later, when the pain had subsided, he made a decision. Somehow, he knew that if he remained in New York City, cycling through ongoing bouts of self-pity while sucking on his emotional poison, he would die. Unpleasantly. The pain had driven him to the edge, and change had become his only option. So, he made a decision. He would go deep into the woodlands—up north, near the place he'd camped as a child, seeking insight or death. Perhaps it was melodramatic, but it was real enough.

With only a basic knowledge of wilderness survival he didn't know how long he'd survive, but he would tell his family members that he'd be gone for a while and that this was something he needed to do. He'd do it on his own two legs, too. No more crutches.

He had not decided if the trip was a vision quest, an opportunity to die alone, or both. Either sounded like a pleasant alternative to his current situation. He'd arrived at a point where he could no longer see hope; life was a dark cavern in which he alone was trapped. Nobody could see inside and it was on him—and him alone—to carry the pain.

He gave in to the desperation and packed his bags that night. There would be no meticulous planning; he would depart tomorrow with whatever he could gather, leaving the forest to welcome or reject him.

But the next day he doubted himself and did not leave. Four days later he still lacked the courage to depart. But on the seventh day, when the pain of not changing his life became too great to endure, he left, and did not look back.

A former roommate, William—dubbed *the Brit* for his heritage—picked him up, driving him ninety minutes to where he'd catch a long bus ride to his entry point, or close to it. William was the silent type, thoughtful and intelligent, and Anax was in a pensive mood during the trip, so there wasn't much conversation. Still, William, with his murky English accent that had somehow evolved into its own dialect through years of international travel, expressed his reservations.

"Are you sure you're up for this? It seems kind of far to be going for just a few days."

Anax paused, looking out the window. "Not really. But I feel like I need to go. To be honest, I don't know how long I'll be gone; could be longer than a few days."

"Do you have a phone?"

"Nope," he said, almost defensively. He'd taken care to leave it behind, choosing to sever all connections to the outside world—avoiding any temptation to call.

William just nodded, unsure how to respond, calm as always.

They neared the drop-off point and stopped for a meal at a country diner. Anax ordered an omelet with avocado and cheddar cheese, with a side of fries. It was the last greasy meal he'd have for a while—perhaps ever—and he took his time with it; his bus wouldn't arrive for two hours. Afterward, in the bathroom, he washed his hands and fussed with his hair for the better part of several minutes before realizing how ridiculous he was being. Perhaps it was an unconscious plea to remain in civilization, where people cared about hair, or worse yet, a concern that nature might look upon him unfavorably should he arrive sloppily groomed. In either case, he was certain that death did not care about his hair.

Saying goodbye to William at the station was tougher than he anticipated; the sudden realization that there was a chance that he'd never see him again sank in, bringing on a subtle wave of melancholy. He was a stalwart friend, forever reliable and always generous.

As Anax limped toward the bus stop, bag in tow, he found himself missing the simpler days when they were roommates, drinking beer and chatting about life. In those days, there was no pain.

Surrender

***

He'd been gone only five days.

Wet with tears and nails clawing dirt, Anax buried his head in moist leaves, twigs and earth. *Is the ground wet, or is it me?* Fleeting thoughts. A branch scratched his eyelid and he did not care. Without the strength to stand or the will to carry on, he was an empty soul. *How can I be crying? I never cry.* He strained his throat, choking on his own despair, and found a strange sense of relief in the process, as if unburdening some unseen weight. Forcing more heaves, coughs and teardrops, he imagined the wetness upon his brow as blood, and again, he did not care. He was nothing—a grain of sand, a speck of dirt at most—a giant, exploding ego releasing a lifetime of nonsense. His heart ached, his throat cracked and he prepared to die. As his eyes opened, he saw only black, but it was not dirt that filled his eyes.

Peaceful here, to die like a wild animal. My body, dinner for the forest. Nobody will ever know. A gentle wave of peace settled upon him and he rolled onto his side, forcing a large gulp of air. Then blackness came.

Sometime later, rustling leaves roused him from heavy sleep, and he squinted his eyes to find its source. A violent, pounding headache racked his senses and he winced. Weakness filled his limbs and he could only watch as the bushes moved and a massive bear, dark as death, lifted its nose into the air, searching the area. Incapable of running and helplessly entranced by the giant's gaze, he lay still. It lumbered toward him, first slowly and then more confidently. Initially overcome by fright, Anax transcended to a peculiar serenity with each step the animal took. Unable to move and in a state of absolute surrender, he closed his eyes. *Not the worst way to die, at the hands of a magnificent creature,* he thought. *God, please watch over my*

The Mystical Village That Rewired Reality

family, my loved ones and all those in need; I have done my best. Thank you for the opportunities. He remembered his out-of-body experiences and felt comforted.

Oddly, amusement flared in his gut and he laughed silently at his predicament. *I'm absolutely insane, laughing at this. Strange things go through a man's head at death. Damn it.* Time slowed, offering space for contemplation, and he considered how far he was from home. A deep loneliness flooded him, evoking a dormant yearning for the community he'd never found. The feeling was not so different from when he'd said goodbye to William at the bus stop. There was both love and regret.

In an instant, the bear was on him. *How did he cover all that distance so quickly?* A large pad pushed at his leg. *My leg—OK, this doesn't hurt so badly. A gentle giant.* His irrational state of mind and inappropriate humor persisted. On the front side of Anax's earth-smeared face came hot, piping air and then a massive, wet nose was in his ear, rhythmically breathing deep, heavy exhalations. *Just like a puppy nose. It even tickles. OK, I'm dead.*

Anax endured his impending death with a suppressed smile and began to let go, trying to see the other side. Trying so hard to see, to disconnect from the sensations of his body. He didn't want to feel anything.

And then, all at once, death returned to the bushes from which it had come.

Lumbering bear; hemp canvas.

Beginnings

***

Basking in a state of humility and wonderment, Anax remained on the ground for nearly ninety minutes, awaiting dawn, just listening. *Leaves rattling, wind singing, critters crawling—but no bear.* He did a cursory check of his limbs and organs. *All present and accounted for.* Perplexed, unharmed and entirely changed, he gathered his thoughts, pushing delirium aside. His head throbbed and his throat craved water, but he was alive. *More alive than I can ever recall. I need water.* Somehow fate had graced him, and he did not intend to die of dehydration.

Scattered belongings lay nearby and he took stock. *Backpack with knife, tent, flashlight, sleeping bag, pad, hammock, tarp, cord, fire starter, water purifier, water container. Check. Headache, check. Dysfunctional legs, check.*

Stumbling along, he watched the sun rise in the East, bringing in a new day and a new life. Birds squawked. *Is that a hawk?* He strained his eyes. Beams of sunlight slithered through the trees and danced on moss, exposing hues of orange, red and everything in between. Dawn's arrival revived him, but he was still lost in the middle of nowhere—miles into the forest. He'd brought no map, leaving his survival to fate. With his back stiff from a twisted and restless night on the ground, he removed his pack and surveyed the surroundings. *Trees and…more trees. What's that? Ahh, brush…and leaves. What else have we got here? Rocks and dirt. OK, then. Time to solve some problems. Like thirst.* The ground foliage was dense, but navigable, and despite sporadic rocky patches that tested his footing, he managed fine. Mostly though, the terrain was a monotonous mix of thirsty pines, sugar maples and beech trees. Having only a vague idea of which way led home, Anax mistakenly walked in the opposite direction.

He glanced skyward in a plea for rain, but blue skies only

reflected disappointment. With his limited wilderness knowledge, he searched for trees that might indicate water, and with each mile that he slogged along he grew weaker and more concerned.

After another frustrating day and a half without water, his concern became so acute that he vowed to accept death again, should that be his fate. It had been only a week since his arrival, but for three days his only water source had been morning dewdrops. His mind wandered, and his tacit acceptance of the situation made the consequences of failure more palatable. *At least I'll die with dignity, and not consumed with fear.* But he did not want to die. Not any longer. Death had already come for him, and death had departed without him. His encounter with the bear had served a purpose. His old life was now dead, and superficial concerns no longer carried the weight they once had. Then again, there was nothing superficial about dehydration.

The lack of water amplified the pain in his bones, and he sought to distract himself with internal dialogue. *The remainder of my life is a chance to live fearlessly and honestly, to trust my own inner voice—for once.* He told himself that old patterns around health, money and rules had simply dissolved. His new life was a free pass and anything that might arise from it an unexpected opportunity. He needed to believe in something to keep his legs moving.

Walking on unstable legs, he willed himself forward, overcoming fatigue and delirium. He fantasized about water fountains and flowing faucets and endless glacier streams. They were the orgasms of life—dripping and spraying and gushing—ready to satisfy his most basic animal needs. If only he could have one swig of fresh water. Just one. It wouldn't need to be cold, either, just room temperature. He'd take his time with it, swishing it around in his mouth, rolling it about, soaking his gums, letting his tongue bathe in its watery goodness.

Stumbling, he reached for a tree as his vision blurred. He scanned the surroundings and the world before him came to life— vibrating like a sentient, electromagnetic being of infinite permutations. *My God...I think the plants are communicating, like they're aware of my presence. Is that...possible? Wait. I don't understa... Oh! They're all connected...and dancing! Dancing! Alive, like a network of... So beautiful.* For ten minutes, he observed a wild boar in the distance drinking from a river. He could hardly believe his fortune. *Finally. Thank you, God. I've found it. Water.* He watched the animal bobbing its head, greedily drinking, and decided to wait until it departed before advancing. Overwhelmed by thirst, he could wait no longer and approached cautiously. When his eyes finally focused, the boar became a round bush rhythmically blowing in the wind, and there was no water to be found. Desperation seized him. *I'm not going to make it,* he told himself.

And that's when he heard it—a rumbling revelation from above—like the heartbeat of the sky, invoking life. With a single clap of thunder, nature's mercy found him; he looked to the dark skies and finally they offered hope. Within a minute, he was fumbling with his ground tarp and anything else that might capture rainwater. Clumsily dropping gear, he directed his last reserves of energy to the task at hand, tying up his tarp between four trees in a clearing and placing stones in the middle so that it would sag and hold water. Twice he tripped and fell. After rummaging through his bag, he pulled out clothing and a towel, and placed them on the ground to absorb water. Finally, he set out his water bladder and metal cup for easy access.

Before long, the sky crackled and droplets began to fall. *Sweet droplets.* Anax looked up, opened his mouth, laughed, and then began to sob, crying without tears. *It feels so good,* he thought. Then, all at once, survival instincts snapped him back to awareness and he double-checked his setup. The tarp looked secure and his knots would hold. Lying flat on his back, he opened his mouth to the skies, spreading his arms and legs, all the while savoring each drop with an appreciation that only a dying man can understand. He grappled with new emotions—a fusion of ecstasy and gratitude for life's most fundamental gifts—and a profound fulfillment settled upon him.

Before it was done, the rain came in torrents, deeply sagging his tarp in the middle. Nearly one gallon of water had been collected. Scooping the liquid with his mug, he savored the first few mouthfuls, as he'd imagined, but then he lost control, gulping cup after cup like a desperate animal. At one point, he burped and vomited and decided to slow his consumption. After his craving ceased, he just sat and stared. Then he mustered the energy to stand and dipped his water bladder into the tarp, collecting all the remaining water. The water bladder was nearly full and his clothes were soaked. Mother Nature had prolonged his life for at least a few days.

***

Nursing himself back to strength took nearly two days. Although still dehydrated, he was vastly improved. After another day, with his water supplies running low again, he took a rest against a smooth tree with a strong curve in its trunk, as if custom crafted for his back. Beset by a sudden onset of fatigue, he didn't realize how tired he was and sleep claimed him, bringing dreams.

Blurry beings, emanating unusual comfort, encircled him, just where he lay, and he, like a child, could only repeat the words, *Who are you?* Instead of voices, they responded with colorful fractals of light, brilliant and flowing, which Anax experienced as ecstasy, love and unquestioned acceptance. The depth of feeling, he realized, was outside the scope of his human experience. As foggy as the figures were, they were familiar. *Who are you?* Still, they offered no words. Unable to tune in to his frequency to directly communicate, they offered love in its place, like a gift of magic. In a way that Anax could not comprehend, these beings felt like home, and he yearned for their companionship.

Upon waking, his head hurt, and he had a vague recollection of an important dream. He could recall only shadow memories—but it was clear to him that he knew the people, as if they shared a family bond. And yet, their faces and features evaded him, like slipping fragments of consciousness. Still, he knew them *so well* during the dream. They had filled him with warmth and restored him. *I wish I could remember more*, he thought with disappointment. Still, the lingering emotions inspired a far-off sense of hope. Rising, he gathered his gear and hiked for several more hours, but the day unfolded without event. After setting up camp in a clearing, he climbed into his hammock and slept deeply.

The next morning went on as the others had. After several hours of scenic, yet uneventful hiking, Anax paused for rest. His mouth dry and throat parched, he finished the last of his food stores. The luxury of drinking water had only reinvigorated his appetite, and he found himself mindlessly snacking on the last of his dried fruit and nuts, which, ironically, only incited his thirst, encouraging him to consume his water too fast. More than three days had passed since the rain, and his supply had dwindled to next to nothing.

I must have walked fifty or sixty miles, and probably in a circle, he considered. *And now I have no food, or water. Still no rain, rivers or ponds. There has to be a water source somewhere. What am I missing?* He was halfway aware that his irrational optimism was just a tool to keep him moving and quell his fears.

That night he built a fire, as he'd done each night since the rains. Stringing his hammock between two stable trees, but not too close to the fire, he stretched out his insulation pad inside it and placed his sleeping bag on top. Next, he strung up his ground tarp in the same manner as he'd done the prior three days, preparing it to catch nighttime rain should it arrive. And last, he erected his tent, just in case he needed it.

When everything was in place, he glanced longingly at his hammock. *So tired and ready for sleep.* The ultra-light hammock—a well-fortified piece of nylon with hooks on each end—had become his sanctuary, a place to exchange survival concerns for warmth, comfort and protection. Although tired from a long day of hiking, he'd regained much of his strength from the last of his water and food. He reminded himself of the consequences of not finding water within the next few days. *I'll find water tomorrow,* he thought with half certainty.

With the fire burning and a light breeze blowing, sleeping in the forest struck Anax as an exquisitely peaceful experience. The firelight cast bouncing shadows on the surrounding brush, animating the darkness, as insect chirps reverberated across the landscape like a well-trained orchestra. He marveled at the contradiction between the locale's harmony and the reality of impending death should something go awry. *I guess this is what it means to be wild, to be an animal of the forest.* Of course, he realized, that his survival instincts were not so well honed as those of the forest animals, and his mood was not consoled.

He pulled up the outer edges of his hammock, swaddling himself. Relaxing his body, he released any lingering tensions. Fear, he noted, had little place in his life now; he should enjoy a good night's sleep. His muscles unclenched and his breathing slowed as he drifted into other realms while listening to the forest's songs.

Before long he found himself in a strange and familiar state of being, where his body slept soundly, but his mind was awake. Almost immediately the vibrations came again, coursing through his body. Noise roared in his ears. *Is my heart rate escalating? Oh well, here we go!* Even though it had been weeks since his last out-of-body experience, it felt like yesterday. He was electrified by the familiar sensation of his energy-body tearing away from his physical body. More barreling noises filled his senses. The separation of his consciousness came fast, but the pullback to his body was strong. He set his astral vision on some trees in the distance and willed himself there, fighting against the gravity-like pull of his physical body; it was a bit like slogging through jello, but the farther he advanced, the easier it got. In an instant, he was free, hovering in a ghostly form near the trees.

It was dark, but the light of the moon illuminated the astral landscape. His awareness grew sharper and he could discern details. Resisting the urge to look toward his sleeping body in the hammock, he shifted his attention from object to object,[7] doing his best to remain calm and maintain lucidity. *Incredible.* He was in the unseen shadow world. *Where should I go?* Before he spent too much time pondering the question, he headed west and set out gliding along the ground, and then flying among the tree canopies. *It's so much brighter up here.* The sky sparkled like four-dimensional, diamond-glitter confetti and the moonlight throbbed with emotion, blending with his being as if it were a part of him. He glided as a wraith in the night, basking in the indescribable empowerment that comes with being free of one's body. Briefly, he contemplated the things he might encounter on his journey, and then he noted a change in the terrain below. Small, rounded structures dotted the landscape. *Familiar.* They blended with the local environment, and he would not have noticed them had it not been for their unusual shapes.

Fifty or sixty feet in the air, he surveyed the land below and was surprised to find two luminescent figures, also floating off the ground. Their silhouettes were chromatic prisms of light radiating impossible colors, and he felt their power, like unconditional love or angelic music. He sucked the sweetness into his soul, as he was drawn to them, like a hummingbird to nectar. The figures glided effortlessly near gardens or foliage, and they seemed to be aware of his presence. Setting his attention on one of them, he arrived at the speed of thought, and found himself hovering next to a woman—or so she seemed. She was breathtaking. Her eyes were green orbs of bottomless warmth, and to gaze into them invited an unquestioned acceptance, a deep sense of community. There was something both familiar and indiscernible about her, and his emotions swelled. She smiled and spoke without moving her mouth. *You are a long way from home. Is this your home, Anax?* Overwhelming excitement seized him and he began to lose focus. How could she know his name? *Wait, don't go*, she said, imploring him to stay. But her green eyes had already begun to fade, and it was too late; the emotions had reconnected him to his physical body and he opened his eyes.

His hammock swayed in the wind. He lay there for some time,

contemplating the reality of his experience; it had not been a dream. It was far too real and he'd been in control. The woman was strangely familiar. *How do I know her?* The dreamy landscape sparked latent memories, like shadows of another life. He racked his brain, but all he found was an intoxicating familiarity that lingered like a secret waiting to be revealed. He pledged to remember every detail. Shortly thereafter, he slept soundly and without dreams.

He woke at dawn to the stirring of the forest's inhabitants. Trees rustled, birds chirped and far off he thought he heard a wolf howl. Upon rising, he noticed that he'd strung his hammock between two elegant birch trees. It had been dark when he set up camp, so he hadn't noticed the trees in detail. But this morning there was something profound about them. Their striped appearance stood out against the uniform landscape, where he could not locate another one like them. Beyond that, though, there was something intangible and ethereal about them.

It was a moment of magic that Anax did not consciously recognize, for these two trees were uncommon. These sibling birch, born of the same mother tree, had just delivered a long-held, sacred message. They had guided him, serving as landmarks on the path to destiny. The message had been received, and the way was open.

***

Without water, there was little choice but to march forward. Reluctantly, and not without trepidation, Anax began his hike, half hopeful for what the day might bring. The trees, despite their stature, were homogenous and lacked inspiration. His legs still suffered significantly from the car accident, and irregular terrain created challenging obstacles, so he directed much of his attention to his footing. His knees were particularly tender, and any misstep or twisted ankle would drastically reduce his chances of survival. After three hours of walking, he took his usual break and leaned against an inviting tree. Broad in girth, it appeared quite old, and its branches reached out to distances that seemed to defy gravity. "Hello beautiful," he whispered. Leaning in to one of its many nooks, he stared out at the landscape, deciding not to sleep that day lest he waste valuable time that would be better spent searching for water.

Moments later, a dragonfly, long, graceful and green, hovered two feet from his nose, followed by another colored like autumn, flaunting brilliant browns and oranges. The green dragon appeared to be in pursuit of the brown-and-orange one and they danced. Several minutes passed as they flew upward, backward, forward, downward; they whirled, and at one point they were connected, flying in space. Dazzling colors reflected off their wings and Anax marveled at their engineering. Observing them with quiet satisfaction, he realized that he'd not encountered dragonflies until now, nor would he have expected to—it was far too early in the season. And yet, they were there, like a divine omen. *They might be a sign of water in the area*, he thought hopefully. He sat patiently waiting for them to depart, and when they did, his gaze followed their track. After quickly gathering his belongings, he walked in the same direction.

His hope rekindled, he strode with vigor. Noticing more birch trees along the way, he regarded them as guides leading him to water, all the while humoring himself with internal dialogue. *Hello friends, I believe my hammock had a rather special encounter with a couple of your brethren last night. Friendly chaps. I'd like to think that everyone was satisfied with the experience. I know I was. And boy did I sleep soundly. So, tell me, which way is water? Ahh, this way, you say? Very well…*

Continuing with his inner antics, he walked fruitlessly for several miles and began to doubt himself. *Those dragonflies could have traveled in any direction after they left me. They're flying magicians, after all; maybe they're just teasing me, or worse yet, leading me in the worst possible direction. Sure, that's it. Hey, let's play with the lost, thirsty human. We can use misdirection and send him on a journey that will lead to certain death. Bzzzz, bzzzz.*

He considered turning and trying a new tack, but it all seemed hopeless at this point. Again, he glanced to the skies in silent desperation but only fair weather shone back. His body wasting, he could only keep moving and speak silent prayers.

All sense of time dissolved, like a blurring of existence, and somehow two more days passed without water. They were a torturous two days. His mouth felt like rough-spun cotton and his limp grew more pronounced. He was a lame animal, destined for death. Stumbling in half-delirium, his mind relentlessly visited old scenes from his childhood. Every long-forgotten conversation, misspoken word or angry conversation returned to his thoughts, like misplaced library books rediscovered in the back of one's closet. They came from nowhere, offering a full-life review. He dissected emotions from long-past relationships, ones he'd not contemplated in years; he reviewed decisions he'd made about how he spent his time, and with whom. He saw the error of his ways in a thousand different shades. Pity and sadness plagued him as he saw a younger Anax, and the life that he'd passively accepted. For young Anax hadn't chosen much of anything, he'd just gone with the flow, content to earn a good income and follow the expected path to adulthood. But he had not been transformed—not really. He'd never shed his skin and taken courageous action on the things that mattered. The major milestones in his life were merely bookmarks; they held no authentic power. They were not true initiations. He never really knew who he was or what he wanted.

Brambles snagged Anax's clothing and he stumbled, lost in trance. As he sought to untangle himself, he paused, suddenly aware of the feeling of being watched. It was a primal sensation, like fight-or-flight, that twisted his solar plexus. He froze and scanned the landscape; all that he saw were trees and rocks. And then, through blurry eyes, he saw what looked like a small boy in the distance, cresting a hill. *I must be hallucinating. Jesus. Is this what happens before we die?* Glancing down at his legs despite a dizzy spell, he noted that they were still moving forward. *Oh good.* Still, he did not feel right. His awareness hovered a few inches outside of his body, adding a surreal sensation to the journey. It dawned on him that he was dying, and he considered setting up his hammock so he might depart in peace. As he descended a particularly steep slope, his knee throbbed with pain, as if firing a final warning, and he prepared to surrender himself to the forest. He was done fighting.

I should write a note to my family, he considered.

And then, as if willed by fate, he heard what could only be a spirit, or perhaps an ancestor, calling him home. The disembodied voice came on a light breeze, like an invitation to death, and he welcomed it. It was a warm voice, the voice of an angel.

"Blessings upon you, friend. We have been waiting for you." The voice came from nowhere, and everywhere, like a bug in his ear, and Anax was now certain that he was hallucinating. Head swiveling, dazed and lost, he could only stare at the gentle woman who had appeared from nowhere and the man at her side. Sparsely clad in strange, fibrous tunics, these people did not belong to Anax's reality. His confusion palpable, he fumbled to ground his erratic thoughts and his words slipped.

"I, I don't understand what is happening. Who? Wha…"

Her soft eyes received him and a gentle hand reached out, offering comfort. "All is well. Come here, darling, sit with us."

"I just don't understand any of this. You—both of you, out here. Am I out of the forest? Where am I? Are you real?"

Her eyes, green like jade, exuded a kindness that he'd never encountered in a stranger, and his tension dissolved.

"You are on the outskirts of a village, a sacred place. A place to which you will soon belong if that is your choice. You need not understand everything now, just know that another part of yourself has visited this place many times before, and we have observed you. We have been waiting for you, Anax. You took action, and now you have arrived."

He fumbled for a response. "How do you know my name? I, I don't understaaa…" But it was too late. Falling leaves slowed, the wind howled and the world became a spinning vortex. A tunnel of darkness came upon him. Anax's leg buckled and he fell to one knee. In an instant, a pair of hands rested delicately on his back, supporting him.

"Do you accept our healing?" she asked.

"Yes, I do." Surprised with the certainty and speed of his response, he could only stare blankly at the ground.

First, she offered a small cup of water, which he drank greedily. Then she placed her hands on his back. Tingling warmth surged from her palms; it was hot and spreading quickly. His first instinct was to resist, but his body had other plans; instead, it soaked in the warmth, surrendering all tension. He was vulnerable and he was open, and he did not care. Letting go, he could keep his eyes open no longer, and within minutes a peaceful blackness lulled him into the unknown.

Healing

***

Hours passed. Assailed by peculiar dreams, Anax shifted and his hand felt leaves. *On top of me. Odd.* His semi-lucid dream state provoked further confusion and he shifted again. This time he felt the leaves on his face, arms and legs, and a primal fear jolted him into awareness. *I'm buried.* He fought himself awake, sitting up with all the energy he could muster. Large green stalks with broad leaves fell away and he emerged squinting into early morning sunlight. Panicked, he quickly scanned the surroundings and spotted two hammocks woven of fiber to his right and a small tipi-like structure not far beyond. He recalled the two people he'd met and relaxed. *I feel better after some rest*, he thought, surprised. Climbing to his feet, he stretched and noticed odd structures farther in the distance. *Where am I?*

"Good morning, Anax. I see that you are more powerful than yesterday; I see light in you. Good." The male voice originated from a cluster of trees behind him.

Anax, perplexed, turned and found the man. His age was indecipherable. Tall, dark-skinned and fit, the man had brown eyes that bore into Anax's soul. *Is he Native American?* His long braid added to the notion.

"Why was I covered with leaves?" Anax asked.

Glancing at the pile of discarded plants, the man paused before responding, "We used them to help cleanse and rejuvenate you; they assist with the removal of heavier energies and also offer a life-force of their own for a time. They are part of why you are feeling a bit better this morning, despite not having eaten or taken much water last night. Come. Everything will be explained."

As the man led him toward the tipi, the gentle woman emerged, greeting him with the same loving, green eyes that she'd graced him with yesterday. She too was of an uncertain age. Healthy and fit, with silver-blond hair and the vitality of youth, she nonetheless seemed older—perhaps much older—but only because of the wisdom that she wore plainly across her persona. Her appearance was more than physical—it was sublime and celestial—defying preconceived notions of how a human should appear. Both she and the man had inviting, mirror-like eyes that conjured Anax's wonderment. She handed him a smooth wooden cup with water, which he gratefully accepted.

"Good morning, Anax. I am Inipia, but please call me Ini. And this is Izeel. You are here because you came to us, whether you realize it or not, and it gladdens our hearts that you have arrived. The village is close by, but before you can enter it is necessary that we work with you for a time. We will require at least one week." She paused, looking him up and down and straight through. "On second thought, we will need at least ten days. Our intention is only to nourish you through our healings and ceremonies, and to help you attain a greater state of balance and power before you enter. We will also explain to you about the village, what you might encounter, and certain boundaries that are necessary for the betterment of all. So, you have a choice. You can turn around and return to your old life, or you can join us here. If you choose to return home, we can provide food and water and show you the way. If you choose to join us, it is imperative that you fully embrace the healings and ceremonies that we offer, that you accept them without reservation and approach them with an open mind and an open heart. Do you understand?"

"Yes."

"Do you accept our help, Anax?"

He paused, attempting to process the information. So much was happening. He looked at them and they were frozen in time, like statues of hope. His hope. But were they? His entire existence pivoted on a decision. His thoughts spilled forth excuses, fueled by fear of the unknown. *This is crazy.* Then his heart responded with warm, tingly music that could be described only as joy and wonder. His mind and heart battled as he attempted to reconcile all that had transpired.

He scanned the horizon, siting the village in the distance and contemplating its possibilities. They were endless. Then he looked back at the couple before once more surveying his surroundings. Fear gave way to excitement, and he returned a bold smile.

"I accept. Thank you both." *I cannot believe this is happening. This is what I have always wanted.*

***

"Were you cut from your mother?" Ini asked. She'd been questioning him for more than an hour.

"Huh? Cut?" Anax was taken back by the bluntness of the question, but Ini's gentle eyes reassured him. "I don't understand," he said, "did you say *cut*?"

"Yes."

"Cut, as in a *c-section*?" he responded, palpably confused.

"Yes."

"Oh. Yes, I was a c-section. Why?"

"You were not birthed properly into this world—you did not journey through the tunnel." She paused, thinking. "It's OK. We will remedy this," she said.

"Uhh…OK."

Each night for ten days Anax slept with large, green leaves covering his body. Insects did not bother him, nor did the cold. And each morning he emerged from his plant cocoon feeling renewed. He was told that the plants provided specific energies and frequencies that were helpful. By day, the ceremonies commenced and Ini and Izeel burned incense, twirling smoke sticks around his body, while humming melodies that permeated his emotions and opened his heart. With equal parts precision and peculiarity, they sprayed scented oils from their mouths—in a fine mist—coating his skin, and activating his energy fields. All the while, they rubbed his body with eggs; afterward, they cracked the same eggs on a flat stone and studied the yolks, as if gathering information.[8]

Then they asked more disarming questions, stripping away any remaining layers of Anax's once-inflated ego. Chanting, praying and singing, they were a constant presence in his life. When he was depleted, they would lay their hands on him and infuse him with energy, reinvigorating him.[9] At other times, he was overwhelmed with emotion and would break down and cry. He had no idea where the emotions came from and his reactions surprised him. Ini and Izeel encouraged him to cry.

After infusing medicinal plant baths with prayers, they delicately poured the water over his head and body, touching specific areas, while singing sacred songs. He never saw where they collected the water, but the songs touched his heart and led to more crying. After inquiring broadly about his family, they acted out different roles in front of him, flawlessly reenacting family dynamics that he'd not communicated to them; they indicated that they were healing ancestral and family entanglements and were simply channeling the information.[10]

"The codes are everywhere," Ini told him. It was confusing and overwhelming, but Anax felt things shifting inside of him. He remained resolute in his commitment to the process. In the afternoons, during breaks, he was challenged to write down all his failings and weaknesses as a human being. This exercise, they said, was important for being honest with one's self, and was the first step toward self-acceptance, and ultimately empowerment. It did not feel empowering at the time, however. After finishing his third page, writing upon unfamiliar paper they said was hemp, he was convinced of his failure as a human being. Every element of his fears, indecision and failures of integrity were laid bare. And each day, he would come up with more items to add to the list. So, he was surprised after several days when the exercise started to make sense, and became strangely liberating. It wasn't until the last day and a half that he was encouraged to create a new list of all his attributes and strengths that he might offer to the world.

At one point, he looked up from his list and said, "So, despite being an abject failure as a human being, it turns out that I have a few positive qualities too. That's good, right?" Ini had appeared amused by his comment, but Izeel just looked passive, or maybe even confused. He could not be certain. Perhaps he was like an alien species to them. Or better yet, maybe they'd revere him as a god. Not likely, he decided, upon further reflection. *Probably more like a lost puppy.*

During this time, Ini and Izeel explained his astrological charts and studied the codes in his hands and fingerprints, divining his soul's purpose in this lifetime while also assessing his weaknesses. Ini explained Anax's fears with ease, casually relaying what she saw, but she rarely used the word "fear" when she spoke of it.

"There are many challenges that confront the minds of humankind in the outside world, she said; most people will be affected by several of them. Some include concerns regarding poor health, failure, judgment, poverty, aging, death and loneliness or abandonment. Each of these tends to take root in certain areas of the body, wreaking imbalance and discomfort. Sadly, the systems of the outside world foster and exacerbate these stresses, leading to a vicious cycle that makes escape quite difficult, particularly if people lack conscious awareness of their own predicaments."

Anax nodded, trying to absorb the swarm of information. He held his attention on Ini who always maintained eye contact. At times, he had to glance away from the intensity of her stare.

"In your case," she continued, "you have suffered from concerns about money, scarcity and poverty. You have also inundated yourself with confused thinking patterns about your health and wellness, making yourself more vulnerable to ailments; this was amplified because you wear your nervous system on the outside of your body and don't know how to energetically protect yourself. In both cases, your greatest challenge has been your own mind. It is particularly unruly and you have not taken care of it. Or, rather, you have not taken ownership of it. Instead, you have lived your life as its servant, allowing *dis-ease* to take root, and now you must train yourself to become its master. When you become master of your mind, such concerns will become non-existent and powerless. You will see them as the illusions that they are. From there you will be empowered to create positive realities. You will be able to do this in both this density and the astral realms. Realities always take form first in the astral layers that surround us before they adopt a denser reality in our world. Do you recall visiting this village while you were out-of-body?"

"I, I...do remember," Anax responded, furrowing his brow while attempting to suppress a smile. Incredulous, he flashed back to his astral projection several days earlier. *Was she...?* Neurons fired in his brain, triggering shadow memories that collided and merged, forming new conglomerates of understanding. His foundation for reality shook like an earthquake, breaking apart the old, moving from solid to liquid, before growing into a raging river that swept away all that had come before.

She continued before he could complete his thought, "In Gylodon, we actively practice such things. It was I who encountered you on your way here, that night, and several times before. We were waiting for you. You were unable to maintain your lucidity and faded away, likely pulled back to your body. In time, you will learn to avoid such pitfalls."

"Wait," he protested, "that, was *you?* That night when I projected into a village?"

"Yes, it was me," she responded as if not comprehending his confusion.

Anax swooned. Trying to remain calm, but completely unhinged, he laughed out loud. Ini had just validated everything he'd experienced following the accident and leading up to his arrival.

"It was *all* real," he said, and his eyes widened. *Real.* He'd

The Mystical Village That Rewired Reality

known it was real, but still, a validation like this eradicated any lingering doubt. It was the final dissolution of old belief systems. His black-and-white world was instantly upgraded to multi-dimensional digital color, and he'd been handed the remote control.

"Yes, Anax. It was as real as our conversation right now; it's just different."

Yeah, it's different all right, he thought, beaming from ear to ear. He could barely contain himself as she continued.

"Understand that astral projection is a natural activity for all human beings. Once you understand that we are not bodies with a soul, but rather souls inhabiting a body, it makes more sense. We all experience multi-dimensional travel at night, leaving our bodies behind, but those who are trained and practiced are best equipped to both remember and prolong these experiences. Most in the outside world will recall only shadow memories and symptoms of their projections, like a feeling of falling, vibrations or sleep paralysis. And when they do have an authentic experience, their mental programming rationalizes it away in short order. Very few people go deep enough to learn the ability. In Gylodon, you'll develop expertise in this area; it seems that you already have a natural aptitude for it. That will make it much easier."

Gylodon? This must be the name of the village. The information came relentlessly, and Anax dug deeper than ever before to process it all. His mind raced to keep up. He always considered himself open, but still he was turned upside-down. After his astral-projection validation, his hunger for knowledge and experience expanded exponentially.

On the fifth night, Ini spoke to him about the village. "Anax, understand that what we are doing here is preliminary preparation for your entry into the village. It is an intensive and rapid healing process, but it is only the beginning. You will continue these efforts, in various forms, upon joining the community. For now, let's just say that we are helping you arrive at a level that we deem safe for the village dynamic and for your own continued growth."

Anax nodded cautiously. She continued, "As one who came from the outside world, by *way of the seed*, you are a special case. It is rare that the seeds send us community members, but it is always important when they do. In my lifetime, you are only the fifth to arrive in this manner."

She paused as if looking for Anax to express surprise, but his face betrayed no signs of emotion. Instead, his mind wandered to the night when he had tied his hammock between the two birch trees. He'd been shocked when Izeel explained how the birch trees were messengers, patiently awaiting his arrival. Someone called the *Seed Bearer* had supposedly planted them long ago.

"Anax," Ini interrupted, as if reading his thoughts, "you will need to give the best of yourself in every capacity. You must be present in all activities. You will learn to reclaim your mind and live by your heart. In many respects, you are at a disadvantage because you come from a society that has already programmed you into limited-thinking paradigms, as well as limited-feeling paradigms. You will need to rewire and empower yourself to gain access to the *four* and *five*. It can be done, but will take some time, perhaps years. Through this process, you will encounter great challenges, but also levels of bliss that you are presently unable to conceive. You will gain access to powers that you have previously only glimpsed, and now they will be a part of your everyday reality."

The thought of such superhuman abilities sent Anax's head spinning and he had to ground himself. He barely grasped the concepts of *four* and *five*, and already he'd been so humbled through the healing ceremonies that he felt shame for his desire to attain such power.

As if reading his thoughts again, Ini continued, "These things, Anax, are your birthright. They are the birthright of all souls who choose to inhabit a body on Earth for a time. The village exists to leverage these gifts for the betterment of the planet. We act to restore balance in all things, allowing harmony and love to flourish. The examples are everywhere within the village—even our plants grow to sizes the outsiders have never witnessed. We are also guardians of several dozen extinct species that live within our village boundaries. The outside world has erased them, but they live on—and thrive here."

That was almost too much to swallow for Anax, and he redirected his skepticism into hearty laughter.

"You'll see," she said.

Briefly, Anax tried to imagine what it would be like when he entered the village, but quickly suppressed the urge and instead held his focus on Ini.

"When you enter," she continued, "you will need to speak minimally about the outside world, even though others might be curious. For those born in the village, you must understand that they come from a very different existence than yours—and much of their power is rooted in these differences. Outside worries are not a reality for them; it is not a part of their model for living. This is a part of what makes them so powerful, but also vulnerable. So, please understand that your interactions with others, excepting a few people, will be limited until you attain a certain level of mind-mastery and heart-consciousness."

***

Anax couldn't sleep. Anticipation rose from his stomach straight to his throat, and then leapt into his dreams. The night, full of fragmented visions and unsettled feelings, was the last barrier before a new world would unfold.

After a time, the first light awakened the forest and he became aware of brisk air moving along the ground to his sleeping area. His skin rebelled against the chill, but then he remembered the day. Slow enthusiasm churned into electric awareness, charging his limbs, and he rose as a man preparing for his quest.

When he stepped outside of the shelter, the woodlands greeted him with its morning bliss, growing livelier as the new sun sprayed fiery pink hues mixed with beams of white that brushed the clouds on their way to feed the forest. The mist spilled through the underbrush, taking humanlike shapes, but Anax could not be certain of what he saw. Stepping onto a glacial rock that merged with the earth, he let the cool moss support his feet and soften his stand. The vista was strange and alluring, and it pulsed with wings and wind, bark and dirt, all of it melding together, coming awake. The light burnished the lands, animating its inhabitants, allowing color to reappear. He smiled and stretched his arms skyward, loosening his muscles while attempting to ground his exuberance.

A month ago, I was shackled to a desk and lived life in a box. Today I will enter Gylodon—a mystical village hidden deep within ancient woodlands. His eyes crinkled, mirroring gratitude, as he gave silent thanks to barely visible stars. He could hardly believe his fortune.

The waiting began shortly after sunrise when Ini and Izeel were locked in conversation for some time, leaving Anax little to do but sit upon the soil—an arrangement he'd grown fond of over the past week. He took several deep breaths and spread out on the ground.

His imagination ran rampant, first sketching, and then painting, all possibilities of what lay ahead. Over the past week, Gylodon had become much more than a location in the woods. It was the genesis of all wonderment, a place with answers to new questions, a portal of transformation. *My imagination is out of control,* he thought, tempering his expectations. *It's probably just a village, like any other.* Still, he didn't believe that, either. His healings with Ini and Izeel had already solidified his belief that remarkable, magical people lived in Gylodon. Even so, he could not shake the feeling that someone was playing an elaborate joke on him. His framework for reality impeded full acceptance of the village; instead it was like a film on a faraway screen, separate from him, and rooted in fantasy. *Nothing to do but wait and see for myself,* he thought, concerned that he might be disappointed.

By midday it was time. Izeel returned from the village after vanishing for nearly two hours. He came as the sun hit its apex and nodded to Ini. She took Anax aside after barely exchanging a word with him the entire morning.

"Anax, prepare your mind for new realities, and open your heart fully." She placed her hand upon his chest and he felt energy. "Remember, only light shines in Gylodon, and you are now a part of that illumination. It is not something that will be. It is not something to hope for. From this day, henceforth, *it simply is*. You are a brother of Gylodon. Embrace this truth as you've embraced nothing else in your life. It is absolute and unshakeable. You will always be accepted here. You will challenge yourself more than ever before, and your efforts will be rewarded with a power that floods your being and lightens your spirit. In time, the worries of the outside will dissolve into the illusions that they are. The elders have embraced your entrance; the omens have been confirmed. I cannot express in words what this means to the members of our community, to the forest and to Spirit. But you will feel it. Let the joy in your heart shine forth and treat this day with reverence and gratitude. Come. Let's walk."

Ini walked on his left, her head just cresting his shoulder, while Izeel, towering over him, strode on his right. He felt their support like unbreakable foundations. It took only ten minutes to reach the outskirts of the village and already Anax felt a subtle shift, a lightening of step, as if the burdens of his body and mind were somehow diluted. He thought, perhaps, it was just excitement but somehow it felt different, almost as if the best parts of him gained confidence with each step; the parts long suppressed or cast aside, the parts that mattered, bubbled to the surface, overtaking the rest. The residual pain in his legs dissipated and he nearly lost awareness of the discomfort that should have been there.

They approached from the east, where a cluster of trees provided shade to several earthen dwellings during the hottest times of day. He noticed that the entrances all faced toward Gylodon's center. Their bare beauty and soothing tones filled him with veneration, magnifying his well-being like inspirational art forms. *What's*

HEALING

happening to me? he thought, in blissful disbelief. *No, I believe it; I believe all of it,* he silently affirmed, as if any doubt risked losing the experience. But the transformation was so rapid that he could hardly process its implications. It was as if someone had dosed him with a drug that induced euphoria. But there was no drug. Just Gylodon.

"Ini," he said, "I feel different. Lighter. How can that be?"

She paused, processing how her everyday reality could be so novel to Anax. "Well, it's the energy, or *consciousness cloud* here, Anax. Collective, high-vibration thoughts and feelings are forged and reinforced on a regular basis here. What you are experiencing is your body's first interaction with the energy fields. The closest you have ever come to something like this was probably some special place out in nature, perhaps a beach or lake. But this is many magnitudes more intense. Gylodon carries more than nature's inherent vibration; it is a co-created reality, united in power and love. We work together to give it form, literally molding its image in the astral plane. That image then becomes a tangible experience for all of us. The changes manifest quickly here. Right now, your physical, emotional and mental bodies are all interacting with its power, recalibrating; it will have a natural healing effect on you. I don't experience it the way that you do. My personal resonance is already calibrated to Gylodon. In time, yours will be too."

She looked toward the village before continuing, "You'll soon understand that there are things in this world that are magical. Things you would not have believed possible. Sometimes they are subtle; other times overt. Most often, however, in your current limited perception, they are fleeting. But here in Gylodon, Anax, we embrace them. Savor them. None of this is religion, by the way. It is not even spirituality, entirely. Everything that we do here is rooted in personal experience and self-exploration. The *Book of Gylodon* provides a framework for learning, a toolset for discovering your own truths."

Anax paused in mid-stride. *"Book of Gylodon?"*

Ini looked thoughtful, as if she'd revealed too much, but continued nonetheless. "Yes. The Book is a well-developed collection of lectures and exercises for assisting outsiders with the transition. It's not designed to be dogmatic, but rather experiential. It will open up your mind, but you'll still need to do the work to remove your negative programming and restructure your realities."

Anax, mind buzzing, was poised to ask a question when Ini cut him off, "For now, know this. In Gylodon, you'll learn to savor life. Out there, beyond the forest, in your old world, countless blessings are lost. A beautiful synchronicity or divine, improbable coincidence is quickly forgotten or rationalized away into an irretrievable oblivion. Out there, too much life is wasted. Like a blur, life sparks and spills, overflowing with sound bites, digital media and all manner of instant gratification. Out there, outsiders are destined to forget their own miracles within minutes of the next distraction. But here you'll find miracles in every passing moment; you'll gather them into your heart's garden, tending to them each day, expanding your consciousness into the realms of bliss. Welcome to Gylodon, the land of waking dreams." Ini allowed her arm to sweep the landscape as if offering all the world's treasures to him.

He half expected her to laugh at the grandeur of her gesture, but she revealed no such intention. Ebullient and open to new possibilities, Anax widened his eyes as he sought to absorb every ounce of the experience.

They had already entered what appeared to be a central area of the village. Vibrant flowers, brandishing every color of the visible spectrum—including new colors that baffled him—were grouped in concentric circles, coalescing in a round rainbow pattern. Stone paths, each aligned with one of the cardinal directions, blazed through the arrangement, uniting in a circular stone slab at the interior. The effect was mesmerizing. Anax caught himself wondering why he'd never seen such an arrangement before; it seemed so natural. *But the colors...*

Then, at once, he felt separated from himself, as if his assessment of the rainbow flower arrangement came from somewhere else, outside of his own mind. *Odd, even my feelings about the world are shifting here. I feel a yearning for beauty,* he thought, smiling uncontrollably. Creativity rose from his lower stomach, just below the naval, and he was overwhelmed with a need to make something new. *Something pristine and gentle, momentous and delicate. It will carry the courage of the bear and the ephemeral embrace of a sun-shower rainbow. Where are these thoughts coming from? This is just so…stimulating, and excessive!* He came alive with poetry and music gelling inside of him, mixing and moving, opening and expanding. At one point, he was nearly debilitated by a sexual energy coursing through his body, like a rogue electric current, but somehow, he breathed through it, dissipating discomfort. He didn't know how to process the emotions, so he stayed close to Ini and Izeel in case he needed assistance.

Passing several people who nodded and smiled warmly, Anax was flooded with their compassion, and returned their smiles as best he could. Ini made no introductions, just kept him moving toward his destination.

After they passed three more villagers, she said, "Anax, when you are ready we will make formal introductions. There is much self-work to be done first. I'll take you to your cottage and let you be alone for a while. In the evening, I will introduce you to your counterpart, Dan. He arrived only several moons back, also from the outside, and you'll be free to converse with him. It is a rare thing to have both of you—two outsiders—arrive in such a close interval. As time passes we'll have a clearer understanding as to why things have unfolded this way. Other than him, you'll be limited to communicating with me, Izeel, the Seed Bearer and your teacher. There may be a couple of elders who will choose to communicate with you before you are ready, as well. Also, you should know that there is one more recent outsider here, but it will take time before you are ready to communicate with her."

He nodded, confused. They stepped around the bend and arrived at a tiny, earthen structure. "Your cottage is here. Make yourself comfortable. We'll come for you later." She provided a quick tour of the modest space before departing.

The outside world had not prepared Anax for the natural state of joy. That state had been whittled away since infancy, dissolved day by day since toddlerhood. It didn't matter. The reality of Gylodon was enough, perhaps made even brighter by the shadows of his old life.

He sat on the bed for some time, hostage to an unbridled curiosity that ravaged his mind and plagued his gut. *How long are they going to leave me here? And how can I feel so good?* He paced, exploring every inch of the small cottage. *It's 121 square-feet*, he recalled, from his brief exchange with Ini. He'd found the number odd and unusually precise, but didn't think much of it. The earthen floors were cool on his feet and the walls were grainy, like sand, to the touch. Colorful blankets captured his imagination and flooded him with warmth. *Simple comforts, indeed*, he thought, as he continued his explorations.

After thirty more minutes of waiting, which included a half-hearted attempt at sleep, he rose to his feet and decided it would be all right to explore the exterior premises. He cracked the door, tentatively peeking outside and was moderately concerned that a pack of super-humans might sweep in, seize him, and teleport him back to his old life. *No, this is silly. Ini said that I am a brother of Gylodon, so nobody's gonna fault me for looking around. Besides, she didn't say that I had to stay indoors.*

He stepped outside, onto a flagstone, searching the near vicinity. Everything was new; even the trees had aspects to them that were odd, reflecting light in unusual ways. But the colors—the new ones—were the most novel of all. He couldn't conceive of how they were even possible. But there they were—making themselves known. A cluster of bobbing wild flowers put them on display, as if proud of their achievement. *Those look like gardens of some sort*, he thought, already en route. The wind shifted and honeyed sweetness flanked his nostrils; he breathed it in with reverence.

***

The village gardens were places of unimaginable magic, and when one gazed upon them with the fourth power, a new world of rainbows, fairies and extra-dimensional beings came into view. It was the only place on Earth where humans, animals, ghosts, thought forms, elementals like salamanders, sylphs, undines and gnomes, and nature spirits like satyrs, wood nymphs and water sprites lived harmoniously, with daily interactions.

Attracted to the light, they congregated here, dancing among their plant brethren, singing enchanting songs and spreading scents that could only emanate from another layer of this world.

Anax strolled through the wild herbs when a gentle, warming wind blessed his cheek. Instinctively, he turned his head to let the sensation caress him; he breathed in the flavor of the forest, and as he shifted, his eyes locked onto what could only be a vision from another world, and his mind spun.

Whoa...how? Is...is she real?

Simultaneously dumbfounded and enraptured, he drank her in with his entire spirit. Eyes of chocolate sitting upon perfect cheekbones, punctuated by delicate freckles that splayed like seeds falling from a flower. Her dark hair fluttered in the wind—the same wind that had graced Anax's face moments before. Even that thought—of a shared breeze—was enough to release a torrent of butterflies in Anax's solar plexus that took flight directly into his heart.

In an instant, his life had shifted.

Preoccupied with rescuing a bug that had fallen into a muddy puddle, she was entirely unaware of Anax's gawking. Emotions coursed through him in a way that he had not previously experienced; at once he felt an urge to cry, to laugh and to be grateful. No words came. Eyes transfixed, he watched as this vision delicately scooped up the insect on her finger and graced it with a kiss before releasing it to a leaf on a nearby branch. *This must be the luckiest bug in the entire world*, he thought, and for a prolonged moment he would have traded all that he was to be that that little creature.

Motherly energy emanated from her core like a gentle lapping wave. She was beauty. She was power. She was love.

"And she is not the one for you," a voice from behind him cautioned. "At least, it does not appear that her destiny is tied to yours from where I am sitting, but what do I know? I've been wrong before." The Seed Bearer released a mischievous smile. Surprised, Anax twisted, pulling his attention from the woman. The man was elderly, with wild white hair and leathered skin, but somehow maintained unusual muscularity—particularly in his legs. They were like tree trunks. He reminded Anax of a Roman statesman; his garment even resembled a toga.

Anax's attention wavered between the elder and the woman in the distance.

"What? But how... What is her name?" Too surprised to even make an introduction, Anax attempted to ground himself.

"She is Tristis, and her beauty is a reflection of the light that shines within her. Like you, she came to us by *way of the seed*. She has been unschooled and re-empowered; she was able to release her traumas, control her mind and find her heart. It took her nearly sixty full moons to get to where she is, and she has finally arrived." He paused, gazing distantly as his eyes watered. "Still, there is a piece of her soul that we have been unable to recover, a soul-split induced by deep, hidden trauma. One day we shall retrieve it. I only hope that it is not too late." Anax, confused by the statement, just listened.

"Your journey is only beginning, Anax. Unfortunately, it is best to minimize contact with her at this stage lest you inadvertently penetrate her new barriers and remind her of the worries she once felt in the outside world. Like you, when she arrived, she was in a delicate state; a state of absolute surrender with a willingness to die, should that be her path. She had to let go of everything to find us. She has worked relentlessly to reprogram herself and gain unfettered access to the *four* and *five*. As will you, Anax, if that is your choice—and from what I can tell, it does seem to be your destiny. You did not arrive here by mistake, young brother."

Anax, silent, returned his gaze to Tristis. "I have heard of the fourth and fifth powers from Ini, but don't know much about them."

"You will, young Anax. I see the light in you. Your teacher will provide the guidance that you require," he said.

Anax turned to ask the old man a question, but he was already gone.

Master Unschooler

***

"The first step toward freedom is thought discipline."
- Book of Gylodon -

Standing nearly six and one-half feet tall with cropped, dark curly hair and fair skin, the Unschooler was an imposing figure. When he stood on the top of the knoll, and the sun hit just right, he cast the shadow of a mountain. His words carried the momentum of a meteor and his eyes reflected a lifetime of doing. Anax knew little about him, or what to expect, but he was ready to learn. *Whatever it takes.* It didn't take long to see that the Unschooler was unlike any teacher he'd ever had. He strode like a general, taking position in front of his students.

"Gentlemen, I see the light in you. Class is now in session," he announced. Anax, excited in a way he'd not experienced since childhood, straightened his posture and sharpened his attention.

"Welcome, Anax. You and Dan will be learning together from here on out." Anax glanced to the student on his right, whom he'd met only once. During that encounter, Dan had exuded profound confidence and solidarity, and in him Anax found a vitality that contrasted starkly with his own weaknesses. Clearly, Dan was a man of action and lived by that code. It was a quality to which Anax aspired. Physically, Dan was short but highly athletic; his hair was dark and neatly trimmed, and his face wore a casual boldness that invited speculation. As best as Anax could discern, he appeared to be of Latin American heritage, but clearly, he'd been raised and educated in the United States.

"Support each other," the teacher continued, "but never lose focus on your own individual growth. Gentlemen, your entire lives you have been schooled. And now, here in Gylodon, you will be educated. Self-educated. I will not dictate right or wrong, truth or untruth; but I will provide a framework for you to know yourself, explore new realities and develop authentic power. Henceforth, your education will be based upon your own experience. You'll learn to dissolve old thinking patterns, destructive cellular memories and constrictive beliefs that hold you in a state of purgatory. In time, you will become sculptors of high-vibration realities. The structure of these lessons is based upon the *Book of Gylodon*, a living document, diligently compiled over centuries to assist non-natives with the transition to mind-mastery and open hearts. Dan, you have heard much of this before, but I am repeating it for Anax. Now, gentlemen, close your eyes and clear your mind," the teacher prodded. Anax followed the towering man's instructions.

"Right now, you have access only to your five senses. In time, you will have access to more. For now, however, you need only concern yourself with these five. *Touch, taste, smell, hearing* and *sight*. *Tools*. Each of these senses exists as part of your physical experience of being in a body; consequently, they exist only in the present moment, so use them to keep your mind from wandering to the past or the future. Use them as tools to clear your mind of undisciplined thoughts. They will be your allies, as you seek to claim ownership of your mind. So, to begin, we will work with *touch*. While you sit on the grass, focus only on the weight of your body on the ground; you may also shift your awareness to the feel of grass under your hands." He paused for a time, before continuing.

"Next, feel the air on your cheek. Feel the air as you breathe it in." Again, he paused for several minutes before speaking, and Anax attuned himself to the sensations.

"Focus on either one of these—one at a time. Focus on nothing else. If any thought should enter your mind, simply observe it and let it pass. Remain detached. Likewise, should an unconscious daydream enter your mind, carrying you away, let it pass as soon as you become aware of it. Become the *external observer* of your own internal dialogues, images and patterns. The objective is to become

The Mystical Village That Rewired Reality

fully conscious of your wandering thoughts. You will see them as they arise, without being attached to them. This is the first step toward *lucidity*. After much practice, you will learn that you can prevent the thoughts from entering your mind at all, simply by focusing on any of the five senses, which exist only in the present moment.

"In time, you'll be able sit in silence for thirty minutes without so much as a single, aberrant thought arising. At that point, you will have gained sufficient mastery of your thoughts and you will be ready for your next exercise.

"Now open your eyes. You will practice these exercises each morning, afternoon and night, at minimum. Perhaps you prefer to work with hearing or sight. You may find that some of the senses are less helpful than others; try them anyway. After that, work only with the ones that take you toward the goal with the greatest precision."

The Unschooler stared intently at Anax before shifting his gaze to the pupil at his side. Perched on the grassy knoll, the students sat in the shade of an old-growth willow tree that had served as a classroom for hundreds of years. Threads of light streamed through the dense foliage, creating a smattering of light and dark. A record keeper, the tree had absorbed all the thoughts, energies and emotions that had been exchanged between student and teacher over the centuries. Underneath its vast wingspan were places of power that served well for higher education.

"Right now, Anax, your mind has no discipline. I want you to think of your brain as a receiver, vulnerable to static interference. Much of that static has come from external sources throughout your life—such as imagery of all sorts, sounds and other portals of communication. But much has come from you as well, reinforcing your own illusions and fears. On the outside, *consciousness pollution* is rampant, coming at you from every angle, always seeking to keep you trapped anywhere other than the *here and now*. Currently, your mind bounces incessantly from one channel to another, daydreaming, devoid of awareness and focus. You are barely conscious of this failing. You lack lucidity, and control. We seek lucidity in all things to direct power in specific ways. It is the warrior's way. Step one is to gain control of your thoughts; after you have mastered this, we will teach you how to consciously create constructive, powerful thoughts that can then be transmitted for specific means. Only then can you truly wield your mind's awesome power."

Excited, Anax glanced right, attempting to catch the gaze of his more experienced classmate. His glance was not returned, as the fellow student exercised greater restraint than Anax could muster. Instead, Dan kept his attention on the teacher with military-like discipline. Anax wondered why the teacher was directing the lessons more at him than Dan, but surmised that Dan did not require the same level of attention, having had several months of training already.

The Unschooler continued, "You must learn that we are responsible for everything that we *think, say and feel*. Every thought, word and feeling that we project has an echo or a consequence, and ultimately, we are accountable for all that we transmit. We must learn to become lucid creators and sculptors of high-vibration consciousness. When we feed the *consciousness cloud* with our own thought transmissions, we must strive to make it lighter and brighter. This is the way of the *warriors of light*."

***

After several weeks of practice, Anax started to notice things. Around the village, he saw wisps of energy, sometimes as balls of light, moving around in various locations. Other times, he deciphered faint outlines of energy beings or simply felt their presence. But nothing had prepared him for his encounter one hazy, ashen evening, during the full-moon cycle.

All in all, it has been a pristine day, he thought, smiling. Despite all the rigorous introspective work he was doing, his energy was at an all-time high, and so were his spirits. There seemed to be no limit to positive feelings in Gylodon. He almost felt guilty—but then thought better of it.

The evening seemed the perfect time to take a stroll down to the winding stream, called *Yara* by some of the villagers. The stream twisted and wandered, like an anaconda, disappearing under brush before reemerging at her next energy point, or so Anax had been told.

The dust kicked up under his feet as he loped along the path. Inhaling, he smelled epazote from the cooking pots across the village. *Must be Mexican night over there.* He was still not permitted to dine, or interact for that matter, with the general village population. But his time would come.

Arriving at the stream, he hopped down its bank onto a wide, reddish rock that pressed out into the water. It was an ideal spot. The breeze was like a soft touch, slightly cool, and calming. He sat down and began to meditate, but before he could immerse himself, he was distracted by a subtle melody coming from an indecipherable direction; in fact, it was nearly on top of him, forcing him to spin around and look in every direction, including upward. The bizarre melody—more flute-like by the moment—grew louder, aggressively pressing upon his consciousness, like the call of a siren. It drew him in, confusing him, enveloping him, disarming him. Completely overwhelmed, he felt his awareness slipping away, as if his thoughts were being sucked into a black hole. And then the evening light did funny things, as if layering on top of itself, and to his right he saw the outline of a person forming, and atop its head were protrusions, which became irregular, elongated horns; at first, it was like a shadow, but then energy throbbed within its outline, pulsing like ripples in water, before morphing into three-dimensional, hairy form. Goat-like legs supported a semi-human torso, topped by an oversized, double-horned head. Anax had never seen a man-goat creature, or any spirit, with such clarity. *My God.* The flute paused and he heard a bone-chilling cackle, and then he felt like meat, as if he were being sexually assessed. Disoriented and dizzy, he attempted to focus. The creature's hairy tail was not nearly as disturbing as its obscene, cherry-red erection, which was nearly the length of the flute in its wiry hands. It cackled again and trotted toward Anax, in bipedal fashion, on two sharp hooves. Anax stood up, his heart beating wildly as adrenaline coursed through his body, and the creature charged, laughing the entire way, coming closer and closer. Bracing for impact, every muscle in Anax's body tensed like iron couplings, and just as he flexed, the creature jumped, taking flight over his head before disappearing into a shimmering hole in the air. Anax exhaled, looking upward, just as it vanished.

Afterward, an eerie silence descended upon the river. He sought to calm himself, slowing his breathing and eventually sitting down. His thoughts became clearer. He could scarcely believe what he'd just experienced. With some concern, he noted the absence of animal sounds, as if they'd vacated the river en masse. He decided to do the same.

The next day he recounted the episode to his teacher.

"Count yourself fortunate," the Master Unschooler said. "That's quite a rare experience—even for the natives. I guess it's mating season for the satyrs. You should feel flattered that he considered you." Anax could not be certain if he was masking a smile.

"Thank you, Master."

"Don't thank me. Thank the satyr." Anax scrunched his face.

"Don't worry, Anax, no spirit can commit physical harm to anyone in Gylodon. It just happens that these particular beings are, for lack of a better word, well...*horny*. It's in their nature. Full moons are the most active times, but full moons during mating season for the satyrs, well, it doesn't get wilder than that. They'll calm down by next month, I expect. Your virtue is safe, for now."

After that, Anax spent more time in the gardens, away from the river, where he was still likely to encounter otherworldly beings, but more important, Tristis. *Beautiful Tristis.* To him, she was an other-

The Mystical Village That Rewired Reality

worldly creature. He'd seen little of her since that first day but she never left his thoughts. She was a white shadow, unseen and elusive. *I'll see her again when the time is right,* he told himself often.

With each passing day, his physical pains had diminished and he no longer limped. His head did not hurt and his body gained vitality. The changes were difficult to comprehend. Sometimes he would sit and contemplate this new reality—not wanting to take it for granted—and he felt immeasurable gratitude. Other times he fantasized about being back home and sharing his miraculous physical recovery with friends. Then he'd catch himself, realizing that he was not in control of his thoughts, nor did they emanate from a place of power. Sometimes he wondered if the pain would return if he left Gylodon, and the thoughts frightened him. At other times, he was seized with guilt for not communicating with his family. He'd spoken to Ini about this and she was going to get a message to them soon; that would allow for improved concentration during lessons.

He embraced his lessons fully, and with each passing sunset he found a growing measure of peace in his heart. The restlessness that had plagued him on the outside was already gone, replaced with a lightness of being that felt so natural that he wondered where it had been hiding all these years. *Is this what happiness feels like?*

✷✷✷

Magic was an inherent part of the village and it mirrored the love that lived within the hearts of its residents. This love suffused all things, including its architecture. From a distance, Anax observed how the people of the village worked together on these projects; often he'd sit within listening range, careful not to interact with anybody, just absorbing impressions. It was a new way of processing information, and he enjoyed it. Today he was perched on a small hill, outside the town center, watching a woman and a little girl at a new building site. Both were dark skinned with jet-black hair that was pulled taut and ornamented with tiny pine twigs. Adorning oneself with pine was common practice, Anax had learned, as the scent of pine was said to enhance self-love.[11]

"Come here, Little One. Pick up the cob ball. You see, just like this. Talk to it, feel it. Feel for just the right consistency—it must have just the right balance of sand, clay, soil and plant fibers. Here, feel this one. This is how strong cob feels."[12]

The little girl reached out and took the heavy ball of mud from her auntie, and her slender arms dropped with the weight.

"Like this?" she said, smiling broadly, arms quivering just a bit.

"Yes, dear, just like that. Come over here, let me show you how we add it to the wall." The girl followed, struggling to hold onto the ball, but not wanting to show any weakness. The elder led her to the wall of the community's latest building project. It was about two feet wide and twelve feet long, but only two feet tall. They were adding to the height.

"So, Little One, you need to use your thumbs to knead the material into the layer below to ensure proper joinery. The plant fibers must be pushed into the layer below. In this way, all the little cob balls merge together to create one solid, unbreakable structure. It's just like all of us here in the village, working together as one. In this way, we are stronger. Do you understand?"

The girl smiled broadly, nodding her head, grateful to be participating in her first community-building project.

Throughout the village, elegantly sculpted houses could be seen. Modest in size and constructed of local earth, clay, sand and fibrous plant materials, these homes followed few of the building conventions of the outside world. Right angles were non-existent as the builders found none of them in nature. These cottages reflected the inherent beauty of the materials with which they were built; wrought with curves, alcoves and magnificently sculpted benches, they embodied creativity and stood as living sculptures. Some of the structures were adorned with geometric symbols, as well, said to hold power.

The Mystical Village That Rewired Reality

Anax learned that these buildings were constructed upon river-rock foundations, and they remained cool in the summers and warm in the winters due to passive solar radiation, thermal mass and the cosmic awareness with which they were oriented.[13]

The thatch roofs, like all building processes, were created through the combined efforts of villagers. Many of them had specialized knowledge of the process and enjoyed sharing their wisdom with the younger community members. Building projects always united the villagers, providing profound opportunities for shared vision and co-creation. They revered it as a deeply spiritual practice and tackled every building task with the utmost dedication, viewing it as an opportunity to blend mind-mastery with communal intention. It didn't matter how laborious or time-consuming an activity was, it was an opportunity for renewal and rebirth—and a chance to bring people together.

Anax was riveted by the psychology of their building projects, how it was not perceived as an undesirable task, but rather an enjoyable pastime. It seemed backward, he'd thought, and yet, he observed it on several occasions. No matter the task, they found joy in working together.

"The best part of these cottages," Ini had told him, "is the healing effect that they have on their inhabitants." On another occasion, she'd said, "Residing in such a cabin is akin to living inside Mother Earth's womb, and the villagers feel the same kinship with their homes as they feel with the earth."

It was a radical perception shift to view his cottage as a womb, and he and Dan had laughed about it. In truth, though, it was damn cozy, and he couldn't disagree.

Bandwidths

✱✱✱

"Our five senses reveal but a sliver of truth in a sea of endless possibilities. Energy is fluid and reality is subject to change."
- Book of Gylodon -

Rain spattered on mud as Anax departed his lodging. *I love this place,* he thought, pausing to look back before closing the door. The cottage, though temporary, was tiny and perfect; it provided everything he needed. With barely room for a bed and table, it was largely free of distractions but contained all the simple comforts. Vibrant fabrics, dyed with local berries and plants contrasted with the tan, earthen walls and the space radiated warmth that could only be described as soulful and healing. Sometimes, when he got too comfortable, he'd remind himself that he had a home on the outside and people who cared for him. *When the time is right, I will return.* He didn't know when that would be, but he assumed that he would have the choice when the time arrived. For now, though, he dared not inquire. He knew only that those born in the village were not equipped to leave, nor did they want to. But he was an outsider.

En route to the Willow Tree of Wisdom for today's lesson, Anax surveyed the skies. *I guess we'll be out in the rain today. Good thing I brought a sweater.* A nervous enthusiasm tickled him, the kind that grips a stranger in a foreign land—an excitement laden with unknown possibilities.

Dan was there when he arrived. "I see the light in you, Brother," he greeted.

"And I in you," Anax responded, still unaccustomed to using the words. He stifled a grin, feeling emboldened by the rain and the challenge of enduring the outdoor lesson, despite the chill. The tree provided more protection than he anticipated, but still the two of them got wet. While waiting for their teacher, they cleared their minds and practiced their thought-discipline techniques.

"Good morning, gentlemen. I see the power in you." The Unschooler's commanding voice cracked the silence, as he varied the traditional greeting to suit his mood.

"And I in you, Master Unschooler," they responded, opening their eyes. Never one for idle banter, the teacher dove straight into the lesson.

"Today we are going to discuss sensory perception. Until now, I have emphasized the importance of using your five senses as tools to keep your mind clear. This is using your body to your advantage. But I want you to understand just how limited these five senses are. In the outside world, much of reality is rooted in these five senses. Many believe that the things they see, hear, touch, taste and smell are the foundations of reality. This is not even close to the truth."

A drop of rain hit the center of Anax's nose and he let it roll, keeping his eyes locked on the teacher. Cold seeped in through his damp clothing, and he brought his arms tighter into his body.

"You see, gentlemen, it is all about *bandwidths of perception*. As you know, many technologies in the outside world can detect energies that are otherwise invisible to us. Think in terms of radiation detectors or devices that detect frequencies when your ears cannot. You'd think that the existence of such devices would be enough to encourage widespread curiosity about what else is out there, but unconventional thinking still exists only in a small subset of the population. Sadly, society has been structured in a way that distracts people from exploring deeper truths; far too often, *consciousness pollution* impedes human potential. Without unconventional thinking, people are relegated to embrace the status quo, without a framework to see beyond. It's the innovators, artists and healers of society who shatter those boundaries, forcing people to think and feel in new ways, to delve into new realities.

"It's important to understand just how limited our five senses are, in the scope of existence. Our eyes see only a sliver of the full spectrum of light throughout the universe. Our bodies sense only a microscopic piece of the radiations that permeate the galaxies. To put it in perspective, our physical eyes see the world through a single grain of sand on an endless beach, and every grain is a new reality and a new prism for viewing the world in countless ways.

"There are endless wavelengths of energy, nearly all of which our five senses cannot detect. A simple example from the outside world includes radiation from wireless routers, microwaves or cellular phones. People cannot see them, but they exist. And this is just a microcosm of an infinitely larger picture. Most of the mass of the universe is completely invisible to us. Some refer to this as *dark matter* or *dark energy*.[14]

"Of course, as you'll continue to learn, when we travel outside of the body new realities are revealed to the astral eyes, varying with our energetic state at the time. We know this through experience." Briefly, Anax's mind returned to his hospital astral projections, when he had noted strange clouds floating in the corner of the room. *Could they be dark matter?* The Unschooler cleared his throat, drawing Anax's attention back to the lesson.

"Everything that we do here is rooted in experience and action. Everything. Take none of these lectures as truth; do the work and discover it for yourself. Otherwise it is simply dogma. And we are creatures of light, not dogma. Leave dogma for those who follow the broken status quo. In Gylodon, we shatter and rebuild reality to our liking so long as it is in alignment with our hearts. Our hearts, by the way, have neurons just like our brains, and carry a consciousness all their own.[15] Listen to them when deciding between right and wrong. The gut is also composed of neurons that communicate information to us."[16]

He paused, rubbing his long, broad hands together, before continuing, "It's ironic that our bodies, marvels of engineering, are also our biggest hindrance. Most people on the outside don't understand how to balance them, slowly poisoning themselves over their lifetimes." The rain slowed. The two students, both outsiders and now closer friends, sat in rapt attention. When no questions came forth, the teacher proceeded with the lesson.

"I have invited a guest to speak with you about a topic that is of the utmost importance." Behind them, leaves crunched, and they turned to find Inipia walking gracefully up the hill, her long hair catching the currents of the wind. She smiled at Anax and Dan before offering a traditional greeting to each of them and hugging the Unschooler.

"Today, Inipia will be sharing some of her knowledge about *energy healing* with both of you," the teacher added.

Anax was giddy. It happened a lot. Finally, he'd arrived into an alien world—*his* alien world—and everything fit. The topics of education were wildly different from his childhood experience, and the methodologies—ones that encouraged experimentation and independent thought—were like newly discovered friends. Where had they been hiding? Even as his body chilled in the rain, he felt more comfortable and more at home than he could ever have imagined.

Instead of standing, as was the Unschooler's habit, Ini sat down on the wet grass, centering herself in front of the two pupils. Her nurturing approach was a welcome change on a cold day. Sparkling like crystals, her eyes were alive and Anax was entranced. Ever since she'd saved his life, and prepared him for entry into Gylodon, he felt a profound reverence for her. He waited patiently as she prepared to speak.

"Good morning, my Brothers. As you both know, we have endless tools at our disposal for healing *dis-ease*, or rather, energetic imbalances in the body, manifested in physical form. Here in the village we use more traditional methods for interacting with energy like herbs, eggs, plants, smoke and music. To the uninitiated, these approaches may seem little more than superstition. But we know through millennia of experience that they are practical tools for altering energy.

"The science of the outside world is still centered on traditional germ theory and chemical reactions; but we, as paradigm-shifters, look at things with a broader perspective. We are not trapped in other people's belief systems that view the body as little more than a biological and chemical machine. Instead, we view it as raw consciousness, physically manifested; it is the electromagnetic essence, forged of water, fire and air—and infused with spirit. It is magic and science all at once.

"The building blocks of our bodies, the elements like carbon, nitrogen and oxygen, are derived from the stars, and the water of our bodies from space. We truly are space beings.[17] But even beyond that, we are beings of organized energy. Even our *personalities* are made of energy."

Ini pushed up to her knees, scanning the hill, before continuing, "I want the two of you to lie down on the ground, head to head and close your eyes."

The ground was wet, but Anax's sweater provided sufficient insulation from total saturation, as he slid into position, pressing the top of his head against Dan's. Icy rain, however, pelted his face and hands, and he was growing chillier by the minute. With his body flat and open, he began to shiver, doing his best to control the reaction. He steadied his breathing, staying open to whatever Ini was teaching. He wondered how Dan was faring and suspected that he was unfazed. Squinting, he saw Ini's hands hovering in the air, two inches above his forehead.

Within moments Anax felt heat, starting in his head and migrating down his back, into his lower extremities. The rain became little more than a secondary awareness, subdued in the background, while the warmth swallowed him. *This is pleasurable,* he thought, smiling behind the neutral lines of his lips.

This continued for nearly ten minutes before Ini spoke, "Within this reality, our bodies are subject to innumerable energetic influences, at different wavelengths and frequencies. Right now, you are feeling radiant energy from my hands, similar to an infrared sauna in the outside world.[18] It is guided by my conscious intention.

The Mystical Village That Rewired Reality

"You see, as *warriors of light*—we are literally made of light—and consequently, we view *dis-ease* as more than chemical and biological imbalances; we also see it as disharmonious resonance, or unhealthful frequencies that are misaligned with our body's natural harmonics.[19] To an extent, we can control these energies, as you've both just experienced."

The warmth was fading, and Anax's soggy sweater was now causing him to shiver. *More warmth please,* he pleaded, hoping Ini would read his thoughts.

"You can sit back up," she offered, instead.

As they rolled into a sitting position, feeling a bit loopy, Dan's gaze caught something in the distance and he pointed. Anax squinted, following Dan's line of sight, and saw what appeared to be a large moose, with massive antlers, prancing in an open field. Scanning further, he spotted a smaller one just beyond it. It was a newborn. The Unschooler turned and watched the animals for several minutes before they slipped back into the woodlands. Anax sensed that the teacher was sending them energy.

The Unschooler beamed. "Those, my friends, are *eastern elk*—one of our protected species that has been extinct in the outside world for more than one hundred and thirty years. We have a small population of two or three dozen of them at any given time. These animals are the last hope for their lineage.

"We do what we can to shield them. Mostly they stay within the village boundaries because there are exceptional food resources here, but also because they are drawn to Gylodon's *consciousness cloud*. Animals can feel the ecological balance here; they are sensitive to the local energies. This has enabled us to safeguard quite a few seemingly extinct species. It's a gift."

All four of them grinned like children; they stood at the threshold of beauty as witnesses to a miracle. It was as close as Gylodonians ever got to feeling pride. But mostly they felt appreciation and awe. Safeguarding a near-extinct species—as its only advocate and steward—was a sacred act, a feat of superheroes. Such was life in

Gylodon; always they would take some time to appreciate a passing miracle, and then they would return to learning and creating, balancing and loving.

Ini looked almost reluctant to return to the lesson, but did so with steadfast professionalism. Each of them was working toward a common goal, whether or not it was fully realized by Anax and Dan. Time was scarce, and she and the elders were at the helm. They needed to make sure that the outsiders were prepared for what lay ahead.

"Now, getting back to the nature of *dis-ease*," she announced, reclaiming their attention. "We already know that physical illness can arise from several different places. Yes, *toxins in the body*. Yes, *parasites in the body*. Yes, *lack of nutrition*. These contribute to many problems on the *biological* level.

"But there is much more than this—we must also look at the *emotional* and *mental* aspects that lead to illness; like suppressed feelings, misguided beliefs, destructive storylines that we tell ourselves, old cellular memories from trauma or even misunderstood sexual energy; all of these can induce illness, or *dis-ease*. Even ancestral imbalances, like a grandparent who may have been part of a war, or genocide, can present as illness in a descendant's body if the fears and energetic entanglements associated with it are passed down through the lineage. The list goes on and on."

Dan shifted, stretching his legs out in front, attempting to loosen his hamstrings. Anax longed to do the same but refrained, keeping his body as tight as possible to preserve heat.

Ini continued, completely impervious to the cold. "Indeed, the greatest opportunity for our healing lies in the emotional and mental spaces, but in the outside world there is also a significant need to shelter one's physical body. Each day, people carry irradiating cellular phones pressed against their reproductive organs while sitting in front of wireless routers for hours on end, bombarding their bodies with dirty electromagnetism.[20] By dirty, I mean that it does not align with their body's natural harmonics. Even the electricity running through their own homes can disrupt their bodies' natural frequencies,[21] although it is the wireless world that poses the gravest threat. In this wireless world people's immune systems are perpetually stressed, and in time they may develop tumors, memory problems, concentration problems, depression or even infertility from constant exposure to these unnatural energies. And still, the outsiders push for more and more wireless radiations, even as they cause cancer, kill bee populations, disrupt ecosystems, confuse and agitate animals, and create the most invasive form of pollution that humankind has ever imagined. And the truth is largely hidden from humanity—nearly as invisible as the energies themselves.

"In the outside world, people rarely escape the wireless radiations unless they retreat into nature, where they begin to rebalance. In the wilderness, people feel strangely energized and their thinking becomes more acute. It's here that they are returning to a more natural state, resonating with the earth's frequencies, and can begin to heal."[22]

She paused, watching her students for any confusion, before continuing, "Interestingly, there are technologies that exist on the outside that are becoming more available to the people, that use frequencies to restore health. These bioresonance devices can identify many of the imbalances in a person's body, including chemicals, pathogens and even emotional imbalances based upon their frequency signatures.[23] They can then neutralize them with frequencies that enable one's immune system to fight back and reclaim its supremacy. As more people reclaim freedom, and the global transition gets into full swing, we expect the influence of these devices to expand.[24]

"Now, I invite both of you to take some time and reflect on the nature of our universe, as well as the energetic nature of your bodies. Remember, we are made of the same thing as the earth—fire and water, mediated by air, and imbued with an electromagnetic essence."

BANDWIDTHS

Both students closed their eyes and wordlessly fell into deep contemplation.

Anax's thoughts drifted into the realm of the unseen, to the land of invisible energies surrounding us, penetrating our bodies and playing with our lives. He saw himself eating, and each bite of food generated specific frequencies in his digestive tract; some were helpful, cleaning the body, while others triggered inflammation. Some frequencies affected moods and still others affected hormones. Each of the chakras, or major energy centers in the body, also had specific frequencies. Even they were affected by food.

Then, from the edge of his consciousness, a black-and-white dog greeted him, wagging its tail with frenzied enthusiasm as waves of happiness emanated from its body. Its body was an electrical generator, he realized, and its joy was transmitted as geometric patterns that danced in space, interacting with Anax's physical, emotional and mental bodies. The dog literally radiated happiness—invisible to the naked eye—but as real as the food in one's belly. Everything was an energy interaction. Then he saw himself in a state of anger, and he irradiated that anger—again, as structural patterns and frequencies—into his surrounding environment, affecting all things. He studied the environment more closely and saw organized packets of energy, arranged intelligently, lingering in space; he bumped into them and felt their subtle overtones but could not discern their deeper meaning. He saw similar energies being drawn to each other, like personalities, building upon collective synergies, and he thought of Dan, the Unschooler and Gylodon. Then things darkened and he was transported to an ancient battlefield of rampant death and destruction, and in the air hung negative packets of energy, ugly things, like old bloody footprints in an abandoned building. Some energy clusters wallowed in anguish, aware of their pain, and still others were unconscious programs, replaying like molecular imprints, or outdated videos. The world was nothing less than a peculiar melting pot—designed for the mingling and remodeling of energy. And it was bright and dark, beautiful and ugly. It twisted on and on.

Then again, Anax considered, it was far too easy to get lost in the world of energy; it was a boundless ocean, encompassing every wave and ripple, fish and plankton, and each plant and grain of sand. It was the language of God, captured in sacred geometry and sound, or love and grief and sex, dancing in the spaces in between, like ballads of beauty. All of humanity was learning about energy, in one form or another, even if they were unaware of it.

Upon completing their meditations, Anax and Dan sat in silence for some time. Anax's thoughts returned to daily life, and a single question bubbled to the surface. *How does the Unschooler know so much about the outside world? Ini, I understand. She's an outsider.* (He'd recently learned of Ini's outsider status and it had surprised him.) But now he was perplexed by the Unschooler's recent revelations. *How does he know about technologies on the outside? From Ini?*

The teachers had departed with scarcely a word, leaving them to sit for more than three hours in silence. The temperature dropped and the damp earth cut through their clothing, sucking the heat from their extremities. *In comes the fire, out goes the cold,* Anax channeled with each breath. It was an exercise he'd learned the previous week, and he suddenly had a renewed interest in developing the skill.

Finally, Dan stirred, stretching his legs and Anax followed suit, as his eyes adjusted to the dwindling light. He looked at his friend.

"How do you think the Unschooler knows so much about the outside world?"

Dan froze at the question, staring blankly as if he were not fully in his body.

"That is something you'll need to ask him," he responded, with a finality that further piqued Anax's curiosity. But Anax did not push the issue. For now, he'd stay focused on his studies. Each day, after all, ushered in new subjects to explore—some more alluring than others.

Animal Energy

***

Anax's entire being vibrated as he watched her. It was as if she were a violin, thrumming the exact melody, or frequency, of his soul. It was intoxicating—like the flute music of the satyr—but far more lovely, and certainly less onerous. Her dark hair played on the breeze, as if the wind had an agenda, and her expressions were gentle, inviting the forest creatures to come forth.

Sitting on the edge of the woodlands with her heart wide open, in a state of fifth-dimensional resonance, Tristis waited. Within minutes they came. First a fawn of unusual coloring, then three gray field mice and finally several birds of different varieties. "Hello, Little One," she whispered to the deer. First it observed her from afar and when the animal felt the energy was right, it gingerly trotted up to her hand and began to feed. She spoke in soothing tones, resonating love, "You have returned, Gentle One. I am grateful, and honored. You are always safe with me, and very loved. Where is your mama?"

The fawn leaned in and smelled her face. Closing her eyes, she smiled and offered her cheek; the tiny nose tickled her, sending a sensation down her back, and she laughed softly.

Anax watched from afar, practicing the fourth power. *That looks a bit like a rainbow,* he thought, as he observed subtle energy transmissions from Tristis toward the fawn. Indistinct swirls of light moved between her heart and the animal, as if she surrounded it with an energetic blanket, putting it at ease. He wondered if she also interacted with the near-extinct species in this manner. *Now that would be remarkable.* In some ways, the reality of "extinct" species still thriving in Gylodon was even more extraordinary than his encounters with the spirit world. The villagers were doing real work—right here on Earth—acting as chief guardians of the animal kingdom. Their service to the planet was inconceivable.

Tristis' hair fluttered in the breeze and Anax was carried away, imagining her soft, loving touch. He grimaced. *There goes my concentration again. Why do I always have a hard time clearing my thoughts? Because of Tristis, of course.* She was sensory overload and all consuming. *Ahhh...to speak with her, to make her smile, to know her.* Once, he'd said something that she'd overheard and he was certain that he'd seen her smile. It carried him for days. But still he was not permitted to speak with her. Just knowing that she existed was enough to set flame to the long-dormant creativity that lived within him. He took to writing poetry; she inspired him in countless ways. Alas, she was also the ultimate impediment to his mastery of the fourth power; every time he cleared his mind of thoughts, she would rise again. Like an oasis in the desert, she haunted him, and he loved her for it.

And she, perfection embodied, barely acknowledged his existence.

His training suffered for his constant longings, and already four moons had passed without his mastery of *four*.

***

Gylodon's relationship with the animal kingdom was a far cry from the outside world. Animals were not commodities to be used and consumed. There was no animal farming, or hamsters in cages—or pets of any sort.

Instead, animals were allies, free to come and go, however they saw fit. If there were any exceptions to this rule, it was with dogs; their bond with humans was ironclad, a marriage that would never dissolve. It had not always been this way—there had been a time when dogs were entirely wild—but those days had long passed. Humans had bred them for disposition and temperament, altering their ancestral lineage, and they'd become inextricably linked to people, in both body and spirit. While they were free to come and go in Gylodon, and largely did so, there were always some dogs that returned to specific cottages to sleep, or to commune with the people they loved. Because dogs were so accessible, they were perfect partners in the development of animal communication, a vital skill in Gylodon. Children would sit with their canine companions for hours, practicing the fourth power. Usually the dogs had little to say, with the simple lives they lived, but sometimes they spoke of imbalances in Gylodon, like a rogue predator violating the peace.

Within the village boundaries, there were only a handful of predatory carnivores, and they tended to wander outside of Gylodon's *consciousness cloud* to make their kills. On rare occasions, though, there were violent animal deaths. They were usually the result of mental illness, too far gone to rebalance, even within Gylodon's energy field. Still, such violence was rarely encountered by the villagers, who looked upon the entire animal kingdom with profound respect, and even a measure of equality. In fact, much of Gylodon's knowledge was gleaned from the forest creatures.

Bears were teachers of strength and stability, as well as family; they were models of solitude, taking time to slow down, reflect and recharge for the new season. Hummingbirds reminded them to find the sweetness in life, to drink in its nectar, to be playful and adaptable to any situation, while foxes were symbols of woodland wisdom, able to adapt, blend and survive—like shape-shifters from the underworld. The squirrels taught them to be industrious and practical, storing provisions for the winter season, while the deer were symbols of gentleness and grace, as well as primal intuition; they were renowned for their fourth power, which was highly attuned to their environments. Even the insects were exceptional teachers. As part of their learning, children would observe spiders for hours, watching them weave, as if they were architecting the web of life, or Gylodon's *consciousness cloud.* But the most revered insects were the dragonflies, with their boundless flight patterns, rainbow wings and multifaceted vision; they symbolized the need for constant transformation and rebirth, and were impervious to the illusions of life—

seeing straight through them, as if gazing directly into the astral planes.

Indeed, the animal kingdom was worthy of respect; it overflowed with wisdom, a biological brew of unrivaled skills, refined intuition and ecological order. The people of Gylodon were grateful for their forest teachers, and for them they would strive to keep the balance.

Falling

***

The woodlands chirped with growing enthusiasm, and the sounds mingled, mixing into a single voice that screamed out, attesting to the day's grandeur. It was a world without judgment—only possibility. Sun crept through heavy clouds, like moonlight slipping through a window, and nowhere was tragedy written.

But there is a reason they call it wilderness. A wild and free existence is not without a price. Nature can reclaim one's body at any time—it is her right, after all. One of the few downsides of being born in Gylodon was an inherent disregard for dangerous situations—a byproduct of fearlessness—that sometimes overshadowed caution, leading to problems.

The twins, Zevi and Huta, enjoyed climbing trees high into the canopies, finding alcoves and nests, or any crevice that another human being had never set eyes upon. The woodlands offered an infinite number of such nooks and crannies, but some of the best were up in the high branches, where the wood thins and branches weaken.

Zevi stretched his neck to see the nest. It was a fine thing, meticulously woven with brown pine needles and sticks, and placed with care. He knew not to touch it, but he had to look inside. Stepping out onto a green branch, he strained to see, and the lithe wood bent under his foot, like a rubbery rod, and he felt it give way, like a slow-motion release. His arm shot upward, grasping for a branch, but it was just beyond reach, and his tiny body slipped, pulled by gravity toward gnarly branches that battered his torso as they slowed his fall, like immovable arms, desperate to assist. Maneuvering to fall feet first, he braced for impact.

Thunk-wump. "Hooooooh!" His left foot hit first, shattering the ankle and breaking the impact of his head bouncing off the soil.

Striking a root, his ribs bounced like a ball, and his lungs contracted violently, like vacuous bellows, bleeding air. His tiny frame quivered, processing the shock.

His twin brother rushed to his side.

"Zeviiii...Brother, how? Oh mama."

Huta felt his brother's pain in his own body, but much less so; the two were energetically bonded and inextricably linked. There was no escaping shared experience. Huta kneeled beside him, relying upon all he knew, and cast an intention for healing while he lovingly cradled his brother's hand. Then tears flowed like a warm-water faucet, and he breathed deeply, hardening his resolve.

"I will return with help, Brother."

But he did not leave right away; instead he remained at Zevi's side, watching his brother's eyelids blink repeatedly, as tears trickled down his cheek and into his ear. His face was pale and scrunched, like a withering flower. Still kneeling, Huta closed his eyes, seeking the calmness that had been the hallmark of his short life. In it he found his power; here he could sculpt reality. So, he sat, intention focused, already setting his brother's healing into motion. When he felt the time was right, he rose slowly, reluctant to leave his twin. His stomach churned, and he felt off balance, but then the earth firmed beneath his feet—and he did what needed to be done.

"I see the healing power in you, Zevi," he said, before departing.

He glided through the forest without tripping once, arriving at the village within minutes, and headed straight to Inipia's cottage. Fortunately, she was home, but Izeel was nowhere to be found. Nor was his mother, Eva. Inipia recruited the help of four villagers who rapidly located the village backboard, crafted from a long piece of thin, unbreakable wood and outfitted with wooden handles and woven ropes that slipped over the shoulder.

The rescuers moved through the village center, passing Anax, who was relaxing with Dan in the sunlight. Dan sensed the group's urgency and said, "Is everything OK? Can we help?" Dan had been an EMT in his former life.

"No," Ini said sternly. "We will handle this." The other helpers looked at Anax and Dan with confused expressions, puzzling them both, before rushing away.

The rescuers moved speedily through the underbrush, adeptly stepping and mindful of every pitfall. Young Huta led the pack, which struggled to keep up, despite its precision. When they arrived, Zevi was just as his brother left him, fully conscious. Several branches lay scattered about, like debris following a storm.

At the sight of the group, he smiled through tears, but his brave smile could not mask the pain.

"Smiling, now?" Ini said, as she approached, feeling mildly relieved. She moved with delicacy, as if any sudden movement or vibration might shatter his comfort. She would give anything and everything for Zevi—it was the healer's way—and there was no higher calling than caring for another in need. She was a divine instrument, living in service to others, and Zevi was a part of her precious ecosystem, the future of her beloved community, and she would not fail him.

Huta laughed when he saw his brother's familiar grin and the others also relaxed at his apparent stable state. Even so, they were at his side within moments, delicately placing their hands upon his crown, forehead, throat, heart, solar plexus, lower stomach and his root. They poured forth energy, like electrical generators, revitalizing his body for several minutes. Afterward, Ini aligned his ankle in one quick movement and applied the brace. Zevi barely cried out, instead launching into hysterical, tear-filled laughter. The group joined in, grateful for the release.

Next, they repeated the hands-on healing, reactivating his energy centers; they did this for the better part of an hour. It dulled the pain, accelerated the healing process and reminded him that he was a part of the whole. The process ensured that there were no blocked or misaligned energies. From years of experience, Ini knew that it was important for Zevi to move through the trauma immediately, releasing it even before they began the transit home. The bone would already start to fuse at the subtle levels from the healing they'd facilitated.

"You've a bit of a bump on your head, young warrior," Ini said, "we'll need to keep an eye on you for a few days, but all is well. No climbing trees for a time." She gave him a stern, motherly look and he laughed at her expression, rolling his eyes in gratitude. In a flush, the color returned to his cheeks, and he looked more like himself.

When Zevi's mood had remained joyful for an extended period, they were ready to make the transit home. The walking was slow, but fortunately the young boy weighed little. Just enough to bend the branch from which he fell, Ini thought.

"Must have been a skinny branch," she joked, delicately pinching a little skin on the boy's ribs.

They returned to the village well before dusk and Ini immediately began brewing several different infusions of comfrey, pine needle, burdock root, dandelion, nettle and skullcap for the boy. Each infusion would be consumed at different times, under appropriate circumstances. The organized process of consuming tea for healing was jokingly referred to as *tealing*, and Ini was a master of the process.

Villagers came to Zevi's side offering him energy, intention and love. Some came and offered music, repeatedly thrumming specific notes that were known to carry healing frequencies. Each who came cradled the boy's hand, offering the traditional message for healing:

"We are all one. We heal together—as one." They believed it too, deep in the fabric of their being; it was, perhaps, their most fundamental truth, a recipe of sweetness and compassion, delicately mixed, and offered from the heart.

This went on for days until the boy was fully recovered. It was the village way. Every person was a part of the whole. There were no exceptions to this rule. Through the process, Zevi's recovery felt like a special occasion, and his mood only brightened with each passing day. His recovery accelerated proportionately.

During the warmest times of day, he was placed outside for hours so Father Sun's rays could fuse his bones and ignite his spirit. All food that was brought to him was imprinted with healing frequencies, as was the water. Once each day, four elders would pray and sing over a single glass of water, creating an energetic cocktail that would galvanize the boy's inherent healing abilities. The life-force was so intense in these cocktails that he could tolerate only one of them each day.

Again and again, people would visit him, offering hands-on healing, spontaneous songs and prayer. The melodies carried frequencies that were known to accelerate bone regeneration and align the body's natural harmonics.

Within eight days, Zevi was healed—and back to climbing trees.

Illusions

✼✼✼

"Darkness is real, but has no place in Gylodon. Mediators must acknowledge their shadows and transmute them into light."
- Book of Gylodon -

Time moved at the speed of thought, leaving Anax baffled that nearly five months had passed since his arrival at the village. Each day offered challenge and adventure. In Gylodon life moved like a dream, blending surreal feats with simple pleasures. Basking in gratitude daily as a natural course struck Anax as odd, but it never ceased to be empowering. It tapped into dormant emotions, pulling them straight from his lower stomach and translating them into poetry.

The previous night, still lightheaded with visions of Tristis, he'd stretched out on his earthen bed, hemp paper and reed pen in hand, and drafted some playful verse. The verse bewildered him; he'd never really thought about having his own family before, but since he'd crossed paths with Tristis, it consumed his thoughts.

Rainbows

In this home, the rainbow rains
Love-filled light through windowpanes.
Color bleeds into our life,
Through our dog, into my wife.

Near the plants, it skips and leaps;
Into Earth, the rainbow seeps,
Then ascends above the crust,
Touching wind's majestic gust.

Through the kids, the rainbow flows,
Graced by light, its bandwidth grows.
Reaching out to humankind,
Rainbow's love is colorblind.

Before long, the dark denies
Dusky light from rainbow skies.
As light ebbs, the kids return
To our home, without concern.

In their hearts the rainbow thrives,
Shining light into our lives.
In this home, the rainbow rains
Love-filled light through windowpanes.

Looking down at the paper, he could not help but feel that a stranger had composed the words. At times, he was confused, or stupefied by his progress, but such feelings were always wrapped in joyful incredulity. Amid his awe, he found a peace that he'd never known was possible. Gylodon had a way of extracting one's authentic nature, peeling away layers of long-suppressed emotions, making room for radiance. It was as if the ultra-individualism to which he'd become accustomed on the outside was suddenly replaced by an inherent yearning for his own community, or family.

He was still thinking about it as he walked to his daily lesson. Spotting Dan up ahead, he was pulled from his family-fantasy reverie. He hadn't seen him all morning; he'd been off on his own, doing his thing, but now the two brothers were arriving at the Willow Tree of Wisdom, exchanging nods and greetings, when the Unschooler arrived for the day's lesson.

"I see power in my students," he said, with a wry smile and honest eyes.

"And I in you, Master Unschooler," came their synchronized reply.

After Dan and Anax were comfortably seated, the teacher paced for several minutes, searching for words. He looked as if he were wrestling with something, unsure how to proceed. An updraft flapped his robe, whipping it like a flag on the edge of a storm. Dan and Anax sat in rapt attention, intrigued by the unusual start.

"Today I am going to speak to you about the outside world," he said, pausing deliberately. He looked at each of his students and his eyes hardened, expelling humor, like a general on the eve of battle.

How can he know anything about the outside world? Anax wondered. Still, it was not for him to question just yet. He was still new, and it was not so long ago that he'd departed the outside world. Even so, his old life felt like a long-lost dream from which he could make little sense. Gylodon had recalibrated him.

The teacher continued, "Gentlemen, because you are born of the outside world and have been exposed to its suffering, it is critical that you acknowledge the darkness that is a part of your history. You cannot hide from it. All dark shadows must be seen before they can be dissolved. I will share this with you one time—so that you may acknowledge the darkness, thank it for its teachings and send it love. You may thank it for bringing you to death's door in a state of absolute surrender. You may thank it for offering you a rebirth, a new beginning. And finally, you may thank the darkness because gratitude will help transform it into light, and that is what we do. I would not speak of this to the village natives, although they have seen some of it during their astral travels and have some basic awareness of it. It is for the outsiders' ears only, and I speak of it only once so that you may heal yourself, and in so doing, help heal the planet."

Anax caught a glimpse of Dan in his peripheral vision. Enraptured by his teacher's heightened intensity, Dan sat like a statue, firm and unmoving.

The Unschooler pressed his palms together, looking thoughtful, and locked eyes with Anax.

"The two of you hail from a bloodied and battered world—a world of agendas, fueled by fear and an incessant need for self-preservation; a world of competition, comparisons and unfettered judgment. It is a reality that has been dominated by the masculine principle of taking control—sadly manifested as warfare, corporatism and the pursuit of money at any cost. It is a world where the feminine, earth-honoring principles of gentleness and love have taken a back seat, leaving wanton animal cruelty in its wake.[25] A world of poisoned water, toxic air and genetically modified food;[26] a place where agenda-driven mental conditioning creates a populace that is unaware and lives in a placid state of acceptance. They accept because they are not lucid. They do not know, and it is not their fault. Their ability to consciously create reality has never been explained or included in their educational system. Instead, their minds are confined to a box—and their power imprisoned—as they are transformed into docile, rule-following workers who are conditioned to become cogs in the machine one day. They deserve better. For too long, humanity's quest for true *personal sovereignty* has been oppressed by destructive illusions. Instead of crafting exquisite realities, too many people struggle to survive.

"Out there, serfdom, or debt, is portrayed as normal, along with the unconscious feelings of helplessness that accompany it.[27] In fact, the outsiders are so conditioned to believe that their system is right and good that ninety percent of them will fight and kill to defend it, while powerful corporations cut down the last of the old-growth trees, poison their water, air and food and drive thousands of species into extinction. At the rate they are going, half the animal species on Earth will be gone within a century.[28]

"Sadly, too many people have lost their connection to nature. Instead, they worship technology, TV pundits and money. They argue fiercely over political ideals, few of which are honored or enacted by the politicians they defend. Still they fight to defend them. Again and again, they fight. In this way, they unconsciously bleed their power, never able to acquire enough to become aware of their own circumstances.

"At its core," the teacher continued, "the problem lies in an excessive consolidation of power by a few. These elites have shaped humanity's reality through media, religion, educational systems and laws. While some frameworks serve a noble purpose, far too many of these pre-constructed belief systems, mandates and suggestive imagery serve only to enslave the collective mind.[29] They have polluted humankind's consciousness in alignment with their agendas of global power, robbing humanity of its birthrights of free thought, self-love, unity and purpose. Gylodon exists to restore these birthrights. That is why we are here—to empower people to become the change they wish to see in the world.

"Remember, everyone on this planet has a worthy destiny. All of us play a role. Beyond the darkness there is always learning, love and spiritual progression. Beauty will always shine amid the darkness because we are beings of light, forged of stardust. In that regard, everything is perfect.

"As warriors, though, we have an obligation to be a force for good in this world, to advance consciousness by seeking balance within ourselves, our families and the planet. Our awareness and lucidity afford us this gift.

"In your cases, you must first balance yourselves before you can truly help the planet. We are more effective this way. In my case, my efforts are best directed at shifting the collective, planetary *consciousness cloud*. Regardless of where we are in our progression, we must live outside of the darkness and seek only to create light.

"And now, let us pay our respects and thanks to the darkness, for it has taught us well. Without it, there is no light.

"Close your eyes and let us begin our exercises in gratitude, as expressed through the fifth-dimensional resonance of our hearts..."

***

Several days passed and Anax grew weary of contemplating the darker aspects of his former life. They were artificial constructs in a confused world, built to deceive and disempower, while serving the few instead of the many. *Why would societies create systems that fostered fear instead of love, anyway? And why would they destroy their own planet in the process?* It made little sense. He was tired of thinking about it. Gylodon felt too good for such nonsense. To Anax, Gylodon was not a place or a thing—it was a *state of being*—his state of being.

Dust kicked up from his hempen slippers as he strolled through the town center, all too aware that he was not permitted to interact with village natives. It was early afternoon, and already he smelled cook fires, and the scent triggered memories of camping, roasted marshmallows and beer.

He paused to watch a group of young women working in a small field, adjacent to one of the cottages. They wore fibrous tunics, each decorated with unique crests or symbols. Singing songs, the women sculpted with some sort of red clay, each working diligently on her own creation; their energy was playful and innocent and Anax was swept away by its power. It was gentle and nurturing, and he could feel it pressing on him, like a feminine tidal wave, or a loving touch, and it filled him up. It was the sweetness of life.

In the outside world, such feelings had been few and fleeting, found only in the throes of love or a moment in time with one's children or best friends, but here they persisted, lingering for prolonged periods of time like orgasms of delight. Sometimes it was confusing, as emotions surged between sexuality and awe and love, overlapping and indistinct. And while his body was not yet equipped to handle all the energies, it had improved significantly.

One of the women looked up at him, smiling broadly, and she was lovely, like a spring day or a wild rose, and he could barely contain himself. Returning her smile, he walked on, feeling her eyes upon him like beams of energy rising in his root, straight through the top of his crown. It was difficult to process.

A curious dog, with short brown hair and disproportionately large, triangular ears emerged from behind a cottage, trotting alongside him. The animal watched him with suspicion, flagging him as an outsider.

"Hey there, Pooch, it's all good. I'm a brother of Gylodon, I promise. I've got my pass right here." He tapped his pocket. Unmoved by the overture, the canine sniffed wildly in the air, keeping its distance, and Anax wondered if he, perhaps, smelled like an outsider. A quick whiff of his armpit dispelled any concerns. *Gylodon fresh…*

Anax turned right, down a short path and arrived at Dan's cottage.

"Hey man, how's it going?" he asked, as Dan opened the door.

"Good. Come on in—I'm almost ready."

"Cool. Thanks." Dan's cottage was larger than Anax's, but had the same feel. On the nightstand, Anax spotted a high-end French press that seemed wildly out of place.

"Dude—don't tell me you have coffee," Anax said.

Dan laughed, looking over at the table. "No, I'm afraid not, Buddy. I had some when I first got here, and I milked it for weeks, but no more. I still use the French press to make tea, though."

"Sure," Anax responded, "lots of tea around here. It's growing on me."

"There really isn't much need for caffeine around here, although they do have it," Dan said, tossing a blanket into his satchel. "This place is amped up enough as it is, though."

"To say the least," Anax responded, pausing. "Hey…well, this is gonna sound a bit odd. So…I get these surges of energy, like sexuality sometimes, and it's kind of painful. Does that happen to you?"

Dan cocked his eyebrows. "Nope—not at all. What are you talking about?"

"Ummm…well…it kind of rises up inside of…"

Dan tried to hide his smirk, but his body was already shaking with laughter. "I'm just kidding, Anax. It's totally normal for outsiders. Our energy channels are being overburdened until they rewire and expand. It takes time. You can try to channel the sexual energy into creative pursuits. That helps a bit."

"Oh, does that work? OK, thanks."

"Sure thing. OK, let's roll." Dan closed the door behind him and they made their way down toward the river. It was the full-moon cycle, and Anax had not returned to the river since the infamous day when he was nearly accosted by a man-goat creature called a *satyr*. Tonight, though, he was determined to face his fear of otherworldly beings trying to make babies with him. And while the Unschooler had informed him that no spirit could harm a person in Gylodon, Anax needed to prove it to himself. Dan was there for moral support, and to see what might unfold.

"I hope you checked your sexual surges at the door, Buddy. That's like catnip to the satyrs. Or *sat-nip*, I should say…" Dan started laughing again.

"Oh, you're just overflowing with jokes today, aren't you? Just wait till *you* have a satyr with a twelve-inch goat-penis trying to violate you. We'll see if you're laughing then."

"OK, OK." Dan raised his hands in submission.

The levity was precisely what Anax needed, and again he was grateful for Dan's companionship. Both men were close in age, and their personalities were a good match, bringing out the best in each other. As inclusive as Gylodon was, it would have been a lonely place without him.

Resting on Dan's blanket, at the river's edge, they both went into a meditative state, just as the light dwindled. The sounds of dusk grew louder, chirping and croaking and hooting, and they blended with the water's flow, like a tribal invocation, calling forth the spirits.

After an hour, Anax felt something behind him, intermingling with his energy field. He remained calm, as he'd been taught, and within several minutes it came closer, and his breath quickened. Dan felt it, as well, and resisted the temptation to open his eyes, or panic. Instead, he wrapped the presence with loving energy, doing his part to displace any fear. But then Anax felt the blanket move, as if a hand, or foot, pressed upon it, and he tensed. Breathing through the fear, he decided to open his eyes. In his peripheral vision, just to his left, he saw a round, hairy outline, and it sent an acute shiver up his spine, from his tailbone straight through to his crown. It was too close. His eyes adjusted to the dusky darkness, and he became aware of an oversized raccoon sitting next to him, as if it were a part of their group, joining them for a casual picnic. Slowly, Anax turned his head. The animal's expression was curious and humanlike, but just like Anax, it was also uncertain. Then Anax felt the blanket move again, and the animal moved to touch him, extending its paw, as if he were some sort of interactive woodlands art display, and all too quickly Anax's discipline gave way to fear, and he pulled back his arm, and the animal shot up onto two feet, before twisting in retreat and scurrying off into the underbrush. Dan opened his eyes just as the creature vanished.

"Everything OK?" he asked.

"Yeah. A raccoon touched me, and I lost focus. Fear got the better of me," Anax replied, calming his breath. "Did you see it?"

"Yeah, I saw it. Don't worry, you did fine. You'll improve a bit each time. Before long you'll be able to reach down and touch the animal."

"That's going to require a serious mindset shift," Anax said, looking toward the bush, regretting his lapse of discipline.

"And *heartset* shift," Dan added. "Remember, you must have total faith in the flow of life—and accept any and all consequences that might arise."

Anax nodded, wishing that he had Dan's fearlessness. In many respects, it seemed, Dan had been born that way. Anax, on the other hand, would have to work for it.

Returning to their meditations with renewed determination,

they wordlessly fell into trance. All around them the landscape was alive, as moonbeams cast long shadows that swayed with the wind, highlighting the unseen, like quartz fragments or tufts of grass, and the tree canopies glowed like soft torches, pointing the way.

Anax and Dan sat for some time before completing their mental exercises. And while they encountered no satyrs or otherworldly beings, it was a good night, the kind where the magic is more subdued, lingering on the edge of awareness, waiting for them.

The Demonstration

✲✲✲

Nobody except the Council of Elders, along with select villagers, knew about the threat to the village. It had been this way for years, an evolving story, but recent events had sharpened concerns. Likewise, the arrival of so many outsiders, destined to become *mediators,* suggested imminent change.

The astral investigations of Honaw and Donja had revealed dangerous trends on mainstream earth, with a disturbing rise in allergies, autism, digestive disorders, metabolic problems and mental disorders—particularly among the young. For many humans, life was wobbling uncontrollably, and people were being forced into awareness of their predicaments, waking to the destructive illusions that society had woven.

In the realms of consciousness, a violent war was underway—and battles raged between love and fear, light and dark, truth and illusion, nature and technology, freedom and enslavement. Both Honaw and Donja knew that humans would face profound pain and trauma before they surrendered to life, acknowledging their own shadows; and then they would look within, into the realms beyond time, through the spaces of the heart, and there they would find the peace that had always been there, patiently awaiting them. Gylodon was destined to play a role in this transition—so long as it remained safe—and was strong enough to defy the darkness.

Of immediate concern to the elders, though, were the technological developments—energy tracking devices—that made Gylodon vulnerable to discovery. They knew that it would not happen overnight, or even within a year, but in the long lifespan of the village, the intrusion was a near-term possibility.

Gylodon was built upon a vortex, an intersection of the earth's energy grids, and this boosted the fourth and fifth powers within its

The Demonstration

boundaries.[30] Nobody knew this except the council members, and this circumstance, they understood, could make the village more visible to tracking technologies.

For this reason, Honaw and Donja were on a follow-up investigation—a daytime astral projection—one that required more skill because it did not synchronize with their sleeping schedules. Today was the day that Dr. Dalton would be demonstrating his technology, and it was imperative that they observe the event. Gylodon's safety was their burden, after all, and they carried that awareness like an invisible cloak, shielding it from the others, giving all they had to protect humanity's finest gifts.

To accommodate the daylight projection, they consumed a relaxing nervine tonic to help them sleep. Before drifting off, they programmed their minds to wake at a designated time, at which point they rose, drank a glass of tea that was mentally stimulating, like caffeine, and went straight back to sleep while their bodies were still tired. As they drifted into sleep, they set the intentions—through mental programming—to exit their physical bodies, meet up, and head to the investigation. The stimulating tea kept their minds awake, while their physical bodies went back to sleep. This facilitated the separation of consciousness. Everything had gone as planned, and again, they found themselves in the laboratory in Colorado, observing events from an invisible wavelength.

Slowly, their astral bodies morphed into humanlike silhouettes, bubbling with aspects of their thoughts and feelings, like complex algorithms of the higher self, or consciousness in motion. Around the edges, however, their energy-bodies reflected an inherent distaste for the environment, and they flashed the colors of dismay, sadness and compassion.

To Honaw, the laboratory was a barren wasteland, like a forest without trees, or a meal without laughter, and it always made him feel out of sorts. Perhaps it was the energy of its inhabitants that unbalanced him, but beyond that, it was the spirit of the place. *Or lack thereof.* The space had no soul, as if it had been bleached away with meticulous care. Donja, on the other hand, struggled with the guilt of spying on other people, and occasionally these moral conflicts intruded upon her projections.

"Gentlemen, please make yourselves comfortable," Dr. Dalton encouraged. He'd arranged six folding chairs for his guests, three of whom he had not met. Introductions had been first names only, and he doubted the legitimacy of those names. By all material appearances, they were well-kempt gentlemen, but there was a lizard-like quality to their eyes that unnerved the doctor; they did not reflect kindness.

After grounding herself in the local astral plane, and firming her focus, Donja glided in behind the seated men, with Honaw close behind. Overshooting her destination, she brushed up against a stodgy man in a blue suit, accidently intermingling energy fields with him, and the hairs stood up on the back of his neck, like a porcupine under duress. He vigorously scratched himself, as if confronting an itch, and she quickly backed off, disentangling herself.

"Thank you for coming today," Dalton continued, "and thank you for your support of this research. My intention is to demonstrate how we can use our directed-energy devices, along with satellite sensors, to identify energetic anomalies around the planet. We can do this in a variety of forms—including heat, light and electromagnetism. Please turn your attention to the large screen above."

A large, digital screen—mounted on the wall, along with an array of monitors—displayed a three-dimensional representation of Earth, crisscrossed with ley lines, connecting in grid-like patterns. Dr. Dalton went into a long speech, using jargon with which Donja and Honaw were unfamiliar. The six observers betrayed no emotion, sitting silently, without so much as a nod of acknowledgment. Honaw noticed that Dr. Dalton appeared especially nervous. Then again, he always did.

As best as the two elders could discern, there was no immediate threat. The technology did indeed identify the earth's grids, as well as vortexes, but there were many of them all over the planet; and from what they could tell, Gylodon's location did not stand out in any visibly divergent manner.

Suddenly, Donja's outline began to fade, wavering between two realities, or two points in space. Back in Gylodon, almost two thousand miles away, some children dashed by her cottage, calling after one another. The noise began to waken her, pulling her back into her body. She struggled to remain with Honaw in the astral plane, but her awareness teetered on the cusp, and she began to feel herself in bed...

"Honaw, I am losing..."

Before she could finish the statement, her energy-body had vanished, and Honaw knew that she'd lost lucidity and returned to her physical body.

He remained for a good while longer, observing, when one of the men asked, "While the visual presentation is nice, I'd like to see the hard data, to identify any outliers. Can you put together that report, Dr. Dalton?"

The doctor shuffled his feet, already uncomfortable at the prospect of compiling such a report and wondering for what purpose he wanted it. It was not his place to ask.

"Yes, Sir. I can aggregate that data for you."

"Good."

For a brief span, Honaw observed the men sitting in chairs, calibrating his astral eyes so that he could better study their energy fields. He was surprised to find their auras completely imbalanced; nearly all their power was concentrated in the head region and the root region. Everything in between was vacant, redirected to the top and bottom. These men, Honaw noted with pity, could feel no emotions or love; they were robots of logic, programmed for extreme materialism. Incapable of compassion, they were like an alien species, devoid of humanity's most fundamental attributes.

He sent them love—a lot of it.

The Mystical Village That Rewired Reality

***

Although Anax had not yet received any formal astral-projection training, he continued practicing on a regular basis, and his efforts often met with success.

Within Gylodon's boundaries, these experiences were natural, at times coming too easily, and Anax often found himself floating around the village at night, encountering other villagers, also out-of-body. These encounters provoked interesting questions—like whether he was permitted to interact with villagers in the astral realms. *Or did the restrictions apply only to waking life?* It was a funny dilemma to ponder. When he presented the question to Ini, she was resolute in her answer—he was *not* ready to interact—*especially* in the astral realms. She did not find his dilemma humorous, either.

Mastery of the fourth power, or mind-space, provided a critical foundation for astral travel. The reasons were manifold; the elimination of fear was necessary to achieve an exit from the body, but beyond that, control of one's thoughts was the ultimate tool in the astral realms. With it, people could stay out-of-body much longer—sculpting realities with greater precision. Anax also suspected that the village's unique wavelength and frequency facilitated the process, closing the gap between material reality and astral reality.

Over the centuries, the villagers had learned that some astral realms were more changeable than others. The layer that surrounded the village could not be significantly altered because it had been created through group consent, over many years, and the energies invested into it were vast and highly concentrated.

But other astral spaces were like blank canvases, and were much more malleable—often transformed by a single thought. This was where the fun happened. The more experienced travelers, while out-of-body, would craft landscapes that could make an artist weep; the effects were mesmerizing and the colors unfathomable. Often, the travelers would enter dark voids of astral space and transform them into masterpieces of light. It was their legacy.

This level of mental mastery contrasted starkly with Anax's old existence in the outside world, where most of his nightly dreams had been low-lucidity experiences, powered by the subconscious mind; the imagery was often jumbled, and rooted in daily fears, or the last thing he'd watched on television. Mostly, though, they were manifestations of *consciousness pollution,* a mishmash of meaningless imagery derived from a world of excessive digital media. During these dreams, he was more like a bystander without control, and recall was poor. These dreams lacked power.

In Gylodon, however, only crystal-clear lucidity would suffice, and Anax constantly sought to improve upon skill sets that he felt afforded him the most profound adventures of his existence.

Consciousness Cloud

***

"We are surrounded by organized, intelligent energy. This is the framework of consciousness—and we are its architects."
- Book of Gylodon -

The learning only accelerated. It was a radical reeducation, built upon personal experience and endless experimentation. There were no academic tests or deadlines; instead, progress was driven by individual desire. *The fire of desire.* Both Anax and Dan felt an internal yearning to inhabit their roles—to align with their unique storylines in the great stage play of life. Each had a purpose in Gylodon—even if that purpose was not yet revealed—and the best way forward was to honor the path of warriorship, making every day of their training count.

They'd arrived early today, taking their usual spots inside the willow tree's droopy embrace, but rogue rays of sun slipped through access points in its foliage, scorching Anax's neck, and he shifted to a shady spot, several feet to his right. He'd yet to learn any magic for averting sunburn. Dan, with his tan complexion, had no such concerns. Today he wore his red-and-black workout gear, which was not altogether unusual for him. As a rule, they were encouraged to wear Gylodonian garb, but Dan liked to go running, and that required outsider clothing and sneakers. So, he bent the rules, as needed, and nobody seemed to mind.

The Unschooler arrived moments later, taking his high position on the knoll, and Anax could swear that he'd grown an inch. The teacher's presence was both imposing and comforting; he was the sort of man who could move mountains with a glance but would step aside for a bug in his path—a true *warrior of light*.

The teacher's last lesson—about the darkness of the outside

world, and the need to acknowledge our own shadows—weighed on Anax. It seemed such a strange thing to consider, in light of Gylodon's grace, and it provoked questions about his own life, as well as the world at large.

"Master Unschooler, may I ask a follow-up question to our last lesson about the *darkness of the outside world*?"

"Very well, Anax."

"Thank you, Master. In our last class, you spoke about suffering in the world and how people are often unaware of the *consciousness pollution* that engulfs them, manipulating their thinking patterns through distraction and fear, while blocking their inherent power. *Shouldn't people be awakened to the illusions that keep their minds enslaved?*"

The Unschooler closed his eyes, summoning an answer. "We are all on our own schedules for learning, Anax. Can you imagine what would happen if the curtain of illusion was lifted all at once, unveiling lifetimes of mental programming for billions of people? The *consciousness cloud*—the collection of all thoughts, emotions and energies that envelop us—would instantly be overwhelmed by fear, anguish and destruction. It would disrupt the natural order of learning based upon our own schedules and abilities. The people's minds would still be programmed, or schooled, to believe in the old paradigms and they would have no framework for dealing with the new realities.

"True power arises from the journey of self-discovery, through our own personal efforts, over time. When we have decoded the negative patterns in our lives, sought change and reclaimed lost power, only then are we on the warrior path. This is the evolution of consciousness; it is how it has always worked.

"This is why we must seek balance within ourselves before we attempt to tackle the world's larger challenges. Most people on this planet are unconscious polluters of thought. They waste more than half of their creative powers on worries that are rooted in illusion and backed by false beliefs—incessant fears of what might happen if they do this, or don't do that. All the while they are sculpting these realities and literally attracting the negative outcomes to themselves. They are victims of societal programming, which feeds their destructive self-programming; the cycle perpetuates itself from generation to generation until someone finds the courage to see through the illusions and undergoes the efforts of rewiring themself. Such rewiring is the art of shifting one's paradigms into an entirely new framework, based on experience, and it is no easy task.

"Always remember that the *Book of Gylodon*, although framed like a lecture at times, is rooted in the spirit of personal exploration and discovery. It presents ideas, but claims no monopoly on truth. Only *you* can decide what is truth, over time, in your own way."

The teacher paused, gazing skyward while motioning toward the celestial bodies above. "All that said, times are changing fast and omens have presented themselves to the elders. They indicate that humanity is moving into an age of transformation, where planetary and solar alignments can alter the speed at which change and self-awareness develop. These new energies from space—presently inbound toward Earth—affect our consciousness in peculiar ways. So, it seems a global awakening might happen faster than we imagined. And while Gylodon will assist with that transition, it will not be the cause of it." He paused again, turning his eyes to the willow tree, and then back to his students.

"Does that answer your question?"

"Yes, thank you," Anax responded. "I do have one more question, though."

The teacher raised an eyebrow, feigning seriousness at Anax's insatiable curiosity. The students rarely asked questions because they were expected to find answers on their own, through their own meditations and internal dialogues. As Gylodonians, they were learning to sculpt realities, and discover truth, through personal trial and error. Still, Anax could not hold himself back, and besides, his question was not about a universal truth. The Unschooler nodded, granting permission.

"Master Unschooler, how do you personally know so much

about the outside world? Do you hail from the outside?" Dan looked down at the ground, as if Anax's question pushed the boundaries of etiquette.

The Unschooler looked pensive before answering, and in an unusual display, walked up to his two students and took a seat on the ground between them.

"Yes, Anax. I come from the outside world. I realize that this may come as a surprise to you, and I apologize for the lack of disclosure. This was not previously revealed because it was deemed more beneficial to your training for you to think that I was a native of the village. I wanted the question to arise organically, when the time was right. Please believe that this decision was made with the best intention for your learning. But yes, I arrived from the outside many decades ago."

Anax was not surprised; somehow, he'd suspected as much. Despite the Unschooler's obvious mastery of *four* and *five*, as well as his unrivaled knowledge about the forces of the universe, there had always been something that separated him from the other villagers. At times his eyes reflected a seriousness that did not exist in the innocent, doe-like gazes of village natives. His were the eyes of someone who'd lived life on the outside, just like Anax, Dan, Tristis and Ini.

"Thank you, Master Unschooler. I understand." *Best to ask no more questions on the matter*, he concluded.

***

His cottage was cool and comfortable, but Anax couldn't sleep. His energy was electric as he lay in bed, recalling life on the outside, contemplating the intimacy he'd experienced in past relationships. He missed it.

Sexual urges had not ceased since his entry into Gylodon. On the contrary, they had grown, at first almost uncontrollably, before he learned to manage the energy. Gylodon had this effect on outsiders, expanding the energies moving through them. Eventually he learned that sexual energy was the same as creative energy, stemming from his lower stomach, and that he could choose how to direct it. He could let it control his biological body, which would invite discomfort and frustration, or he could use it in a productive capacity. He chose the latter. Since he did not have any options for loving companionship at present, he directed the energy into his creative works, as well as his self-healing.

He and Dan had discussed the topic on more than a few occasions, not without humor, and both had come to the same conclusion—to channel the energy into creative acts. Dan, resultantly, had become a prolific cook, doing his best to bring Latin flavor to Gylodonian dishes. In between cooking and studying, he enjoyed extreme sports, like climbing; often he'd find new rock faces to traverse or caves to explore. Once he had repelled down a sacred mountain to the astonishment of the villagers. To them, it was an important omen. To Dan, it was Tuesday.

Regardless, both men viewed the challenge as just one more test on the path to self-mastery. That said, mastery of self had never been more challenging, amid Gylodon's powerful pull, and they both relished the day when companionship again would be available.

For Anax, one afternoon, that day arrived sooner than he anticipated. Her name was Metea, and she was a wild river, young and frictionless, ebullient and assertive.

He was walking back to his cottage, taking an alternative path through a stretch of the woodlands when she came up behind him, gingerly, and confidently, taking his hand. He recognized her; he'd seen those big brown eyes looking at him on more than a few occasions, but he was never permitted to interact, nor did he think much of it. In truth, he wasn't sure what the customs and rules were for physical attraction in Gylodon. In that instant, though, he knew only that her flawless brown skin, wild black hair and soft beckoning eyes matched the gentleness of her touch with goddess-like precision.

Power rippled from her tiny frame, carrying with it a raging storm of femininity that wrapped its delicate limbs around Anax's will—befuddling him, luring him, tempting him, owning him.

What is she doing? My God, she is so gentle.

"Where are you taking me? I'm not really supposed to…" *I can't very well pull away from her. That would probably just make the problem worse. Don't want to offend.* So, he walked with her, and she led him deeper into the woods, not entirely out of view of the village, but down into a gulley, behind some thickets. Pine needles coated the ground. It was getting dark, and things were moving fast. His first instinct was to resist; he was not yet permitted to interact with village natives, it was forbidden. But her energy was unlike anything he'd encountered; it slithered like a snake and it wasn't even sexual. *Or is it? Yes, it is sexual.*

His next thought was of Tristis, and his feelings for her, but this experience was already feeling independent and uncontrollable, bound by nothing. *Besides, I'm not in a relationship with Tristis. She doesn't even know me.* His next thought was that he would be expelled from Gylodon for breaking the rules. *I'll just have to tell them that I, as a weak outsider, was ill-equipped to resist her power. It's true, anyway.*

He was glad for his decision. The next forty minutes were a melding of color and sensation, a sharing of energy unlike anything he'd ever experienced.

She came to him, wide open and devoid of expectation or inhibition. Pulsing ecstasy and innocence, she came in waves, vitalizing the nuclei of his being. Her lips were as gentle as her touch, and every cell of her body came alive as he stroked her hair, his fingers finding the way to her scalp, pressing just enough before sliding down her back, discovering the next point of vibrating flesh; voltage jumped from her skin as he pressed her points, and she, alive with the fervor of Mother Earth moved to the high position, taking control. The pine needles were like gentle acupuncture upon his back, as her magnetic being merged with his electric self. It was a blur of rainbow and breath, pure perfection, free and true.

Afterward, she left as quietly as she'd arrived, leaving him to understand what had taken place. She'd spoken not a single word. For twenty minutes, the smile upon his face was all he knew, and he was unable to assemble a coherent thought. Then, as he gathered his wits and rose, he realized that she had given him a sacred gift—far beyond physical intimacy. He could scarcely believe it, but he felt it, moving through him like a serpent. *A gift of energy.* She'd shared her power with him—as an energy transference—and it swelled in his root, climbing up his spine before entering the crown of his head, where it exploded outward, connecting him with new levels of awareness. The world felt different, bigger somehow, as if the fruits of wisdom hung on every tree, finally within reach. He was being reconfigured, or rewired, for a new reality.

I will keep this to myself, he decided.

ELEMENTS

***

"All of reality is built of water, fire and air—forming earth—and blessed with electric and magnetic attributes. But there is a fifth element, the heart of all things, which only can be deciphered in our own way."
- Book of Gylodon -

The weeks sped by, and to Anax's relief, nothing ever was said about Metea. He saw little of her. He likened the experience to a lucid dream, and accepted it for what it was—a cherished teaching, a gift of power—but one that had not altered his feelings for Tristis. Still, sometimes, the memory seized him like a tornado, and he felt the energy rising within him. And while he struggled to rationalize it, in the end, he had to throw out any thoughts he had on the subject. They were all rooted in past realities, none of which applied to Metea. Instead, he sharpened his focus and lengthened his stride along the path to spiritual warriorship.

The day was mild and dry, with a soft breeze that carried the scent of pine pitch. Anax and Dan sat cross-legged on the earth, beneath the willow. In front of them, in the waving grass, lay an intricate altar. Its foundation was a red cloth and upon it sat a burning candle, a bowl of water and a variety of rocks and crystals. Scattered around the candle and the water were red and white flower petals. Their teacher, atop the knoll, towered over them.

"Both of you, before too long, will begin your intensive astral projection training. Anax, you appear to have natural gifts in this area, but there is much you need to learn to become truly effective. To gain mastery, it is important to have an understanding about the nature of reality, and energy, so you know how to alter it. This applies to everyday life but particularly when you are projecting, where thoughts and feelings can take form much faster." Both students leaned forward.

"When you gaze upon the altar, what do you see?" The Unschooler paused to let them consider.

"I see the elements of fire, water and earth," Dan replied.

"Good. Anax?"

"I see the symbolic representation of the universe, but I don't know how to express it."

"Good. The elements are foundational to understanding the nature of reality. When we look upon the altar we see a candle; this is the symbolic representation of fire, but it is much more than a flame. Likewise, we see the water principle embodied, which is much more than something you drink. Let us begin there.

"*Fire*. If ever there is something born of magic, it is fire. Conjured from thin air, it appears, providing life-sustaining warmth, but it must consume and destroy to do so. Cause and effect. Fire embodies the masculine principles of vitality and action, but like everything it has both positive and negative qualities. Creator and destroyer. Transformer. It is *Father Sun*, which gives and takes life."

The Unschooler paused, turning toward the river. "*Water*. Yet another element of pure magic—it makes up sixty percent of our bodies. It can store information like a liquid crystal. Upon the altar before you it is represented in a physical form, but this is merely symbolism, as well. For water provides life-sustaining moisture. In its positive form, it is essential for all of life. When it is removed, life cannot survive. It embodies the feminine principles of emotions, feelings and creativity. It is *Grandmother Moon*, which pushes and pulls the oceans.

"Fire—masculine. Water—feminine. These are foundational to all realities, even throughout the astral realms."

Laughter emerged from the far side of the hill where Zevi and Huta, along with several other children, were running full speed through the fields. The Unschooler kept his gaze locked on his students.

"Now, what floats all around the altar, but is invisible? Why air, of course. Air, the *intermediary*—the bridger of fire and water. Air seeks balance—equalizing fire and water. In its physical representation, air can extinguish or grow fire by providing or removing oxygen; likewise, it can cause water to evaporate, taking it away, or it can help condense water, providing moisture where it is needed. Through the mechanism of heat transfer, or convection, it seeks to cool something that is hotter than its surrounding environment, thereby reestablishing balance. All things must seek balance.

"As I have told you, our world has had too much fire for too long, so now is the time for water to return. The emotional and creative elements of water can help to rebalance the planet by dissolving archaic power structures that seek to enslave nature or harness weapons of destruction.

"It is our role to assist with this transition. As human beings, all of us are intermediaries, just like air. When we speak, or take an action, we can seek balance and harmony or we can choose to be disruptive. The choice is always ours.

"Now, the bottom of the altar—the red cloth—symbolizes *earth*, the fourth element. Earth is the physical manifestation of fire, water and air combined, united through the power of electric and magnetic."

Anax and his classmate sat in silence and the sound of the wind upon the leaves was particularly jarring. The information was difficult to understand, but both students knew that their super-conscious awareness would absorb it. It was the kind of thing that one could grasp when it was being explained, but afterward, some of the understanding would drift away.

"Now, enough lecturing today. We have discussed four elements. But there is a *fifth*. I want you to go out into the woodlands, to your meditation spot, and consider what this fifth element is, and how it interacts with the others. Go deep into your consciousness,

The Mystical Village That Rewired Reality

and seek answers for yourself. Repeat this process every day until you have defined your own personal truth on the matter. Go now."

As Anax strolled into the woodlands, seeking his meditation perch, he could not help but feel the urgency of global change, as if it pressed upon his abdomen, jumping up and down, begging him to do his part. He felt the call to service like a visceral craving, but still he lacked clarity on what form it should take.

***

At night, when he was alone, Anax sought a deeper understanding of the lessons that he'd been taught. He'd let his thoughts run on a course, around specific questions, and pick up answers along the way. Tonight, he considered the *consciousness cloud* and the nature of reality.

Information was everywhere, he knew. A couple of years back, while lounging in his cubicle, wasting time, he'd come across a scientific study that demonstrated the ability of scientists to record, store and retrieve vast amounts of data in DNA strands. And not just your run-of-the-mill DNA data, either—but entire works of literature or extensive audio files could be uploaded, stored and retrieved from DNA.[31] What appeared as a speck of DNA dust could hold millions of pieces of information. To say the least, it was intriguing. For Anax, these scientific breakthroughs had confirmed his suspicion that the human body stored nearly infinite amounts of data, like galactic hard drives. And that was just the physical body.

But what about the non-physical spaces? What about the spaces all around us? How much data might they hold?

As he lay in bed, setting his intentions for the dream state, he contemplated the *consciousness cloud,* seeking to better understand its makeup, or its energetic structure. At its core, he reasoned, it was composed of vast amounts of information that somehow remained coherent and clustered, like *codes of consciousness.* It stretched everywhere—through time, space, and alternative realities of all sorts.

Understanding the codes, or the fabric of reality, was a daunting endeavor. In his own mind, he likened the codes to packets of information, arranged by wavelength, frequency, shape and color, protruding into six or seven dimensions, at the least, and always surrounding him, attracting him, repelling him and penetrating various aspects of his being—like air on skin, or breath carried into the lungs. He knew they were there. They had to be. Love, hate, joy, sexuality—always they were there, moving through him, like rising storms carrying torrential rains, followed by the inevitable calm—and the empty spaces in between. And while a part of them might arise from within a person, there were also parts that came from outside of a person, moving around them—and then through them.

The codes could be passive or active, sentient or otherwise, and they had infinite permutations and synergies, like mathematics or exquisite works of literature, floating in the *consciousness cloud,* like tiny gods unto themselves. Works of art were their own worlds, and their bits and pieces drifted in space just waiting to be reabsorbed by an inspired brain so they might be reinvented into some new creation. The codes came to open and willing minds, of similar vibration—and they connected to one's central nervous systems through feelings, images and language; they mixed with the stew of life, in a bubbling pot of creative juices—while passing through the artist's intellectual filters, blending with layers of history and experience, before being refined, altered and ultimately rebirthed into a new work of original proportions.

There were highly intelligent forms of consciousness, as well, in all manner of shapes and forms, from gnomes to sylphs to sexually deviant satyrs...to darker forces loitering in the astral layers like energy vampires desperate to pillage one's soul.

But the high-vibration, loving entities had aspects of their souls that could exist across six or more dimensions at any given time—bleeding across multiple *consciousness clouds* like runny watercolors. They were constantly evolving into finer and finer layers of space that somehow held larger and larger amounts of information, like quantum computers with infinite cloud storage. And always they were moving toward unity.

Across the layers of reality flowed the universal life-force that enlivened and transfigured all the *codes of consciousness*, like a parent generating and nurturing new life. Air, water, fire, earth and electromagnetism were the tools of its trade, and it used them like clay or brick or mud, to build frameworks for new realities. Invisible to the human senses, this universal force—*the fifth element*—was the source of material creation. And it was known as *Akasha*. It was the dark matter of the spaces in between—and the foundation of all form. This hidden element allowed sound, or vibration, to exist—and only from vibration could physical forms arise. Its very existence allowed consciousness to be created, as similar vibrations could synchronize, collecting molecules and building worlds.

Of course, Anax realized, there were certain vibrations that influenced the world more than others. Like *love*. Love was God's purest vibration. Potent beyond measure, it served as fuel for constant transformation, growth and connection. It was the reason for the proliferation of life.

Anax squinted, noting that he'd left a candle burning; it spun dancing shadows off earthen walls, and just above the flame, riding the wall's curves, the shadow split into a symmetrical form, projecting a heart-like shape stretching toward the ceiling. *What is love? Does it have shape and form? Is it simply vibration?*

It's more than that, he knew. It was the life-force that moved through all things. It was the power that unified all things. Without it, life would cease because mothers would abandon their offspring like burdens unworthy of attention. Perhaps a mother's love was the very essence of love—the sense of unity that comes from being part of something greater than oneself. Perhaps even a tiny field mouse understood this, cuddling with its mother and siblings, forming a single ball of fur, in a warm cubbyhole just below the earth's crust. That was community, after all. With love, there came a lightness of being—a freedom that only authentic interconnectivity can offer. It is the realization that *we are never alone.* Indeed, love was the vibration of *connection* and *unity.*

Anax turned over on his pillow, taking in its scent and adjusting his body on the bed. He considered the loneliness that he'd felt in the outside world, after the accident. He'd isolated himself, blocking the flow of love, severing his community. He'd felt real pain.

Was it a self-imposed prison?

Perhaps the concept of "loneliness" was nothing more than a self-generated reality—a distasteful, heavier reality experienced by so many—but by no means the end of the line. Perhaps loneliness was the antithesis of love, serving as a breeding ground for fear. But in the end, he knew, it was all just blocked energy, awaiting reconnection to community, or Spirit.

Anax had wanted love badly; he'd yearned to know it, to bathe in it, to suck it into his soul.

Gylodon had pointed the way; it had become his reservoir. The community had reconnected his soul into the web of life, where it belonged, on the superhighway to love.

Changes

✶✶✶

It was an unusually bright morning in Gylodon, as if sunbeams were amplified through a lens, with no clouds to soften the glare. And just as the earthy scent of tea drifted across the village, and breakfast was soon to begin, the panic erupted. Within moments, small children sat down on the ground crying, as they wrapped their arms around their knees, rocking back and forth, while adults zipped around, moving to and fro, like ants in a colony under attack.

At first nobody knew what was happening. All at once they felt a deep agitation, like an itch they could not scratch, and it tore through their serenity with knifelike precision. Most had no idea how to process the discomfort. They'd never had to do so before. So, they squirmed. And chatted. And tried to meditate.

The problem, some determined, was a new frequency from the skies, ripping through the village *consciousness cloud* like a razorblade through paper. The incoming energy agitated the animals, as well, which had long grown accustomed to Gylodon's gentle embrace, but now took to running, scurrying and standing on high alert, just like in the outside world. Even the bees panicked, colliding into one another, as their navigational instincts were rendered useless.

Anax and Dan watched as villagers ran about, and elders held impromptu meetings in the town center, glancing skyward, gesticulating wildly with their hands. The inbound energies were man-made, coming from the skies by their best estimates. The villagers were highly sensitive to any shift in energy, more so than Anax or Dan, but even the two of them noticed a subtle discomfort.

"What the hell is going on?" Dan asked, placing his hand over his stomach.

Probing his body, Anax recognized a strange pressure in his diaphragm, something both alien and disturbingly familiar—it was the feeling he used to get when he was running late on a project deadline. "I'm feeling *stress*. Do you feel it?"

"Yes. And I don't like it." Dan looked angry.

Many of the children, feeling unwell from the energies, returned to their cottages to be with their families. The thick earthen walls provided protection, offering substantial relief. Anax and Dan watched helplessly as the all-powerful Gylodonian villagers struggled to understand the predicament.

And then, all at once, the unwelcome energy ceased.

Mostly, life returned to normal for the villagers, but some people had changed, just a bit, as fear touched Gylodon for the first time, tainting the wellspring of love. The elders became more vigilant—doing whatever was necessary to maintain the balance. There was much to do.

***

The elders trickled into the room. "Brothers and sisters, I see the light in you. Welcome." Honaw greeted each council member with a hug—four women and three more men, for a total of eight. They wore casual cotton tunics, most of which were deep red or cream colored. Chosen by village consensus, the elders represented a vast collection of wisdom, born of lifetimes of love and lucidity. More than a millennium of collective experience existed among them, but nobody counted.

They seated themselves on reed mats, in a circle, atop a cold, earthen floor, awaiting Tristis' arrival. It was rare for them to extend an invitation to anybody, let alone an outsider, but all agreed that it was necessary. The meeting was to be practical, not ceremonial, so only a small hearth fire burned and there was no altar.

"Tristis needs to understand," Honaw entreated. "We have all seen the portents of changing times, and with so many outsiders now in Gylodon, she needs to know what is happening. Donja and I have seen much during our astral investigations, as have you all,

The Mystical Village That Rewired Reality

and the time is now. The outside technologies are advancing. And now we have experienced them here—in our home. In time, they may discover our location. In addition to these new risks, the astrological alignments—for the entire planet—are now falling into place; the grand transition is under way for all of humanity. But still, the people are held back, overwhelmed by *consciousness pollution*." Never had Honaw's Native American heritage been so evident; the fire in his eyes was that of his ancestors—a powerful lineage that had long revered freedom and nature, and one that had been hunted throughout the ages for it.

Donja, authoritative by nature, with silver, peppery hair and stout stature, chimed in, supporting Honaw, with whom she'd shared many investigative astral projections. "As an outsider, Tristis is better equipped to process any fear that may arise. We all know about her destiny as a village leader, as does she, but she has yet to embrace it. Of all people in Gylodon, she needs to know."

The elders nodded, mostly silent, with only the eldest woman suggesting that they use storytelling to convey the message. Donja concurred, offering to take the lead. A woman, they all agreed, should deliver this message.

After receiving the invitation to meet with the council, Tristis was unsure how she felt. She assumed that it was about the markings in her hands and fingertips that forecasted an important role for her, but she was not comfortable with the implications. In a way, she was irritated by the invitation. It felt presumptuous. But that emotion came from somewhere deep within her, somewhere still broken.

The knock came sooner than Honaw anticipated, and he rose with an agility rarely witnessed in a 102-year-old man. He was the youngest elder, so the task of receiving people at the door fell to him.

"Ahh...Tristis, please come in, welcome to our circle. I see the light in you," he said.

Donja also rose, offering a reassuring smile before escorting

Tristis to her place on the floor. Tristis' black hair was untethered, and it dangled loosely below her shoulders, partially obscuring her cheeks, but it did little to conceal her uncertainty. The elders wrapped her in love.

"Come, my dear, please make yourself comfortable." Donja took her place beside her, and Tristis waited patiently as the focus turned back to Donja, who remained pensive while considering the best way to proceed. Tristis breathed deeply.

"Tristis, have you ever heard the story of Gylodon's history? It is a short fable, explaining the origin of our village." Tristis shook her head, eyes widening at the prospect of learning something new.

"Very well. It will be easiest if I just read it to you. Ipupiara, would you be kind enough to pass me the parchment?"

Ipupiara reached back to a knotted wood shelf, half twisting, and removed the scroll, which he passed to the Seed Bearer on his left, sending it around the circle to Donja. She removed the string and took a deep breath before reading:

There came a time when power had consolidated into the hands of wealthy aristocrats, as well as large religious institutions, both of which sculpted realities in unnatural ways. They wanted others to conform to their rules—their versions of truth—and, to this end, they sought to enslave the collective mind. They brought violence upon open-minded folk, punishing all forms of free expression and eradicating those who did not ascribe to their religious practices. With spear-like precision, they thrust their spiritual rules upon humanity, and hunted those who did not comply.

During this era, the religions of the world institutionalized spirituality—carving and chiseling it to their liking—before forcing it into a cage where the people might follow.

Science tried to set it free—by bridging the gap between science and spirituality—but science had too many rules and guidelines, thus progress was slow. The scientists who rattled the cage were thrown inside.

The spiritualists tried to set it free through demonstrations of faith and love, but faith was not enough for many. And love evaded others. The spiritualists who bent the cage bars were ostracized and burned.

Ultimately, it was the "travelers of astral" who freed spirituality—everyday people who learned the art of leaving their bodies to explore new dimensions and taste new realities. It took but one lucid experience to know its power, and suddenly the world became a multi-dimensional wonderland.

The spirit, they learned, lived inside and outside the cage, omnipresent, forever flowing through all things. And they were a part of it. Their new awareness was not based on science, faith or love—it was grounded in simple, repeatable personal experience. Spirit, they learned, is wild, and such things cannot be caged.

In a single out-of-body experience the travelers proved to themselves that consciousness could exist outside of the body, that alternative realities abounded, and that death was nothing to be feared. The world was not at all what they had previously perceived. Not even close. Bodies were simply vehicles for the cosmic, eternal soul, capable of sculpting reality through the powers of thought, emotion and energy manipulation. While traveling outside the body, astral environments were highly responsive to thoughts and intentions.

In time, the travelers gained expert proficiency in navigating the astral realms, and the universe became their playground. They were transcendental pioneers, rewiring reality, and their experiences were both natural and practical.

The governments, commercial interests and religions alike did not appreciate the empowerment that astral travel afforded individu-

als. The travelers were no longer spellbound by demagoguery, but rather defined reality through their own personal experiences. Forming their own innovative concepts about the world, free of judgment or boundaries, they had tasted their own truths, and would honor them henceforth.

The institutions came for the travelers, swiftly and brutally, decimating their way of life. Some were thrown in cages, and others fled to the forest, to hidden corners of ancient woodlands, forming small villages hidden from the societal constraints of the outside. Most of the villages were found and burned.

But one survived. It was called Gylodon, and few knew of its existence.

She paused, re-rolling the scroll, before looking at Tristis.

"This, my dear, is how Gylodon came to be. Back then, the villagers were mostly limited to the fourth power. Since that time, the village has evolved into much more, discovering the fifth power, or heart-consciousness, and the need for balance and harmony throughout all of nature. Mastery of both the *four* and *five*—together—has empowered us to alter realities in unprecedented ways. With these gifts, has come both awareness and responsibility. We became aware of humanity's plan, driven by its evolution of consciousness, but also by galactic cycles and planetary alignments, which are presently under way. There is to be a *grand transition*, Tristis, and it is already beginning, during which humankind's consciousness is destined to expand at an accelerated rate, freeing minds and opening hearts, and paving the way to a new multi-dimensional age. We, as Gylodonians, can no longer remain in the shadows, hiding."

Tristis shifted, nodding uncertainly and Donja continued, "When the time is right, we will need to rely upon the outsiders in Gylodon, like yourself, to act as *mediators* between the wisdom that we guard and the people of the outside world."

The Mystical Village That Rewired Reality

Tristis sat still as stone, her breathing barely perceptible. Donja put a hand on her shoulder. She considered telling Tristis about the threat to the village, that its invisibility might not last amid the technological advancements of those who hunted them, but in the end, she thought better of it.

"There is one more story that we would share with you, Tristis."

Tristis nodded assent, suddenly conscious of the centuries of wisdom that surrounded her. The elders sat like children upon the floor—flexible, agile and smiling—but still their faces bared rings of knowledge like ancient redwood trees. There was no hierarchy in Gylodon, just a voluntary acceptance of the Council of Elders, but Tristis felt like an infant, nonetheless.

Donja looked down before continuing, "There was a time when water ruled the planet. Emotions ruled alongside water, and people were largely guided by feelings and creative impulses. But life was out of balance, without structure and order—and it was only a matter of time before fire would rise to displace the water, along with humanity's gentler sentiments, in favor of logic, profits and the enslavement of nature. Like a see-saw, fire and water battled for supremacy, and with fire's rise, humans stole power from each other—and from the earth—and people came to trust their minds over their hearts."

Donja paused, thoughtful. She looked at Ipupiara, across the circle, before addressing the elders.

"I think perhaps it would be best to share the prophecies."

Two of the elders shifted, and Tristis felt the weight of silence upon her, as Donja looked to each council member in turn, seeking their approval. When she was convinced of their consent, she again turned her attention to Ipupiara. He nodded, again reaching back to find a scroll, which he passed to his left, with noticeable delicacy and reverence.

The document came to Donja, and she carefully unrolled it, looking Tristis in the eyes, with unusual firmness. "This is both a history and a prophecy, scribed under trance by a council member more than three hundred years ago." She pursed her lips and read:

Water and Fire

*When water was Queen, submerging the earth
Emotion drowned logic, leaving a dearth
Of structure and method, planning and form;
Life was unbalanced—an orderless norm.*

*Water's wild oceans defied all constraint,
Dripping and roiling in colorful paint.
Art flowed freely, without reservation,
Formless and flowing, life lacked foundation.*

*Immutable laws demanded correction
To counter the culture's lack of direction;
King Fire ignited a rapid transition
Claiming and taking his newfound position.*

*With Queen Water's untimely defection,
King Fire's ire provoked resurrection
Of logic and order, thinking and rules;
Weapons and coin became viable tools.*

*Planning was paramount, progress a joy,
To tally and count or build and deploy
New slings and muskets to conquer one's foe;
Fire burned nature so bankrolls could grow.*

The Mystical Village That Rewired Reality

They lived in the mind and ousted the heart,
Warfare and coin banished rainbows and art.
Amid Earth's vast change, King Fire grew forceful
And, with coin and drink, few were remorseful.

But, alas, such change created a void;
Human empathy was nearly destroyed.
The hole was immense, devoid of emotion,
Long lost were the lessons of Mother Ocean.

But love only hid where fear abided,
Soon it would rise upon waves that glided
Unto humanity, quelling the flame,
Calming King Fire and cleansing the blame.

Queen Water rose to rebalance the scales,
Unhinging prisons and shattering jails
Of broken beliefs and mental pollution—
*The power of **six**—a new revolution.*

The drought now sated, doubt soon abated
As love stormed walls, mankind had created.
Hearts expanded and illusions dissolved
As the earth's new mandate swiftly evolved.

Blessing and guiding the human rebirth,
Spirit cast rainbows unto Mother Earth.
The grand transition was now underway;
Never again would they be led astray.

Fluid emotion joined lucid notion,
As Father Sun embraced Mother Ocean.
King Fire, Queen Water—of mind and heart—
Blended and evened, avowing their part.

Embracing its role, and its new mission,
Gylodon's goal, and the Earth's transition,
Spirit entered into the sixth new age,
Breaking illusion, collapsing the cage.

Humankind, now sculpting reality,
Became light, transcending duality.
Freedom emerged, forever expanding,
Warriors of light, always commanding.

Donja paused, re-rolling the scroll.

"So you see, Tristis, civilization has lived too much in its mind for too long, held captive by destructive illusions. The motherly, nurturing energy of water was relegated to a back seat in favor of profits, process improvement, bullets, bombs and war. This is now changing, and we are to play a role.

"As water rises again—which it is currently doing—it seeks true balance with fire. This balance will symbolize the unity of mind and heart, logic and emotion, masculine and feminine, driving humankind to its greatest achievements, while allowing the planet to blossom into a garden of free thought, self-love and purpose—along with a reverence for nature. This balance is the source of the *six*, a power that is rarely discussed, with few Gylodonians even aware of its existence. This power—the *six*—is your birthright, Tristis."

Tristis tightened on the inside, suddenly recalling the revelation of her destiny and the discomfort that it brought. She did not understand the origin of her resistance, but always it was there, pushing at her, driving guilt into the hollows of her heart. She was not equipped to lead Gylodon. She had not even conquered her own darkness. She was a child among giants; and for reasons she could not fathom these giants gazed upon her without judgment, reflecting only love and unwavering belief. Somehow, they believed in her. They believed in her more than she believed in herself.

The rest of the meeting was small talk. It was clear that the elders would not press her anymore today, and for that, she was grateful.

She departed as she had arrived, unsure and off-balance.

Initiation

***

Within the village, people were largely free to explore their passions and unique gifts, but they were expected to maintain an ongoing level of personal growth and excellence. Fortunately, they held themselves to the standard, finding endless fulfillment in their own growing power.

At first, Anax had been puzzled about who carried out the various village responsibilities, particularly undesirable ones. One day he asked the Unschooler, "Who gets stuck taking care of the composting toilets?" The Unschooler had appeared perplexed for an entire minute before exploding with laughter.

"Anax, you make me laugh," he said, tempering his amusement. "When you have complete mind-mastery, churning compost is as enjoyable as a steaming cup of nettle tea on a cold day. It's all a choice. Try it."

Eventually Anax learned to make a ceremony out of churning compost, and could find some enjoyment in the process; it was not, however, as good as a cup of nettle tea—particularly on a cold day. Nonetheless, it was a revelation at the time, of how a different mindset and heartset could shift his reality. Everything was an opportunity for learning, and increasingly he strived to integrate himself into the village activities, soaking up knowledge, but also finding gratification in the labor.

Gylodon's existence required an ongoing commitment from its members, both individually and collectively. While it was mostly a consensus environment, with recommendations from the Council of Elders, it only remained hidden from the outside world through the collective intentions of its inhabitants. Everyone understood this. Together they molded the local energies through communal meditations, creating an impenetrable shield from the outsiders.

The Mystical Village That Rewired Reality

Only those who were destined to join the village could breach its *consciousness cloud*. It had existed this way for hundreds of years, since the Dark Ages, some said.

The recent intrusion by unnatural frequencies was the first of its kind in Gylodon's history. Still, the village was well protected from outsiders, and people could not simply walk in. Any outsider who approached the village boundary would feel an overwhelming need to walk in the opposite direction. The process was mostly unconscious, leaving intruders unable to analyze or understand their visceral need to retreat. Animals, on the other hand, were free to roam in and out of the village boundaries, without ill effects. Their energetic purity—living only in the present moment—afforded them such freedoms.

Of all things, Anax was most mystified by how the village had remained hidden for centuries. He understood the principles behind it, but its undeniable reality never ceased to impress him. He was still shocked—and profoundly honored—that he had been permitted to breach its shield.

To date, his efforts had focused on his personal development, as was needed, but more and more he expressed an interest in contributing directly to the village. For both him and Dan, giving back to the village was as critical as their own personal development; it was a deep need, driven by gratitude and service. They seized every opportunity to lend their assistance, and even began to offer their own intentions—through meditation—for the village's well-being and growth. Without realizing it, they had already begun to shape the village's *consciousness cloud*, offering their own power to the collective cause.

Their efforts did not go unnoticed.

INITIATION

***

Time looped and days became nights; before long, it was all a blur, moving with natural cycles, embracing each moment, living in a natural state of joy—even in dreams.

They came to him just before sunrise. *Music.* A gentle knock at the door pulled his consciousness into waking life, and for an instant he was certain he'd imagined it. Dreamy music filled the void. Anax closed his eyes and listened, and the knock came again. *Not a dream.* He rose, noting the hour, and feeling slightly startled at the occurrence. *Hope nothing is wrong.* He dismissed the thought almost immediately. Opening the door, his jaw dropped as he saw the entire village, with Dan at the forefront, gathered outside. Donning ceremonial cloaks, carrying flutes, and apparently laughing at Anax's utter shock, they surrounded the cottage. Shirtless and disheveled, he made quite the ragtag appearance. Two middle-aged women of Asian descent walked up and slid a colorful cloak over his head, each taking an arm. *Am I dreaming or am I awake?* It was a mantra he used regularly to train his mind to become lucid within the dream state. But this was no dream.

The women whisked him toward Dan, who wore similar garb and an unflinching smile. In fact, his smile was so robust that Anax needed a double take to confirm what he was seeing. Flute music filled the air and they marched as one just as the sun peeked through the trees and the forest awakened. The pebbles were cool underneath his bare feet. He looked to Dan for insight, but Dan just smiled back, revealing nothing. They marched for some time when Anax became aware that they were heading toward the Willow Tree of Wisdom. Both he and Dan were escorted to the top of the knoll, just under its branches.

As the realization set in that he and his friend were the center of this ceremony, his heart and throat tightened, transforming emotion into tears. Never in his life had he felt so supported. The villagers, now directing their love at the initiates like a high-pressure fire hose, cleansed them, and any blockages that their bodies had been holding were dissolved, leaving them lightened and burden-free. Their hearts blew open, gracing them with a new understanding of unity. In front of them stood the Unschooler, the Seed Bearer, two village council members, Ini and Izeel. The music paused and the elders, along with the villagers, closed their eyes, welcoming the rising sun. For Anax, the tears kept coming, while Dan just smiled.

The Seed Bearer spoke first. "This is a time of new beginnings. Today we honor our brothers, Dan and Anax. Our brothers have honored Gylodon with their ongoing efforts to achieve mastery of the *four* and *five*." He paused, scanning the village, before continuing.

"We are all one. Together we rise. Together we heal. Together, our power builds worlds. In Gylodon, nobody is ever left behind. Today we honor Dan and Anax by declaring them worthy initiates of Gylodon. No longer shall their village interactions be limited to a few. They are now free to be one with all."

Anax, stunned at the new opportunity, not the least of which included freedom to interact with Tristis, silently began to question their decision. *But, I don't have mastery yet. How...*

As if reading his doubt, the Seed Bearer continued, "You are indeed ready, Brothers. Understand that your initiation does not connote absolute mastery of anything. But it does suggest a basic level of proficiency that we feel positions you to truly become productive members of Gylodon. You were always our brothers, but now you will help us to forge the *consciousness cloud* that defines our village. We welcome you with open arms. We are all one. Together we rise. Together we heal. Together, we build worlds."

The music began again and the two women, who had temporarily stepped aside, returned to remove Anax's cloak, exposing his skin, before placing a garland of miniature red and white flowers around his neck. The tiny stems had been woven together with meticulous care, forming an intricate wreath. Dan received the same. Both men were encouraged to kneel, hands and foreheads in

INITIATION

the soil, and, one by one, each village member approached them from behind, placing a hand, or two, squarely on their backs, just behind their hearts. One by one they came, silently offering prayer and infusing energy. By the third person, Anax was audibly sobbing. Dan, likewise, began weeping within minutes. The acceptance they felt was unlike anything they'd ever encountered. There was no comparable love in the outside world.

Every single member of the village, including young children and infants, placed their hands upon them that day, welcoming them with heartfelt acceptance. Anax could only weep, his mind sometimes visiting his old life, and he felt sadness for the suffering that it had imposed. *Why do we suffer?* he wondered—over and over again—and he could make little sense of it. *Why does everyone not experience this joy?* He cried more, for the first time feeling only love for the old Anax, and it felt wonderful. *I love you,* he said to his former self. *I embrace you. We are one. We are all one. Nobody is left behind. Nobody is ever left behind. Thank you, Teachers. Thank you, Guides. Thank you, Spirit. Thank you, God. We are all one.*

All sense of time ceased and the two brothers, overwhelmed with gratitude and an unerring sense of service to the community, curled up in the soil. Day became night, and they slept on the earth, wrapped in blankets provided by their new family. When they awoke in the morning, like newborns, it was just the two of them, and it all seemed like a dream.

Initiation ceremony for outsiders; hemp canvas.

Readiness

✷✷✷

Barriers breaking. Lightness of being. Power. Anax basked in his feelings. He glided on air, carrying the determination and poise of a warrior. His white linen shirt captured the sunlight, drawing attention to the handsome beaded necklace that Ini had given him. The necklace's pattern included one of the new magical colors found only in Gylodon, and marked the first step of his personal evolution. He coveted it. Upright and full of smiles, he radiated the fifth power, touching every creature he encountered, like a passing gift of grace. It was the day. Today he would speak with Tristis.

His training had progressed far enough that he was no longer deemed a threat to the community balance. *Or to her,* he thought. He was initiated. His awareness and focus were finely tuned instruments and his daily meditative practices had only enhanced his power. *I have attained a basic level of self-mastery*, he told himself. *Still, my one weakness is HER.*

But she had also proven to be his greatest inspiration, firing his will to push forward with his training. *It is the only way that I will ever get to know her*, he'd reminded himself during the hardest times. Somehow, when it mattered, he'd set thoughts of her aside—the ultimate test of training—and he had grown vastly more disciplined through the process. And while he could set aside thoughts of her, he could never set aside his feelings.

Thoughts we control, but emotions must flow. He remembered the teaching. The emotions pulsed in his heart center, inspiring hope, presence and connection. His solar plexus, or power center, was vulnerable to her and fluttered, while his lower stomach, or sacral space, thrived—driving him to new heights of creativity. He was a new man.

The morning had a slight chill, the kind that awakens the soul.

The Mystical Village That Rewired Reality

Along the path, he sought permission from a cluster of wild flowers before picking them. *Perhaps taking flowers is a bit odd, since I don't even know her,* he considered. In his old life, such an act would be perceived as eccentric, over-the-top and foolish. But here, in the village, such things were welcomed, so long as they were authentic and given from the heart. Ego and fear of rejection had no place in Gylodon. *She is such a wild thing,* he thought. *Wild flowers suit her.* His stride lengthened, carrying confidence, and he hummed a tune he'd heard somewhere, breathing in the forest's essence, before exhaling the energy to his beloved trees. *The birds have a haunting melody today. Perhaps they know.* He laughed in silence and floated along.

Before long he arrived at his new eating area. He had earned it. Designated for those who had developed basic competency with the powers of *four* and *five*—those who were initiated—the dining space was open and cheerful, with a smattering of handcrafted tables and ground cloths for those who preferred to sit on the earth. He felt proud, but did not hold tightly to the emotion, as he knew it was rooted in ego. *Such things have no place here. Remnants of my past,* he mused. *Let it flow. Let it go.*

His eyes swept the area, but he saw no sign of her. Briefly, he was disappointed, but then unimaginable warmth swallowed him, coming as a prism of light and selfless love; it was the *five*, raw and pure. First smiles, then fellow Gylodonians approached, hugging him, acknowledging the light that he had become. But above all else, he could feel, and to some extent see, the rainbows approaching him from all sides. They swaddled him, and he humbly accepted and returned the energy with love from his heart. Savoring the magical interplay, he only wished that she had been there. She could have sent him energy and he could have returned it with all his being.

Anax's world had been restructured in profound ways. No longer did he live in a concrete jungle, disconnected from nature, where competitiveness and ultra-individualism strangled community. Instead, he lived in enchanted woodlands—unified with nature—as a brother of Gylodon. Life was a dream.

He placed the flowers in a vase near the eating area for all to enjoy.

He learned that Tristis had taken her meal early and retreated to the forest to be alone. Apparently, she craved time with the forest more than with people. It was her way, they said.

Still—hearing somebody speak about her—somebody other than the Seed Bearer, was a thrill, and Anax was not discouraged.

They dined on the living food of the forest—wild spinach, amaranth and burdock root—but only after infusing it with intention and gratitude. Raising their hands above their meals, each person performed their ritual. They did the same with their water, taking care to charge it with unique blessings. Some charged it with power, others with healing intentions and others simply with love. And when they drank it, the vibrations flowed through their bodies and became part of their energy fields.

***

His favorite beverage as of late was nettle tea. With a steaming cup in hand, Anax walked to the far side of the hill and was surprised to find his classmate already basking in the early morning light.

"Oh, c'mon," Anax said, chuckling. "*Really?* How'd you get here before me?" Determined to arrive before Dan for once, Anax had taken special efforts to rise earlier that morning.

"It doesn't take much, my friend, just a dash of willpower and an ounce of action." Dan paused. "You look strong; it seems like you're making good progress these days. How are you feeling about things?"

Anax found a patch of grass and sat, eyes fixed on the rising sun. "Good. I feel more energy each day. I'm keenly aware of my mind's bad habits now and can stop them in their tracks. My control is much better. Even my dreams seem more meaningful, and I have better retention. As for astral projecting, well, I have no problem slipping out of my body now, and I can hold it longer and longer."

"Yeah, I know what you mean," Dan responded. "I feel like I can do anything now. I do wish that my projections were more frequent, though."

"In time, Brother. This whole extra-dimensional reality thing—well, it's just limitless. Hard to process that it's real sometimes—it changes so much." Anax paused, looking down, "By the way, I was wondering, do you know anything about Tristis?" he asked, abruptly shifting subjects, and instantly regretting his lack of subtlety.

"Tristis? Hmmm." Dan cocked his eyebrows before chuckling. "She's beautiful, isn't she?"

Anax squirmed, "Yes, she is."

Dan continued, "Well, I know that she likes time alone. Seems to have a way with the animals—that's kind of her thing, I guess. Always out in the forest with them. Caring for them." Dan squeezed his hands together, as if considering something.

"Between you and me, I heard someone mention that she needs something—some kind of healing—which is odd since she completed her preliminary training, but I don't really know. People are kind of hush-hush about these kinds of things, as you know, honoring the code of *personal sovereignty*. Honestly, she doesn't seem to enjoy time with people all that much, but she seems pleasant and is diligent about her duties. It's almost like she's working on her own private project when she's out in the forest. Like she's looking for something. Why do you ask?"

"Just curious," Anax responded quickly. Dan snorted, and Anax continued, "She seems to enjoy working with animals. They trust her."

"Yeah, I've witnessed it. Strong mother energy. You could ask her, or perhaps the Seed Bearer could tell you more, I suppose. I know he's one of the few people she speaks with regularly. She trusts him."

READINESS

"That's an idea. Thanks." *I just might do that.*

✳✳✳

The breeze collided with the green hilltop, flapping blades of grass, just as they completed their meditations and opened their eyes.

"I just went thirty minutes without a single thought," Anax announced, grinning.

"Sure you did," Dan replied. "If you did, you'd better start injecting some thought forms in there and sculpting some realities. Otherwise, that's kind of a waste of a free mind." He smiled and playfully flicked a pebble at Anax. "I had about five thoughts, but they lasted only a couple of seconds. Three of them were about flying off that mountain over there." He pointed and laughed. "Anyway, shall we stretch?" Anax nodded.

They worked through their muscle groups—stretching, massaging and relaxing every part of their body. Next, they used tactile imaging to direct energy anywhere that they still felt tension. [32]

"Strong body, strong mind," Dan declared. It was their daily refrain.

"Strong spirit, now arriving," Anax responded.

"Warrior on the way!" Dan countered.

"On the way?" Anax jested. "Oh, you're not a warrior yet? Let me know when you catch up."

Their friendship had grown significantly over several lunar cycles. Close in age, each had only a few people with whom he could interact until recently, and both felt a natural gravity toward each other, spending more and more time together. Dan had proven himself a loyal friend on countless occasions, and Anax was extraordinarily grateful that fate had allowed them to share this journey.

In the outside world, Dan had been a daredevil, living an adrenaline-fueled lifestyle and routinely engaging in extreme sports. He was never reckless, though—always maintaining focus and absolute precision—but the risks were high. Despite his calculating mindset and uncommon intelligence, he pushed boundaries that were inherently deadly. He crossed lines that few on Earth dared to approach. The disparity between Dan's old life and his new existence within the village fascinated Anax and it was a source of ongoing discussion, although they both understood that it was not prudent to linger on the past. Still, their time alone invited banter and they wanted to learn about each other's lives prior to the village.

After stretching, Anax couldn't resist his usual line of questioning, a source of great humor to him.

"How are you doing with sitting in silence these days, Brother?"

Dan smiled softly, as if to laugh. "Well, it's getting easier. Honestly, when I first started I didn't think that I could do it. I thought, man I must've arrived at this village by mistake. Not enough action here. Fate must've misplaced my destiny or something. But after immersing myself in the ways of the village, I realized that there really was a lot of action here. It was just a different type of action." He paused, looking down.

"You know, Anax, I used to do some wild things."

"Oh yeah? Like what?" Anax moved closer.

"Well…let me think. There are a lot of stories to choose from." Dan looked toward a mountain in the distance, choosing his words. "I once base-jumped off a skyscraper in Panama City in broad daylight before landing in a parking lot and fleeing in a get-away car. That was fun and all, kind of a rite of passage, but not as dangerous as some of the other things I've done; like getting knocked unconscious while skydiving, only to wake up moments before it was too late to deploy my chute. I landed in some far-off field and couldn't remember my name for about an hour. That was *not* so fun."

"Seriously? That's scary stuff, dude."

"Yeah, I know it seems that way, but I had long since accepted the consequences of my actions. One day I just decided to live each day as if it were my last, and I did—from that day forward. Of course, I did do a lot of stupid things along the way; in college, I outran cops on my motorcycle more than once, only to have to hide my bike for the duration of my time in school. I hate to admit it, but the worst part about that experience was losing access to my bike. Being a fugitive from the law was kind of an afterthought.

"And later in life, when I was moving to Mexico City for a job, I drove my luxury sports car straight through hostile drug-lord territory in northern Mexico—cruising at a steady 110 miles per hour the entire way, through the night, unwilling to stop for anyone."

"*What?* That's nuts!" Anax said.

"And that's not all. My mom was in the car with me."

"Oh c'mon!"

"Well, she wasn't gonna let me go alone. I tried to talk her out of it, but she insisted. She's a strong woman."

"Yeah, clearly. She'd have to be, in light of your extracurricular activities."

Dan nodded, smiling. "I'll tell ya, though, the most powerful experiences I ever had were my wingsuit flights off mountaintops, gliding like a bird, feeling the elements in their rawest forms. Every flight was like a new pathway into awareness.

"In hindsight, I think the reason I did these things was to attain a Zen-like state of clarity—a pure transcendence—that I found nowhere else in life. In those moments, I was truly alive, lucid beyond compare. Each experience was like a prolonged orgasm of awe; it was pure ecstasy, measured and controlled, but driven by pure passion. I did not believe in God at the time, but now, looking back, I believe that I was seeking a God-like state of being. I sought my truth through personal experience, much like we do here in the village. But I was wrong to believe that this experience existed only in extreme sports. If I am being completely honest, I have to admit that I was also a bit of an egotist, a showman, and I reveled in the challenge, achievement and recognition of it all."

Dan paused, looking back at Anax before continuing; "Finding a similar state of transcendence through imagination, astral travel and plant-medicine ceremonies has been a true awakening for me. I'm no longer overwhelmed by a need to seek adventure outside of myself, when I have all of it right here—infinite universes and exploration at my disposal. All I need is mind-mastery and an open heart. If you'd told me I'd be saying this a couple of years ago, I would have laughed at you. Of course, I was never afraid of death, and I'm even less afraid of it now. The only difference now is that I covet living more and feel like I have a purpose as a *warrior of light*. I'm not sure that I ever had a clear purpose before. It's been a shift, for sure. That said, I still miss my motorcycle on occasion." He paused. "Women, too. They were always quite nice." He smiled.

Anax stared pensively at the ground, nodding his head, momentarily recalling his experience with Metea. He guessed that Dan had not been as fortunate as he'd been to find female companionship in Gylodon. He considered sharing the story, but instead pivoted back to the discussion.

"Yeah, the shifts have been strange and came on faster than I anticipated too. It's amazing how quickly we change when we're in the right environment. It's a constant state of learning—and being. My mind and body feel so cleansed and unfettered; it's like having access to a whole new set of tools."

"Yup, and *new truths*," Dan responded. "Looking back, I think the only thing that I ever really feared was ending up alone, and now I know that we are never truly alone."

Anax smirked, "Yeah, must've been terribly lonely with all of those women in and out of your life."

"Hey, I was just waiting for the right one," he responded.

Dan chucked another pebble at him, and they continued stretching before migrating out into the woodlands to gather wild greens for lunch. Anax took pleasure in the lessons on local, wild-edible plants. Dan, on the other hand, was still adjusting to a meat-free diet, an ongoing source of humor between friends.

I AM

***

"We must all do our part to heal and liberate our light bodies. To heal oneself is to heal the lineage of life, through the cosmic web of consciousness."
- Book of Gylodon -

Every day was expansion and learning, transforming and rebirthing. Each moment became a new adventure, revealing previously unseen pathways into meaning.

Today, Anax sat astride a bulbous rock formation, his body merging with its curves that flowed seamlessly into a natural lounge chair. For several timeless minutes, he leveraged the *four* and *five* to touch the rock's spirit, opening his consciousness to explore its history. He saw a slew of random travelers over the millennium; they too had discovered this special resting place. Each had taken time to relax here, building a fire adjacent to the formation. The spot was obvious. The stones had held the fire's heat, providing temporary warmth to the travelers' weary bodies on cool nights. He reached out to the travelers through time, calling upon them for strength and guidance so that he might choose wisely. But no response came, so he returned to the present, shifting his attention to the task. It was vital that he approach it with absolute sincerity and truth.

When Ini had approached him several days earlier to advise him that it was time to craft his "I am" declaration, he'd welcomed the exercise. However, it was to be much more than an exercise, she'd said. His declaration was to become a tool of transformation—a perfect reflection of his heart, purpose and aspirations. "Choose your words wisely," she'd said, "for they will alter your reality." Today, Anax was finalizing his work.

Having developed proficiency in mind discipline, he was now freer to inject intentional thought patterns into his consciousness, coupled with feelings, to mold life into his chosen version of the human experience.

"We are born with life blueprints," Ini had told him, "but it is our responsibility to paint our reality, to dress it with color. We choose the materials with which we decorate our life, even if the skeleton is already in place. We also have the right to change things, if we choose. We are the creators, after all. So, Anax, with your declaration, I invite you to craft a poem to yourself, worthy of an emperor, and let its content flow from your soul. Let it express all that you are to become in this incarnation—all that you are now. It shall serve as the newest version of your blueprint for self-generated reality."

She'd explained that the process was designed for outsiders only, to counteract the detrimental programming of modern society. It was a tool for rebuilding oneself through self-love, energetic release, power reclamation and for reinforcing one's life-purpose architecture. He was to repeat it every day, absorbing it deeply into his cells, his heart and his personal *consciousness cloud*.

As he finalized some of the sections, he looked down at the hempen paper, embracing its personal significance. It was just for him. It reflected not just who he was to become, but who he was, in the depths of his being, in the expression of his eternal self. He knew that the document was incomplete. It would always be so, changing and growing with him, as his priorities shifted throughout his life.

I AM

I am raw power, centered and light,
I steer my soul, by clear inner sight.
I am aligned to all things divine,
I write the script for my life design.

I AM

My body floats lightly as I stroll along,
With fervor and clarity, I sing my song.
I am vibrations, directed in space;
My purpose is guided by Spirit's good grace.

Conjoined with the fabric of this universe,
I face trials with courage and fully traverse
Boundaries and limits and broken illusions;
Charging forward with faith, I craft solutions.

I am precise memory, focused and clear—
I am forward momentum, destined to steer.
I am innovative and totally free,
I sculpt reality with unfettered glee.

My chakras are balanced, and all well-aligned;
I am health incarnate, my power enshrined.
I energize my water and bless my food,
I am spirit in the flesh—I'm raw and nude.

My projects are pure, and aligned with the heart;
Aiding the universe, I freely impart
My counsel and healing, to people in need,
Traversing a pathway of virtuous deed.

Astral projecting with ease and with focus,
I ride the wind to my life's chosen locus.
Easily gliding to any dimension,
I breezily ride to sacred ascension.

I am built of earth, water, air and fire—
A thrumming electromagnetic choir
Of resonant sound, floating in space;
In Gylodon's heart, I've found my place.

I am the light, defying the dark
I walk my path, I leave my mark.

I am healed, I am whole
I am bliss, I am soul.

A shiver trickled down his back, into his legs, but there was no chill. It was pure energy that moved through him, straight into his *consciousness cloud*. Already crafting new worlds for himself, he immersed himself fully into the great mystery of reality, dissolving illusion and energizing his destiny.

He was, after all, a sculptor of high-vibration consciousness, a *warrior of light*.

Astral Museum

***

The moon was full and the vibrations came on for the third time in a single evening. He barely felt the exit, just sudden flight and air streaking across his cheeks. *Not alone,* Anax realized, with controlled enthusiasm. He knew who it was—who it had to be. Long strands of brown hair fluttered in his face as he was escorted across a dark, sparkling skyline. The night had come alive with astral flair and he'd left his physical body behind. His spirit guide led the way, and so far, had not communicated a word. It was as if the cosmic gods had granted him access to the playground of immortality. He absorbed the scenery and felt tiny amid the vastness.

The scenery shifted and it was daylight. *Indoors.* The building was uncommon; vaulted ceilings more than two hundred feet high met bright glass panes, firing light on the milky interior. *I can see so clearly.* It was as if he saw the world through crystal filters that captured every reflective particle—a confetti-glitter universe. He was in awe. She led and he followed; there were hundreds of other people, or spirits, or astral travelers touring the space.

It's a museum, Anax realized, stupefied. *Did I just figure that out, or did someone plant that thought in my mind? Look around,* a voice said inside his head.

Massive sculptures of well-known superheroes, born of humankind's earthly imagination, filled the space. Some were fifty feet tall. Vibrant colors adorned their costumes; the detail was flawless. *They look different.* Nearly alive, the statues extended beyond three dimensions, rippling with light. He recognized many of them from his childhood. His spirit guide directed his attention to one on his right. No voice came, just a gentle force redirecting his attention. It was Batman. He stood there, speechless, admiring the sculpture's craftsmanship, and the way it was wrought with stardust, or some

The Mystical Village That Rewired Reality

otherworldly material. *How do I know that it's stardust?* It was as if the knowledge was right there—second nature.

Turning his attention back to his guide, he observed how her figure was semi-transparent, brimming with a white luminescence, and accented by oily rainbow patterns that slithered, constantly moving. She was exquisite.

Anax—she telepathically communicated—*understand something. I brought you here because you are ready to know the universal truth.* She paused. *The truth of life is that we are all superheroes.*

In a flash of insight, he suddenly knew why this museum existed, and why superhero lore throughout history existed. It reflected the inherent power in each of us to sculpt the dream of life—to mold energy and craft consciousness. It all made sense. Then, all too suddenly, his ego grabbed him, and he made a joke that perhaps Superman was more appropriate than Batman, since they'd just been flying moments before, but he felt small and silly like a child afterward. Walking alongside his guide made him conscious of his own lack of development. *I have a long way to go*, he thought.

Still, the marvels of this extra-dimensional museum sent his spirit soaring. This *was* reality—a universal reality. And he was here, fully conscious. Suddenly, his excitement surged, and the museum blurred. *Oh no! I hope that I don't wak...* And then her voice, *Stay with me, Anax, hold on...* But it was too late. His awareness came and went, between spirit and flesh, and he tried to hold on, focusing on the environment, but then he felt his body. He opened his eyes and found himself in bed.[33]

He lay in silent wonder, his joy curbed only by the realization that he should have remained in the astral realms for much longer. He was improving, but he should have performed better considering his mind-mastery progress. He needed to subdue his emotions in the astral state, while letting them flow in his waking state. It was tough to balance.

Still, the message awakened his warrior spirit and his solar plexus surged with determination. *I will become one of the greatest astral travelers of all time. Beyond time, even,* he thought, smiling. And he'd use his skills to heal others and help balance the inequities of the world. *Just like a superhero.*

Tonight was special because he'd called upon his spirit guide for assistance—and she'd come. She could not manifest physically in Gylodon because her vibration was several amplitudes higher than what the village could support, and her astral home was several layers away, so any direct contact in this manner was deemed a success. It pushed him to explore finer and finer layers of space. During several extended projections, he'd had no astral body whatsoever and experienced 360-degree vision—just like a dragonfly.

✷✷✷

Since he began his mental exercises, his decisions had become firmer and he no longer second-guessed himself. It was as if self-doubt and fear had been dismantled. He was a man of action. Simply trusting his intuition and accepting any consequences that might arise was a new sensation, and one from which he drew confidence. Life had become a pedestal that lifted him skyward, offering boundless power. No longer was it a place that beat him into the ground. His destiny was his, and his alone, to fulfill—wherever that path might lead.

Before heading to lunch, Anax made a decision. It was time to speak with the Seed Bearer. During their initial encounter—on the same day that Anax first set eyes upon Tristis—the elder had mentioned things about her that continued to intrude upon his imagination. Although his interactions with the elder had been infrequent, he now resolved to seek him out for answers.

Tristis continued to confound him. On a couple of occasions, he'd attempted to initiate a dialogue, but almost immediately she'd excused herself. He could not explain his overwhelming need to know her. Aside from her beauty, she had a magnetic power—like an invisible force that intermingled with the very molecules of his soul. He speculated that there was a part of him that was meant to help her, but he was unsure of how. At least that's what several of his meditations had revealed. *It's foolish thinking, it's all in my mind,* he'd chide himself. But then he'd reconsider, acknowledging that his unceasing gravitation toward her eclipsed foolishness; it was visceral. Besides, his heart would not allow him to cease searching. His intuition told him that there was a reason for it all and that he should seek the answer.

She's worth the fight—even if I end up burned by fire. I control the extent of my suffering. It's my choice, and I learn from everything. Still, sometimes out of desperation he would seek to create distance between his thoughts and her, consciously severing his energetic attachments, but they would only reappear within a day, leaving him agitated. While it seemed he could control his mind, his heart had a consciousness of its own, and it would not be denied.

Before he could deal with that, though, he had an afternoon lesson to attend.

LOVE + LUCIDITY

✶✶✶

"To wield true power, we must master our minds and open our hearts. From there, only light may shine."
- Book of Gylodon -

The day was prickly and it was unclear if it would rain. Static was in the air, but so was the immutable, light-filled energy of Gylodon. Anax made his way to the willow tree and could not help but be awestruck at his body's lack of physical pain. He'd noticed his distress starting to fade as soon as he'd entered the village, but now after a stretch of months, he no longer noticed any discomfort whatsoever. Pain that he'd previously accepted as inevitable and destined to plague him for a lifetime simply had departed. It was like being reborn. Sometimes he wondered if it would return if he left Gylodon, as if the village's *consciousness cloud* was the only thing that kept it at bay. But none of that mattered, because in Gylodon fear-based thoughts were merely illusions awaiting transformation. Whenever he caught himself drifting, wondering about the past or future, he'd remind himself of that.

He skipped over a dirt mound and made his way up the hill, keen on observing every detail around him, absorbing the energies and tuning in to the day's hum. A jubilant goldfinch dived-bombed his head, swooping perilously close, as it blazed a blurry yellow line not a foot from his face; he followed the creature as it sped to a high branch in the canopy before re-launching into playful flight. He felt its joy as his own.

Anax arrived before Dan, eager for the afternoon lesson. Taking a seat, he closed his eyes, and before long he sensed Dan's arrival.

"Who's that radiating all that light over there?" Dan said.

Anax released his focus, smiled, and responded, "I feel the light in you too, Brother." Never opening his eyes, he simply enjoyed the interaction for what it was. *Brotherhood.*

He sensed Dan take a spot on the earth nearby and commence his own mind clearing. It was a crucial step before any lesson.

The first leaves of autumn coated the ground like an eclectic quilt, and both students heard their teacher arriving, as he stepped through the discarded foliage.

"Gentlemen, I see lucidity, love and light in you. And that will be today's topic." As usual, the Unschooler's voice was strong and reassuring.

"And I in you, Master Unschooler," echoed the students' simultaneous response. The teacher granted them several minutes to open their eyes. There was a glow about him today, more so than usual, and it lent radiance to his sturdy, military-like stature. He was a force of nature.

"Welcome. Today you will learn the equation that defines us. It transcends our life purpose, and is universal to humanity. It is our foundational precept for living within Gylodon. To put it simply, the equation is *love plus lucidity equals light*. I'll say it again. *Love plus lucidity equals light*. Take some time to sit with this."

After ten minutes of silence, the Unschooler continued, "Now, see how your understanding aligns with mine. For me, it means that heart-consciousness, or love, is infinitely more powerful when it is united with a disciplined and focused mind. Together, these two elements can sculpt high-vibration consciousness, or *light*, as we like to say. This is the same light we refer to when we say that we are *warriors of light*.

"We are all born with selfless love, pure and unpolluted; but it is our mind, over time, that shapes, squashes or amplifies it. An undisciplined mind allows fear to take root, and this, in time, can dilute the power of our love, by blocking or suppressing it. The mind will create alternative variations of love like co-dependency, selfish love or sexually focused love, rather than the purest form of selfless love. There is nothing wrong with alternative forms of love, but they lack the power of pure, selfless love. And pure love, when offered to the *consciousness cloud*, transforms wastelands into gardens.

"As outsiders, we first learned about fear from our parents, and later from our community and society. We developed undisciplined minds, fertile for fear, and then planted with worries. Our lack of lucidity shapes the types of love we experience, which is fine learning for most of humanity, but for *warriors of light* it is not enough. For sisters and brothers of Gylodon, it is insufficient. It will not shift darkness into light. It will not build bridges across vast, dark crevices.

"As *warriors of light* we assume full responsibility for every thought, feeling and action that we radiate to the world; we act consciously, and always with the best intention. The truest path is easily navigated with the heart, but if our mind is polluted we will second-guess it. Naturally, there are times when the mind must take the front seat, such as problem-solving and deeply analytical tasks, but still, your heart can always navigate deeper truths if you are willing to listen. These two powerhouses, when wielded in harmony, are more powerful than anything. They shift realities on a grand scale. Your mind is like a blade and your heart is a rainbow. Sculpt with the blade, with careful precision, and feed your realities with the rainbow. Always choose your words wisely, for they are sharp. A simple, well-placed word to the right person, spoken with love, can emit a ripple of change, an echo of transformation, tipping scales and shifting paradigms. Our words, and thoughts, are the building blocks of reality, and love is the fuel. Together, they mold the dream that is life."

The Unschooler sat in silence, allowing the students to absorb and explore the lesson. Briefly, Anax's thoughts, like a rogue log amid wild rapids, drifted to Tristis, but he let them pass and returned to the lesson. His attention became razor sharp after that, and time seemed to dissolve, or bend, just as the teaching penetrated his cells, like a beam of light.

After a long while, the air chilled and Anax opened his eyes.

Darkness had descended upon the skies, revealing lustrous stars on an infinite, cosmic canvas. The dusky grandeur evoked emotions, like lunar love, and he felt his heart open just a bit. New animals would be afoot—the night dwellers—and Anax felt their power like nocturnal firestorms. Looking around, he did not see the Unschooler, but he did find Dan, ever the brother, sitting patiently nearby, also in meditation. He heard Anax stir and welcomed the break from the long exercise.

"Master Unschooler just left us in meditation? Hmm. That makes for an interesting day. Perhaps he just wanted to emphasize the lesson in some way?"

"Whoa, I was deep," Dan responded, stretching his legs, "yeah, perhaps he wanted to see if we'd allow fear or anger to take root, or if we would continue in the spirit of lucidity and love."

"Or perhaps he just went to the bathroom and decided not to come back," Anax quipped.

"A warrior's task, indeed," Dan responded, pursing his lips. "Bathroom duty."

Anax lingered in the moment, ebullient, bubbling with reverence for his entire existence in Gylodon. Seeing his brother still there with him, sitting in the cold after several hours in darkness, evoked a deep sense of camaraderie, and it filled the voids in his heart, like pools of water, following the rains.

Hunters

***

Outside of Gylodon, where the fabric of humanity was twisting and ripping, where concepts of power were still medieval things of dastardly proportions, darkness still loomed—and it held far more sway than it deserved. Sometimes it cloaked itself in a white collar or a dazzling suit, like camouflage, and other times it was reminiscent of the vilest forms of ancient tribalism. But always it was there, seeking dominion over people and nature. Already the outside world had entered a new age—an epoch defined by human destruction and pollution—and all of life was in imminent peril.[34] Humankind had set a trajectory to eradicate half the species on Earth within fifty to one hundred years, and the collective consciousness had barely even flinched. It was no wonder the nature spirits held humans in low esteem. They ravaged everything they held dear.

Humans mistreated each other, as well. Love was forced to fight for its rightful place at the table of life. The caste systems stood as timeless prisons of poverty, abandoning the bottom dwellers, leaving them to slog around in the mud, to fight for survival. And just as they struggled in the quicksand of life, others climbed atop their shoulders, kicking wildly, battling for their "rightful" place. Nature was treated as a toy to be played with and discarded, just like humanity's most vulnerable souls.

And while the scales were tipping and the time of change near, darkness was a powerful adversary; it would not go quietly into the night.

***

Clouds hung in the air like a gray wool blanket as Anax rounded the turn. Dan was far ahead, running at a leisurely pace, and Anax struggled to keep up. The terrain was irregular and demanded constant vigilance. Exercise of this nature—that is, setting aside time to simply run—was uncommon in Gylodon. It was an "outsider thing," apparently, and local villagers were prone to both confusion and laughter when they contemplated the ritual.

The energy of the village was so conducive to natural stamina and longevity, and the lifestyle already so active, that "exclusive exercise time" simply wasn't necessary. But old habits are difficult to break, and Dan had always been an endurance runner. Anax joined him on occasion, just to push the limits of his legs and see how they held up under the pressure. They'd been running for the better part of forty minutes, in a straight line away from Gylodon, dodging trees and rocks, and Anax wondered just how far the village *consciousness cloud* stretched. So far, his legs felt better than his lungs, but he wondered what would happen if he breached the invisible threshold.

As he crested a small hill, he was nearly tackled by Dan who had taken a sniper-like posture behind a tree stump.

"Get down," he said.

Anax froze, slowly kneeling.

"Look over there, on the horizon."

As Anax caught his breath, he spotted a man and young boy, clad in tan hunting attire, hiding behind a tree while sighting a rifle on something that neither Dan nor Anax could see. Before Anax could assimilate the scene, the boy fired the rifle with his father's assistance, and a large animal, previously concealed, stumbled forward revealing its location. The creature attempted to walk, but already the front part of its body was collapsing from the pain. The man rubbed the boy's head in a congratulatory fashion, and they walked cautiously toward the struggling creature.

Something dormant flared in Anax, like a long-forgotten dark shadow. He hadn't felt it for quite some time. It was anger, hot and expansive. *How dare they desecrate our woodlands and celebrate cruelty.* He watched them laugh and hug each other, all the while shifting their attention between the animal and the rifle, celebrating their achievement. Worse yet, Anax knew that the man and boy were far too deep into the woodlands to be hunting for food; they wouldn't be able to carry even a fraction of the meat. They'd done it for sport—perhaps as a "coming of age" ritual for the boy. The thought sickened him.

Anax rose, along with his fury, and Dan grabbed his arm, attempting to pull him back down. Twisting his wrist, Anax slipped away, starting on a beeline for the pair of hunters whose backs were turned. Before he could reach them, another shot rang out, ripping apart nature's hum, as a kill shot put the animal to rest.

Anax felt fire and adrenaline pumping wildly as he lost control and accelerated toward the pair. Everything he'd learned about self-mastery came unraveled.

"How dare you hunt for sport!" he screamed. His voice was loud and booming, but only the boy appeared to hear anything, and even he barely showed any recognition.

Now within twenty yards of them, he screamed again, "How dare you hunt for sport!" This time, they both paused, listening more closely, as if they heard a peculiar whisper from nowhere. The pair scanned the area, confused, uncertain as to the sound's origin, or if they had imagined it entirely.

As their line of sight crossed Anax, he saw their eyes lock onto him, squinting and deciphering, just as abject terror spread across their faces. The man instinctively raised the gun while telling his son to run in the opposite direction. The boy was on the edge of tears, yelling at his father to come with him, screaming something about a ghost. Again, Anax attempted to speak but they did not appear to hear him. The man sighted the rifle on Anax and just at that moment, he felt Dan pull him forcefully behind a tree.

"Anax, stop! He'll shoot you. He thinks you're a ghost."

"What?" Confusion flashed across Anax's face.

Dan took a tactical posture and peeked around the tree, while maintaining an ironclad grip on Anax; the hunter was slowly backing up and beginning to turn in retreat. The boy was far ahead.

"Thank God, they're leaving," Dan said, noticeably relieved.

"What the hell was that about?" Anax asked. "Why could they not hear me? And don't tell me that I'm dead, please. Please tell me that Gylodon is not heaven."

"Lucky for you, you are not dead. But they could've shot you, and I have no idea what would have happened. Maybe the bullet would have gone straight through. I don't know. We are at some kind of boundary or wavelength change in the village *consciousness cloud*. It's still strong enough to repel people from walking toward Gylodon, but when you and I transit through it, our bodies are literally transitioning from invisibility to solidity. I think we appeared as ghosts to them."

"Jesus." Anax said.

"Yeah, something like that. He was going to shoot you in self-defense. Did you see how scared he was?"

"Yes."

When the hunters were no longer in sight, they made their way over to the animal. They stared at it for the better part of a minute before either one spoke.

"They have no idea what they've done."

"No...they don't."

It was an eastern elk, one of the near-extinct species that were usually safeguarded within the village boundaries. They'd seen one several weeks ago. This one had wandered too far.

Dan and Anax said a prayer and called forward energies to help the animal transition smoothly. They did the best they could to heal the spiritual trauma that the animal's soul was likely confronting, and called in guides to assist the animal with a painless transition.

The walk back was an odd affair; they both carried the heaviness of the day's events, feeling nature's loss as their own, but with each step they took back toward the village, they were wrapped in more and more love. By the time they returned, the anger that

Anax had felt was gone, and it was replaced with a deep appreciation for life.

They ran into Ini in town and explained to her what had happened. She was surprised, although this had not been the first time that something of this nature had occurred, she said. If she was concerned about the proximity of the hunters to the village, she did not show it.

"For whatever reason, you both were meant to experience this," she said. "Consider it a lesson that the eastern elk has chosen to teach you. I suspect that the hunters also learned something." She said little else, except that she would relay it to the elders. Her eyes could not hide sadness as she departed.

Dan and Anax returned to their lodgings to contemplate the fragility of life. The ill-conceived rituals of the outside world—taking the life of another creature to make one's self feel more powerful—felt like alien realities from a forgotten age.

Humans can do better.

Answers

***

A couple of days passed, and outside of the Unschooler's brief inquiry, nothing more was said about the elk. Somehow life felt more precious. It was a gift that was experienced by many, but promised to none. Life's delicate nature hardened Anax's resolve to know Tristis, and he decided to act.

En route to the Seed Bearer's cottage, Anax walked with authority. *Need to know*, he silently affirmed. *One way or another I'll get some answers.* For a little while he was embarrassed to be seeking guidance about Tristis from an elder, but she'd been off limits for so long that he didn't know how else to proceed. A lot had changed, and a lot had not—she still bewildered him.

The day was mild and sunny as he trekked along the unkempt path to the Seed Bearer's cottage. Upon arriving, he approached the door and knocked. No answer came. *Hmmm. I know that you're in the village, Master Seed Bearer. Where are you?* He walked around the cottage and admired its craftsmanship. Its details were flawless, replete with eye-pleasing curves and astonishing artistry. *How can such a small structure feel like a cathedral?* The rounded windows and sacred geometric sculptures evoked wonder, nearly distracting him from his purpose. Crossing the southern exposure of the building, he spotted the elder sitting in the gardens, deep in meditation. He approached respectfully, taking care with each step, and then slowly took a distant seat.

"Anax, I see the light in you." Without opening an eye, and with his back turned, the Seed Bearer called out.

Startled by his immediate recognition, Anax rose from his half crouch, offering the traditional response, "And I see the light in you, Master Seed Bearer."

"Come over here, young man."

ANSWERS

The elder signaled him to join him by the garden. Opening his eyes, he turned his attention to a dandelion sprouting from the ground, beckoning Anax to do the same.

"What do you see here?" Questions like this were common in the village, challenging its inhabitants to see beyond the surface of things and to transcend any preconceived notions they might hold. Seeing with the physical eyes was only a small part of the picture. It was more of a feeling, divining information through the fourth and fifth powers. Anax practiced countless exercises like this, clearing his mind of his own thoughts, and simply absorbing insights from the object of attention. Whatever he perceived was accepted as meaningful. Occasionally, his own random thoughts intruded, but this sort of distraction—a temporary lack of mind discipline—was infrequent for him these days. When it did happen, it posed few problems; he could easily make a distinction between an erroneous thought emanating from his own history and the real essence of the object.

He took a closer look and closed his eyes. "A dandelion. I see a symbol of the sun, a plant that takes action, is resilient; a survivor that has been mischaracterized as a weed."

"And in your old life," the elder asked, "what would you have seen?"

"A weed, or simply a dandelion."

"Right. Now look at this rounded seed head." He pointed to the fluffy seed topper next to the flower. "Do you see how perfect it is?"

Anax nodded, looking closer, and the old man continued, "It is a miracle of nature, a perfect sphere constructed of hundreds of elegant, little flying machines; each one built only to carry the destiny of its seed. Each seed is a passenger, seeking a home, putting its full faith in the wind and these miraculous, fluffy wings. In this respect, Anax, they are of the air element. And in their flower form they are more like the sun, as you said. Did you know that the dandelion plant extracts toxins from the earth, as well? They are stewards of the Mother. They transform poisons in the soil into something positive, just like an alchemist. And when we consume them, they assist with cleansing our own bodies, but the toxins do not harm us. They have been *transmuted*." The Seed Bearer paused, brow crinkling. "These plants have deep roots. We should be so lucky." Anax remained silent.

"Speaking of plants," he continued, "I would like to one day visit the particular birch trees that guided you here. We should offer them thanks for delivering our message after so long."

"Yes, that would be nice," Anax responded, contemplating the journey and the beauty of such an action. He loved those trees—they'd pointed him to his new home.

The old man bent lower, momentarily directing his attention to the plant. Anax was certain he saw his venerable eyes misting. A breeze blew through the garden, playing with the elder's thinning white hair, just as several dandelion seeds took flight.

"So, what brings you here, young Anax?"

"Well Master, it's kind of a personal issue, perhaps it's silly to bother you with it."

"There are no bothers here, Anax."

"Thank you, Master." He paused, feeling a bit childish. "I have tried on a few occasions to speak with Tristis but she seems unwilling to open up to me. Do you recall that day you told me that you did not see her tied to my destiny?"

"Yes."

"Well, you might be right, but what I can't explain is a constant and consuming need to know her and to help her somehow. It's hard to explain but I have this sense that I'm destined to know her on a deeper level, yet it seems as if she doesn't even enjoy my company. Perhaps I'm a fool, but I don't know how to move through these feelings. The more that I try, the more they grow."

"I see," responded the elder. "This sounds like *love*." Anax blushed. "Have you used the powers of *four* and *five* to divine clarity during your meditations?"

"I have, Master, and I keep arriving at this fierce feeling that I can help her in some important way. I can't deny that I have feelings for her, as well, but this is something else entirely."

"Are you *sure* that it is something else entirely, Anax? Certain kinds of love can be most consuming. It is only natural to seek union with a woman, to yearn for lovemaking. This is one of the benefits of having a body."

Anax's cheeks flushed hot—he was startled by the old man's forthrightness about sex. The elder read his reaction, "This is strange to you? Our sex, in the village, is very open, rooted in the present moment, inviting energy fields to merge for active creation. In most instances, we redirect the climatic energy of sexuality into planetary healing. It's quite effective, I assure you."

Anax stuttered, suddenly recalling Metea and the softness of her skin. *Active creation?* He was struck by the possibility that Metea had redirected the energy of their intimacy into his own personal healing—as a gift of power—and he was grateful. It had certainly seemed that way. But that had been a while ago and much had changed since then. He knew that Metea would always be a world apart, unable to relate to his reality. *Tristis, on the other hand, is someone I can relate to.* Imagery steamrolled his consciousness, taking his mind adrift, and Tristis came to him, naked and untethered, leading him deeper into the woodlands. *Enough.* Catching himself, he stopped the daydream in its tracks. Looking up, he found the aged eyes of the Seed Bearer penetrating his psyche, like a parent reading the needs of an infant.

"I am not accustomed to sex being so open, Master. That said, it sounds pretty good." *Can't wait to tell Dan about this one.* He snorted at the weirdness of it all, but the elder only looked pensive. Anax shifted topics, displacing visions of the virile, 130-year-old elder engaging in "active creation."

"Regarding my insights about Tristis, Master, I am driven by my intuition and feelings. It is a message that I am receiving about her, again and again; it's unrelenting. Even when I turn off the thoughts, the feelings still flow. What does it mean? I don't know if she even needs help with anything. More than likely I'm the one who needs help."

The old man looked him in the eye. "Have you addressed these sentiments with Tristis? In this village, we do not guard emotions, Anax, even if they may be received in a way that disappoints—even if she does not wish to merge her energy bubble with you."

Oh, dear God. Did he just say that?

The elder continued, "But honesty should never lead to prolonged disappointment. You should speak with her about this. Then it will be her choice if she seeks or desires your assistance. As for your feelings for her—you are of the *four* and *five* now, so there are no restrictions on your interactions. Still, tread lightly with her, of all people. Despite her mastery of the mind, the heart can still carry wounds if they are deep enough and still serve a purpose for learning."

The elder nodded, suggesting the conversation had come to an end.

"Thank you for your counsel, Master Seed Bearer. I will speak with her soon. Oh, one last question, if I may. When we spoke on the day that I first encountered Tristis, you mentioned something about a piece of her soul that you were unable to recover, and that you hoped to recover before it was too late. What did you mean by that?"

His eyes impassive, the elder turned toward him, considering the question. "Anax, on that day, I spoke too freely and should not have revealed what I did." He paused. "Still, perhaps there's a reason why this came to light." His words slowed. "Speak with her. But still…do you recall how Ini and Izeel read your fingerprints, hands and face, among other things?"

Anax nodded.

"Well, they discovered something special about her. She carries rare fingerprints—markings of a natural-born shaman, or *Chief Mediator*, as we call them here.[35] And encoded in her hands are the stars of high leadership—suggesting an extraordinary life purpose.

We have not encountered such a thing in more than three hundred years. So, there are those who believe, myself included, that she is destined to lead this village. And perhaps more important, that she is destined for access to the *sixth power*."

"Sixth power?" Anax was incredulous. "I've never heard of a *sixth* power."

"It is not discussed because only those with these markings are able to attain it. It's difficult to describe, but as a *mediator* with access to *six*, well...Tristis would be able to create a perfect union between mind and heart. She'd become a balancer of the masculine and feminine, not just within herself, but also throughout the world. With the *six*, her energy field would be magnitudes larger than any of us can attain. She would have an uncommon ability to restore balance anywhere, mediating and rebalancing all inequities within her presence. The effect is not permanent, but it is profound.

"So you see, Anax, she is quite a woman, and it is no surprise that you are drawn to her." He smiled. "To assume a role as *Chief Mediator* in this life usually requires a willingness to experience traumas that the average soul is not equipped to handle. This accelerates learning, but there is a price. In some cases, it can be years or an entire lifetime before one heals the trauma and can assume the power. Often, they do not. Unless the soul has been restored in full and all parts rebalanced, she cannot assume power. In some cases, the blockage is caused by ancestral trauma that is passed down through the lineage and is more difficult to identify.

"In Tristis' case, however, it appears to be from this lifetime. Even with all the healings that our village provides, there is still a part of her heart that we could not reach. A part she is unable, or unwilling, to reclaim. It's missing, you see, ripped from her during a challenging time in her life. This part of her soul is lost in the lower astral dimensions, and neither she, nor any of us, has been able to recover it. Despite her love of the forest and the animals, she has great difficulty trusting people, and to some extent, she has even lost her faith in humanity."

The Mystical Village That Rewired Reality

Anax stood silent, staring. Things made a bit more sense. Still, hardly believing what he'd heard, he felt small next to the image of this woman, and all that she embodied. *What could she ever see in me?* He could barely process the implications.

"I have probably said too much," the elder continued, "but I trust that there is a larger meaning to all of this. I will speak with Tristis, and inform her of what I have shared. We are not a village prone to gossip, so I trust that you'll guard this information appropriately and use it only for the highest good. Use it only to create light, young Anax."

"Thank you, Master Seed Bearer, I understand." Anax nodded respectfully and departed the gardens.

Nightmare

***

His pillow was soft and fibrous, with just a touch of scratchiness; he likened it to nature's grit. Some said it was stuffed with dried mugwort and lavender. Whatever it was made of, it brought vivid dreams. His mind was on a rampage lately, bouncing between the elk-slaying and his recent learnings of Tristis, and all manner of imagery and emotions spilled forth.

As he dozed deeper, into the layers of the subconscious, where fear sometimes resides, he stumbled through dark woodlands in search of the missing parts of Tristis' soul. He tripped several times, but each time he rose. He knew only that he wanted to help her; he wanted to find the source of the sixth power. But he was not strong enough. Or wise enough. As he traversed the bleary landscape, shadows seemed darker and the land felt diseased, quite unlike Gylodon, and he felt the presence of a predator, eyeing him like a toy, ready to strike. He was going to die before he'd done whatever he was destined to do. His life was forfeit, payment for some unseen debt. Perhaps it was a wildcat that sought his life as recompense for the dead elk, or perhaps it was something far more sinister. The threat felt heavy, like darkness itself stalked him, or Gylodon, and never had the exquisite nature of Gylodon felt so fragile and vulnerable. It would crumble under the weight of what was coming.

He saw the illusions of the outside world—polarizing belief systems that inspired violence, negligence and horrific planetary imbalance. Mixed in were value systems that promoted poverty, sickness and the desecration of nature. Humanity's darkness bore large holes into Mother Earth, twisting needles into her body, extracting her blood, while defecating poisons into her waterways and mutilating all that was precious with robotic efficiency.

Society's destructive illusions were invisible prisons, mixed into life like artificial ingredients in a boxed meal. People consumed the poisons with smiles—oblivious to its presence and grateful for its convenience.

Anax watched in horror as mercenaries stormed Gylodon, bearing semi-automatic rifles, just as the innocent eyes of Gylodon's inhabitants offered curiosity and acceptance. The outsiders infected the village like a black plague, gutting the land, seizing the lumber, shaving the earth's body bald; by the time it was done, Gylodon was a barren wasteland where only the crumbling remnants of its earthen cottages still stood. The thatch roofs were burned to ash, and the gardens vaporized. The last of the "extinct" animals were exterminated, caged or scattered to the outside world.

The shadows seeped into the land, growing like tumors, and before it was done the invaders planted the gardens with genetically modified food, sprayed pesticides liberally, erected overpriced condos, and established schools that taught fictional history from textbooks of illusion. The *Book of Gylodon* was seized and locked away in some aristocrat's safe as a souvenir.

The *consciousness cloud* of Gylodon was dissolved bit by bit, as darkness filled the void, displacing the heart of humanity's unrealized gifts. And just as the blood of the innocents fed the soil, Anax writhed in agony, and he awoke in his cottage, drenched in sweat. His heartbeat was like a war drum, portending cultural annihilation and the end of Gylodon.

Never had he been so overjoyed to wake from a dream; but in Gylodon, dreams were the fabric of reality, in one form or another, and the thought brought tears. He prayed that it was only his imagination that spawned the nightmare.

He breathed in the lavender scent of his pillow, calming himself, and lay there contemplating just how different his old life was, both the seen and the unseen, the known and the unknown. When compared to Gylodon, the outside world was another planet; but the outside world had given birth to Anax, and he would not deny his history or his heritage. Love still lived there—in the hearts of mothers, fathers and children—and there it would remain, for all days to come.

There was only *one* humanity, after all, and it was both darkness and light. He would live for its light. It was the warrior's way.

★★★

The next day, sitting on the village outskirts, obscured by eight-foot green stalks, Anax and Dan prepared for a meditation to connect with the plant spirits. The broad, green leaves carried frequencies that connected with the heart-space, and both men let the tones soothe their energy fields. The wind had died, leaving an eerie silence inside the plant fortress, like a vacuum in space.

Dan turned, setting intense hazel eyes on Anax before breaking the silence. "Do you ever feel like you don't belong here? Different?"

"Different?" Anax paused, taken back by the question. "I don't feel excluded, if that's what you mean. Everyone has been remarkably inclusive and kind. I really don't think they see much difference at all, which is incredible, and a bit odd, actually."

His eyes fixed on swirling energies in a nearby plant patch, Dan responded, "Yeah, I don't think so either, but they *are* different. And so are we. They run on a different computer program. Their code is clean, and ours is messy. I know we're rewriting it, but you can't just delete the old parts. It takes time to get things running smoothly."

Anax laughed. "How poetic. Did you just use a computer analogy amid the natural beauty and wonder of Gylodon? Haven't thought about those machines in months. Thanks for the cubicle memory." Instinctively, he put his hands on Mother Earth, just to make sure she was still beneath him, and that he wasn't sitting in an office chair.

"Memories of the past are not all bad," Dan countered. "We both have family on the outside. I was as much of an individualist as you were and had even fewer attachments, I'd guess, but I still have people I love out there." He paused. "Many, many women, in fact."

"Ha." Anax laughed before getting more serious. "I know what you're saying. About family, that is."

Having family on the outside was tough. Memories persisted and guilt followed. Abandonment guilt. To counteract the sadness, family members were held as part of their daily meditations, usually at the end, when they'd attempt to reestablish energy cords and send love. Afterward, they'd sever the cords. The ritual brought peace of mind and opened the heart-center; it also brought palpable relief to their families, hundreds of miles away. Anax was grateful that Ini had managed to mail his letter letting his family know that he was well, and would be out of touch for some time. *It was something, at least,* he told himself. Ini, as a former outsider, was one of the few who could leave, if necessary, although the outside world had become increasingly foreign to her over the years.

"Well you know, Brother…" Dan paused, as if reconsidering his tack.

"What is it?" Anax finally asked, after a prolonged wait. He didn't want to pry—it wasn't the warrior's way—but it was different with Dan; he was freer to follow his impulses with him.

Dan took off his sandals as he sat down on a patch of dry grass. "We get to leave, you know. When the time is right."

"Huh? Leave? Leave the village?" The thought made his legs ache.

"Yes, the village. Once you've attained a high level of mastery it's the duty of the outsiders to take their power back to the outside world. You didn't know?"

Anax looked confused. "No. I mean, I've wondered, but nobody ever said anything about leaving. I figured nobody would stop me, but I didn't know if there was an honor code concerning staying." The thought of leaving triggered old fears and he shivered.

"There is an honor code…of sorts. You stay as long as it takes to attain mastery and to contribute your gifts to the village. When the time is right, and you are ready, then you depart, if you wish. As outsiders who have been trained in Gylodon, we are equipped to act as bridges between the village wisdom and mainstream earth. We'll be able to go out there and build new worlds. Better ones."

"Gifts?" Anax asked.

"Yeah, different for everyone. It might just be whatever your role is, something you do, or it might be more specific. You know—walking your path. They believe that any outsider who has arrived here has an important aspect of himself to contribute."

Again, Anax shivered. A foreboding sense of destiny pushed his thoughts back to Tristis. He still hadn't shared his feelings about her with Dan; it never felt right to do so. Besides, he didn't want to provide him with endless fuel for the inevitable prodding that would follow.

A branch cracked above.

Looking up, Dan spotted it first. A large, red-tailed hawk was perched proudly just twelve feet overhead. Anax noticed the mighty bird almost simultaneously and both men wordlessly went into a meditative state. First calming their emotions, they then opened their hearts to the bird, projecting the fifth power.

They sent green light, mixed with rainbow, and with each breath the energy surges expanded. *In through the pores, out through the heart.* In it came and out it went. Each of them opened an instant communication channel with the animal. *We are all one. Hello, Brother Hawk,* Anax thought. The bird remained seated, just watching, for several minutes. Then it hopped down two branches, now within six feet of them. Both could palpably feel its energy; neither had ever been so close to a majestic, wild bird. They kept their excitement in check, projecting only calm, loving energy. Continuing in their own way, each silently conversed with the hawk, asking for guidance and offering their respect. The bird examined them for several minutes before a distant rustling sent it into flight. Dan and Anax just sat, eyes closed, smiling. *Gratitude.*

The rustling intensified and they spotted Zevi and Huta in the distance, running from tree to tree.

"I heard that those two manifested a configuration of hummingbirds, in perfect alignment." Dan said.

"Yeah, remarkable," Anax mumbled. "Remarkable." Such abilities seemed far away, leaving Anax to feel inadequate next to these two young *reality sculptors*. He consoled himself with a story he'd once heard from the elder, Ipupiara.

In the story, a hummingbird is lying on the ground with its legs straight up in the air when an elephant walks by, nearly stepping on it. The elephant looks down on the tiny bird and asks, "Why are you lying on the ground with your legs like that? You could get stepped on."

The hummingbird replies, "Well, I'm holding up the sky, of course, making sure that it doesn't fall."

The elephant laughs before responding, "But you're too small to hold up the sky, Little One."

The hummingbird sighs, as if he's been told this before, and responds, "Well, I can only do what I can do. So, I'm doing my part."[36]

Anax closed his eyes and smiled, feeling gratitude for meeting a magnificent hawk. It was a good day—a Gylodon day.

Elders

***

Within the council chambers, a fireplace forged of river rock and earth burned scented wood; incense clung to the air, inviting contemplation, and a bowl of water sat on the mantel above the fireplace. Wild flowers, red and white, adorned the altar cloth on the floor, and the ground's coolness provided welcome respite from the fire's heat. The elders filed into the room, welcomed by Honaw.

In addition to the eight members that comprised the Council of Elders, there were two more unofficial members—former elders who had transitioned into the spirit world, remaining in the lower astral realms to watch over the village. They offered special insights, drawing on broader dimensional awareness to provide clarity when needed. Sometimes these spirits visited in dreams, and other times they simply communicated through the fourth power. Tonight, however, they appeared with notable clarity, drawing energy from the upper realms and the circle, and were easily visible to the well-trained fourth power of the council members.

The group assembled to hear from one of the eight elders, Ipupiara, who'd been experiencing a recurring dream for more than ten nights. He felt it carried a message for the village, so the council had assembled to discuss its implications. Taking seats on blankets and reed mats, they formed a circle, joining hands and calling upon the spirits for guidance. They made offerings of tobacco, berries and seeds. After some time, one of the elders, an old woman, wizened and white-haired, began the sacred chant, calling in the four directions, and opening the circle to Spirit's counsel:

Eastern air *carries eagle's flair*
With feast of mind and broad insight

For those who rise with Father's light;
The spring is king and all is right.

Southern fire *projecting heat,*
Crawling through on lizard's feet,
Taking action, task complete;
Transformation, summer's treat.

Western waters*, all granddaughters*
Of beloved moon;
Seeping, weeping and soon sleeping,
Dark arriving soon.
Land of astral, space of dreams,
Reality bending at its seams;
Autumn's colors and the bear
Taking rest within its lair.

Northern earth*, the land of ice,*
Hard with bone and sacrifice.
Ancestors talking,
A lone wolf stalking—
Winter's biting touch.

Spirit above, Mother below,
Heartfelt center, celestial glow.
Mind and heart—all of creation,
Mediating incarnation.

The chant completed, they unclasped hands and sat in silence for several minutes. The fire's crackle rose above the stillness, drawing their attention. A pipe was passed, and Honaw spoke first.

"Brother Ipu, we are here because of your visions; please share your experience with the council."

Ipupiara paused, as if waiting for his thoughts to come, gazing at the altar, lost in trance. He sighed, looked up, and his voice intoned quiet compassion, "It came upon the Mother, burning and consuming. Each night the flames came closer to the village, and each night I awoke, skin burning, as if scorched by fire. I decided to explore deeper, and on two nights I projected to the local astral layers around the village to seek evidence of any evolving realities. I found nothing, but I remain unconvinced. The dreams continue each night. They've been unrelenting—I thought perhaps we could ask our spirit brothers Ohan and Asku to explore in more depth."

The council members turned their attention to their two ghostly counterparts, who in turn looked at each other and nodded before fading from sight. At the speed of thought the spirits were gone, exploring the nearest layers of the astral world.

Donja took the opportunity to share her concerns. "I too have had dreams—dreams of trees burning, where mother bears search frantically for cubs that have fled into the night. Three times I have had this vision. My astral projections have likewise revealed no evidence of this in the local vicinity around Gylodon. Still, I feel something is amiss. Like a tipping point—the world is changing. Perhaps it is a message of the larger world. Perhaps it is a message that we desperately need water to balance the fire."

It was a message with which they were all well acquainted. Donja was not one to miss an opportunity to express her concerns, particularly among a group of sages who were generally loving and impassive about such things—perhaps too much so—a side effect of fearlessness, which left them vulnerable. But things had changed since the man-made frequencies had cut through Gylodon, sending its inhabitants into fits of discomfort. Some had even experienced fear for the first time. It had been a one-time experience, fortunately, but that did not detract from its implications, or from the healing work that had been required to rebalance things.

"Indeed," contributed Honaw, "it seems that things are speeding up since the outsiders have arrived. I don't understand the connection, but I trust that we will soon gain clarity on what their roles will be."

The group sat in silence until the pipe was passed to the Seed Bearer. "I had a conversation with Anax some time back," he related. "It was curious. He came to me and seemed to feel that he was destined to assist Tristis with healing, or perhaps recovering, the missing part of her soul." Murmurs and nods of assent followed the circle, while the group processed its implications, and two members appeared doubtful.

"How does he even know of this?" asked Honaw.

"One day I mentioned it to him, rather inadvertently, and I guess that it stuck with him, he responded. "In fact, he was adamant about his desire to assist Tristis, claiming to experience unceasing indications of this from the fourth, and perhaps the fifth powers. I don't think that he is ready, by any stretch, but perhaps we should consider the possibility of him going to the mountain."

The oldest woman, bony and bent, and usually silent, looked up with fire in her eyes. "But he is not ready."

"No, he is not," the Seed Bearer agreed. "But things are happening quickly; the outside world is twisting faster than before, and as we all know, Tristis carries the marks of *Chief Mediator*." Again, murmurs of assent filled the room as each member looked to the faces of their counterparts, reading each other's eyes, as if the truth lay coiled inside.

"Brother, we do not send people to the mountain before they are ready. It is not the way." The other woman, with steel-blue eyes, a rarity among villagers, looked saddened by her own words.

"No, it is not," added Donja. "Still, Tristis carries the power of the *six* within her and she needs our help to become whole. We all play a role in supporting her healing; she needs it. The world needs it. Even now, after attaining a notable level of self-mastery for an outsider, she still cannot hide the sadness in her heart. If Anax feels that he can help, I say we need to give this serious consideration. No outsider has ever arrived without a larger meaning." Again, nods of assent and subdued murmuring filled the space as the elders stared at the altar, searching for answers among the scattered carnation petals.

"We will need to see if Anax is open to this," said the Seed Bearer. "Still, we'll need to give him more time. As much as possible. I will speak with him when the time is right."

The oldest woman's face still reflected careful concern when she spoke, "My brothers and sisters, the mountain will break young Anax if he is not ready, but I will defer to the council's judgment on the matter, and of course, Anax's wishes. Let us pray that he is ready." The group consented and the matter came to rest.

"The next matter for discussion," added Honaw, "is our immediate course of action for Ipu's and Donja's visions. While we await feedback from our spirited counterparts, I feel that the village should come together to reinforce the local *consciousness cloud*. We must not be discovered by the technologies of the outside. I propose that we double or triple our ceremonies, and call upon everyone to further raise the village frequency." He paused, awaiting agreement. Nods all around. "Good, then the matter is settled. I will make arrangements."

***

Donja was the first to exit the council meeting, and autumn's air greeted her skin with cool kindness. She heard an animal-like whimper, something out of place, and rounded the edge of the building in search of its source. Nearly tripping over herself, she encountered Huta and Zevi, isolated, distraught and crying. The anguish on their faces was an alien thing, unsettling her. Never had she seen such twisted expressions, let alone on these two carefree boys. She was a powerful figure, not as nurturing as some, but a master of the heart, nonetheless. She kneeled down to the boys.

"My little twins, what has come of you?" Her expression was firm, but loving.

Zevi could hardly put two words together and Huta was not much better. Panting, Huta spat words between heaving breaths, "Why the fire? Why is fire coming to the village?" Then they cried more and shrunk down into each other, forming a tight ball, as if the closeness could alleviate the pain.

In an instant, Donja realized what happened—the boys had overheard the village meeting. How or why they would do such a thing, she had no idea. Zevi and Huta had lived in purity and light their entire lives; they'd never had anything to fear, and all at once, they had overheard stories of fire coming to the village with animals fleeing. She realized that their reality paradigms had been rocked and they had no framework for processing what they'd heard.

She hugged them close for more than a minute.

"It will be OK, Little Ones. Breathe in the light. Breathe in the love. You are loved and protected. All is well."

Her words did little to console them as they tightened their amalgam of bodies. She could scarcely see their faces, each trying to burrow into the other. She spent a few minutes sending them energy, then rose to go speak with the elders still lingering inside.

"Fellow council members, we have a situation. Zevi and Huta have overheard our discussion and have lapsed into despair; they don't know how to process the imagery and darkness that we discussed."

Honaw rushed outside, as did the other women, and Donja remained inside with the Seed Bearer and those who had not departed. The Seed Bearer revealed no expression as he said the unthinkable, "Perhaps it is best that the illusion of pure light in the world be dissolved just a bit. If they are the chosen ones, as prophesied, they will have to face the darkness of the outside world eventually."

Donja and the others remained silent, nodding solemnly, feeling the tide of times rising against their backs. Things were under way.

Woodlands Encounter

✳✳✳

To Anax, Tristis was a strange and exotic creature. Even more so than Metea, who'd escorted him into the woodlands like a magical nymph, emancipated his energy channels, and left him in a state of rapturous stupor. How Tristis could exceed that, he did not know. But she was dear to him in ways that defied both common sense and physicality.

Born on the cusp of the fall equinox, she was both the sun and the moon. She carried the fire of summer, the water of autumn, and as a *mediator* of worlds, she also carried the air of spring. Above all things, though, she was a woman of the earth.

When the Seed Bearer and Ini had revealed her destiny as a future leader of Gylodon—with access to the sixth power—she'd only sat in stubborn silence. Afterward, she'd disappeared into the forest for the better part of a rainy day. The responsibility weighed heavily on her, and her teachers gave her space; ultimately, it was her choice to accept her destiny or deny it.

Even more challenging had been the revelation that the trauma she'd experienced in her past, along with the part of her soul that had been severed, left her handicapped and incapable of assuming her full mantle of power. She valued people of action, and having her own power blocked made her feel inadequate. She worked doubly hard to remain positive and it made her stronger. Still, it challenged her daily.

Not a day passed that Tristis didn't do self-healing work. Today was no exception. Deep in meditation, lost in the invisible spaces of memory, she sat cross-legged upon a round gray boulder as she journeyed to places in her past, searching the dark corners for any information that might help. She turned over stone after stone and sifted through trauma after trauma—all in search of answers—but none came. Looking upward, she sought divine guidance, and the sunbeams highlighted the softness of her features, revealing oval cheekbones, pliable lips and tiny pink ears partially obscured by lustrous black hair that played with the breeze like an enchanted pendulum. But her beauty did not mask her frustration.

Astral projection, she was told, was effective for searching out the other realms, but she'd never been able to leave her body. She'd come close a couple of times, experiencing the vibrations and some sensations of energy expansion, but she could never complete the process. It was disheartening. She assumed that it was the missing piece of herself that held her back; in its place lingered deeply buried fear and mistrust. Fear, she knew, could block out-of-body travel. That was a cardinal rule. Perhaps she unconsciously feared what she might find. So, she looked deeper. And still, after many moons, she was no closer to the redemption that she sought. Sometimes she felt envy for those born in the village; they never knew fear. They could exit their bodies with ease. It was as natural as breathing.

Despite her commitment to personal healing, her devotion to the creatures of the forest—ensuring that they were loved and cared for—often took precedence over her own personal needs. They filled a place in her life that humans never could. They were easy. She trusted them because they would not betray her, and their innocence was rewarded with her unconditional love. It was a comfortable exchange.

Sitting upon a boulder nearly three miles from the heart of the village, Tristis felt a prickling energy on the back of her neck, as if she was being watched, and her diaphragm clenched. She relaxed, accessing her fourth power, connecting with her surroundings. Leveraging both her astral vision and empathic sensitivities, she was certain that she was not alone. The energy was strong and humanlike. Opening her eyes, she scanned the area. Again, the hairs prickled on the back of her neck, bristling with the blustery breeze. The autumnal crispness was the kind that chilled and comforted all at once. The leaves had changed, presenting a mosaic-like appearance that provided ample cover to anyone trying to hide. She turned slowly and swept the landscape, her eyes opened wide.

Anax realized that she sensed him. He was doing nothing wrong; he was merely seeking a meditation spot, same as her. He was shocked when he'd stumbled upon her, lost in trance. Admittedly, he'd fantasized about such a chance encounter in the woods. It seemed that he had now manifested it into reality. *I guess my focused intentions are growing stronger*, he reflected silently upon seeing her. *They are now coming true.* Still, childlike nerves kneaded his gut. His warrior mindset dissolved in her presence, replaced by old insecurities.

He approached tentatively so as not to disturb her, but he was about to be discovered. Stepping out from the trees, he revealed himself, holding up a hand in greeting. He approached slowly, trying to find his bearings. No words came. His mind blank and body pulsing, he fumbled for something heartfelt, or even profound to say, but found only the traditional village greeting.

"I see the light in you," he called. His voice quavered awkwardly, croaking like a frog's, and he shook his head in disbelief.

Tristis studied him, invisibly stoking his discomfort, as if he'd trespassed into a forbidden world. "And I in you," she finally responded, rising to her feet.

Against the backdrop of changing leaves, Tristis was like a woodlands goddess, and the bouncing light played on her features, exposing every dimple, crease and freckle, and Anax looked up at her, feeling her power, as a tide of emotions coursed through his body like a pulsing magnetic field.

After sliding feetfirst from her perch, she approached more confidently, apparently recognizing him, or at least confirming that he was a member of the village.

"Hello," Anax said tentatively.

"Well, hello," she replied, as her eyes cut to his core. "What brings you out to these parts?"

He paused, surveying the surroundings, all the while feeling her eyes upon him, dissecting his intent. "Well, I was out seeking a new spot for training, and it's such a beautiful day that I kept walking. I haven't been this way before." *And it seems that I am here to finally meet you, Tristis.* Her birdlike glance penetrated his psyche, unbalancing him, as if she'd just tapped his thoughts. Fumbling for words, he continued, "I was surprised to run into someone else out here from the village." He paused, watching her.

She glanced upward, then set her dark, knowing eyes upon him. *My God, those eyes,* he thought, completely devoid of any self-mastery whatsoever. Luminescent pearls—perfectly shaped and endlessly knowing—paralyzed his body and quickened his heart. She was the essence of femininity, and she wore it like an invisible cloak, unaware of its presence. It was the most potent kind of magic.

"Yes, it is rare that I run into anybody out here," she responded, already missing the solitude.

Anax smiled. *Get to know her now or never,* he thought. Still, he knew that delicacy was warranted. Despite all the inherent power and leadership that was part of her destiny, she was still vulnerable. He would not lose her trust before he'd even had the chance to know her.

"So, Anax, how has your transition been?" she asked, disrupting his thought.

He smiled. She knew his name, at least. Then again, how could she not? The village was not that large.

"It's been indescribable," he responded, searching for words. "The shift, as you know, is so empowering. I feel like a superhero sometimes—more natural than ever before. Just lighter." He took a breath and shifted a stick with his toes. "And what about you? What was it like for you?"

Her jaw clenched and then relented. "It was hard work—and still is. You know how it goes. It's an entirely new way of life, a different existence. Superhero abilities, as you said." She forced a smile, as if concealing something. "Who could ask for more, right?"

Anax laughed in agreement and moved closer to her boulder.

He reached to touch it, feeling its curves, and it was cool on his fingertips.

"Life has certainly opened up in unusual ways," he said. "Still, you're right, it really does take a great deal of daily discipline and practice. There are no shortcuts. For me, the out-of-body travels have become a favorite activity." At his words, she furled her brow, turning away, and regret stuck in his throat. He attempted to shift the subject. "What about you? What are your favorite parts?"

She sighed, her mood lightening. "So far, my favorite parts are the interactions with nature and all her creatures," she said. "It's beautiful to me how close and intimate our interactions can be with wild animals, simply by calming our mind, eliminating doubt and projecting love. It's like they're completely domesticated when they approach. I've even had wildcats approach and allow me to stroke them! Twice! One of them was an eastern cougar, thought to be extinct in the outside world. But we have a small population of them within the Gylodon boundaries." She paused, shaking her head and expressing awe as she recalled the experience. "In the beginning, I'd sit for hours until the animals approached, but I couldn't maintain my calm state of mind when they got close; they'd sense my tension and flee. But in time it just became natural. You surrender to whatever happens and just project the *five*. It never fails."

Anax gaped. "Wow...*wildcats*. That's extraordinary. Do you think it could be done with a bear?"

"I don't see why not. If you're in the right heart vibration and keep your mind still it shouldn't be a problem. I'm sure it happens from time to time around here. Of course, if you falter for even an instant—before you've built trust—it might pose some problems."

"Yeah, I almost touched a raccoon once," he said, looking down, feeling a bit silly. "What's your secret?"

She paused. "There's no secret. It just takes absolute belief and daily practice. Some people are more natural than others, but everyone is generally capable of these feats. Here it is a way of life. Out there, where you and I come from, it's much more difficult, with little community support, and systems and people that keep us living in a state of…" She looked away, cutting herself off, and Anax saw pain flash across her face.

Perhaps I can help with that, he thought, again blanketed with an uncontrollable sense of love and service to the woman.

"I'm sorry," he offered, "I didn't mean to pry." Feeling a twinge of guilt, he remembered the Seed Bearer's advice about treading lightly. It also occurred to him, with momentary panic, that the Seed Bearer may have told Tristis about their conversation and he needed to address that. *Soon.*

"It's OK, Anax. You did nothing wrong. It's just hard sometimes to remember the outside. It makes me sad to think about all the suffering out there—for humans and animals—when there is a better and more natural way of living right in front of us. Species should not be going extinct as quickly as they are. Biodiversity should not be dying because governments and corporations place profits above life. They have no right. A balanced earth-honoring existence is our birthright—as it is for all the animals. Out there—in the outside world—they keep trying to advance technologies, claiming to improve life, but it seems that so much of it only serves to distract us from our own power while poisoning our ecosystems; and we suffer for it. It's like *TVs before trees,* or *distraction before compassion.* People are energetically amputated. It's sad, that's all."

Anax nodded. For the first time, he saw the hidden leadership in Tristis, and he wished that he could feel things as deeply as she did. He'd always been analytical, but through his training he'd learned the importance of feeling things.

He appreciated the way she felt things—and how he felt when he was around her. Until recently, his training had focused only on himself—as was necessary—but he could not recall ever having had such a natural, deep-rooted community concern as Tristis had expressed. It was inspiring. Perhaps she liked people, as well as animals, after all.

Still, he needed to tell her about his intuitions. She probably already knew, and besides, it was his duty—a promise made to the Seed Bearer. He searched for words. "Tristis, this might sound a bit odd, but for a long time I have had intuitions about you."

"Yes, I know," she responded, without hesitation.

"So, the Seed Bearer told you." His shoulders relaxed. "I apologize for speaking with him first; I wanted to speak with you on several occasions but I was unsure how to broach the subject, and we have interacted so little."

"And what subject is that?" she prodded. "That you can help me in some way? Honestly, Anax, I'm grateful for the good intentions, but I'm unclear how you'd be able to help me heal. Healing is kind of…a personal thing." She paused. "And honestly, I don't like to rely on people for help."

He faltered, but found his ground. "I know it's strange. But the feelings I've had about this have been unrelenting. I feel as if I'm meant to help you in some way."

"Do you think that something is wrong with me?" she asked, testing him with a challenging tone. "Do you feel that I need help?" He couldn't tell whether she was half serious or entirely affronted. The subtle acrimony was unsettling.

"Well I'm sure that I need a lot more help than you do," he responded. "But it seems like you're destined for big things in this village and that you might have a few impediments along the way, as we all do. I don't understand it, but I feel that I can help. It's more than just wanting to help, as I said. I'm trying to honor our code here by paying attention to my inner guidance." He wanted to relay his personal feelings as well, but that would only undermine the credibility of his message. Besides, he needed to get to know her before he'd dare to mention something like that. He sincerely hoped that the Seed Bearer had omitted that part of their conversation.

"Well, Anax, I don't know what to say. Thank you. I guess I'm open to this. I don't know what you intend, but we'll see how it goes. Sound good?" She looked away, severing the short-lived synergy between them, and Anax, inspired a moment before, was deflated. It was the first of many highs and lows for him in Tristis' presence. There was a communication gap, a clashing of personalities, or perhaps just an emotional disconnection that left him unbalanced in their conversation. He could find no rhythm in their discourse.

"Sounds good," he said more confidently, "and thanks for understanding—we'll see how things unfold. You gonna be out here much longer?"

She nodded, looking back at her boulder.

"OK then, I'll be on my way. It was nice to see you, Tristis."

"Likewise, Anax." She smiled and turned.

Her subtle rejections only intensified his longings, stirring up a tornado of emotions that ripped through his being. He noticed his legs were a bit wobbly as he departed. *Jeez.* Making his way back to the village, he resolved to write some poetry; he surely couldn't meditate.

The trail back brightened, as did his mood, and he set his thoughts to finding tangible solutions to Tristis' problems. She had some kind of energetic blockage; more than that, though, she was missing a part of her soul. He'd begin searching for it. He'd seek answers through his meditations and in the astral realms, or maybe he'd just stumble upon them during one of his projections. The prospect thrilled him, as if he might win her heart by helping her heal. It was selfish, but she was more dear to him than ever before, and now he had permission to begin his quest. Driven by purpose and fueled by passion, he knew that his mission would propel him through the grayest of shadows. He would not yield until he found what he sought.

Returning to his cabin, he sat down at his table with a reed pen and wrote the following:

Ode to Tristis

Through soulful prisms of endless seeking
Shines lovesome light that's prone to streaking

WOODLANDS ENCOUNTER

Athwart the sky, betwixt the trees—
Blessing lands and noble seas.

And just below, upon her face,
Are scattered freckles that embrace
The lips below, before they splay
Like seeds on breeze that tend to stray.

She's coy and cautious, yet aware;
She's fierce and graceful, oh so rare.
Her heart's well tested—one that's pined,
A stalwart spirit, oh so kind.

A friend to creatures, large and small,
To those that pounce and those that crawl;
To those that fly and those that walk,
To those that slither, those that stalk.

Shy, alone and quick to flee,
With earthen eyes that yearn to see
Nature's creatures roaming free—
Where, alas, lies your heart's key?

He knew that the verse wasn't finished, but the rest would come when the time was right.

* * *

The days moved fast, too fast really, and Anax had no answers for Tristis after three weeks, despite several successful out-of-body explorations. He needed a new strategy for finding answers within the astral realms; he also needed to improve his concentration, which faltered under the weight of his Tristis-borne fantasies.

Following one of the community meals where he'd exchanged

casual courtesies with her and several village natives, he left for a hike. Seeing her always evoked new determination and today he was roaming the local woods, seeking answers. *Spirits…show me the way. Please show me how I can help her assume her role as Chief Mediator. Help me to help Gylodon. I trust that the answers are close. Please guide me.* After several hours of effort, he sat down and pulled a biscuit from his pocket to replenish his energy.

Sometimes he doubted his ability to make such a grand contribution to the village. He was new and inexperienced. He lacked the mastery of the natives. What could he offer? But such doubts did not linger long; instead, they were swept away by the wind and transformed by sunlight, only to return as power. Such was the code—as written in the *Book of Gylodon*.

He sat within a cluster of birch trees, reminiscing about his journey. A simple decision—to flee into the woods with barely functioning legs, a simple act of surrender and willingness to die, had charted a new course for his existence. It wasn't simply external circumstances that had changed; it was mostly he who had changed. He could no longer relate to his former corporate self; nor could he relate to the physical pain that had ravaged his body and poisoned his spirit. In essence, he was reborn. And now all he wanted to do was to play his role—to do his part.

He felt the call to service, and it fed his desire to help Tristis and Gylodon. He would give back, no matter what, and he knew that helping her claim her mediator-borne powers was the greatest contribution he could make. He felt it deep in his core. Each day his fire burned hotter, and he channeled his will into a single point that contained enough energy to rip a hole in the cosmos and open a doorway to answers. He'd find them.

Leaves rustled behind him. "Anax, I see the light in you," came a voice, "and I see that you've befriended some more birch brethren." The voice carried gently to his ears, sending a trickle of energy down his spine. He turned, and to his surprise found the Seed Bearer only three feet behind him. He rose.

"Master Seed Bearer, I see the light in you, as well. Good afternoon."

"Yes, it is a good afternoon." The elder surveyed the landscape as if searching, and Anax waited. "And for you, young Anax, the afternoon is about to get more interesting." The intensity of the elder's stare, now laser-focused, was curbed by a gentle sadness, as if he were about to deliver disheartening news. A shiver ran through Anax, and he felt a sense of foreboding, like destiny wrapped in trepidation. The fear was alien and he released it, instead returning the Seed Bearer's stare with equal intensity.

"Young Anax, your progress has been watched closely by the elders—both here and in the astral planes. You've worked hard, clearly driven by a goal. Do you still carry the same intuitions that we once discussed—to help Tristis inhabit her role as *Chief Mediator*?"

"I do, Master Seed Bearer. Stronger than ever."

The old man nodded, as if he already knew the answer. "Good. There are few things more powerful than a focused and unceasing intention. It seems that your learning is to be accelerated, if you feel that it is right for you. It will entail leaving the village for a time, to a place where the vibration is not as high as Gylodon; a place where you may face your own deepest fears all over again, without the energetic support of the village cloud." He paused, looking down, choosing his words. "It's a place where you can take your astral projections to the next level by fully immersing yourself in a challenging environment, in the darkness of a cave, inside *the mountain*." He paused, gauging Anax's reaction, but Anax's face betrayed nothing.

The elder continued, "It is a journey that can help you find the answers that you seek, and to discover questions that you have yet to ask. You will see healing in a new light, but understand, you first will be plagued by darkness; you'll need to rely upon every ounce of your learning thus far to conquer the ensuing madness of the mountain. You'll be vulnerable and crippled again before you find your balance, Anax. It is a great deal to ask of any man, and so it must be your decision." The elder's eyes shone with fiery compassion, and his emotions pressed to the surface. Anax stared, his face like stone. The concept of darkness was difficult to conceive in his new life; after months of soaking in Gylodon's energy fields he'd been desensitized to it. The thought of darkness in the world triggered an avalanche of memories and suddenly his head ached. The pain was subtle, but real.

The Seed Bearer looked Anax in the eye. "The council does not take this suggestion lightly. Throughout Gylodon's history, there have been only a handful of villagers, all outsiders, who have ever faced the mountain. Understand, young Brother, that there is no assurance of physical survival, but there is an unrivaled opportunity for accelerated learning. Within the mountain, you'll die again and again, living many lifetimes in a single incarnation; you'll face the blackness of the caves, the bite of the cold and the pangs of hunger. But through it all, if you—or when you—maintain ownership of your mind, despite the madness, and continue to open your heart, you will emerge victorious. I believe in your ability to do this, if it is your wish."

Clouds covered the sun and a chill blew from the West; Anax found himself turning toward it. *The West. Land of dreams and darkness, bears and caves. Realm of moon and water.*

"Sit with it, young Brother. Feel it. Let your heart guide you." With that, the Seed Bearer departed whence he'd come, and his footsteps left no sound.

Anax sat listening to the babbling brook for some time. His mind emptied and filled with black—just listening. New awareness filled the void. Somehow, he knew that his teacher, the Unschooler, was one of the few who had braved the mountain. It made sense— the pieces fit, coming together in a burst of clarity. A feeling of destiny blew straight through him, bringing the cold with it, and just as he began to shake, he saw that courage also came with it, and that all would be well.

Tristis and Twins

***

The air was moist and carried the sweetness of decay. Autumn's transformation carried death, and Tristis inhaled it. Resting atop her perch, deep in meditation, she battled her shadows. The emotions moved through her, like a turbulent ocean, begging for release. Pain pulsed in her solar plexus, spreading into her chest, moving upward, and when it reached her throat she wept, clutching tightly to the rock. Encounters with deep sadness were rare in Gylodon, but she had an uncommon vulnerability to them. They came on like a sickness. On top of that, the animals had not come today. It seemed they sensed her melancholy and kept their distance.

Brisk air brushed across her rosy cheeks and she pulled her sweater tighter. She took solace in knowing that the twins would be arriving soon. She'd played a vital role in their recovery after their exposure to darkness and fear, and felt more bonded to them in light of their vulnerabilities. Fear was something she knew all too well, although she guarded that truth with vigilance.

Since her arrival in Gylodon, Huta and Zevi had been drawn to her as if by gravity. She'd known them for most of their short lives, and in her they found a rare and uncommon outsider who bled motherly comforts, showering them with love. In a way, she was a novelty as an outsider, but they coveted her company for reasons beyond that.

Often, they sought her in the woodlands, during her meditations. The twins were among the few humans in the village with whom she shared affection. To her, the youngsters were as precious as her own children on the outside, and since she could not physically be with her own children, she poured much of her heart into the boys.

Zevi and Huta also shared a special bond with the animals, and that only strengthened their connection with Tristis. To her, the boys were a gift from God, available for endless hugs and smiles when the animals were not forthcoming. Innocent and pure, they were just like the woodland creatures.

But the twins had changed since their exposure to darkness. For the most part they recovered well, but a switch had been flipped, and they were not the same. They were sturdier, slightly less open, and a bit more serious. Fortunately, they were still prone to laughing fits, for which Tristis was immensely grateful.

During their recovery, their relationship with her had intensified. Despite their youth, they sensed her gifts. Tristis was raw potential energy, untapped, awaiting a tipping point that might never arrive. And it seemed to them, perhaps, that their destiny was tied to hers. Nobody had uttered a word about such a thing, except Tristis, who told them privately how much she would love it if they could meet her own children one day. Such dreams were near impossible, she knew, but still she shared her wish with them.

Whenever she made such comments, the twins smiled, shifted shoulder-to-shoulder and went silent. Then they would erupt like twin volcanoes, giggling with effervescent eyes, while hugging Tristis.

She also knew, on an intuitive level, that her life was tied to theirs. Perhaps they were simply there for love, but maybe there was more than that. She felt it, deep and beckoning, obscured and unrevealed. For now, though, she accepted the hugs with gratitude, while sharing wild fruit and laughing until her belly ached. Their youthful laughter was powerful medicine and it healed bits and pieces of her broken shadows. She loved them for that, and for so much more.

Plant Medicine

✱✱✱

*"Authentic mystical experience is the path
to understanding consciousness."*
- Book of Gylodon -

The grand tipi was a place of transformation, and tonight the fire burned hot. The ground was littered with colorful blankets, and beneath them, layers of dried plant fiber provided insulation from the cold ground. At the center, a meticulously maintained fire raged, warming the space. With a forty-foot diameter, the tipi could hold many people. Tonight, there was plenty of extra seating space, and more than enough opportunity for healing.

Despite Tristis' self-healing efforts, she remained incomplete, and sought other channels for answers. Plant-medicine ceremonies—aligned with the lunar cycles—afforded such an opportunity, occurring monthly in Gylodon.

After entering the grand tipi, she walked the ceremonial circle in a clockwise direction, minimizing eye contact, and took her seat in the southwest portion of the round, a place of power for her.

Plant medicine never provided what one expected, but always provided what was needed, so there was little point in anticipating how the process might unfold.[37] Ripe for introspection and self-discovery, and best attained through the ceremonial process, these events were not easy for beginners, and they challenged the mind and body in unusual ways.

The participants sat in relative silence, preparing themselves for the medicine. Tristis scanned the circle and noticed the two other outsiders in attendance. She'd seen Dan at the circles before, but had not previously seen Anax in attendance. She chuckled quietly at the prospect of not being the only one to purge this evening. Purging was the release of blocked energies through vomiting, and was an integral part of the process. It was usually villagers who hailed from the outside world who purged. Those born within the village held a purity that did not require the same degree of cleansing. Likewise, their bond with the mother-medicine was strong—through their relationship with nature—and it was unlikely that an outsider would ever reach that level of connection.

When Anax saw Tristis, his heartbeat quickened and his solar plexus tensed; she wore two long braids, black as earth, contrasted by colorful lanyards that secured them at the tips. Her freckles stood out against the firelight, as did her cheekbones, and her bright white garments exuded sacred purity. He was thunderstruck by her feminine power. Already he was having visions of exquisite beauty and the ceremony had yet to begin. His enthusiasm overflowed, and he considered what lessons the medicine might bestow upon him. Looking again at Tristis, he thought, *I get to share my first plant-medicine experience with her, even if she is sitting across the room and cares little for me. Life is good.*

The ceremonies, an all-night affair, were facilitated by one of the elders who acted as a guide through the process, relying upon spirit songs, prayer and energetic support from the group. The elder's short, stodgy torso was anchored by dark, muscular legs that were adorned with sacred rainbow beads and tiny rattles—crafted from the shells of local nuts. The old man had led countless ceremonies over the years—some said for more than a century—and had become one with the medicine. In both heart and mind, he was the medicine, embodied in flesh, and so he carried the authority to hand out the dosages based upon what he felt was right, as the participants lined up to receive the sacrament. The sacrament, derived from local vines and alchemically mixed with prayer and song over many days, was bitter in taste but unrivaled in power. Depending upon the cleanliness of one's digestive system, the medicine took effect anywhere between minutes and hours. For the villagers, it took only minutes.

Tristis drank and reclaimed her seat. Within five minutes, everything began to change, becoming more fluid. She closed her eyes and the world moved; she opened them and everything vibrated, like a single organism. The truth of all things was revealed through a new lens, as multi-dimensional awareness rose to the surface, unmasking the hidden side of life—in the astral and etheric realms of consciousness. Staring at the fire in the center, she thought she understood it—she sensed its intelligence—but she could not quantify her understanding. She certainly couldn't explain it. The thought was fleeting as a wispy cloud manifested before her, drawing her attention. It morphed into a fully embodied female form, donning a dark-red ceremonial robe with intricate, queenly embroidery that flowed seamlessly to the ground. Tristis laughed, wondering if others could see the apparition. Although her ability to see spirits had grown significantly, seeing one with such colorful detail was rare. The spirit's robe was from a different era, but still bore the hallmarks of clothing worn by village elders. The queenly figure signaled to her, flourishing translucent arms. "Are you looking at me?" Tristis responded, quietly.

She laughed again, unable to contain her giddiness at seeing with such clarity. A lightness of being enveloped her as her energy-body expanded, like a balloon without boundaries. Silently, she asked, "Who are you?" The spirit, young in appearance with waist-length hair, pointed at Tristis before shifting its eyes downward and deliberately tapping each of the last three fingertips on its left hand; and then, to Tristis' surprise, the spirit turned and pointed directly at Anax. *"Anax?"* she whispered, confused. Then the apparition pointed back at her, once again staring into her eyes. Tristis shuddered at the intensity of its gaze, which flooded her consciousness like a violet river, washing over her soul, understanding its essence—as if becoming a part of her. To balance the onslaught of intense energy, Tristis grounded herself with humor, giggling softly while awaiting more information, but already the spirit was fading, like a rainbow after the rains. In the wake of its exit, she was left only to contemplate the message. The emphasis on the fingertips, she knew, was related to her own destiny—and the codes written into her fingerprint markings. Nobody else had seen the ghostly figure, except the elder leading the ceremony, who nodded knowingly at her.

Anax vomited, releasing stagnant energy onto the soil in front of him. *Please take it away, Mother Earth,* he pleaded. *I don't need it any longer.* He retched loudly, and his face twisted into animal-like forms, but nobody seemed to mind. With every purge, he was getting well, and it was good. A young male helper, not more than twelve years of age, arrived to aid him, raising a hand over his vomit and reciting an incantation before sweeping the waste onto a long, thin stone. The boy departed the tipi, presumably for the stream. "Thank you," Anax managed to mumble. The boy nodded, blinking kind eyes that exuded maturity.

I feel good now. Powerrrrrfullll. Anax's posture, now upright, reflected his mood. He was a warrior, dancing in the realms of light. Inside his visions—in the spaces of expanded reality—every small movement generated a ripple of change, echoing throughout the cosmos. A dance sequence, properly timed and divinely coordinated, could call forth rains, or move clouds. It was the specific sequences—or codes—that were unknown. But he saw them plainly, like words on paper, or melodic frequencies crafted long ago by higher intelligence. He could play with the ether and mold the astral, and it would bend to his will. All of life was a magical dream of his making.

Ominous flute music, played by a ceremonial apprentice, filled the space and the melody suddenly lightened, shifting to a sacred Gylodonian song—the *Song of Power.* Anax's visions soared into the cosmic realms, amid a sea of stars, and he found himself hovering in space, legs crossed, gazing down upon Earth. She was a living, breathing consciousness. The planet seemed small and fragile amid the vastness, all her majesty relegated to an illuminated ball, floating in an infinite pool of galaxies. She was a child—vulnerable and precious and growing. And humanity used her, cut her, and bled her, as if she were an object without a soul. He could give back to her—he knew it. He looked to his energy-body, and it glowed white, even as he floated in space, gazing upon Earth like an astronaut with no ship. He wept with joy. Feeling particularly emotional about Mother Earth, he resolved to help her. Within an instant, he was floating over Africa, in a barren desert where dust drifted across a dying land. *Water here*, he said, as he swept his hand across the landscape. Within minutes, water bubbled up through cracks in the ground, like liquid crystals, carrying the codes of life. Somehow, he knew that a massive body of water would form there. Again, he swept his hand. *Vegetation here*. Green plants, first as sprouts, began to dot the terrain, and before long the color of the desert shifted to shimmering greens, dark and light, and the energy began to change. *Flowers here*. Smatterings of color blended with the greens, bringing it all to life like a sentient sculpture. In no time the landscape became an oil painting, teeming with life and again, Anax knew it was real. And while the creation might not manifest immediately in the earth dimension, it had been constructed in the astral realms, like a god, and it was a reality, biding its time.

He opened his eyes and was instantly transported to the present. Peering around the circle, he found Tristis, eyes closed, deep in trance. She glowed like a goddess—a daughter of Earth. It was apparent that she'd had a second cup of the sacrament and was journeying deeper. Anax had journeyed as deep as he needed to go. Transformed by medicine, music and magic, he thought, for the hundredth time since his arrival, *I can't believe this is happening.*

But he was not done. For the next couple of hours, he experienced the accelerated learning of plant medicine. It was a revolution of reality. He shifted between mind-consciousness and heart-consciousness, exploring each in turn. When he focused on the mind-space, he encountered an endless magnitude of geometric patterns, complex fractals, lines and shapes. Logic and intellect, like children of mathematical truth, ruled this space, but it was dark and colorless. Shades of gray dominated, and he felt little, if any, emotion.

When Anax shifted into heart-consciousness, color expanded around him like multi-dimensional watercolors, and it moved like a river; there was none of the rigid structure of the mind-space; it was far more fluid and alive. Rainbows pulsed and new frequencies moved through him, inspiring ecstasy, love and sometimes sadness. *My God, the colors,* he thought. Many of the colors, and the forms they took, were not something that his waking, rational mind could conceive. *Even the shapes are different, pulsating with emotions. They are alive,* he realized. *The colors...are they spirits?* Rather than trying to figure it all out, he just observed in awe as new awareness touched his spirit. *Even if I don't understand this,* he thought, *perhaps my higher self can make some sense of it.*

At once, the music changed and the scene shifted; his vision tunneled through rock, dark and cold, and he was pulled deep inside. *The mountain.* Somehow, he knew that it was "the" mountain. *Do you welcome me, strong mountain? I extend my love and I thank you for all that you will teach me.* No response came, and then he was dizzy and purging again, uncontrollably, and the mountain became frightening. He battled with the fear, calling upon colors and inviting his heart to illuminate the darkness. *Let love enter here. Let it in—please God.* It worked, but only when he held it. Otherwise, the darkness returned, enveloping him, blocking love while stealing body heat and leaving him exposed. He shivered violently. The fright of the darkness was almost too much to endure, and his heart raced. Somehow, he knew that the darkness reflected the darkness within him, the shadows yet to be acknowledged. He needed light to expose them; it was the only way to find and confront them. His breathing became labored as his body shook, and then, at once, he felt a hand on the back of his neck, sending warmth. It was the ceremonial leader.

The darkness got the better of him and he purged violently once again. *Let it go. LET-IT-GO. I let it go. I, I, I...* He weakened, growing suddenly tired, and then, at once, had nothing left. Instead of battling, he surrendered to the darkness. In his surrender, he found a measure of peace, a sliver of light. A silent contentment lay upon him and his breathing slowed; it was as if he'd just faced the final battle of light and dark, and was now better equipped to handle the journey ahead. On the edge of his awareness, he felt a hand release from his neck. "Thank you," he whispered.

Nobody but the elders knew of the mountain plan and even they did not know his decision. Dan would be saddened by his departure, but Anax knew that he'd understand; it was in Dan's nature to understand such things, having traversed much of the world on his own, prior to his arrival in Gylodon. Anax was not as strong as Dan, nor as adventurous, but he was as ready as he'd ever be. The remaining hours passed like a dream, and finally he slept, plagued by a kaleidoscope of visions that he did not understand.

He awoke with unusual vigor and it surprised him, as he anticipated some sort of hangover from the purging, but there was nothing. Just power. A floating feeling, like the one he'd first experienced upon entering Gylodon, enshrouded him, complementing the comfort he felt while swinging in his hammock. *Hammock.* Somehow, following the ceremony, he'd crept into a hammock, strung between two nearby trees that were located just outside of the ceremonial tipi. *How appropriate.* The air was crisp, and for a time he lay there, just listening to the forest. Indeed, life was perfect. *Perfectly mysterious.*

"Come find me!" The words echoed from behind him and he knew that some of the village children were frolicking nearby. *What a life.* A smile graced his face. The wind carried the forest's song, and he relaxed, just listening. Each forest sound merged with the next, into a single stream, and Anax discerned a repeating melody and rhythm—like a natural heartbeat. He could not bring himself to rise, and instead savored the majesty of the moment.

Eventually, he sat up in his hammock, stretching his back, and turned to watch several of the village children playing nearby. He waved and they barely noticed, instead running into the woods, intent on their game of chase.

Placing his feet on the cool soil, he twisted his body and felt an unusual surge of energy in his torso. To his surprise, the surrounding vegetation gleamed with strange aberrations of light, revealing their hidden aspects, like divine reflections. The grass, likewise, exuded a vivacity that was almost humanlike, as if it poured forth emotion. *Whoa. Hello, Earth.* The world had removed its mask, unveiling its true self. Or, perhaps, he'd finally opened his eyes.

Hungry, Anax made his way over to the eating area; breakfast would still be happening. He floated through the entrance.

"Hello, my brothers and sisters, I see the rainbows in you," he announced, seeing them with notable clarity. *Residual benefits of the medicine,* he realized. *That's why everything looks so magical.* Feeling playful, he could not shake his smile and several of his brothers and sisters nodded at him, silently acknowledging his experience from the night before. They knew that he was new to the medicine. He looked left, and to his surprise, found Dan sitting with Tristis. A couple of other villagers sat at the far end of the table.

"Good morning, guys," Anax mustered, "May I join you?"

"Good morning to you too, my light-filled brother. Wow—will you look at the size of that grin? My God, it's ear-to-ear!" Dan joked, as he shook his head.

"Someone's been rewired," Tristis offered.

Anax nodded, still beaming, "It's a beautiful day, what can I say?"

Tristis looked down at her empty plate, and Anax felt a pang of disappointment at her imminent departure. He could sense it. On the few occasions when he did sit down with her, it rarely lasted long. Dan read his thoughts as Tristis picked up her plate, forged of red clay, and stretched her arms skyward while preparing to depart to the dishwashing station.

"Well, Brothers," she said, "enjoy the day." With that she rinsed her plate and left for the woods, taking a measure of Anax's joviality with her. In truth, he enjoyed being called *Brother* by everyone except Tristis.

"She still drives you crazy," Dan said, shaking his head. "What happened to all that warrior self-mastery?"

Anax looked down at the table. "I wish I had a good answer, Brother, but I have none. But thank you for calling me out on it—I just love having my vulnerabilities laid out on the table."

Dan grinned, "Better to know where your holes are so you can patch them up."

"Ha. Well, you know, we all have our weaknesses."

"Speak for yourself," Dan countered, feigning seriousness. Anax raised his eyebrow, a near-perfect imitation of the Master Unschooler, and Dan unleashed a laughing howl that drew the attention of the others at the table.

After selecting some food and sitting back down, Anax called upon the power of last night's ceremony and began energizing his meal, but the ritual was short-lived. Instead of savoring its nourishment, he played with his food for several minutes, as the mountain weighed on his thoughts. He did not relish sharing the news with his friend, and didn't want to spoil the good mood. Nonetheless, Dan had become his closest ally and it was better to deal with things than to let them linger.

"So, I have some news to share."

"Ahhh...news," Dan responded, crinkling his eyes. "Slightly foreboding tone. OK. Out with it, Buddy."

Anax took a deep breath, choosing his words, "Well, I was approached by the Seed Bearer the other day about going to a place they call *the mountain*."

The color drained from Dan's face and he looked down at his food. "The mountain! Anax...that's a serious matter. What do you mean, *going to the mountain*?" He quieted his voice. "Are you actually considering it?" Dan looked his friend in the eye.

"I'm going, Brother. I feel it's the best way I can contribute to the village."

Dan interrupted, "You do know that you have a choice, right? And that there's absolutely no judgment if you decide to just stay here? None."

"Yes, I know," Anax responded. "I know it's crazy, and believe me, I hate to leave you for a time, but my intuition is guiding me to embrace the challenge."

"Damn," Dan countered, lowering his voice, "I don't want to dissuade you in any way, but living in the mountain is far more than a challenge. Honestly, I don't know all that much about it, but the few legends that I've heard indicate that it has driven both men and women to madness, more times than not. People more prepared than you. It's like taking yourself to the edge of death physically, but more important, taking yourself to the edge of darkness, to a space where your own consciousness will be pushed to its limits. It can traumatize your spirit if you are not prepared. I mean, from what I've heard, people have out-of-body experiences for long periods of time just to escape the harsh realities of solitude—like a coping mechanism. Other times they're pushed out without their consent, because their physical bodies are literally dying." He stared back down at his food, his eyes like glass.

Anax smiled. He'd never seen his friend resist a good challenge before. "So, basically you're saying that the prospect of me sitting still in one place for hours on end frightens you? As in—your worst nightmare?" Attempting to inject some humor, Anax raised his eyebrows in a professorial manner, but Dan did not take the bait.

Anax sighed, grateful for the concern. "I guess I'd better make sure that I'm prepared, then."

"You've already made up your mind?"

"Yes."

Dan continued, as if the decision were still up for debate, "What is your motivation for this? How do you expect to help the village by doing this?"

"Well, for one thing, I can develop my skills at an accelerated pace. And for another," he looked out to the woods, "I'm going to help Tristis."

Dan's eyes widened and he swallowed hard, choking back words of incredulity.

Anax continued, "I know it sounds crazy. Believe me, I know. But Tristis is destined to play a very large role in this village, and perhaps even on a planetary level if I can help unravel whatever is holding her back."

Dan regained his composure. "You would risk madness and death, just for a shot at helping Tristis attain her destiny? To *unravel* what holds her back?"

"Yes, Brother, I would. And will. This is my role to play—my gift to offer. Isn't that what it's all about? We're all one."

Dan just shook his head in disbelief, but could not help smiling. "I knew there was a wild man inside of you. I just can't believe it took the mountain to unleash him." He breathed deeply, expelling some tension and beginning to accept the new reality. "So be it, Brother. I'll miss you, but I'll support you however I can. Our time together went by too fast." He looked down at the table, his eyes vacant.

Anax nodded. "It *has* been too fast. Good company has the unintended consequence of accelerating time, Brother. Thank you for your support. I knew I could count on you."

***

He hadn't yet told the elders of his decision. It felt strange to be guarding such a secret.

After separating from Dan, he made his way down the narrow path, stepping mindfully toward the place where he'd spent so much time. The sky was clear and the willow tree towered formidably over the empty hillside. Time alone here was humbling, and Anax felt a lonely solitude, a sadness to be departing such nobility. Pressing his back against the tree's massive trunk, he imagined himself absorbing its rings of knowledge, embracing its strength and courage. *Wise Willow, please stand by me on this journey I'm undertaking.* He looked up at the drooping branches, which enveloped him, and felt protected. Sitting only feet from where he and Dan had absorbed countless teachings by the Unschooler, he felt his emotions pushing like high winds against stubborn stone. He sat against the tree for some time, with the occasional tear pressing to the surface before finding its way back to the earth. When the time was right he rose, and continued up the crest, going where he needed to go.

It felt odd approaching the Unschooler's cottage; he'd done it only twice before in all these months. The path was rocky and after he rounded the third curve in the trail, he saw the structure. The dwelling was much like a hobbit house, built into the earth, and partially subterranean with a moss-covered roof. The gardens were wild and unmanicured, but the stone path closest to the home had been laid with precision, in stark contrast to the unkempt portion of the path. He reached up to knock and the door swung open.

"Hello, Anax. Come in."

"Thank you, Master Unschooler." He dispensed with the usual greetings and walked in, admiring the space. Some of the woodwork was spectacular, particularly the rounded arches that seemed to support the dwelling. Timber framing was a coveted skill in Gylodon.

"Some nettle tea?"

"Yes, Master. Thank you." He took a seat next to the small fireplace, recognizing the design—it had been engineered to maximize heat with a minimum of fuel. Built of rugged earth and stone, with a timber mantel and accented with sacred geometric patterns, the fireplace was an altar. Anax had seen some of the geometric patterns before—they were used as portals into other realms during meditations—but many he did not recognize. Again, he felt sad to be leaving such wonder behind.

The teacher poured the cups and took a seat across from him. "You're here about the mountain?"

Plant Medicine

Mildly startled at being so easily read, Anax just laughed. "Yes, Teacher. Have you been there?"

"Ha! Oh my. That's funny, Anax. The way you projected that, like it's a resort that I've visited. Very good. Very good. A bit of levity goes a long way in dark places. I'm impressed that you figured that out. That I've been there, that is. You know, there are only a handful of us, and none living except for me, who've been. Then again, it's only a place for outsiders, and there are relatively few of us these days. But yes, I was there. A long time ago."

Anax assumed that the elders had relayed the possibility of his journey to the teacher. It was odd seeing him in such a casual mood.

"Well, Master Unschooler, I'm going to the mountain. I've only told Dan so far, but I wanted to speak with you before making it known to the elders."

"I see." The teacher's laughter shifted to thoughtful reflection. "I see that you've made up your mind, as well. Firmly. That's good, Anax. This is not something to be uncertain of. I trust that our lessons will serve you well."

"Thank you, Teacher. I trust that they will. I was hoping you might offer me some advice. Perhaps even tell me what drove you to embark on your journey?"

"Ahh," he took a long pause, pulling his tea close. "Well, for me, the decision came from an insatiable desire to expedite my learning. I was an eager student, as you might imagine, and I wanted nothing more than to attain absolute mastery. I wanted to make the most of my opportunity to learn in this life. At the time, I was the only outsider in the village, and I wanted to develop my skills to a level where I could more easily fit in. I had no other home or family, so I needed to fit in."

Anax nodded, intrigued by the opportunity to access this part of his teacher's history, and stricken with the awareness of how difficult it must have been to be the only outsider in Gylodon.

The teacher continued, "Despite all of the acceptance here in

The Mystical Village That Rewired Reality

the village, it is easy for an outsider to feel inadequate in power. That was not acceptable to me. As for advice," he paused in his customary fashion, opening himself up to the flow of information, "the best advice I can offer is to never lose sight of your power. Practice and use all your tools. Call upon all your helpers, and never, ever lose faith. Trust in the process. Listen to your heart. Your heart will speak the truth when all else seems lost. If you lose control of your mind, you will need to rely on the heart to rebalance. Likewise, if you lose control of your emotions, you will need to rely upon your mind to rebalance.

"The journey is what you make of it. It's yours and yours alone. Nobody will ever know, or understand, the battles that you will wage and the lessons that you will learn. You will come to know yourself, and love yourself, in an entirely new way. Be open to the visions. Remember to trust the inner voice but know which one you are listening to. If it is from the heart, you can trust it to be true. Other voices are not to be trusted; they can lead you astray. Be wary of the mountain spirits, they are not like the ones in Gylodon—they dwell in the lowest astral realms. They are made of shadow and fear—and you must, under all circumstances, transcend their influence. Do not yield your energy to them, or they will latch onto you, sucking your life-force.

"*Love* and *lucidity* remain your most powerful tools in this environment. When you raise your personal frequency to that of love, by entering the heart space, the darkness cannot touch you; it will be rendered impotent. Remember—the mountain spirits have not a fraction of the power that you hold within you. Earth is *your* realm, *not theirs*. Only by giving away your power are you rendered vulnerable—and warriors don't do that.

"Also, do not neglect your nutrition too much—including a bit of sunlight each day. By now you know which wild plants you can consume. Make them your allies on this journey. If you are there during the wintertime, well, you will learn about survival, and slowing things down. Including your metabolism.

"There is a village priestess in the area—she is the caretaker—and she will keep an eye on you. She can help you subsist when food is sparse, perhaps even guiding you at times. Do not misjudge her tiny, frail and youthful appearance. She is the Cave-Keeper, Holder of Shadows, and within her she holds the world's darkness. Her life is the ultimate sacrifice, dedicated to transforming the world's darkness into light. She is most commonly known as the *Transmuter*. First, she draws in the darkness, pulling it into herself and the mountain, and then she transmutes the energy into love. The work is tedious and dangerous, but her power is extraordinary. She will give you space to learn, but will also be available to teach. She's a tougher teacher than I am, by far." The Unschooler winced in recollection.

Anax reeled at the Unschooler's revelations. The Seed Bearer had not mentioned anything about a priestess, let alone a *Holder of Shadows* and *Transmuter of Darkness*. Nor had he mentioned anything about fear-inducing spirits that can suck one's life-force. Before he could dwell on this new information, the Unschooler continued, in casual fashion, as if he'd revealed nothing more than the day's lunch menu.

"Learn to make fire, and keep fire. Know your water source. Get to know water. Know the land. All in all, get to know yourself, Anax," he said smiling, his tone softening. "There is much to uncover. And much to do, I'm sure." He said the last with a knowing smile.

"Yes, there is much to do," Anax responded thoughtfully. "Thank you, Master Unschooler, I'm grateful for your counsel. And thank you for all your teachings these many months. I don't have the words to express my gratitude. You've taken so much time with Dan and me, given us so many gifts…"

"Anax, it has been my honor to serve you and the community. It is my role. I trust that there will be more to come."

"Yes, I trust that there will be." Anax responded, feeling reassured.

"Good. Is there anything else that I may help you with?"

"Well...this *Transmuter*, can you tell me more?"

"Only that she will be your teacher, if she so chooses." Anax recognized the intonation of finality in the teacher's voice, and he knew that no more information would be offered.

"Anything else?" the teacher asked.

"No, I don't think so," he said, pausing, reluctant to depart so soon, as if he were forfeiting his final opportunity to glean knowledge from someone who had experienced the mountain. But the reality was that it was a unique journey yet to be written and his teacher had already given him the tools he would need. He nodded to the Unschooler, then rose and carried his mug to the counter. Hesitant to leave, he admired the woodwork one last time before stepping toward the door.

"Anax," the Unschooler said, sensing his student's hesitation, "you are ready. We stand by you. Remember, you are a brother of Gylodon. We are all one and nobody is ever left behind. Do what you need to do, then reemerge stronger and more balanced than ever before."

"Thank you, Teacher." Anax smiled, departing with a measure of confidence.

Mountain Preparation

***

His last week in Gylodon was spent re-learning some of the basics of wilderness survival—making fire with sticks, bow drills and flint, as well as the basics of water purification, incorporating a variety of techniques. Boiling water was simple, but making filtration systems using local sand, gravel and charcoal was more fun. It made the water taste cleaner. He doubted he'd need every technique, but it comforted him to have some of the basics down. *There's probably a natural spring nearby, anyway,* he thought. Nobody gave him any specifics in this regard; that was for him to figure out. He'd been practicing these techniques throughout his time at the village, so nothing was new. He also brushed up on all the local, edible plants. Still, he did feel a slight trepidation about winter. The Unschooler had said he'd learn about survival and subsistence when the bitter weather came. He breathed deeply. *Trust.*

Tristis softened over his final week, offering smiles and even light conversation. Her attention served as a reminder of his promise, fortifying his courage when it wavered. He tucked her smiles away, deep inside, so they might serve as waypoints, should he lose his path. Three times he'd found himself staring into her eyes, utterly lost, only to snap back to the present, awkwardly looking away. And each instance had been a brief journey into the heart of the ocean, to a wild and treacherous landscape. Each time, he wondered if he hadn't just glimpsed the answers that he sought. Whenever his unspoken love bubbled to the surface, he'd re-center himself, remember his imminent journey and focus on the harder realities. But thoughts can be comforting—and memories magic—so he stored them away.

The Mystical Village That Rewired Reality

***

The Seed Bearer was tending his garden when Anax delivered the news. The elder led him down into his seed cellar. The shelves were lined with wooden casks, baskets and countless jars, each of them overflowing with seeds and dried herbs.

"Young Anax, look here," he said, expressing unusual emotion. "Inside this vault. Millions of seeds, each imbued with a unique blueprint. Like people, there are countless types of seeds in this world. Each one is capable of self-replication, beauty and nourishment—all pieces of the earth's story. A bit of water brings them to life, while the sun's fire helps them transform and grow. Once they become a plant, they act as *mediators*, balancing the very air we breathe. But it is the earth that is their foundation.

"Now, understand, most seeds will not survive to become adult plants, despite their potential. Life is a gift. Those that adapt, those that are blessed by timing and circumstance, those that create a proper relationship with their environment will thrive, becoming sturdy, full-grown plants capable of offering their fruit to the world. But even a growing plant is vulnerable. You, Anax, are a growing plant, so you mustn't forget to water yourself each day, to let the fire transform you and the earth support you. Grow toward the light. When you find yourself out of balance, just breathe. And remember, young Brother, we take care of all our plants in Gylodon. *All of them.* You understand?"

"I understand, Master Seed Bearer, thank you for your kind words and support."

"Good. When you have a moment, I want you to plant the seeds of your heart in Gylodon's garden, where we may all tend to them. Do this before you depart."

The Seed Bearer had become a grandfather figure to Anax, and he could not express how comforting it was to be supported. It was extraordinarily humbling, as it is when someone feels undeserving of another's unconditional love. But sharing love was as natural as

Mountain Preparation

breathing in Gylodon, and Anax inhaled its sweetness with humility.

***

When he spoke with Ini, she smiled warmly and hugged him, telling him how far he'd come, and how far he would go.

"Anax, I still remember you, stumbling through the forest, lost and preparing to give up. But you never did. And we will never give up on you. When you're in the mountain, you must work on your own healing as much as your mission for Tristis. Until you rebalance yourself, you will have difficulty finding all the pieces to help Tristis. You have come a long way, but there is still much work to be done. Remember, we must first heal ourselves—only then are we best equipped to heal our families and communities.

"Your heart is beautiful, but it has not yet cleansed itself of darkness. There is still anger, lack of self-love and a loss of trust that haunt you from your past. And while you keep these vulnerabilities well guarded, they still live deep within you. You will learn to embrace your shadows, but first you must recognize and acknowledge them. Get to know them, understand their purpose, their lessons. Send them love, and when they are ready, when you are ready, these pieces may be transformed and reintegrated back into your soul. *That*, dear Anax, *is healing*. Bringing light to the darkest displaced parts of self. *Becoming whole*.

"I know why you go on this journey. But do not forget that this is as much about you as it is about Tristis and Gylodon. Do the work, whatever it takes. Be kind to yourself. Learn to love yourself. Love yourself as we love you, as I love you."

Ini's final words brought a surge of emotion into his throat, mixed with a sense of unworthiness, and she smiled, offering a reassuring hug. Her hugs were warm and special, like healings unto themselves.

"Thank you for everything, Ini. For rescuing me, for helping me to heal, for inviting me into Gylodon."

"You are very welcome, my dear. You are meant to be here, among us. We are stronger for your presence."

Afterward, Anax made his way toward the door, again reluctant to leave. Stepping outside, Ini touched his arm, turning him around to face her. "Remember, Anax, with love we shatter the illusions of fear. With love *and* lucidity, we build new worlds."

He nodded solemnly, hoping he had strength enough to honor the path.

Ode to Tristis

***

Rising early, Anax planned to savor his last few moments in Gylodon before his departure. The sun was cresting over the eastern pines, slipping through the needles like water through gravel. Self-love, gentle and light, swaddled him, and he was grateful for life. Although sad to be leaving, he felt confident in his decision to go. That decisiveness carried comfort and acceptance.

He stepped lightly upon the flagstones as he made his way to the gardens, his bare feet collecting the morning dew and its coolness livening his step. His journey was beginning anew. *What better place to start than the location where I first saw her?* He recalled his vision of Tristis on that day—a ghostly beauty unrivaled in all of nature, at least to him. It really didn't matter that she failed to see him in the same light. Love was love, expressed many ways, and he was about to play his part in the grand stage play of life. At least that's how it felt to him on his final morning in Gylodon. It had been nearly eight months since his arrival and already he was departing. He breathed deeply.

Arriving at the gardens, he admired the droplets glistening upon the exotic flowers. For him, the plants never failed to inspire awe. Winter was nearly upon them and still they bloomed. He could only attribute it to Gylodonian magic; then again, maybe it was just nature's resilience, adapting and reinventing itself—that was magic too. Either way, they were gifts, and he inhaled their redolence, storing it away in the cabinets of memory, like a dried flower.

The village was quiet, with very few people afoot, and he welcomed the solitude. He found a stone, took a seat, and instantly went into a meditative state, directing his awareness to his family on the outside. He'd written more letters to them, which he left in Ini's care, should his physical body not survive the upcoming ordeal.

The guilt of separation, knowing how distraught his family must be, was his greatest challenge in Gylodon, and it was only softened by the realization that he was working toward a larger cause, in a world of new paradigms. Still, he felt the guilt coming on strong, squeezing him, so he transformed it into light, sending it back to them, as a gift of energy from his heart.

He took his time, silently speaking with each family member back home, expressing his love and gratitude for all that they had provided for him growing up. Parents truly were a marvel; no matter how much they frustrated their children, there was always a silent, unbreakable bond of love; no matter how deeply buried, pulled or stretched, the thread always endured. It stretched through the cosmos, an immutable part of the ancestral lineage of life. He saw this clearly since his entrance into Gylodon.

When he was done connecting with his family on the outside, he brought his attention to the mountain, continuing to build a relationship with it, as he'd done for the past few weeks; he pulled energy into the mountain, creating a sanctuary of power that he later could call upon should the need arise. For now, he shared the energy with the mountain. *We are all one. Family.* The mountain would become family, he told himself. The stone was cold and hard and dark at first, but with time, it had warmed and illuminated. There was still much to do, but the process was under way. He called upon the spirits who supported him throughout his time in Gylodon, a collection of guides, masters and angels; they would all be at his side. Already they'd empowered him so much, and he'd only needed to ask. There were no words for his gratitude, only a shared sense of love and unity.

When he completed his meditation, he roamed the gardens for some time, again recalling his first sighting of Tristis. And now, here he was, about to embark upon a journey of healing—for himself, Tristis, Gylodon and the planet. Sometimes it seemed utterly fantastical that such a thing was possible, since he had only recently lived in a state of hopelessness, bound by a cubicle, less than a year before. But then he'd dismiss the old patterns of his mind, enter the heart space, and know without doubt that it was true. Somehow it was true. It just was. He could do anything. *Trust*, he told himself. *Power*.

He departed the gardens, passing a wild raspberry bush, and approached a cluster of birch trees for which he'd developed a fondness. Upon inspection, he noticed new markings on one of the trees and felt protective of it, as if it had been injured. Peering closer, his eyes focused and the markings moved, then came alive, flying straight at his face, only to pause in mid-flight, hovering, as they danced for him—like flying acrobats. Two dragonflies, one orange like autumn, and the other an electric green, were mating in mid-air. They separated, only to continue the chase, all the while holding Anax's head as the center of their universe. He smiled, not the least bit surprised, and thanked the spirits for the omen. Dragonfly season, he knew, had long since ended. This display was a divine act—from another layer of reality.

When the dragonflies departed, he followed them into the woodlands and came upon an unusual cluster of wild flowers—reds, oranges, yellows, greens, blues, purples, as well as the three new colors, visible only in Gylodon. He spoke with the plants for some time, asking permission. Then he rose, selecting several of each and arranged them into a concentric, rainbow bouquet.

He made his way back to the village, now aware of the time for the first time in recent memory. He would be departing Gylodon within hours. *The village will be up by now*, he realized. As he entered the village periphery, he saw people gathering outside, and knew that they were gathering for him. Still he remained hidden on the outskirts, just watching. *All these beautiful people.* He looked down at the flowers. *We are all one. Each a piece of the whole. Even me.* He remained hidden, taking a back path.

There was one more errand to tend to before his departure. When he came upon her cottage, he peered inside the window, and to his relief she was gone. He looked around outside, just to make certain. *Gone.* Stepping out from behind a bush, he walked up to her front door. From his pocket, he pulled a sheet of hemp paper, which he placed on the doorstep. Next, he pulled a smooth river rock from his pocket, placing that on top of the paper. Before it was done, he placed the colorful flower bundle atop them both. He'd memorized what was written on the paper after he'd finished it; he would need to recall it while inside the mountain.

Ode to Tristis

Through soulful prisms of endless seeking
Shines lovesome light that's prone to streaking
Athwart the sky, betwixt the trees—
Blessing lands and noble seas.

And just below, upon her face,
Are scattered freckles that embrace
The lips below, before they splay
Like seeds on breeze that tend to stray.

She's coy and cautious, yet aware;
She's fierce and graceful, oh so rare.
Her heart's well tested—one that's pined,
A stalwart spirit, oh so kind.

A friend to creatures, large and small,
To those that pounce and those that crawl;
To those that fly and those that walk,
To those that slither, those that stalk.

Shy, alone and quick to flee,
With earthen eyes that yearn to see

ODE TO TRISTIS

Nature's creatures roaming free—
Where, alas, lies your heart's key?

Oh, dear Tristis, of the faerie,
Find your power, be not wary.
Though your path may twist and bend—
With snakelike grace, it does ascend.
And though it slithers through the dark,
Its shadows lighten by your spark.

To you I pledge to play my part—
To feed the light inside your heart.
To heal you whole, restore your faith
I'd leave this form—become a wraith.
I'd travel through black astral space
To light the path unto your grace.

To try, or die, it matters not.
Your light ignites what Earth forgot.
We are one, but you must lead;
By God's grace, you are the seed.

Afterward, he made his way back to his own cottage to gather his supplies for the journey, and to say goodbye to his new family. Of course, he wasn't really saying goodbye. *There are no goodbyes among brothers and sisters of Gylodon. We are all one, and nobody is ever left behind.*

A sense of peace settled upon him, and with it came a gentle northern breeze, carrying the voice of his ancestors, the voice of strength. It blew straight through him and whispered into his ear.

Destiny.

I am ready, he replied.

Departing

✱✱✱

His pack was relatively light—outfitted with his original gear, which he was grateful to have, along with some village additions, including a warm sweater, a blanket, writing implements, hemp slippers, a small pot, dried teas, powdered greens, several medicinal salves, nuts, seeds, salt and honeyed granola treats.

Gifts were generally not given, he was told, because he was destined to return. If his departure had been of a long-term, or permanent nature, then gifts would have been appropriate. To give them now, though, would suggest a failure to return. The exceptions were food and survival necessities, and that is how he'd acquired the few supplies he had.

He stumbled down toward the town center in a daze, and his sense of confidence morphed into a mixed bag of emotions. Doubt already had made a brief appearance, before passing, when he recalled Dan's warnings. *Will I be able to find this cave priestess—this Holder of Shadows?* His concern was frustrating; it was too soon—he'd not even left Gylodon's powerful vibration yet.

The rainbow flower arrangement in the town center had been replaced with more hardy greenery, accommodating the seasonal cycles, and he found the contrast stark, foreboding colder weather and the challenges ahead. *Will I be able to adapt like the plants? Adapt or die.* Briefly, he was maudlin, recalling his arrival. Then he laughed at the hilarity of it all. It had been such a peculiar shift of life circumstances, to arrive here now, in such unimaginable fashion. And yet, it was so.

A long line of villagers had assembled to say goodbye, and Anax took his place at the front of the reception. Behind him stood the elders and the Unschooler, wearing ceremonial garb; mostly they wore long, flowing white tunics, accented by beaded jewelry. But his teacher brandished one of the sacred Gylodonian rainbow necklaces, and Anax could feel its power, as if it offered him protection from the travails ahead. Others were attired in long garments of deep red and brown. Anax stood out, wearing a combination of outsider clothing, namely his shoes and pants, along with some more casual village garments. He didn't think they'd mind that he was underdressed for his own departure; nonetheless, he was deeply humbled by their more formal clothing, and found few words to express his emotions.

As the villagers approached one at a time—nearly three hundred of them—each hug became more difficult to endure as the end of things drew near, and the chasm in his heart widened. *It's not the end*, he reminded himself. *It's just for a while.* In truth, he had no idea how long he'd be gone. The idea was to remain until the healing work was complete; it was unclear how long that would take. Nonetheless, the departure was proving more emotionally depleting than he'd anticipated.

Dan hugged him for the better part of a minute, before placing his hand on his sternum and saying, "Warrior on the way." The words stung, a reminder of how much he was going to miss the camaraderie. Again, he reminded himself that separation was just an illusion, that all villagers were connected in a seamless web of energy, able to communicate at a distance. Still, it was not the same, and he already missed his friend. It made him think of his family on the outside, as well, and how far away they were—in every respect.

Metea, of whom he'd seen little, kissed him on the lips, startling him—and arousing him—and again he was reminded of that dreamlike day. Her lips awakened a current of energy along his spine, and it rose like a fire-breathing serpent, making its presence known. It was a reminder of the gift of power she had shared with him—and how it still lived within him. Now that he was going off into isolation, he wondered why he hadn't sought her again. But then he spotted Tristis in the line, and remembered.

His heart fluttered at her approach, bracing for a subtle rejection, but also hopeful for a hug. He was surprised at the openness with which she embraced him, and kissed him on the cheek.

"I have something for you," she said. Opening his palm, Tristis placed a small gemstone inside, before curling his fingers around it with delicacy. "It is to assist with astral projection and healing." He looked down at the stone and smiled, seeking words that did not come. And then she was gone, leaving a void, after which the remaining villagers became a blur of love, embraces and blessings. All the while he could focus only on the stone, burning a hole in his hand. Her simple gesture had given him something of profound importance. She had acknowledged him, and the gift provided a tangible connection to her, one that would burn warm when the nights were frigid. She probably had no idea of the effect it had on him, but that was of no consequence. He felt more prepared to face the mountain—and that was a blessing.

It took nearly three hours to receive everyone in the line; by then it was nearing lunchtime, and the town center had mostly cleared. Slowly, loneliness—a long-forgotten sentiment—crept in, carried by fear. He attempted to shake it off.

After final embraces, the elders departed, leaving only Dan. He was to escort Anax several miles down the path before returning.

***

The path was moist, heavy with earthen decay. Slimy stones glistened with green algae, daring intruders to mount them. Anax stepped softly, noting that the sun had moved beyond its zenith, and was barely visible behind hazy, ashen clouds. The forms mirrored his mood, somber and colorless.

The map, handcrafted by the Unschooler, rested comfortably in his pocket, providing a small measure of security against a slew of newfangled emotions. It seemed that with each mile down the trail his knees began to ache. *Can it be?* He cleared his mind, instead turning his attention to Dan. Dan returned his gaze with

DEPARTING

expressionless stoicism. Then he spoke.

"You're going to need to make camp within five hours or so, but you can make it a good distance on this terrain until then." He looked ahead, down the path; it was a natural clearing—an ancient riverbed, long since dried out—with no sign of man's presence. Along its edges, Anax noted the last remnants of wild spinach growing, defying autumn's chill. Insects had gutted the leaves, eating excessive portions, but there was still dense nutrition there, minerals that he would need. He estimated that the plants would be around for a few more weeks, and he hoped he would be as well—and then some.

He sighed, looking at Dan. "Yeah, nightfall will come sooner than I realize, I'm sure. It's gonna be strange camping in isolation again. *And cold*. My memories of it are not particularly fond. This time, however, nature is my ally." He forced a smile.

"Good," Dan responded. "Listen, Anax—above all things, stay safe—I know you can handle this. Find a way. You and I, and the other outsiders, are needed more than ever. I don't know if you are fully aware, but we—all outsiders, actually—are considered *mediators*. There continues to be talk among the elders of imminent planetary change, I have heard only bits, but it is to be a revolution of consciousness. All of us who arrived in Gylodon are at the center of this, somehow. I can only assume that by going to the mountain now, this is part of the process. But I will miss my friend."

Anax was jolted by the reference to *mediator*. "I have heard that term before, about Tristis, but not myself. It does make sense, though, if the *mediators* are bridges to the outside." He paused, pensive. "Thanks for the reminder, Bud. I'll be sure to keep myself alive for the greater good. Ha."

"Good," Dan said. "So...I have an idea. Maybe we can attempt to meet up in the astral realms, during the full moons. How does that sound?"

The suggestion was both intriguing and comforting; Anax paused as the implications sank in. "Yes, absolutely. Sounds perfect.

The Mystical Village That Rewired Reality

Let's shake on it." He extended his hand and clasped Dan's forearm; Dan returned the gesture, holding firm and looking his friend in the eye.

Anax continued, "So each full moon, we'll set the intention to astral project and meet. How about if I come to you, in Gylodon? It'll be a nice little retreat from the mountain for me."

Dan smiled and nodded. "Yes. Agreed."

"And you'd better be able to maintain lucidity. I'll not tolerate amateur hour in the astral realms."

Dan laughed and nodded assent. They walked on, silent, each feeling more content. After four miles, they came upon a natural stopping point, a rock outcropping with a smooth, flat surface. The stone was cool without sufficient sunlight to warm it, but they spread out nonetheless and had a snack of nuts and freshly picked apples.

"I think this is where we part, Brother." Dan said.

"Yeah."

After a bit, Dan rose, as did Anax. Without words, they clasped shoulders and embraced, and then Dan turned toward Gylodon without a backward glance. As he watched his friend depart, it occurred to Anax that had he known Dan in the outside world, with his extreme and dangerous lifestyle, he would have been the friend most likely to get him killed. He laughed at the irony; Dan also would have been the friend to whom he'd most willingly entrust his life.

He found himself wishing that he had his friend's vitality, fearlessness and sturdy disposition. But, alas, he was Anax, and that would have to do.

Suddenly, his knees ached, and he felt the onset of a headache. He drank water, mixed with a bit of mineral salt, and pulled out his map. The journey would take three days.

Departing

***

It was, most assuredly, the road less traveled. In a way, it felt a little bit like returning to hell, to the illusions that had once imprisoned him. Within an hour of Dan's departure, and a few more miles of distance between himself and Gylodon, old pains crept back into his bones and they frightened him.

The painful awakening alerted him to how much healing work still lay ahead. He understood now that the exercises he'd undergone had provided the tools he needed for self-healing, but he had not yet cleansed the ancient stresses, broken beliefs and destructive storylines of his life. The traumatic cellular memories were deeply embedded, and it became apparent to him that Gylodon, with its higher vibration, had been a crutch, taking away the physical pain so that he could master his mind and expand his heart-consciousness. But outside of the village, he was feeling like the master of nothing. Physical pain had a way of derailing even the most disciplined of minds.

He reminded himself that he'd only begun the process of rewiring his reality, and the mountain was the next step toward true *personal sovereignty*. There he could find freedom, and seize the opportunity to eviscerate his broken parts. Darkness and solitude, within cold stone, would be his classroom. It was an opportunity to purge the mental pollution buried within his personal *consciousness cloud*.

Still, the physical pain sickened him, taking him back to a darker time. *Is this what life is like outside of Gylodon?* It was a stark reminder of suffering in the outside world.

The sun had migrated toward the horizon and it was time to make camp. Already the temperature had dropped noticeably. He'd gathered some nettle and spinach along the way.

He strung his hammock between two gnarly trees, at a heightened elevation—nearly five feet off the ground. The setup was adjacent to a large boulder, which acted as a stepping-stone into the hammock.

Foraging for firewood next, he toted a medium-sized bushcraft knife. Knives were among the few implements permitted in Gylodon from the outside world; they were indispensable allies in the woodlands.

He split some small pieces of wood for the fire. Then he shaved thin wood strips from a branch that would readily ignite with a spark. The fire started with ease, and when the flames were blazing he set about soaking the wild greens and softening the stingers on the nettle, before sautéing it all with water in a small saucepan. He added salt for taste and topped it off with an assortment of nuts from his supply. *Dinner of the forest.* It was delicious; wild greens were energetically potent food sources that connected him to the land.

Leaning against the boulder, he pulled the map from his pocket while sipping his tea. It was a work of art. The lines were laid with elegance, but the scale, and detail, were lacking.

The Unschooler had instructed him to make any improvements upon the map that he felt were appropriate. The exercise made him feel like an explorer, and in truth, he was. Cartography was a bonus. He didn't want to ruin the original, so he set to making a copy, tracing the outlines upon a fine sheet of paper. When he'd completed the exercise, he made a few additions, with notes.

In his old life, he had a poor sense of direction, a failing that he'd used as a crutch for too long. Now he proceeded with confidence, adding several key markers to the map. When he was satisfied, he climbed into his hammock and made himself comfortable. From his pocket, he pulled Tristis' gift, and he rolled the stone between his fingers.

As he drifted into unconsciousness, he thought, *I wonder if it's a bad omen that Tristis gave me this gift. Does she think that I will not return?* The thought dissolved as the pull of sleep was more powerful than fear.

Anax's mountain journey; hemp canvas.

Valley of Below

✱✱✱

Dawn's animations eased his consciousness into a waking state, and for several minutes Anax lay there, considering the outside world. Millions of people would be rising soon, reporting to jobs that few of them enjoyed, climbing into their cars or boarding a train to a business of somebody else's creating. They would not forget their coffee. Their minds would be filled with concerns about bills, deadlines, health, relationships or being late. Many of them would space out for an hour or two after arriving, before getting started in any kind of productive capacity. After lunch, they would space out again for a while before summoning productivity. When the designated hours had passed, they would make the trek home, pick up the kids, cook dinner for the family and then sleep, resetting the cycle. Two or three weeks each year, if they were fortunate, they would deviate from this routine with a trip to somewhere new.

Anax felt grateful to be so far from *normalcy*. The story of normalcy needed to be rewritten. *Then again, I'm heading to a cave in the middle of nowhere, on the cusp of winter.* And again, the lines between lunacy and non-conformity blurred, and he understood the pull toward normalcy. *Of course, normalcy rarely allows for a free mind and an open heart.* Not in his old existence, in any case.

His mind returned to the place where all things begin, the present moment. Rousing himself, he stood and stirred the fire's ashes before preparing a light breakfast. After eating, he packed his gear mechanically, pausing only to relieve himself in the bushes, before heading out, searching for the next waypoint, map in hand.

The soil was gentle on his knees, but when he stepped on a rock, he was harshly reminded of the weak points in his bones, and his nerves were only too willing to admonish him about the journey ahead. Pushing the unpleasant implications from his mind, he searched for softer footing. Otherwise, the journey was pleasant.

He'd grown comfortable being out in the woodlands, and this was just an extension of the same, excluding Gylodon's *consciousness cloud*, of course. But Anax still carried Gylodon's power in his heart, and it helped. More than ever he understood that boundaries were illusions created by thought patterns—human choices, in essence—and he could write his own rules.

According to the map, the next milestone to reach before nightfall was labeled the *Valley of Below*, which kindled Anax's curiosity. Already he was probing the area with his mind to gather impressions, and he sensed a primal, earthy vibration. It was the energy of death and decay, in its most primordial sense, offering rebirth through a never-ending cycle of transformation. It cared not if one's body survived, but it did love and nurture the spirit. This realm was ruled by animals, he sensed, both contemporary and mythic, available to share wisdom with any human who ventured below. *The spirit of the bear lives here,* Anax recalled from a previous astral projection. His mood lifted at the prospect of exploring the area in more depth. He marveled at how much his fourth power had expanded, and he was grateful, remembering that despite the pain in his legs, he had a new set of tools at his disposal for transmuting adversity. He was no longer a slave to his mind or body. Gylodon had prepared him well.

He reached out to several birds along the way, brushing up against their consciousness, but they simply pointed him onward. Even with the pain, his legs were far more functional than when he'd first arrived at Gylodon. There had been some significant healing, after all. But he knew it was not complete.

By late afternoon he approached the waypoint, looking for a rock formation that marked his turn. He could not shake the feeling that the Unschooler had checked in on him, somehow, and his sense of community bloomed. Images of the Unschooler popped into his mind with subtle, yet overwhelming, force; he felt the teacher's familiar energy move right through him, pressing upon his awareness for some time. He relished the interaction—they had practiced such exercises—and he was profoundly grateful for the support.

The trail, lined with loose riverbed rocks, inclined steeply and the temperature was beginning to drop. He came upon a large patch of wild spinach, unspoiled by insects, and took nearly one quarter of the lot. Never had he taken more than one quarter of any bunch, out of respect and balance. He wondered if others, before him, had feasted on the same patch.

Pressing on, he saw that the trail curved around a swamped gully, and he took care not to let his shoes get wet. Although he'd not worn his original hiking shoes from the outside world during his entire stay in Gylodon—opting for woven hemp slippers, or bare feet, instead—he'd reclaimed his old footgear for the journey. He wondered at the wisdom of the decision. For now, though, they served him.

A large rock outcropping, nearly thirty feet tall and one hundred feet wide came into view. *The turn.* He took the footholds with escalating enthusiasm, now beset by a sense of urgency to establish camp before darkness arrived. Behind the rocks, the land sloped steeply and the trail challenged his knees; he grabbed a large stick to assist with the descent.

Down the hill was the *Valley of Below;* it was somewhat green, although it had begun to change. There were fewer trees and several interesting rock formations—some of which seemed to defy gravity. At the bottom on the western side were two natural springs, both of which fed into a small pool that bled into the earth before disappearing.

The spot for camping was obvious—two large trees growing inside the rock formations, which formed a natural barrier to the wind. He moved to set up camp.

The site's resonance was vastly different from that of the trail. Right away he sensed that several different energies had been anchored to the location, perhaps through ceremonies, or events. He felt a reverence for Gylodon's history and the intrepid few who had made this journey. They'd left large footprints—far broader than his—and it was humbling. He turned his attention to making a fire, which came easily, and then he strung up his hammock in the center of the formation. While the water boiled, he roamed the narrow and clearly defined valley.

Suddenly, chills shot up his spine, one after the other; he separated the experience from fear, noting that it was only the harmonics of the area interacting with his own energy fields. The valley was both life and death, he sensed, bringing new buds to bloom when those before had been consumed by nature. It was a repeating cycle of infinite arrangements; it was home to the animal spirits, forever mastering the present moment, in service to their evolving ecosystems. Mixed with it all was a raw, feminine essence—Earth—loving and deadly. It was the body and its cells. There was no distinction between the elements of the earth and the physical body once the cells dissolved. The energy of the cells, however, remained intact, even after physical dissolution, carrying the *codes of consciousness*, like batteries of wisdom. Here, in this place, Mother Earth and animalkind fed each other, timelessly intermingled in the cycle of transformation.

He returned to the fire with some more kindling, again considering how, and who, had intentionally planted the lessons at this site. Clearly, the energies had been anchored here for a reason, perhaps even as a lead-in to one's arrival at the mountain. It occurred to him that he should honor the tradition, and reinforce the energies of the site, along with making offerings to the animal spirits that lingered there.

After eating, he updated the map and prepared a second cup of tea. He was considering how he might leave an offering when an acute stress thrummed in his trunk—from his tailbone straight down his legs. It was a survival stress, but instead of clenching, he breathed deeply into his stomach and radiated the *five* into the surrounding brush. Something—or someone—was watching him. He became perfectly still, listening at another level, probing outward, and sure enough, his mind touched a life form; he ascertained with fair certainty that it was an animal. Casually tossing several more sticks into the fire, he rose and slowly turned. An exploding cellular memory produced an image of a bear, a residual effect, and he laughed silently at the prospect. He did not fear bears, or any animals, for that matter. Woodland creatures were family now.

Dusk arrived, bringing blackness, and the fire's light bounced off the brush, projecting erratic illusions of movement. Between the shadows, he sensed the presence again and wondered if perhaps it was a spirit, and not an animal, after all. But then two tiny orbs returned the fire's light—hallmark signs of an animal's eyes.

Surprised at how little concern he felt, he walked toward the brush. Something skittered to the right, averting his approach. Again, he radiated love, inviting the animal to join him around the fire. When no response came, he returned to his seat and just listened.

An hour later he saw it. It crept around the other side of the campfire, as if seeking warmth, defying expectations of how an animal should behave in the wild. *What are you?* He saw a silhouette with a tail as he continued projecting the *five*. It approached with caution, low to the ground, haunches spread, and tail down. It was afraid, but desperate for connection. Anax could scarcely believe it when a wolf—*actually, more of a dog*—tentatively approached, keeping the fire as a barrier between them. The dog had a wolfish appearance, but was too small to be one, probably not more than fifty pounds. It was rangy and missing some patches of hair on its hind legs. As best as he could see, it was black, with a white patch that stretched across its left eye down to its stomach. The hair along the ridgeline of its back was lighter in color, and stood erect, forming a wild mohawk.

The dog hunkered down on the far side of the flame, its shoulders tense, and Anax spoke gently, "Hello, friend. You are safe here—no need to fear anything. Enjoy the fire and stay warm." He paused, thinking, then slowly picked through his bag. "Let me see what I have to share with you."

He poured some water into a cup and placed it halfway between himself and the dog, which remained still, albeit rigid. Next, he pulled a piece of granola, lathered with honey and nut butter, and tossed it within a foot of the animal. The dog made no move to take it, instead keeping its gaze locked on Anax. It clearly did not want to leave the fire, despite its anxiety. Something had spooked it, perhaps, or maybe it was just cold. Still, it was odd to have a wild creature approach him in this manner, especially outside of Gylodon. Maybe he had changed more than he realized, and his energy fields had become more inviting to animals, even out here. It made sense, considering his training and exposure to Gylodon's *consciousness cloud*. Still, it was remarkable.

Anax returned to his seat on the opposite side of the blaze. He watched the animal slowly turn its attention to the food. It sniffed the surrounding air for several moments, reluctant to move, again glancing uncertainly at him, before shimmying along the ground toward the morsels. Sniffing suspiciously at the foreign scent, it clasped the food in its jowls, and quickly returned to its former position, locking its eyes on Anax.

"So, you're a girl, are you?" The dog ate the granola in a single swallow and hardened her stare.

"Well, it will be nice to have some company around here. Where did you come from, anyway? I can see that you're wild—and yet, your instincts seem almost domesticated. You're an oddity, Kiddo. Then again, I probably am too, eh?"

Two soulful eyes, betraying humanlike sentiments stared back, rattling him. He sensed raw emotion emanating from her.

"What's your name? I think we need something a bit more fitting than *Kiddo*." He closed his eyes and opened his mind to the *four* and the name came in a flash. *Nika*. "Ahh, so you're called Nika? I like it." Again, he examined her from afar and noted that her mohawk extended all the way up to the top of her head, and she wore it like a war helmet. It did not, however, match her scraggly body.

"You don't look so tough to me. Although I suppose you could be a scrapper." He smiled, satisfied with the name.

"Nika it is. Well, Miss Nika, here is one more snack before sleep." He tossed another piece of granola. But instead of moving toward the food, her spirit spilled forth anguish, fresh and bloody, and he felt her pain, heavy upon his sternum. Fire that should have been in her eyes had been dampened by grief—the sort that only true innocence can carry.

"You keep staring at me like that and I'm bound to cry. What happened to you, Nika?"

Reluctantly, he moved to his hammock. It felt good to be floating in the air, off his feet; but the warmth he felt came not from his blanket, but rather the prospect of a new friendship. He wondered what brought her to him, and hoped she'd still be around come morning. As he drifted to sleep, he reached out to her—using the *four* and *five*—and for a moment she let him in.

And then he wept for her—and her loss—before sleep overwhelmed him.

***

As Anax's dreams bounced between mindlessness and lucidity, a small, dark woman approached him; thin of bone and youthful in appearance, the woman had inhuman eyes that contrasted with an otherwise normal figure. He stood there, becoming clearer—awake in the dream—and she strode with increasing aggression, casting cataclysmic, black eyes upon him. Paralyzed, he felt fear and hopelessness permeating his awareness with each step she took, and he attempted to speak, but no words came. The woman lunged like a cat, pressing her face within an inch of his own, opening jaws that revealed the fangs of a snake, as her head split wide along the jawline. All he could hear was a hissing throughout his entirety, loud and sharp, and he tried to scream, but instead he woke. It took him a full minute to gather his bearings, certain that he was still hearing the hiss. But the sounds of the forest had commenced with the sun's ascent, and they grew louder, gradually muting the snake's call, which screamed from the depths of his slipping consciousness. He lay there, processing the nightmare, trying to calm himself.

Still dizzy, he glanced around the campfire from his hammock, grounding himself. His eyes searched for Nika, but there was no sign of her. The food he'd left was gone.

Animal Companion

***

Walking alone—in wild territory far removed from humanity's footprint—livens the spirit and fires the blood. Anax was connected to nature's hum, a web of death and life, and it unsheathed his vulnerability, exposing him to its peril, while sharpening his awareness of the beauty around him. Beauty could be found, he knew, by looking just beyond danger's demarcation line. Dan had taught him that. Crossing that line had been central to Dan's lifestyle before Gylodon. *And even in Gylodon.*

Anax smiled. The day was warmer than the last as he stumbled from his hammock, half awake, circling to the far side of the ashes. Nika's tracks disappeared into the woods on his right, he noted, as he stirred the coals and prepared his tea.

Taking down his hammock as the water heated, Anax scanned the trees for any sign of the dog, but there was little movement. Likewise, his fourth power revealed nothing in the near vicinity. Disappointed, but not disheartened, he pulled the map from his pocket to confirm the next waypoints and camp destination.

He hoped to arrive at a location labeled *Middle Ground* by nightfall. Needing to make haste to reach the site by dusk, he gathered his gear quickly and headed out on the path, noting the sun's position as reference.

A large part of his awareness kept watch for Nika as he attempted to shape-shift his instincts into that of an animal. It was a game, of sorts, where he sought to assume the vibration of a dog, observing how his thoughts, feelings and awareness transformed during the process; it created a primal sharpening of the senses, making him the hunter. At one juncture, he was pulled off the path by a nagging need that would not cease. At the turn, his body weakened, like a weight upon his soul, but he pressed on, following his instincts. As was often the case, he was surprised when his instincts proved correct; he was also deeply disappointed.

The morning's tea curdled in his stomach when he stumbled upon Nika's shredded body. Wolves had acted out of sport, barely taking any meat, and the body was already firm. Anax squatted, sorrow swelling in his chest, as he reached to touch the animal. She was ice cold. The spirit was gone; he'd seen the spirit depart before—as a swirl of light that died in the eyes, vacating a useless body. The image of mangled flesh was so far removed from the perfection of Gylodon that it left him stunned. But that was nature, he knew—equal parts exquisite and deadly.

As he delicately brushed her mohawk, admiring its wild irregularity, a passing confusion beset him. He reoriented himself to ensure that he wasn't hallucinating. The white patch, previously over her left eye, rested roundly upon her right. Looking more closely, he moved around the dog's body, allowing hope, for just a moment, to rise. *Oh my God...it's not Nika. It's not even female*, he realized, his relief profound. *A near replica of her—but not Nika.* Expelling a sigh, he loosened the tension in his chest, but before the breath had departed, an empathic loneliness, deep and unsettling, infiltrated the void; the energy emanated from nearby. Turning slowly, he spotted Nika watching from the underbrush, just five feet away. Immediately, he realized that she'd been sitting with her companion's body before he'd intruded. Her bearing displayed no ferocity, only defeat. She should have fled at the sight of him, but the pull to her canine companion was too strong.

"Nika. I'm so sorry." It was all he could say. Her eyes were even more sunken than the night before. She'd lost her tribe, the last of her pack. *Her twin and leader—destroyed.* Anax felt as if she was already conceding her own death, so heavy was the despair she carried. In a way, she reminded him of himself, not so long ago. He sighed, pity carved into the lines of his brow. "You shall rise again, Little One. This is not the end of your story."

He considered how to proceed. She would not leave the body if it were left there, he knew, so he took to digging a hole, hoping it was the proper course. He used a stick and flat stone to pry the earth, which reached a depth of one and one-half feet before he hit roots. *It will have to do.* Looking to Nika, he asked permission before placing her brother's body into the hole. Then he gave a short invocation:

May your spirit transition with ease and grace, releasing any contracts and energetic attachments that do not serve the highest good. May love travel with you, as the unbreakable bond that unites a pack, even in death.

Although Anax had never been religious, only spiritual, he called upon St. Francis, the keeper of animals, to accompany the dog's spirit into the rainbow, and to assist with the release. When it was done, only love would remain. He asked St. Francis to heal Nika's heart, as well, so that she might let go, and find hope again.

As a beam, he felt the fifth power pass straight through the top of his head, through a vortex into his back, filling his chest and then traveling farther down, through his root into the earth. It came on like a warm blanket, a wrapping of God.

Gracefully, he covered the body with soil, to the top; then he collected round stones to protect the site, before topping it with a layer of pine sprigs. He hoped that Nika would understand. Animals were better suited to letting go than humans, he knew. Acceptance came sooner when they saw and smelled the deceased; then they could accept their passage as a natural course of existence, rather than forever seeking or awaiting their missing companion. But the wounds were still fresh, and Nika looked broken.

Nonetheless, Anax was grateful that Nika had seen her sibling's body. A direct meeting with death would eventually help her to accept, and let go, so that she might return to the present moment—where dogs belonged.

His thoughts carried to his own family and he sent them love. Then he thought of Dan, Ini and Tristis. He still had the people he loved, and Gylodon; few were so blessed.

***

He would not make it to *Middle Ground* before dusk, given the events, so he resolved to spend the night at the site, even with the risk of wolves in the area. While building a robust fire, he spoke soothingly to Nika, doing everything in his power to provide her with a measure of safety and peace. She would not accept any food until late into the night, but she'd come closer and closer—a sign of trust—until finally she ate. The victory had evoked laughter, even as his supplies dwindled.

He hoped that she might travel with him. More time to bond would be helpful, but as much as he wanted to linger, an unwavering sense of urgency called him to the mountain, and he knew that there was no time to waste. *Still, a companion would be most welcome.*

In Gylodon, the notion of community had been redefined—it had become a mystical utopia of ubiquitous acceptance, in all regards, from fellow humans to animals to plants. His soul had merged with that community, and he felt its absence like a phantom limb. When he reflected upon his recent experiences, Dan was always there, learning with him, sharing in an indescribable sense of fulfillment. That sort of fraternity—bonding as two people of shared heritage in a foreign land, amid challenge and achievement—was like a drug. Anax craved it and knew that he would do everything in his power to return to it.

Shifting in his hammock, he drifted into unconsciousness as Nika rested just outside the hammock's breadth, tuckered out and curled into a ball, almost within reach.

***

He rose just after sunrise and scanned the perimeter. The morning was moist, leaving a layer of liquid beads atop the foliage. On first pass, he searched for Nika but saw nothing, and a dank loneliness settled upon him. But then, farther to the left, a shadow moved and she was there, alert and on her haunches, studying him, from the camouflage of a tree. He smiled at the disheveled appearance of her mohawk; it made her appear wilder than any dog that he'd ever seen, and he suspected that she was.

He packed, and then re-checked the map before setting out.

"C'mon, Girl. Let's go." Nika stared, dumbfounded, cocking her head as the alien command sailed by, echoing into the forest's abyss. He sighed, recognizing the dilemma. So, he tossed her one last piece of granola and walked toward the path without her. She would either follow or not. *Follow me, Girl,* he pleaded silently.

After ten minutes on the trail and no sign of her, he found the solitude intolerable; it was not loneliness for himself that he felt, but for her. *How can I leave her?* It occurred to him that her ability to hunt and acquire food was probably reduced without her pack mate. She wasn't a wolf, but a dog. Despite being born in the wild, her heritage was that of a domesticated animal, and she likely lacked the instincts to survive on her own. Still he pressed on, doubt growing with each step, whistling now and again, as he'd done at the campsite, hoping she'd hear. Three times he called out, eliciting only confused glances from several birds.

His mind drifted to the mountain and slammed into stone, icy and unrelenting. *Still so much ahead.* He'd not even arrived at his destination, which might kill him yet, and already his legs ached with the pain of loss. The dog's loss, he realized, was his own. It was apparent to him that his empathic sensitivities had expanded multifold in Gylodon; this was a blessing and a curse. On the one hand, he could feel and process energies in any location—reading them like a book; on the flip side, being so sensitive was overwhelming at times, making him vulnerable to his environment. Out here, he was inextricably linked to the web of life, no better or worse, part of the same local *consciousness cloud.* Within that cloud loomed earth's harmony—gritty and nurturing, playful and melancholy. He too lived in that cloud, his own being intermingling with it, sculpting and blending, leaving its mark.

His mind searched for Nika, and he sensed her, far off, and on the move. *Good Girl.*

Middle Ground

***

He arrived at the campsite well before dusk and assessed the terrain. *Middle Ground* was plain and unassuming, mostly flat ground with a variety of trees, including some birch. The site lacked proper protection from the elements, and an unforgiving breeze swept straight through, prompting Anax to add another layer of clothing. The presence of the birch trees was comforting; like stalwart, old friends, they were a good omen, and perhaps a portal into the dream realms. He strung his hammock between them as he'd done many times before.

With the fire crackling and tea in hand, Anax cruised the site, tuning in to the fourth power. The energies were strangely familiar, a mixed bag of human and natural rhythms. For an instant, behind him, he sensed a spirit—*an ancestor, perhaps*—and he turned just as the hackles on his neck stood erect. The experience was brief, as the cold air disrupted his concentration, and he pulled his sweater tighter to him.

As he recalibrated to the site's pulse, tuning in to the invisible, it occurred to him that the area was a mirror of Earth, overlapping energetically and physically, but much less dense. In fact, this dimension was familiar; he'd been here before, through many of his astral projections. Known as the *reflection realm*, it was an easy access point for astral travel because it was so closely aligned with the earth's plane. There were distinctions, of course, like clouds of dark matter, or concentrated thought forms that hovered around the otherwise normal earthen structures. But mostly, it was the same. Within this realm, a variety of nature spirits and human spirits resided—mirroring earth's makeup of animals, plants and humans.

A wolf howled in the distance, breaking Anax's flow, and his mind turned to Nika. *Come to me, Nika. Find my scent. I have warmth—*

and a bit more granola. Again, he radiated the fifth power toward her, and like a laser, he pulled the energy in through the top of his head and pressed it out through his heart-center, synchronizing it with his breath. *She felt that one,* he knew, and smiled. *Come, Nika.*

Darkness arrived with no sign of the wild dog, accompanied by a more aggressive breeze, cutting his sweater with its bitter blade and forcing him closer to the flames. So, he added wood to the fire, and left out some water for the dog.

Shortly after climbing into his hammock, Anax fell into unconsciousness. At some point during the evening his mind awakened, just as his body slept. He immediately transitioned into a vivid dream, one that was both dark and disconcerting—but not without hope.

What is this world?

He was teleported to the outside world—to an undesignated time in the future, he sensed—as he became the observer of another reality. The information poured in to him, both as a witness and an indescribable knowing.

A nameless man, with manicured nails, perfect white hair and an ash gray suit sat down at a table, joining more than forty wealthy industrialists and politicians, to discuss their agenda. Mostly they were white-collared men, along with a handful of women, who controlled the major industries and injected money into governments through banks, bribery and coercion. They routinely merged their corporate agendas with governmental interests across the planet, all in the name of power and control. Anax sensed that they had robbed humanity of many gifts, including low-cost energy solutions, frequency medicines, affordable healthcare and education. They preferred to keep the populace unaware and dependent upon their broken systems. Sadly, they felt justified in their clandestine power games; some even believed that they served the higher good. In truth, they were delusional and out of touch—empty shells of humanity who made sport of other people's suffering.

A vision of a chessboard flashed before him, a symbolic

representation of their strategic plans. He sensed that a new set of international trade agreements would expand their influence over humanity, or so they believed.

Despite this, Anax could not shake the feeling that it was all quite laughable, that none of it mattered; all of life was just a big stage play, anyway.

And yet, it does matter, he realized.

These people were creating an invisible prison of suffering for too many humans, across too many cultures, and it was not necessary. They were consciously choosing to structure human existence in this manner, supplanting human rights for corporate interests. And it was a game to them.

We should move away from suffering, not toward it. He knew that humankind had the resources to eradicate poverty, global warming, animal abuse and many diseases—all causes of suffering. The solutions existed. And yet, putting an end to the needless suffering was not a priority. Only the illusions cast upon humanity made it appear a priority; but to the elite industrialists, humanity's suffering was preferable. Their personal interests were aligned with a caste system—one that permitted poverty and sickness. It fed their power structures and financed their ventures. So, they institutionalized humanity's suffering through their choices.

Anax was beset by an overwhelming sense of service to Gylodon—and to life. *Warriors of light seek the dissolution of suffering, always moving toward a high-vibration consciousness!* He tried to scream it, but no voice came.

Instead, he was transported to a new cityscape, where water had grown scarcer due to erratic climate shifts, as the wealth gap had widened, dissolving the middle class into oblivion. As the elites moved to gain control over water resources, the planetary caste system ripped apart, creating the obscenely wealthy, and everyone else. Governments and corporations merged, blurring lines like never before—and the people paid the price.

However, when the elites had denied water as a human right,

they made a drastic error. Humanity had crossed a threshold from which it would not return. Too many minds had been freed and too many hearts had been opened. The invisible prison bars could now be seen, revealing long-held beliefs to be false illusions that collapsed under the weight of expanded consciousness.

Humanity decided to stop playing by the rules—and the false choices—they'd been given, and instead rewrote them. The movement was young, barely a seed, but the shift in consciousness was well under way.

Anax's perspective then shifted to several townships, where small communities had banded together relying upon local resources in private sharing models. They practiced earth stewardship, planting trees and gardens, and drastically cut animal agriculture. Leveraging innovative permaculture techniques, hydroponics and sprouting methodologies, they perfected local, small-scale food production. Perhaps most important, though, was the creation of new unions—peaceful, standing armies—that spanned entire townships. Whenever a commercial-governmental entity sought to unseat their solutions—voted upon by fair democratic process through the Internet—they called upon the entire union to stand in the way. The elites were vastly outnumbered in this respect. The rules had been rewritten, and were predicated upon fair majority rule, through peaceful process. They called it *community progressivism*.

There was a movement to ban television news, or to simply turn off TVs for extended periods of time, to fast from the endless mental conditioning. Many people volunteered, seeking freedom of thought, and new societal plans were hatched from rediscovered creativity, latent for too long, as the people reclaimed *personal sovereignty* and sculpted new realities.

In one town, people worked collectively on various tasks, and each person chose explicit activities that were aligned with their personal gifts. *Amazing! The tasking is self-assigned and based upon individual skill sets, personal fulfillment and creativity!* It was a revelation of the inherent power—raw, potential energy—in every single human being.

And then, as if struck by a hammer, Anax was stunned to observe Tristis, clad in modern clothing, walking among the crowds. Waves radiated from her body, enveloping the people, rebalancing their fields. Her presence awakened minds, inspired creativity and aligned hearts in a spirit of service—to humans and animals alike. Anax felt joy, ebullient and fierce, as her energy penetrated his own; it was much like being back in Gylodon, intertwined with its healing *consciousness cloud.*

The bustling sounds of the town began to blend with flowing water. *What is that water sound? It's bubbling.* It grew louder, overshadowing the scene's bustle, until it filled his ears like a rabid slurping that thrust him back into a waking state, just as the sun crested the horizon. His brain was paralyzed by the overload, as he opened his eyes, forcing inhalation. And just beyond the embers, on the far side of the fire's debris, loomed Nika, voraciously slurping the water he'd left out.

For a full minute, he lay there, observing her in the dawn's red light. Her fur was wirier than he'd realized, and she was malnourished. The missing patches of hair on her haunches were not so bad after all, but still he considered applying the sulfur salve he'd packed at the last minute. *Perhaps that might help.*

She finished drinking, now aware of being watched, and lifted her head, returning his gaze with uncertainty.

"Hello, Nika. It's very good to see you."

For several more minutes, without rising from his hammock, he spoke to her in calming tones before singing three Gylodonian songs that had been created for soothing and connecting with animals. The tones were of critical importance and Anax did his best to replicate what he'd been taught. Afterward, he swung his feet around, slowly touching the earth and rising. She tensed, but made no move to flee.

He retrieved his bag and rummaged around inside, keeping his eyes on the dog. When he located one of the pieces of granola, he pulled it out, offering it by hand, as he squatted to Nika's eye level.

She made no move to take it, so he tossed it halfway between them.

It took a minute of consideration, but then she timidly trotted to the food and ate it without retreating. It was the closest he'd been to her. Anax's excitement surged, but he quickly shifted back to equanimity and calmness as he reached for another piece, again tossing it halfway between them. Again, she approached and took the food, this time retreating only a foot. He smiled broadly and commenced speaking to her in soothing tones.

"You and I are going to be great friends, Girl. Trust me." She cocked her head, curious, and more confident.

Again, he offered food from his hand, and she approached, pulling back three times after coming within a foot of him. So, he altered his strategy, turning his eyes away from her, head bowed, feigning submission, as he extended his hand. And then he felt the tickle of a gentle mouth upon his palm and the treat was gone. This time he allowed his excitement to surge.

He'd won a basic level of trust with her, and it had happened faster than he could ever have imagined in his old life. It was the lessons from the *Book of Gylodon* that had expedited his bonding with this creature, and for that he was grateful. Humbled, he recalled that all of life was energy—a molecular playground of thoughts, feelings, frequencies, electromagnetism, water, fire, air and earth—molded into consciousness. Indeed, all things were possible.

HIGHLAND

***

When Nika finally retreated to the far side of the fire to clean her paws, Anax brewed some tea and began the process of breaking down camp. Once things were in order, he sat down on the ground and pulled the map from his pocket. Delicately unfolding it, he admired the fine paper. He'd always had a fondness for maps—especially old ones—as if each chart held forgotten secrets leading to long-abandoned treasures. The hand-drawn kinds were the most personal, and exquisite, crafted through the eyes of a single explorer daring to traverse ancient jungles or tread some far-off ice field. Such maps held power, and were historical accounts of a unique journey, marking the fulfillment of an uncommon destiny.

In a way, Anax thought, he was on his own treasure expedition, and the treasure was nothing less than uncovering his true self, doing his part to heal and find power, so that he might assist Tristis and Gylodon. Looking down at the map, he noted that he'd failed to update it the night before, and he felt a pang of guilt. Fortunately, most of the relevant markings had been inputted along the trail, and he was content.

He chewed some seeds while studying the next waypoints. The final destination was labeled *Highland*. That was where the map ended. The mountain was not listed anywhere—by design, he'd been told. "Just get to Highland and you'll find the way," the Unschooler had said. Anax calculated the distance using a piece of thread along the track, then compared it to his previous transits, accounting for a wide range of error.

Highland. It will take about eight hours of steady hiking to get there, he estimated.

"You up for a little trip, Wild One?" Nika, with one ear folded inside out, ceased her grooming and again cocked her head, much to Anax's amusement. "You're quite the lady, aren't you?"

They set out after a shared breakfast, during which Anax touched her muzzle. She had not flinched. On the trail, she traveled alongside him, ranging out to twenty or thirty feet on his right or left flank. Occasionally, she charged ahead; and sometimes, when the terrain was more challenging or the way unclear, she followed, close on his heels.

His departure from Gylodon left a vast void; only now, back in an individualist mindset—one of isolation and survival—were its implications fully realized. But the universe had responded with kindness by uniting him with a dog. The scruffy companion brightened his day; no longer did solitude hover, pressing on him. Instead, her presence invited laughter, diverting attention from the aching in his limbs. Out here, she was the heart of his community.

By mid-afternoon the trail had grown rockier, forcing Nika to fall behind, trotting tentatively across the loose terrain. Anax did not fare much better. Twice they stopped for water, as the higher altitude took its toll along a slow and perpetual incline. Eventually it crested into a flat plateau, dotted with sporadic patches of grass and few trees. On the far side, it dipped, leading into a sunken gulley that was fed by a crystal-clear spring. Anax noticed that the afternoon light played on the land in unnatural ways, as if bending and casting shadows that should not exist. He squinted, trying to decipher the landscape's oddities. Something was not right.

While scanning the horizon, his foot snagged a root and he stumbled forward, raising his arms to catch himself, but his hand scraped against something in mid-air, something that should not be there, and before he could comprehend it, his shoulder slammed into an unforgiving surface, causing him to twist, and he tried to counterbalance, but it was too late as his nose collided with a wall of stone, inciting a rush of blood that momentarily blinded him. *What the...*

He shook his head to clear the shock. Stunned by the spontaneous appearance of a sheer rock face—one that was invisible moments before and was now nearly on top of him, he gawked at its proximity. So close was he to the wall—which disappeared into luminous, peculiar clouds—that he tasted its gravel in his mouth. Clasping his nose, he stepped back and attempted to rationalize the illusion; it had appeared from nowhere. As he studied it, waves of energy, similar to the gardens of Gylodon, permeated its walls, seeping in and out, flashing and bleeding color like oil; they spun and vanished, only to return, repeating the cycle.

Nika drank heartily from the spring, oblivious of the surroundings.

My God. "Looks like we've arrived, Nika."

As with his experiences in Gylodon, the wonder of existence was upon him, and reality was bending at its seams.

***

After restocking their water supplies, Anax walked the perimeter, repeatedly glancing skyward, entranced by the swirling clouds. Nika's nose touched his calf, and he, surprised by her closeness, looked down to find her tail tucked between her legs.

"You spooked, Girl? What is it?" She pressed a little closer, and he put himself on heightened alert, trusting her instincts, while searching for an access point. Resting for a moment, he leaned against the mountain, placing his hand on a stone slab. Almost instantly he started to feel ill, as if anger and sadness and confusion wrapped themselves around him, draining his life-force like thirsty leaches or hungry ticks. Recoiling from the stone, he stepped backward, breathing deeply, and recalled the Unschooler's warnings about the mountain spirits. "*They can latch on to you,*" he'd said.

Not on my watch, Anax thought. He called upon Gylodon's power, and he felt it encase him, like armor built for a *warrior of light,* and he knew that he was protected.

After another fifteen minutes of walking he came upon a break in the rock, jagged and irregular, and he reached into his bag for a flashlight. The entrance narrowed at the top, blocking light, while bending awkwardly into the shadows on ground level. Anax's stomach twisted at the prospect of climbing into the tight space, but still he touched base with his intuition for guidance, and the answer came in a flash—*Yes, this is the entrance.* "Shoot. I guess we're going in, Girl."

Briefly, he considered changing the plan and camping on the plateau—the sunlight was already fading—but he pushed forward, trusting his inner voice. The flashlight gave him confidence, and as he rounded the third curve, turning sideways to fit, he spotted light on the other side. Nika followed him without hesitation, reluctant to be left behind.

It occurred to him what a challenge it might have been had he needed to turn around with Nika in the narrow space, but fate had favored him. Having called upon Gylodon's power to shield them both from any low-vibration energies residing in the stone, he felt reassured, and when he was forced to touch the rocky surface, the negative emotions were more subdued.

At the far end of the cavern, the light grew brighter, and after thirty feet, and crawling at one point, they emerged into sunlight on the far side. The sandy trail widened before narrowing, as they climbed a path uphill that was surrounded by smooth gray rock faces on both sides.

They had two hours before darkness, he estimated, and he chastised himself for not grabbing some firewood on the way in. "We'll make do, Girl." They climbed steadily, and the air thinned just as the walls became more imposing. The narrow corridors induced solitude, cutting off any sense of the outside, as man and dog navigated through the stony labyrinth.

Anax experienced déjà vu, as if he'd been here before, and with it came a resurgence of humor, and he laughed at life's absurdities. Again, he recalled life in an office cubicle, and its peculiar metamorphosis into Gylodon, and now a remote, magical mountain pass. As if his distance from humanity wasn't sufficient, the steep enclosures and foreboding walls ensured total isolation.

"Bet you haven't seen terrain like this before." Nika wobbled on a loose rock before regaining balance, and he offered her one of the last remaining pieces of granola. She took it from his hand without hesitation. "You're committed, Girl. I'll give you that." There was probably no going back for her, either, he realized; he hoped that she'd be able to navigate back to the entrance if the need arose.

Finally, they arrived at a large overhang that would serve as a shelter. It protruded precariously, out to fifteen feet, but appeared to be stable. Anax felt palpable relief at the lucky break, and wondered if others had camped here before. He did not have the energy to find out. With exhaustion racking his body, he found himself more unbalanced and achy than he could recall since before Gylodon. "I hope you're faring better than I am, Nika." She looked tired as well, and he offered her water and some crumbs.

There were no good hang points for his hammock, so he set up on the ground. By a twist of fortune, he found a dead bush nearby and harvested the wood for a small cook fire.

"Look what I found, Nika. Yup, that's right—*fire time.*" He dismantled the dead plant into small, functional pieces and then gathered stones to throw in the fire, knowing that they would hold heat even as the flames died out. It was not a moment too soon, as the sun fell below the walls, and darkness intruded. The fire cast a subtle glow upon the walls, creating comforting ambient light.

He added green powder to his tea, for additional minerals and vitamins, and took a cold supper from his meager supplies. "Nuts and apples, it is." He'd stocked up on fruit when he and Dan had discovered an apple tree along the trail a few days earlier. It had been a lucky break. He paused, looking at Nika. "You're good company, Girl. I like our conversations." He considered how he might feed her, and himself, in this rugged environment; the prospects of food were bleak. *We will deal with those challenges soon enough. For now, we sleep.* But the question gnawed on him, and he could not shake a sense of responsibility to the dog—a creature that had unwittingly followed him all this way, on a quest of unknown peril. She was his responsibility now.

The fire turned to embers, and he rolled over, attempting to sleep. Nika curled up beside him, a body length away.

***

He woke just before dawn to semi-darkness. Something stirred, and his stomach clenched; he listened, eyes closed. When the sound abated, he slowly scanned the site and saw no sign of Nika.

Sitting up, his eyes adjusted to dawn's dwindling darkness, and for a moment he thought he was dreaming. Rubbing his eyes, he refocused, but still she was there, becoming clearer. A small-framed woman, a silhouette just seconds before, stood not more than a dozen steps from him. He froze, observing her. Her eyes moved like morning mist—as morphing smoke brushing lenses of obsidian glass. She was the woman from his dream.

Calming his heartbeat, he breathed deeply, looking closer. The air was crisp and the woman wore no shoes. She wore barely anything at all, he noted, only a cloak that draped her body like a ghostly garb from a bygone era. Her body was petite, almost fragile in appearance, but the energy she exuded was like… He tried to place it. *A mountain.*

When she said nothing, he slowly rose to his feet, again scanning for Nika, feeling incomplete without her.

"She'll not save you, but she will assist you," the woman said.

"*What?*"

"*The dog.* She will eat your shadows and transform them into light."

Anax shifted uncomfortably under her gaze, confused, and again he searched for Nika.

"She hides in the boulders," she said, nodding to the rock formation fifty yards behind him. As he turned to look, the woman inhaled deeply before exhaling tones that rattled the rock beneath his feet and traveled up through his bones, like an all-powerful resonance permeating his being. *A human tuning fork,* he thought, shaky, as he felt things shifting inside of him. The sound subsided and she began whispering into the air indecipherably, inciting a new sequence of vibrations, like a language unto itself. All he could discern was that the language—both in its inflection and tone—was unlike anything he'd ever encountered. It was a full-body sensory experience. This went on for several minutes, as if she was having a conversation with an unseen spirit, or the mountain itself, and he wondered if perhaps she'd been alone for too long. Her snakelike eyes pierced him, as if reading his thoughts, and she exhaled one final tone that reverberated into the surrounding stone, immediately putting him at ease. It was as if he'd just walked back into Gylodon. All tension and pain dissipated as his energy fields expanded, buoyed by some unseen power. *Did she just recalibrate the consciousness cloud here? How...*

He heard Nika trot up behind him and turned to greet her, but she passed right by, walking straight to the woman. Kneeling to the dog's level, the woman gestured in a manner that implied respect, or even deference, while reengaging in her whispers. Nika nuzzled her leg, as if she were a long-time companion, while the woman brushed her lightly between the eyes with her thumb.

Anax stared, dumbfounded, but open to any reality at this point. After a prolonged silence, the woman noticed the confused look upon his face and spoke, "We took her fear and dissolved her illusions. Temporarily, of course."

"We?"

She paused, unclear about his confusion. "Myself and the mountain, of course. I took them and dissolved them, and the mountain ate the leftover."

Right. "Yes, I see that," Anax said unconvincingly.

She returned her attention to Nika, as if instructing her, and Anax shivered in the brisk morning air, again mystified by the woman's bare feet and minimal clothing. The entire scene was disorienting.

After a few minutes, she said, "She promises to do the same for you. The contract is set."

"*Contract?*" Anax was thoroughly confused.

"Yes, *the contract*—between you and Nika. Why else do you think she's here? Did you think that you rescued her? In a way, you did, I suppose, but it is she who is here to rescue you."

"Oh?" He felt like a child. The fact that the woman had discerned Nika's name was unsettling, but also strangely gratifying; it confirmed that he too had uncovered the dog's true name through intuition. In a way, it gave him confidence.

In a sudden shift, the woman's expression hardened and her eyes flashed black, like a lunar eclipse heralding darkness, and the aches returned to Anax's body in a rush, like an avalanche of agony. Fear flashed across his face as he wobbled uncertainly, struggling to maintain balance, and he turned toward the woman, feeling betrayed.

"From now on, you will need to transmute your own pain," she said, "but Nika has agreed to help you. That is the contract."

Breathing deeply, Anax attempted to dispel his body's tension. He couldn't speak. The sudden shift back to the mountain's *consciousness cloud*—and its darker energies—was jarring, and his physical body struggled to adjust. The woman studied him with an air of disapproval.

"All dogs are *transmuters*, like myself," she said. "They live in service to humanity by absorbing our negativity and transforming it. Likewise, when you give them love, they will mirror and amplify it."

Anax held eye contact as the woman rose, walking toward him.

"When dogs absorb our dark energy through our hands—from our stroking—we often feel our tension relieved. This tension does not disappear. It travels to the dog, where it is transformed and re-released. With each wag of the tail they both clean and move energy outward, as a wave, cleansing our environments. In this manner, they are constantly cleaning our local *consciousness cloud*, on our behalf, by removing pollution and turning it into selfless love. We refer to dogs as *shadow-eaters* because they agree to consume—and cleanse—the darker parts of our personality so that we may find relief. Humans are in their debt."

Nodding in confused deference, Anax looked at Nika, feeling wonder. She cocked her mohawk-topped head, in her quirky manner, and he laughed out loud, relieving some of his tension. His body was already feeling a bit more stable. He waited patiently for the woman to speak.

Gazing at the horizon, she said, "I know your name, *Anax of Gylodon*, but you will not know mine. I have no name, nor shall I ever carry one so long as I am here. Some have called me the *Holder of Shadows*, and others have referred to me as the *Transmuter*. However, I give my true name to nobody, lest the darkness have an advantage over me. Understand?"

Again, he nodded uncertainly.

"Do not nod unless you actually understand." To this command, Anax nodded in earnest.

She paused before continuing, "Names carry power, like a specific frequency that is aligned with our bodies. The energy of a name coexists with us, intermingling with our own identities. If the forces of darkness discover one's name, then we are more vulnerable, and our personal energies can be manipulated. While there is no such threat in Gylodon, here in the mountain these threats are everywhere, and I must guard all my personal frequencies, including my name. I advise you to guard your own name, perhaps even take a new one, something common."

She looked down at his footwear—from the outside world—and then firmly into his eyes. "Remove your shoes. Do not block the earth's pulse."

The air was already biting his hands and tightening his joints. He looked to her as if to protest, but thought better of it. When the shoes were off—leaving only socks—she looked as if she were going to tell him to remove them, as well, but decided otherwise.

She continued, "My feet are built of new realities; down to my very cells and mitochondria I am adapted to endure the deepest cold. I have achieved this by reprogramming my body's control systems, and altering my DNA. This is your first serious lesson, Outsider, so listen closely. All of reality is predicated upon your belief systems, the building blocks of your illusions. Some of them you are conscious of and others are invisible to you, but still they are your beliefs, and your responsibility. All these beliefs can be altered to sculpt new realities. You will not wear shoes again until you have redesigned your belief systems around the cold. You will need to shift your paradigms to achieve this."

Anax shuddered, suddenly fearful. This teacher was far more severe than any he'd encountered in Gylodon. She did not carry compassion as they did, at least not that he could discern. Anax looked at Nika, who bowed her head and tucked her tail, her confidence dissolving, as if the order had been directed at her.

"Pack up and follow me." She led them around a winding trail, and the stone floor was icy and sharp upon his soles, even with socks. He found himself seeking the sun, calling upon its warmth; silently, he reverted to breathing in its fire, disseminating the heat to his limbs. It helped.

The woman looked at him, seemingly amused, "Fire breathing is just a crutch—a Gylodonian learning tool. It's far from a restructured reality."

Anax gaped. Stunned at the precision with which she'd read his thoughts, he suddenly felt excited by the prospect of learning from her. He hoped she'd be willing to teach.

"You still carry your shadows about you like an outsider," she said. "In your heart, I think you are still an outsider. Your time in Gylodon was insufficient; you've not even learned to restructure belief systems and sculpt realities." She paused, scanning the mountain, as if reconciling his lack of preparation. "You are not ready for this environment, but you are here, nonetheless...so you will need to learn quickly. From this moment forward, do not think of yourself as an outsider; that will only make you vulnerable. Think of yourself as a brother of Gylodon. Call upon that power often. In time, perhaps, you will become a brother of the mountain."

She pushed ahead, leaving him to trail several body lengths behind, with Nika on his right flank. At one point, navigating a steep decline, he slipped and his flesh snagged rock, ripping his sock while slicing his leg from his anklebone upward—a four-inch gash. He pressed on, deciding to address it later.

They walked for hours, breaking only once for water, at which point the woman walked over to a bush, removed some leaves and instructed Anax to chew them for energy. She took none for herself.

For the duration of the hike, which included paths along several narrow cliff faces, he was struck by her stamina. Physically, there was barely anything to her, and yet she was like a machine, perpetually pressing on, every step precise and well placed, while he stumbled along awkwardly, straining to keep her in sight. Nika stayed with him, as she too struggled with the low oxygen.

"What have I gotten you into, Girl?" he said, looking at Nika. He stopped briefly to offer her some water and she consumed it gratefully. Glancing upward, along the sloping rock, he noticed the same ethereal, roiling clouds mutating into patterns that he'd seen earlier. The clouds were denser than they were in Gylodon, and on several narrow spots along his path the misty forms spilled out of the walls, reaching toward him like grasping hands, and he had no choice but to pass through. Their energy was sticky, causing his pulse to escalate, and he quickly worked to cleanse himself by calling on the fifth power.

Otherwise, the terrain was monotonous, and had he not had to focus on every step to avoid injury, he might have appreciated the mystical scenery. Instead, the journey became a test of will—keeping his feet warm and safe without shoes, regulating his leg pain, tending to Nika, and breathing through the burning in his lungs while straining for adequate air. With each hour that passed, his hunger for air grew more acute, and his feet felt heavier.

Finally, as late afternoon arrived, the unlikely triumvirate came upon a stopping point, nearly at the mountain's apex. The path opened onto a plateau, where several garden beds had been established, much to Anax's surprise. There was even grass in several areas, although the green had begun to fade. He wondered if soil had been toted up here to allow for all of this. It seemed out of place.

The nameless woman disappeared into a hole in the rock face, signaling Anax to remain behind. She returned with more water, along with some dried berries, which she offered to him. Much to Anax's shock, she also had some dried fish, which she fed to Nika. Nobody in Gylodon consumed meat or fish. He had no idea where she would have come across the fish. Still, he knew not to ask questions; for now, he would observe and learn, as he was taught.

He took a spot on the ground, sitting cross-legged, and Nika happily joined him. The woman likewise took a seat. She stared at him as he ate.

"You have a strong dependence on food. That will require some reprogramming." He swallowed hard on the last berry, making sure to appreciate its flavor.

"Up here, you must carry courage like a shield," she said. "Love—and fearlessness—will be your greatest defenses against the darker energies. Any fear, any doubt, will leave a chink in your soul's armor, and that will not serve you, or Gylodon. Always remember, there is no good or evil. There is only light and dark, and infinite shades of gray in between. As a *transmuter*, I absorb the world's darkness so that it can be turned to gray, and then to light. The mountain holds—and recycles—these energies, as does the earth below. You are not equipped to handle these darker energies, so do not take on more than you can process."

"I understand," he replied with more confidence.

"If you have any questions, you may now ask."

"Thank you. The fish—the people in Gylodon do not eat meat. Where does it come from?"

She sighed heavily, as if the question pained her. "There is a

The Mystical Village That Rewired Reality

place nearby, a mountain lake, where fish are plentiful. On occasion, I eat some fish, because I must. The fish have chosen to feed me, and in return I feed the earth. That is the contract. Much like Nika will be to you—your *shadow-eater*—I am to the planet. I also derive much of my energy from sunlight, and can live on it alone—along with water—if I desired. But that is not adequate fuel for the strenuous work that I do. You too will learn to reprogram your body's control systems to derive sustenance from sunlight."

Anax stared blankly.

She continued, "Just as I feed the mountain, you will feed Nika. She will require energy and sustenance to assist you, so you will fish on her behalf, and feed her. Do you understand?"

He grimaced. "Yes, I understand." In Gylodon, he'd been so conditioned to respect all of life that the thought of killing fish was repulsive. He pushed the discomfort down, sending love to the darker reality, while deciding to adapt to nature's larger plan.

She read him with ease, nodding, as if he wore every thought, feeling and intention on the outside of his skin in plain lettering. "Good. That's the spirit. Tonight, you will sleep in the cave entrance and at some point, I shall take you deeper. The rock is built upon crystals that are critical to the work that I do. There are more of them deeper inside, but your body will need time to adjust to their intensity. They exist both underneath, and in the walls, and they make this work possible. Without these crystals, I would not have the power required."

A crystal cave. He could scarcely believe that he stood at the fulcrum of light and dark—a secret so well kept that few in Gylodon even knew of its existence. Nobody had mentioned a crystal cave. Somehow, he knew that it acted as a supernatural computer for reprogramming the world's ills. Again, he was reminded that he'd arrived here for no reason other than playing his pivotal role in the world's grand transition. Everybody has a role to play, and his was as a *warrior of light*.

Of course, all of humanity carried a shadow side, and Anax was no exception. But dark shadows are not all evil; they were just cruel and ugly—misguided energies awaiting transformation and redirection.

***

The priestess retired into the cave's depths, leaving Anax and Nika huddled on the cavern's cusp, as the light grew dim and temperatures dropped. Anax tugged a wool blanket from his bag, which he folded with precision, fashioning a bed for Nika that would provide insulation from the rocky floor. But Nika remained perched in her spot, sitting upright, as visibility waned. Her silhouette was like a small mountain peak, awaiting a storm. Perhaps they were both in awe of the solitude, the mountain's silent pulse. Or, perhaps, they both contemplated their unexpected partnership—one that strengthened their resolve.

Anax braced himself against the wall, upright, swaddled in his sleeping bag. His feet stuck out awkwardly as he attempted to tend to his wound without the benefit of light. He paused, staring into the depths of nothing, and wondered how he could feel so small and insignificant, here at the apex of Earth's healing, and yet be so important at the same time. Within him lived love and intellect—capable of building new worlds. All the codes of creation could be found in a single cell of his body, and he had an endless supply of them. His existence meant something—he was taking action—and for better or worse, it would lead to somewhere important.

No matter how long he sat with his eyes open, they did not adjust to the blackness. He peeled back his sock, revealing the cut, and was struck by a chill. He slipped Nika's blanket over his feet, and blindly fumbled through his supplies, searching for a salve. When he could not locate the medicine, instead coming upon the stone that Tristis had given him, he sighed, laughing to himself, as he leaned his head against the stone slab. Palming the gem in his left hand, he thought of Tristis and Dan, family and community, and then he searched for Nika in the darkness. He discerned only her shadow. Her breath was soft, but audible, and he radiated love in her direction. She would still be there come dawn—they were a pack now. Her unconditional fidelity, a foreign sentiment until Gylodon, dissolved the darkness, and for one fleeting moment fear did not exist.

He closed his eyes to escape the chill, still amused by life's folly, but instead of warmth, he found a verse:

What is love, but loneliness
Transformed into community?

What is light, but a black-and-white shadow-eater
Transmuting darkness into rainbows?

They are everything—and the only things—worth living for.

He felt a gentle pressure upon his feet as Nika climbed onto the blanket and circled into position before settling down. And then, a warm tongue tended to his wound.

***

And just as the warmth comforted him, cleansing his pain, so too came the cold. The battle of shadows—in the land of dreams—had only just begun. The world's darkness was now his bedfellow, and it lingered within the very stone upon which he slept. Its ghosts clung to fear and doubt like tar on skin, seeking any vulnerability; they came in all shapes and ills—penetrating dreams—violating one's consciousness. Either Anax would assume ownership of his mind or his spirit would be eaten piece by piece. The mountain was a tumor, awaiting evisceration, and it was no place for amateurs.

Exhaustion ravaged his body, demanding sleep, and his mind

drifted into the realm of dreams, down into dark stone crevices, places of insignificance and irrelevance; he was but a speck of light in a gray and endless void. He could scarcely remember what love was. Nobody could see him for who he was. Nobody could see him, at all. He was nothing more than a pawn—a bug to be squashed— in a world of giants. He sat with the realization, feeling his worthlessness, draped in helplessness. The world moved around him, effecting profound change, but he was too busy trying to survive, to find basic food and resources, while the ecosystems upon which he relied withered around him. And his back hurt. Something was burning there. The pain awakened an idea—a radical one—and he became awake and alive within the dream. He remembered that reality is fluid. And ideas are the architecture upon which change is built. And love? Love is the fuel.

He looked at his arms, again feeling the pain in his back, and they were more like legs, gangly and segmented, like an insect. *How peculiar.* He felt strong, strangely so, but still something dug into his back. Again, he looked at his legs; he had several of them. Six, in total. *They are attached to my thorax*, he realized, as if it were obvious. It dawned on him that he was, in fact, an *ant*—piddling and small— and quite near getting squashed by the giants above. But there was something else too. Pound for pound he was the strongest warrior on earth, and when he merged his power with his community of fellow ants, they were unstoppable. They could build anything. Even worlds.

And here he was now—alone, and in the dark—and still he was powerful. His mother and father ants had given him a strong body and a relentless spirit. He might be squashed, but then again, probably not. Once more he felt the pain in his back. He turned his head to see what was boring into his thorax. To his surprise, a long, slender needle dug squarely into his back, nearly piercing his armor, and it extended upward and upward into the worlds above. On top of the needle's head, high in the clouds, in the seemingly untouchable places of power, a platform rested. Upon the platform, large feet created even larger footprints, and they altered reality on a grand scale. They stomped around on the platform, laughing and drinking, setting policies into motion, making deals and claiming power over the masses. The more they stomped, the more he felt the pain in his back. They looked like self-appointed kings and queens, patting each other in a congratulatory fashion before turning and stabbing each other in the back. Their realities were selfish and ugly, methodical and blind, and they left humanity in a perpetual state of suffering.

But what could he do? He was but an ant in a world of giants. Then again, he realized—as he marveled at his body—ants can carry more than twenty times their own body weight. He flexed his legs and felt their power. He had an idea. Sidestepping to the right, he tested the boundaries, and the needle upon his back swayed, swinging slightly to the left, and the giants on the platform above stumbled, trying to regain balance. He re-centered, steadying the world above. For now, he'd be the world below. He had leverage here. He may be just an ant, he realized, but he was also a fulcrum of change. Just by the choices he made, and the actions he took, he could send ripples across the world above, altering realities in profound ways. He too could effect change. His change would be positive and respectful of nature. It would be fair and just. The pain in his back felt good now; it reminded him of all that he could do. He'd carry that pain—for a while, anyway—as a reminder of his strength. And just like that, with his acceptance, his skin peeled away—like the ripping of a band-aid or an astral body—and he was transformed.

When he emerged from the cocoon, he found the remnants of his thorax discarded upon the ground. He looked at the crusty old shell, and then he looked to his new body and it was long and slender, with electric greens and iridescent wings of rainbow; he could see all of it. He could see in all directions. His dragonfly eyes saw straight through life's illusions, broken beliefs and rampant *consciousness pollution*. The joy of his new body initiated a wild, fanciful flight in all directions, like a puppy exploring new smells, and then he knew where to go, and settled upon his course. His vision sharpened as he flew straight into the dark clouds of pollution—with love in his heart—and he seeded them with joy, spreading it liberally, doing his part to bring light into the world.

***

Morning arrived with lines of gold, drawn straight from the rising sun, cresting the crystal mountain and warming Anax's face. He opened his eyes, recalling his first dream inside the mountain; it had been a visceral experience.

Turning his head, he spotted Nika, sitting upright like a sentinel. He pushed up on his elbows and squinted into the morning's first light when the soft pattering of a tail captured his attention. Again, he looked at Nika, who bobbed her head rhythmically and shook her hindquarters in a full-body wag before taking several steps in his direction. He nodded back at her, inviting her closer. Instead of approaching, though, she spread her haunches, lowering herself to the ground, before springing into a playful dance. She looked like an awkward bounding deer. Anax chuckled, slowly rising and walking past her toward the mountain's edge, where she followed on his heels.

Gazing upon the expanse below, he found mostly balding trees that had shed their autumnal baggage, littering the forest floor with next season's nutrients. But some trees, Anax observed, still clung to their leaves, unwilling to accept winter's impending arrival. They would resist the change until its inevitability became too much to endure, and then they would surrender, becoming part of the cycle, doing their part to feed the next generation of seedlings.

Change cannot be stopped, Anax noted with quiet resignation. *Sometimes we must surrender—and accept the flow of life.* Brushing aside some pebbles, he sat down on the rough soil next to Nika and rested his hand upon her back.

"I'm glad we're in this together, Nika. This journey won't be easy."

But we will embrace our destiny, nonetheless.

Dear Reader,

Please accept my boundless gratitude for your attention, time and energy.

Thank you for coming along this far.

Now I invite you to go a little bit farther. Please read the *commentary*; it is an important part of the work, offering expanded insights on many of the concepts introduced in the book.

And please connect with me @
www.JustinNathan.com and **FB/JustinNathanBooks**.

(You're invited to download a complimentary copy of *Decoding the Hidden Symbolism in The Mystical Village That Rewired Reality*—available through the website.)

Commentary

*Only your heart can navigate truth.
Enjoy the journey.*

***

---

[1] **Astral travel and astral planes.** These terms refer to the subtler dimensions of existence to which our consciousness (often in an astral body) travels during out-body-experiences (astral projections). These dimensions overlap our world, in parallel, but exist at wavelengths and frequencies to which our five senses are not attuned. However, during astral projections, we can shift our consciousness into more subtle levels, exit our bodies, and transit through these alternative realities. The lowest layers closely mimic our physical earth and its energetic structures. However, proficient astral projectors, who have attained sufficient consciousness control, can raise their energy to more subtle levels and experience higher-vibration realities in the upper planes. These planes become more colorful and beautiful. Amid the different dimensions, there appears to be endless alternative realities. For more information on astral projection and astral travel, I encourage you to explore the works of William Buhlman, Robert Bruce and Jurgen Ziewe, all of whom are prolific, modern-day astral explorers and writers. For a more social experience, I recommend the *International Academy of Consciousness*, which actively teaches astral projection and energy work in a classroom setting and at retreats. I've taken classes with this organization in the New York City office, and found the teachers to be professional and well informed. Other organizations, like *The Monroe Institute*, also offer numerous learning opportunities for the astral explorer.

COMMENTARY

² **Life purpose fingerprint diagnostics.** I highly recommend *Lifeprints: Deciphering Your Life Purpose from Your Fingerprints* by Richard Unger. Richard is among the foremost experts in the world in hand analysis. I've had several personal experiences with Richard and studied his fingerprint system. It is a statistically validated, potent resource for self-realization. It is believed that the fingerprint shapes—much like the contour lines of a map—are in fact, mappings of the brain, which reveal specific information about one's personal blueprint when studied. Ten *whorls*, as written into the Seed Bearer's fingerprints, indicate a broad life purpose of *service*. The shapes of his hands and fingers have relevance to his earth connection, as well. Earth stewardship is a large part of his life's purpose.

³ **Impossible colors.** If the cone cells within our retinas could be adjusted to new settings, under special circumstances, it is conceivable that we could experience new colors. In the case of the Gylodonian rainbow, new colors were visible because the brain's visual cortex mixed color signals from the two eyes, allowing for the presence of bluish-yellow and reddish-green. Then again, Gylodon does funny things to people.

⁴ **Life purpose diagnostic systems**. There are probably too many to count, but for those who seek guidance, it is a worthwhile pursuit. At a younger age, I went on a quest to better understand my purpose, using a number of different systems including astrology, fingerprint analysis, personality testing, life-path numbers, Mayan destiny system, etc. They have all proven deeply insightful. For me, a key realization on this quest was to understand that one's purpose might not align with a specific job or clear means of income. This is often the case. Life purpose transcends these paradigms. Of primary importance, in my experience, is to just start somewhere. Start working, in any capacity, on the things to which

your heart calls. If you are honest, authentic and open to the process, the other parts will open from there. The path will become clearer, and you will sculpt it with increasing ease. Do not rely upon an exact job or activity to define your purpose. The path is for you to create, through the guidance of your heart, once you understand your personal blueprint, and the tools at your disposal.

[5] **Ice comets and water on Earth.** Nobody seems to know for certain the origin of water on Earth. One theory is that ice comets from space delivered water to Earth, lending itself to the idea that we too might be from outer space, partially, at least, since our bodies are composed of more than 60% water. And now NASA has acknowledged the presence of water on Mars. Keep your tinfoil hat tuned for more on that.

[6] **Near-death experiences.** These experiences are well documented and share common characteristics throughout the world. Conventional science often attempts to rationalize these experiences into limited-thinking paradigms of biological and chemical processes, but there is much more to the story. How do I know? I know from personal, repeated experiences during my astral projections. There are many similarities between astral projection and near-death experiences, with the exception of nearly dying, of course. I can speak only for myself, but I challenge doubters to have their own astral experience. It's really not so difficult for those committed to the process. (Again, astral projection experience, that is, not a near-death experience). Perhaps the most well-known researcher on NDEs today is Raymond Moody, a PhD and MD who has written numerous books on the subject. Check him out.

[7] **Lucid dreaming and astral projection technique.** Shifting focus from one object to another is a technique used by both lucid dreamers and astral projectors to maintain focus and enhance

astral vision. It can help you to sharpen your vision during a projection into a crystal-clear, multi-dimensional viewing experience, while grounding yourself, ironically, in the other layers.

8 **Indigenous shamanic healing techniques.** I have explored shamanism for many years now and it is a topic so deep and vast that I continue to be awed by its teachings. There are many tools used in different cultures, some of which are mentioned here. Different types of smoke can be used for cleansing a person, while others can be used for invoking spirits; eggs are used for cleansing the body's energy fields (they are rubbed on the body, absorbing energy, becoming heavier, and sometimes rupturing in mid-rub near areas requiring attention); candles can be rubbed on the body and used for diagnostic purposes by reading the flame; likewise, the yolks of eggs can be read by experienced practitioners after the eggs have been rubbed on the body. In truth, skilled practitioners can read just about anything, so long as they have a system and know how to decipher the codes. Green plants are used to cleanse and repel lower energies, while rum and Agua de Florida are common tools for energizing the body's aura. Whether using stones, feathers, sacred objects/places (huacas) or powerful altars, the list goes on and on. All the items have a practical purpose. I have been a part of some powerful apprenticeships (and healings) over the years, but one can always go so much deeper. If you are in the New York City area, I invite you to explore the *New York Shamanic Circle*. I had the honor of serving as one of its core members, for a time, working closely with powerful healers who continue to inspire me.

9 **Energy-healing with hands.** Most commonly known as *Reiki*, this healing modality enables practitioners to act as vessels, channeling energy through their bodies from the universal source, before offering it to others through their hands, or by other means. Physical contact is not necessary. The energy is often felt as a

pronounced heat, whether offered in person, or remotely. The transference of energy transcends space and time, allowing for healings at a distance. Practitioners generally receive *attunements* as part of their training, which opens them up to receive and share the energies. I have been trained in Reiki and have used it countless times on my pets, friends, spaces and food. I have found animals to be very receptive to the energy.

[10] **Ancestral-lineage healing**. Some say our ancestors live in our blood. If we establish a relationship with them, they may serve as guides and helpers, walking before us, pointing the way. Understanding our linkages, in a practical framework, is important. Sometimes ancestral energies, as well as those of our living families, can be entangled with our own in ways that do not serve the highest good. An example might be a father who served in a war, and experienced deep trauma; this trauma is then energetically passed down to his children—on conscious and unconscious levels—presenting as irrational fears or stress responses. This same trauma then passes down to the next generation again. Consequently, a grandchild might have an unexplainable fear of someone sneaking up behind them, trying to commit harm. New and emerging studies in epigenetics reveal that genes can be turned on and off when trauma occurs. These genetic alterations can then be passed down through the lineage, altering behavioral patterns, without changes to DNA sequencing. Powerful therapies such as Family Constellation Therapy® which has been reignited in recent decades through the work of Bert Hellinger, a German psychotherapist, lead the charge in healing these kinds of imbalances. I have personally participated in more than a dozen multi-hour constellation sessions over the years, assisting other people, as well as receiving personal healing. It is deep and life-changing work that taps directly into the fields of energy around us, channeling unseen information, healing patterns, reestablishing hierarchies and disentangling that which

does not serve the higher good. If you are in the New York City area, I highly recommend experiencing a session with Natalie Berthold, a talented facilitator with whom I've worked.

11 **Pine scent enhances self-love.** Plants carry frequencies, as well as biological and chemical components that interact with one's moods, health and general wellness. Essential oils derived from plants are commonly used to assist with healing; perhaps the most well-known model for this is the *Bach Flower Remedy System*. Pine oil is often prescribed to people who assign too much blame to themselves, or carry guilt too readily; they are often unsatisfied with their outcomes and can be their own worst critics. Pine oil can create an energetic state that seeks to rebalance these negative emotions, helping a person move back toward self-love, which encourages physical healing.

12 **Cob natural-building techniques.** I have had the pleasure of building a cob cottage from the ground up, mixing all material by foot and placing each cob ball by hand. Cob building exemplifies a balanced approach to construction, using the low-cost, natural materials on hand, primarily earth, clay, sand and straw (or some type of fibrous plant material). Sometimes people need to have some of these materials delivered (like straw and sand), but largely you are using resources from the land. It is an ecologically responsible building technique that leaves almost no waste as a byproduct. The homes are strong and can last hundreds of years, if properly maintained. Sadly, it is not an approved building technique in the United States, even though one-third of the homes in the world are constructed with some kind of cob, even small skyscrapers. Permitting it would likely get in the way of commercial-developer (and lumber-industry) profits, I'd guess, which is totally unacceptable reasoning, as are so many of the lobbyist-pushed, profit-driven restrictions in our society. Regardless, the beauty of cob, in my view, is

unsurpassed, as everything is sculpted by hand. You'll never have a more personal relationship with a home, and likely you'll never receive more robust healing from being inside a home. Its natural energy is profound. I highly recommend *House Alive!* workshops for those considering a natural-building experience. They've served me well.

[13] **Cosmic awareness and home planning.** This is an important topic and one with which natural builders are in tune. It deals with how a home is positioned to optimize the seasons, passive solar radiation and cooling, natural light, moisture, earth energy, magnetic fields and even planetary and star alignments. It is an area that I am not qualified to speak about in depth, but can safely say that we could use a bit more of it in modern society. Homes are sanctuaries and they should be constructed to optimize happiness and well-being. These variables play a greater role in our health than we might realize. With a bit of forethought and knowledge, a home can integrate with nature in a way that amplifies its power and blends with the heart of its caretaker.

[14] **The universe is invisible.** Most of the universe's mass is completely invisible within our limited sensory experience. Check out *dark matter* and *dark energy*, which, when combined, are said to make up 95% of the universe. We can't see them, but they exist nonetheless. Yup, there's a lot out there beyond our "five-sense" paradigms of reality. *Dark energy* can be likened to the term *consciousness cloud*, used throughout this book. In my view, *dark energy* forms the vast neural network of all realities, connecting every aspect of creation in a vast web of information, like a matrix, or infinite cloud storage organized into countless permutations of frequency, wavelength, color, thought, emotion and so much more. To some, this energy is known as *akasha*, or *ether*, and it is the foundation of universal consciousness.

15 **Hearts have neurons like the brain.** Science now validates that the heart has approximately 40,000 neurons that learn, remember and feel things. Like the brain, the heart is capable of so much more, serving as another seat of conscious awareness. No longer is "heart-consciousness" a nebulous term about love, but rather, a proven practical tool for accessing information, just like the brain. The heart also sends messages to the brain, creating a pathway for the unification of mind and heart. It is my belief, through personal experience, that the heart is best equipped to navigate truth, through feeling things, while the mind is too often clouded by societal programming, fear and illusion. (The false stories that we, and those around us, tell ourselves to accommodate the needs of our ego). Gotta love that heart. I know I do. Check out any number of scientific journals on this subject for more information.

16 **Guts have neurons like the brain.** The gut is lined with so many neurons that some scientists have taken to calling it our "second brain." It plays a role in stress response and likely our emotional responses. Who knows what else it can do? It does a lot of things independently of our brain, apparently, keeping things running smoothly. Really makes you think, eh? Or feel? Consult any number of scientific journals on this subject for further exploration.

17 **Our bodies are derived from stars.** According to astrophysicist Neil deGrasse Tyson, "The atoms of our bodies are traceable to stars that manufactured them in their cores and exploded these enriched ingredients across our galaxy, billions of years ago. For this reason, we are biologically connected to every other living thing in the world. We are chemically connected to all molecules on Earth. And we are atomically connected to all atoms in the universe. We are not figuratively, but literally stardust." Ain't that stellar?

[18] **Radiant energy from hands.** The radiant energy from one's hands has been found to be within the far-infrared wavelength, which is the preferred energy wavelength for many saunas, used for detoxification and cellular healing. Chi gong masters and Reiki practitioners, in particular, have developed the ability to radiate this energy with notable potency.

[19] **Disharmonious resonance as a cause of *disease*.** Disharmonious resonance is a term that I have chosen, but it can be described in many ways. Think of it as dirty electromagnetism and radio waves in their most common form, interfering with your body's natural frequencies. We are electromagnetic beings, operating at certain frequencies, and yet we are living in a world of artificial lighting, non-ionizing radiations, cellular towers, wireless routers, etc. Our bodies are constantly inundated with unnatural frequencies, without reprieve, disrupting our body's natural harmonics. Those in cities will find no sanctuary from these radiations. But if you consider electricity-free lifestyles, like the Amish, for example, you'll find no prevalence of ADD in children and extraordinarily low levels of cancer. And while this does not prove causation, as many variables can be at play, many scientists have found noteworthy correlations with regard to the absence of electricity and improvements in health. In fact—regarding wireless energies—a recent large-scale, $25 million federal study by the National Toxicology Program has found an increased risk of cancer with cellular phone exposure, so the dangers are officially documented. And now the FCC—seemingly operating in the interests of the telecom industry instead of consumer safety—is relentlessly pushing forward with its 5G agenda, which aims to irradiate vast sections of the United States with new high frequencies, creating a massive communications grid, potentially capable of every Orwellian nightmare imaginable. This is happening right now, with the first new towers slated for 2017. Imagine a cell tower on top of

every telephone pole, collecting data on everything you do, while polluting your body and home, and you might have a small vision of the future. Children and those who already have compromised immune systems may be more vulnerable to wireless irradiations. Animals and insects are also sensitive to these irradiations. More than two hundred scientists from forty-one nations submitted an appeal to the United Nations and the WHO in 2015, seeking improved public protection from wireless exposure. The current safety standards in the United States are outdated, and omit many key risk factors. Nonetheless, the FCC is pressing forward with its 5G plans. It appears that the 5G grids will require significantly more towers than the older technologies, potentially creating the greatest health (and freedom) risks that we have ever encountered. Explore "5G dangers" and do your part to raise awareness and reach out to your politicians and consumer safety advocates. This is a big deal, and being pushed on the population very quickly without proper considerations or public consent.

[20] **Dirty electromagnetic frequencies engulfing us.** Your body is an energy vehicle where cells, tissues, and organs communicate with each other via bioelectrical transmitters and receivers. Now insert your body into an artificial environment that is constantly irradiating it with new frequencies (wifi, cellular, and home electrical meters, for example) that are not in alignment with those natural processes. The result? Health imbalances, like radio static, opening the doorway to disease. Check out Dr. Mercola, MD's site for more information on how this is affecting health on a large scale. Imagine living in a state where your immune and nervous systems are constantly stressed, unable to recover, even when you sleep, because your wireless router is still turned on and your cell phone is parked next to your head on the night stand, constantly irradiating. Not good. Now imagine yourself living in a major city. Guess what—you are being inundated by twenty different, local wireless

routers in your building and neighboring buildings, twenty-four hours per day. And with the FCC's new 5G agenda, this is likely to expand multifold. If your immune system is strong, then maybe it's not a major problem for you. But if it is compromised already, perhaps this pollution impedes healing, or exacerbates physical pain. Or if you're a child, with tissues still developing, perhaps the detrimental effects are amplified. The long-term ramifications are unclear—and have not been properly tested. Believe it or not, there are entire cellular-free zones now, in certain parts of the country, as more and more people develop sensitivities to the radiations. What happens when allergies to wireless radiations become more widespread? How will anyone escape? There are even physicians who recommend disconnecting one's wireless router as part of the healing regimen for certain health conditions. Unfortunately, irradiations are becoming increasingly difficult to escape. We are poisoning ourselves in the name of "connectivity."

[21] **Dirty electricity in homes**. It seems that when higher frequency "noise" or "transient" energy gets mixed in with our current 120-volt, 60-Hz systems, it might be creating problems with our own energy fields and bodies, manifesting all manner of medical problems. This "noise" is related to all our new gadgets, which no longer draw power in a steady manner, but rather draw power in a non-linear, high-frequency fashion, creating inconsistent, transient energy that is not aligned with our wellness. Other areas of concern include the new electrical meters that are being installed on homes today. These are part of a grid system that wirelessly communicates with other electrical meters in the neighborhood, blasting us with more radiation throughout the day. Beware if one gets installed near your sleeping quarters or a space where you spend a lot of time. While there have been studies by the NIH regarding power-line frequencies as possible human carcinogens, these dangers pale in comparison to the wireless threats that we face every day. A large

COMMENTARY

ongoing federal study has now linked cell phones to cancer—so wireless transmissions are indeed a serious threat to health. And how do they affect animal, plant and insect ecosystems? Scientists have found significant destructive effects on plants, funguses, bees, frogs and birds. And that's just the beginning. Unfortunately, not too many people are paying attention to the destructive effects of wireless radiations; the reasons for this are two-fold—first, the radiations are invisible; second, people like their wireless toys. But just because the radiations are invisible doesn't mean they don't exist and affect the environment. Since all of this is somewhat new to humanity, we need to really pay attention. How about we find a way to have frequencies in our homes that boost the immune system rather than hurt it? Yes, frequencies can be (and are) used this way. For more on dirty electricity, read Dr. Sam Milham's book on the subject, *Dirty Electricity: Electrification and the Diseases of Civilization*.

22 **Schumann resonance, earth resonance.** The Schumann resonance is a global electromagnetic resonance in the extremely low-frequency range, generated and excited by lightning discharges. It is nature's vibe, as I like to think of it, and measuring it requires extremely sensitive equipment. Some believe it has a health-balancing effect on all of life. *Earthing*, or walking barefoot on the earth, particularly in wet areas like a beach shoreline, or dew-covered grass, can help bodies connect with these natural energy fields. Some people swear by *earthing* for pain relief and general health.

23 **Bioresonance diagnostic and treatment devices.** Imagine yourself walking into an office, holding a couple of electrodes, putting a little saliva or blood in a cup, and getting a printout within minutes of every parasite in your body, chemical imbalances, nutritional deficiencies, allergies and even emotional disturbances. The equivalent of fifty blood tests—and so much

more—in ten minutes. Sounds like science fiction, right? It's not. It's frequency/bioresonance-based science, used throughout Europe, Asia and the less-monopolized medical markets of the world. It's based on decades of research and frequency database development. Medically progressive Germany is leading the charge, making the technologies widely accessible. In the United States, these devices have made it only into the hands of veterinarians on a limited scale. Perhaps one day Americans will get a bit more health freedom and be afforded access to these amazing devices. I had to seek an alternative medical professional to get my reading done. Sadly, he couldn't promote his service because of the threat to his license, so he hides in the shadows, waiting for others to find him. He originally purchased the device to help his family with medical needs that were not being met by the western pharmaceutical model of treatment.

[24] **Future of medicine: frequency-based, vibrational medicine.** I think that pharmaceuticals are not the future; built upon a monopolistic, patent-profit system, to the exclusion of alternative technologies, as well as basic herbalism and nutrition, their days are numbered. Large, retrospective studies already have revealed the price they cost society in lives and dollars (check out one critical study on this subject titled *Death by Medicine*, compiled by a number of MDs and PhDs). Look, I'm not saying that synthetic drugs don't work; I'm just saying there are (and could be) better, lower-cost alternatives—without the side effects—if western doctors were allowed to learn about and utilize them. But these alternatives were written out of the United States medical curriculum a long time ago, probably because they can't be patented. Health freedom (and honest choices for patients) will eventually gain a foothold in the United States, though. Right now, sadly, physicians are demonized and threatened for any suggestions outside of the acceptable pharma-script. No pun intended. I have chatted with a billionaire

COMMENTARY

family who will go only to Europe for cancer treatments because they are not given a full range of options in the United States. Sad. Anyway, I digress. Back to the future of medicine—remarkable bioresonance devices are being used throughout the world now, offering new insights into non-invasive, natural energetic treatments. I have read dozens of case studies (and some clinical studies) on these devices and I am encouraged by the results. For example, studies on allergies have revealed that by holding some electrodes and receiving the appropriate frequency patterns (that neutralize those that are out of alignment) people can heal their allergies with an efficacy that surpasses antihistamines. I have read case study after case study, by physicians, on all manner of disease treatments with these devices and I am floored by their revelations. None of this has been fully permitted to touch the *consciousness cloud* of humanity yet—at least not in the medical-profit-monopoly markets. Instead, they are mischaracterized as "pseudoscience," despite studies that support their importance. Of course, these devices do require a highly skilled practitioner to do things properly, and the technology is still evolving. But when used in the hands of a capable physician and bioresonance practitioner, science fiction becomes reality. Welcome to the future. For more information on some of the history of frequency-based medicine, explore the story of Royal Raymond Rife, a revolutionary scientist whose discoveries were—you guessed it—suppressed.

25 **Institutionalized animal cruelty**. Talk about a topic that people ignore. I've been a vegetarian for many years now, although admittedly, I do eat a bit of fish from time to time. I still have a long way to go. But my imprint is small and I accept responsibility for the food decisions that I make. I will never turn a blind eye to the mass-produced, institutionalized cruelty that is the commercial meat industry. It is an appalling expression of humankind's darkest shadows—shadows that few can discuss comfortably for more than

The Mystical Village That Rewired Reality

a few minutes before they go out and purchase their factory meat for dinner, or lunch. Don't get me wrong; I am not entirely against meat consumption, when done in a natural and ethical way, like small, family-run farms. I don't personally choose it—and I don't like it (or believe that it is necessary)—but I have respect for people who practice environmentally responsible farming and remain connected to their food, accepting responsibility for what it represents. I think that if one chooses to eat meat, then one should have the experience of personally killing the animal at least one time. And eat it afterward. In this way, people are at least assuming responsibility for what they are eating, understanding what it represents. This, in my view, is far more honorable than the blind, disconnected state of those who buy nice little packages of chopped supermarket meat while ignoring its origin. It's irresponsible behavior, and many goodhearted people are guilty of it. If these people visited just one factory farm, many of them would cease eating meat on the spot. Instead, they live in a state of ignorance, tacitly complicit in the torture of animals, while smothering any underlying concerns with ketchup. Before long, the uncomfortable becomes comfortable, and new paradigms for acceptable animal abuse evolve. As humans born with reason and compassion, we are better than this. I love animals. They are conscious, sentient beings. They are not commodities to be mass-produced, tortured, injected and slaughtered for the sake of fast food. If that practice is not bad enough—it is now more widely recognized (although not in the public consciousness) that the commercial meat industry, through its massive environmental imprint, is the leading cause of global warming on the planet. Yup, *number one*. Simply eliminating cheeseburgers in the United States would have the impact of pulling all the SUVs off the road. I won't go too deeply into details, but you can look into it, and find the math. Commercial meat is an extraordinarily inefficient food source, requiring 2,500 gallons of water to generate just one pound of beef, while simultaneously calling for the destruction of old-growth rainforests to make room for more. These sacred, old-growth trees filter out carbon dioxide and toxins from the air to provide *us* with clean oxygen. They serve *us*! So, what do we do? Cut them down to make room for more tortuous, inefficient, global-warming-inducing beef production. And yes, there are alternatives for adequate global protein with an ounce of innovation and effort. For example, spirulina (algae) farms could offer tremendous, low-cost protein sources. So could portable bean-sprouting systems. They might not taste as good as chicken, but they don't desecrate nature while leaving a legacy of blood and torture in their wake, either. It's time for us all to become conscious creators, and it begins by acknowledging our failures as a species.

26 **Genetically modified food**. As a culture, we are not living in balance with Mother Earth, and so we find our personal lives out of balance. Sadly, this imbalance is most heavily perpetuated by certain business entities that place profits above human-, animal- and plant life. These companies employ mostly good, well-intentioned people who generally do not acknowledge (or understand) the destruction that their employing institutions reap. The employees are dependent upon these institutions, or so they believe, for the survival of their families. This, of course, is an illusion. A mighty, powerful one, and one that keeps much of humanity locked in a state of placid acceptance, through their fear and societal programming. And so, the problems are perpetuated—*air pollution, water pollution, soil pollution* and *food pollution* (genetically modified food with excessive pesticide usage), just to name a few. These corporations have similar rights to humans, but they lack any moral compass and are motivated only by a higher stock price. Besides the increasing scarcity of clean water—due to climate shifts and other factors—genetically modified organisms (GMOs) and their dangerous pesticides continue to emerge as significant threats to human civilization. Genetically modified organisms are not simply hybridized plants, as

The Mystical Village That Rewired Reality

some might believe, but rather, are the results of altering DNA in unnatural ways (and potentially disrupting naturally ordered ecosystems and immunity) across the planet. Perhaps the worst part is that the use of toxic herbicides has only increased through GMO agriculture, spawning mutant super-weeds that require increasing varieties and volumes of weed killer, while poisoning our foods. The threat is real. The effects of this grand experiment on humanity (and the animal/plant kingdoms) are unclear because they have not been fully tested. In the United States, we see strange digestive disorders and allergies rising in increasingly young populations, without good explanations. While this does not prove causation, it warrants serious consideration. Some scientists have even drawn correlations to a decline in the IQ of our children with growing pesticide usage. Ask yourself—by what logic has one of the major pesticides—increasingly banned in Europe—only grown in use in the United States? And why have many countries in Europe banned GMOs? On top of this madness, it is alleged that GMOs have not led to any significant increase in crop yields, as they were once promised to do. A recent study by The New York Times, using data from the United Nations, found little difference in yield performance when the U.S. and Canada (GMO nations) were compared to European nations (non-GMO, lower pesticide usage). So, it seems that we are being poisoned for *nothing*, and are threatening naturally ordered ecosystems for *nothing*. All so these agricultural-biotech companies can have a higher stock price. It's imperative that we become aware of our circumstances; only then can we unite our power and actively dream new realities into being. New innovations can replace these outmoded, insidious systems, leaving them remnants of the past. In my view, the answer does not lie in simply *fighting* these systems; rather, we, as beings of infinite creativity, must dream alternatives into reality, find ways to deliver them into mainstream consciousness, and allow these new innovations to replace the old systems that do not serve the highest good. These shifts may come with disruptive new energy technologies, innovative non-toxic pesticides, or with advancements in home sprouting systems, hydroponics and permaculture. Or, perhaps they'll come by finally electing a candidate who can curb or eliminate the influence of money in politics. Corporate interest groups have no right to make decisions for humanity, especially when it relates to health and welfare. Increasingly, people are becoming aware of these hard realities. In my view, it doesn't serve to waste too much energy fighting Goliath; instead, let us unite our power and replace Goliath with innovative alternatives that make him obsolete. *We the people* hold the power when that power is organized and properly channeled.

27 **Debt as normal.** What a strange paradigm. There is normal human debt, like credit card bills and student loans. Then there is banker debt, like derivatives and leveraging money hundreds of times over to play in the grand casino. It has evolved to such an extent that people are penalized if they do not have debt! (Or credit, as they like to call it). You want a loan? I'm sorry, you don't have any credit (debt), so I can't give you a loan. Go out and get some debt, then come back and we can talk. The term *credit* is another illusion. They call it *credit* because it gives a more comfortable feeling to the people who blindly embrace it, thereby committing themselves to a modern form of indentured servitude, where they work to pay the interest on their debt. Yup, just like the peasants living on the lord's land. The system has just become more civilized, is all, and so has the societal programming, making it appear to be normal. It's called institutionalized thinking, created by design, and it is all illusion. Recent examples of evolving consciousness attempting to replace the old, outmoded monetary systems have arisen through alternative, virtual currencies like *Bitcoin*. Currencies like this seek to avoid the exploitation of those who control the money supply, by decentralizing the process. Avoiding debt is difficult in a society that endorses it; nonetheless, we see a growing movement in self-

sufficiency, off-grid living and smaller homes. Perhaps eco-village systems (and lifestyles), with resource sharing and smaller living will play a role in the solution.

28 **Extinction rate.** It seems unfathomable, but at the rate we are going we will lose half the biodiversity on Earth within one hundred years. It's shocking, I know. The rate of extinction is increasing exponentially; we are currently killing off species with such alarming speed that it has been compared to the same effect that the meteor had on the dinosaurs. It seems that we are in the sixth mass extinction event of our beautiful planet's history and few are even paying attention. While elitists like to blame overpopulation, I personally hold the wealthy institutions and governments that drive public policy and industry accountable. It's their exploitive industrial practices—and policy agendas—that have poisoned the environment, blocked the rapid adoption of clean-energy technologies and created an economic caste system that punishes the environment—and people—as they strive to survive. It's not the average Joe who's done that. Rather, it's the institutions that have controlled—and far too often manipulated—policy, production and industry in favor of profit at any cost. Properly regulated capitalism is OK, but unfettered capitalism, devoid of morality and constraint, is a time bomb. We can still change things. As consumers, change starts with our buying decisions, but as humans it climaxes with a revolution of conscious awareness and action. This is a call to all innovators, healers, and environmentalists who feel that the death of an entire species at the hands of industrial abuse is an unacceptable—and unnecessary—price to pay for anything. Time is scarce, but possibility for change is everywhere.

29 **Media manipulating consciousness.** We live in a world of powerful direct-to-consumer marketing that routinely sculpts our belief systems because we are not taking control of our lives. Our

conscious awareness has been on autopilot, unconsciously absorbing billions of pieces of spoon-fed information because we are too tired to think for ourselves. Television has been the ultimate tool of unconscious programming, and yes, it happens all the time in many ways. From politicians spinning stories (say something enough times that is an outright lie, and half the population will believe it to be true, arguing on its behalf), to sensationalized news stories that promulgate deep fear, to demonizing people who speak out against any of the established, corrupt systems. Even friends and family will demonize each other for saying something that is outside of their acceptable societal programming paradigms. The platforms for societal programming (manipulating consciousness) have grown stronger in recent years. What was once a diversified portfolio of more than fifty media (news) conglomerates in the United States has consolidated into a tiny handful of massive, monopolistic platforms—leaving them free to manipulate mass messaging however they please. Pure oligopoly. Yeah, look that one up. This consciousness manipulation extends into social-media platforms, as well, which have been caught running experiments manipulating consumer emotions and thoughts. As we increasingly consume digital media we become more vulnerable to messaging. The more inundated we are with media sound bites and fear-based news, the more disconnected we become from the earth and our true natures. As beings of raw consciousness, with unlimited potential, we are destined for much more. We are all capable of taking control of our consciousness and sculpting new realities. The first step is filtering out the *consciousness pollution*.

30 **Earth-energy grids and vortexes.** The human body emits various energy fields that converge at certain acupuncture points, where effects are amplified. The *earth-grid theory* postulates that the earth also has energetic grid lines that converge at certain acupuncture-like points, like the chakras in the human body. These can be

considered vortex points. Allegedly, these points have been identified and used throughout history by various civilizations. Some researchers have even speculated that many of the pyramid locations correspond to these points, to leverage their power. Other sites have been known to have detrimental energies, like the Bermuda Triangle. There are many theories, but with an ounce of creativity one could make the leap to viewing Earth as a macrocosm of the human body with rivers like arteries, mineral-rich oceans as blood and wind like breath—a sentient system of self-regulating forces that strive toward homeostasis.

[31] **Data storage in DNA.** Using artificially synthesized DNA, scientists have successfully stored—and retrieved—vast amounts of data, using simple codes. The beauty of this evolving technology is that DNA has extraordinary longevity—potentially enabling data to be stored for a million years or more in the right conditions; consequently, some have labeled this form of data storage "apocalypse-proof." Scientists have stored books, audio files and even images before successfully retrieving them with near-perfect data integrity. The costs are still high but are expected to fall significantly within a decade. Information is all around us. Get your DNA flash drive today!

[32] **Tactile imaging.** This technique leverages the power of touch to help focus energy to a designated place within the body. Robert Bruce, a pioneering researcher in astral projection and author of *Astral Dynamics,* discusses this technique quite extensively. I highly recommend his books.

[33] **Museum astral projection.** This is an account of an astral projection that I experienced, with full lucidity, while projecting three times in a single night. At the time, I was using binaural frequencies to assist with the process. I set the intention that my

COMMENTARY

spirit guide would assist me with the projection, and sure enough, she did. She took me to the most awe-inspiring museum I have ever visited, and yes, I made a silly comment about Superman and felt small afterward, in the wake of her extraordinary lesson about our own superhero abilities.

34 **New epoch for Earth.** Several scientists have called for the declaration of a new geological epoch in Earth's history called the *Anthropocene*; this epoch marks the rapid onset of irreversible planetary destruction caused by human behavior over the past seventy years, characterized by rising carbon dioxide levels, climate change, massive animal extinction, radioactive waste, plastic pollution, and even animal remains from commercial farming. If approved by the scientific community, this new marker would end the previous *Holocene* epoch, which had provided Earth with a stable climate for 12,000 years. It begs the question—*What right do we have to kill everything? None.* Some would like us to believe that excessive human population is the cause. While it's true that we need to curb the growth rate of the human species, it is the rapid onset of destructive technologies that has been the biggest problem. Technology is what allowed for the growth of human populations in the first place. Remember, nearly all the destructive products, technologies and toxic waste on Earth were pushed by corporations and permitted by governments—through policies or mass-marketing channels—not by the average human being. It is unregulated capitalism, greed, government corruption, lack of education and misplaced priorities that are the problems. Our entire educational system should be revamped to change the thinking of our youth—encouraging them to hold environmental stewardship as their highest priority. Ask yourself, *why hasn't this happened?* Solutions are out there, and each of us can contribute. We can do big things or small things—but every bit helps. Start by being mindful—decline the plastic bag at the checkout counter, eat less meat, ride a bike, and make informed

choices about the products you buy. Together we can shift humanity's *consciousness cloud* toward balance. But it all starts with our own individual choices. It's time to stop following the herd; each of us must become the solution.

35 **Fingerprints of natural-born shaman**. According to Richard Unger, author of *Lifeprints: Deciphering Your Life Purpose from Your Fingerprints*, the markings of a shaman can be indicated by highest ranking prints appearing on the left pinkie, left ring finger and left middle finger (healer + innovator + mentor = shaman). Tristis exhibits these prints. I highly recommend seeking Richard, or somebody who has trained with him, for a life-purpose reading.

36 **Hummingbird and elephant story.** I first heard this story while working with shamans in the Amazon rainforest. The storyteller was named *Ipupiara*, which translates to *fresh water dolphin*. He was a shaman, anthropologist, teacher, elder and friend. I learned from him both in the jungle and in the United States. Even after he transitioned to spirit, he visited me in my dreams. He is dearly missed and this short story is recounted in his honor.

37 **Plant medicine.** This is a reference to *ayahuasca*, or similar plant medicines, widely used for healing and spiritual development throughout South America, and other parts of the world. These medicines are extraordinarily powerful, opening portals to other realities—through visioning and body purging, while simultaneously leaving one's energy bodies more open (and vulnerable, in some cases). This is an enormous topic, but I will offer my feelings on the subject. I have had profound, life-changing experiences with plant medicine, specifically *ayahuasca*, rewiring me into new realities. Some of them are accounted for in this novel. My personal feeling is that this medicine should be used sparingly (occasional ceremonies) for most people, but not as a regular protocol. I see it as a tool for

spiritual development, but not as the answer to it. In my view, we must find the answers through our own work, leveraging our own inherent powers. I also feel that lessons learned during plant-medicine ceremonies should have time for integration before other ceremonies are undertaken. Of course, many people will have differing opinions on this subject, based upon each person's unique path. More power to them. This is just my view, based upon my own transformative plant-medicine experiences.

THE MYSTICAL VILLAGE THAT REWIRED REALITY

The End

(And… *The Beginning*)

FIND YOUR LIGHT AND ILLUMINATE THE WORLD.

Dear Sisters and Brothers,

Thank you for reading my debut novel! You are forever a part of my story, and for that I am bursting at the seams with gratitude.

Now, alas, I have a small favor to ask—*would you consider writing a review?* As an independent artist, I rely upon your insights and opinions to spread the word. Without you, this work would be relegated to the dustbins of obscurity. But with your voice, perhaps it can play a small role in making the world a better place—shifting paradigms and tipping scales toward love and light.

I see the light in you…
Justin

Made in the USA
Columbia, SC
24 December 2019